the
Wren
in the
Holly
Library

the
Wren
in the
Holly
Library

USA TODAY BESTSELLING AUTHOR

K.A. LINDE

Entangled Publishing, LLC
644 Shrewsbury Commons Ave., STE 181
Shrewsbury, PA 17361
rights@entangledpublishing.com

Red Tower Books is an imprint of Entangled Publishing, LLC.

Visit our website at www.entangledpublishing.com.

Edited by Liz Pelletier and Molly Majumder
Cover art and design by Bree Archer
Deluxe Limited endpaper illustration by Melanie Korte
Deluxe Limited case design by Elizabeth Turner Stokes
Stock art by vladymyr/Depositphotos, alex_skpr/Depositphotos,
Explorer/CGTrader, Tithi Luadthong/Shutterstock, ulimi/Gettyimages
Interior design by Heather Howland
Interior formatting by Britt Marczak

Standard HC ISBN 978-1-64937-711-1
Deluxe HC ISBN 978-1-64937-407-3
Ebook ISBN 978-1-64937-422-6

Printed in the United States at LSC
First Edition June 2024

10 9 8 7 6 5 4 3 2 1

RED TOWER BOOKS™

MORE FROM K.A. LINDE

To the girls who fell for the library
before the beast.

Author's Note

It was raining on my favorite day in Ireland.

This should surprise no one. It didn't surprise me.

I was bundled up in a purple raincoat beside my mom, walking down gray cobblestones from the bell tower of a church to a gilded castle to the ancient library of a school. We'd traveled to Dublin to retrace our Irish roots and as a first stop to a book signing in Paris. But it quickly dissolved into me taking furious notes in my phone at every new location.

Notes that would become the beginning of this book.

About the heart of Laurence O'Toole, which was kept in a locked metal cage and stolen from Christ Church Cathedral. About the soaring library at Trinity College that housed a book so old it belonged behind glass. About Irish fairy trees that were so sacred the roads had to be built around them.

It began with a thief, a library, and a monster seeking ancient treasures.

But it didn't end there.

When I came home, myths, legends, and fairy tales were absorbed at rapid pace. I delved into a realm of magic, where Druids walked among us, the turning of the seasons was controlled by primordial beings, and mythical weapons were used in battle.

As I wandered the streets of New York City, I knew that I wanted to take this magic and mold, layer, and infuse it into a new kind of story.

Where the library is always open.

And darkness lurks behind every corner.

So, pull up a chair. Sink into the cozy softness. Let the black cat next to you hiss gently. There are hundreds of books, thousands of books, more books than you could ever read. Green ivy growing in the dim light.

Now let me spin a tale for you—of monsters and magic and little thieves.

The Wren in the Holly Library is a tale of monsters, mystery, and romance. However, the story includes elements that may not be suitable for all readers. Combat, violence, sex, drug and alcohol use, sex work, and gang violence are depicted. Abuse, genocide, and colonization are discussed. Readers who may be sensitive to these elements, please take note, pour yourself a cup of tea, and enter the Holly Library...

PART I

THE HOLLY LIBRARY

Chapter One

*I*t's now or never.

Kierse crouched low, pressing her back against the stone in the shadows.

Across the street was the largest Upper West Side brownstone she had ever seen. Every detail looked original to the Victorian house, from the wrought iron banisters to the holly bushes lining the walk and clinging to upstairs balconies. Even the intricate door knocker and the bronze sconces looked original.

Kierse slowed her breathing and crossed through the slushy brown mess that was New York City after a snowfall. Fresh powder was coming down again, and she obscured her footprints before peering through the first-floor window into an enormous shadowed study. Nothing was out of place—as if it were staged. Only a sliver of light bloomed through the crack under the door.

Her job was simple: steal a diamond ring, get paid.

"Please *try* to be careful," Ethan's voice said into her earpiece, which attached to the radio at her hip. A cell phone would have been better, but she'd never been able to afford one.

A smile hit Kierse's features. "I'm always careful."

"Since when?"

Never. She glanced up to Ethan on the neighboring rooftop where her lookout had binoculars trained on her. She gave him a double-finger salute and got to work. She whipped out a set of tools, flicked the lock on the window, and slid it up soundlessly. She'd investigated the nonexistent security system on one of her first reconnaissance missions, and she still didn't understand how no alarms were present and nothing tripped. She checked her surroundings, then slipped into the study, closing the window behind her.

This was the part she had programmed in her mind. After constructing a mock interior layout of the house, she'd run through her plan again and again. She was prepared, but she'd broken into enough places to know that nothing ever went exactly to plan. Her benefactor, Gregory Amberdash, had given her all the information he had, which admittedly wasn't much. The ring was kept in a locked box in the library. A library seemed an unusual place to keep a ring with a diamond the size of a robin's egg. But what did she know about rich people? This guy didn't even have a *security system*. A library probably made perfect sense to him.

Kierse steeled herself for what could be the first sign of trouble, but everything was as it should be. She maneuvered around a mahogany desk with a gilded lamp and sleek black leather insert, between a pair of couches, and to the silent grandfather clock that showed the time was nearly midnight. With a breath, she eased the door open and peered down the hallway illuminated by soft, bracketed light. Her eyes darted everywhere at once—taking in the sitting room at the end of the hallway that she'd only ever seen through binoculars, the grand staircase to her right, the polished wood floors, the lush, filthy-rich interior. On silent feet, she crept down the smooth hardwood floors and flipped the front door lock.

The first rule of thieving: always have an exit strategy.

"So far, so good," she whispered to Ethan as she stood in the empty house.

"Monster?" he asked.

She shook her head even knowing he couldn't see her. "Not yet."

Ethan's investigation into the owner had been fruitless. John Smith was clearly a fake name, and it linked to a business that didn't exist. The house was enormous and had two regular staff who showed up rain or shine. Yet not a single look at the owner. In her line of work, that meant one of two things: a wealthy human who was out of town or a monster.

A monster would be a *big* problem. If she was caught in a monster's house, she'd be subject to the Monster Treaty just like anyone else. And the consequences of breaking the Treaty were typically life-threatening. Which meant she couldn't get caught. She'd keep her fingers crossed for an out-of-town billionaire.

"Keep me updated," Ethan said. "Gen would kill me if something happened to you."

"Gen knows me better than that."

Her heartbeat thudded in her ears and adrenaline fired through her veins as she snuck through the empty house. A smile lit her face. It was a wrong smile. She'd been told that too many times—because she wasn't supposed to think that this was the fun part. Sneaking, thieving, and most of all, getting away with it.

Her devious smile grew as she hurried up the staircase and stopped before giant wooden doors. A bronze sign hung over the doorway that read THE HOLLY LIBRARY. Intricate whorls and swirls were carved into the frame. She could make out a string of holly vines and berries in the design, and then something almost shifted as she stared at it. It felt like a familiar language that tugged at the recesses of her memory, but she had never seen anything like it. She shook the cobwebs out of her mind and reached for the cold iron knob. She was prepared for it to be locked, but to her surprise, the handle turned.

Kierse rolled her eyes skyward. No alarms. No locks. What's next—the jewels just sitting out in display cases?

Still, she dragged it open just far enough for her to slip into the place of secrets.

Her eyes widened. The sign over the doorway suddenly made perfect sense. Holly vines crawled up the shelves and over the top of the wood of the largest private library she had ever seen. They should have been a hazard to the collection, but none of the books seemed hindered. Everything was exceptionally well cared for. But the real beauty of what lay before her was that each and every one of the hundreds of bookshelves was packed full with book after book after book. Rows of old leather-bound volumes to brand-new hardbacks with pristine dust jackets.

All she wanted to do was pull them off the shelves just to smell them. Crack open those perfect spines and devour the contents. She wanted to live and breathe a different world. Something, *anything*, other than her own horrid reality. It would be easy to spend a lifetime in this room and never read every volume. But she didn't have that time. She only had a few minutes to find a diamond ring and get the hell out.

Kierse's gaze narrowed on the large window at the other end of the massive library between rows of bookcases. She passed a cozy sitting area with a table, couch, and set of chairs at the center of the room to the window and flipped the latch. Exits were always a priority.

"In the library," she told Ethan. "Anything on the outside?"

"All clear here. Hurry up."

She rolled her eyes. Leave it to Ethan, sitting comfortably on the outside, to hurry her along. She went in search of the safe. Amberdash claimed it was nestled into a bookshelf on the left side of the room. She was just realizing how little description that was in a place this size. Kierse walked the stacks, peering into corners and moving vines about to see if the safe was hidden. She was just getting frustrated with the search when she brushed aside a string of holly and revealed the safe on a shelf at eye level. She frowned at the innocuous box.

"What the hell?" she whispered into the stillness.

It was a simple safe with a hole for a tiny key. Only a two-pin tumbler. The kind of fireproof carrying case that anyone could have in their home for paperwork. It was too easy. Almost insulting. There had to be a trick to it. Who kept an enormous diamond ring in a safe with a lock a *child* could break?

A sensation like cold water through her veins hit her fresh. Something wasn't right here. She'd had plenty of jobs go to shit, but the prick of nerves that raised the hair on the back of her neck wasn't normal. She touched the silver wren tied around her neck on a black silk string to dispel the feeling. In the end, it didn't matter why this was so easy.

She retrieved her tools out of her pocket and gently touched a rubber piece against the safe. One safe she'd broken into had been rigged with electricity. Not a pleasant feeling. But nothing happened this time. Not even a sizzle.

She fortified her nerves before inserting her tools into the lock and jiggling the two pins, clicking the safe open. She'd been able to do that since she turned seven years old. Breaking the lock had only taken her a matter of seconds. The safe released upward without a sound, revealing the contents within: a stack of folded paperwork, an unfamiliar stamped silver coin, a hunk of black metal, what appeared to be a human fingernail, and the giant diamond ring.

Well, at least Amberdash hadn't been lying. It was here. Kierse pocketed the ring and stared at the rest of the contents. What a bizarre assortment of things. Kierse shut the lid, carefully relocked the box so that it wouldn't look disturbed, and moved the holly vines back into place. She shivered as she righted herself. This library spooked her. There was something off about it, and she couldn't put her finger on it.

"Well, well, well," a cold, dark voice said from the shadows, "what do we have here?"

She stilled, a chill skating down her spine. *Shit.* She'd been wrong. Someone *was* home.

And now, she was nothing more than prey caught in a predator's trap. She could hear it in the sound of his voice. It was the carefully precise speech that set her on edge. He had a slight British accent. Silky smooth and devoid of any emotion, just pure, unbridled male. Power lurked dark and hungry in every syllable.

Panic clawed its way into her chest where cool, calm calculation normally resided. She needed to collect herself and lean into her carefully honed instincts. Without them, she was dead. There was no alternative.

He took a step into the light, his body framed by the closed library doors. His pale face was all sharp angles, hard edges, and dark shadows. His cheekbones were high and cut out of marble, while his eyes were carefully shrouded in the dimness. He had hair as dark as pitch, so dark it nearly blended in with the surroundings.

Kierse took a slow, deep breath, shifting her weight to the balls of her feet. She was closer to the window than he was and thanking whatever god would listen that she could make it there before him. Time to employ the second rule of thieving: run.

She darted across the open length of the library. Where before the window had been a dozen long strides away, it now seemed an interminable distance. But as adrenaline kicked in and her blood pumped faster and faster through her veins, everything else slowed down to a crisp, clear picture as if in slow motion. She was still quick, moving at lightning speed that hours and hours of training had prepared her for, but *this* was something else. Something that Ethan always said was her unfair advantage when they were sparring. It got her out of most situations.

Kierse focused on the approaching window she'd unlatched earlier. Her gloved fingers dug into the bottom of the window and wrenched it upward. The well-oiled gears made no noise. She looked down at the two-story drop to concrete with growing dread. She'd done worse, but she hardly enjoyed it.

As she climbed onto the sill, she ground her teeth. The height was dizzying. She remembered her former mentor's training sessions, when he'd tried to break her irrational fear of heights. It wasn't a good look for a would-be master thief.

Jason had made her walk on every skyscraper in the city.

He'd had her jump rooftops.

He'd pushed her *off* of rooftops.

It wasn't the worst thing he'd ever done to her, but it brought back the old feelings of righteous anger.

In this moment, *only this moment*, Kierse thanked him for allowing this drop to not completely paralyze her, and with a breath, she released.

She went weightless in midair. She was flying and braced for her landing. On concrete, it would be a *bitch* to roll out of. Just last year, she'd wrenched her knee on a misjudged fall and hobbled around for weeks. She couldn't afford the same misstep tonight.

She'd just cleared the ledge, gravity pulling her down hard and fast, when a hand reached out from above and grasped her arm. She heard her shoulder pop and screamed. She prided herself on her stoicism, but she'd had no warning. No expectation. No one, no *human*, could move as fast as he had. It just wasn't possible.

She dangled helplessly in his grasp, then gritted her teeth against the pain, and to her dismay, she was hauled back through the window. Even worse, he was using just *one* arm to lift her. Once she crossed the sill, he threw her across the room. She bounced and bumped her way down the carpet. Her earpiece was torn from her ear on the way, radio smashed under her hip, disappearing into the depths of the library—so much for radioing Ethan when she was in trouble—before she jarringly collided face-first into the back of the couch in the central seating area hard enough to see stars. She bit back a groan. Her dark hair came free of its tie and sprawled across her face. She jerked her head to get it out of the way but had to close her eyes against the pain.

Fuck. This wasn't supposed to happen. It had all gone to shit so fast that reality was just now catching up with what her body knew from every bump and bruise.

So much strength. So much brutality.

In her world, that meant just one thing. One horrible thing—monster.

Nope, not the easy route tonight. Not even close.

Sometimes it was unfathomable to think that she lived in this world with monsters. When she was a kid, living off the south Manhattan streets, monsters had been nothing but a scary bedtime story. Men were monster enough for her.

Now, all the stories were true.

Thirteen years ago, they came into the light, as swift and furious and brutal as the stories imagined them to be. Suddenly, monsters and humans were forced to coincide. It was about as bloody as imaginable, and the world collapsed practically overnight.

Every manner of beast roamed the streets, killing humans at will. Monsters destroyed large swaths of cities. Shelter became scarce. Food even more so. Police, firefighters, healthcare—all of it became nearly impossible to navigate. Humans fled the cities in droves, heading into old bunkers and trying out rural life. But monsters weren't confined to Manhattan, and the world quickly narrowed. Kierse's parents were already long gone by the time the monsters appeared, and she survived by ingratiating herself into the thieving guild of her late mentor—Jason. But the population had been decimated, and if it weren't for the recent Monster Treaty, no one would be alive today.

And she had just broken the Treaty.

"Bravo," he said dangerously.

He clapped twice, slow and condescending. He didn't even bother closing the window or locking it. He left it open to the frigid night air, and then he stepped casually, confidently forward.

"What a daring escape plan."

Kierse came to all fours. Her popped shoulder protested. Her head spun. Possibly a concussion. Gen and Ethan were going to be furious. She used the couch to lift herself unsteadily to her feet. She swayed slightly, and blood trickled out of her nose. She hoped it wasn't broken.

Then she tilted her chin up to look at him.

He just smirked. A lethally stunning killer. Now, in the light, she could see that his hair had a tinge of midnight blue. His eyes weren't depthless dark orbs as she had believed. They were swirling gray, as temperamental as the weather and as fatal as standing in the ocean in the middle of a hurricane. He strode forward, slipping black-gloved hands into the pockets of his pitch-black suit.

She ran through the types of monsters, trying to place him. The main forms of monster were vampire, werewolf, mer, wraith, shifter, and goblin. Other manner of monsters remained but were far less common, such as nymph, phoenix, incubus/succubus, and troll. She felt none of that coldness of the vampires. Even from a distance, he was primordial fire. Werewolf was more likely considering the heat he was producing, but she had run with a wolf pack once, and he seemed ever the loner. Wraiths always gave off a slightly uncomfortable sensation of death, as if at any moment they were going to suck out your soul. He was too small for a troll. Too large for a nymph. No water nearby for the mer. A shifter, maybe?

"What is your name?" he asked as he stepped before her.

"None of your fucking business."

"So, she does speak." He reached forward with one hand as if he were going to assess her bloody nose, but she acted on instinct, deflecting the touch, and then leaned forward to throw a punch. The first worked. His eyes flashed in raw anger as she knocked his hand away from her face. Then he blocked her punch as if she had barely moved.

"That isn't very nice," he growled.

She didn't care. She locked deep into that place within herself and moved like water. Settling into her center of gravity and using every ounce of her training to bob and weave as she tried to hit him. To find an edge to get away from him somehow.

But he hardly seemed to register her thrown punches or swept legs. He stepped and sidestepped. He dodged and countered. He moved with a grace developed from years and years even though he only looked about twenty-five, same as her.

After only a few minutes, she was huffing. A slow smirk stretched across his mouth. He was toying with her. He had no intention of letting her get a lick in edgewise. And then he stepped into her momentary blind spot and jabbed a hand into a trigger point at her shoulder. Her arm fell dead. She couldn't pick it up.

He flipped her effortlessly and dropped her down onto her back, hard. All the air rushed out of her lungs in a big whoosh. Her head spun. She couldn't move her arm. Her other arm throbbed from the joint displacement. She'd been training nearly her entire life, and he made her look like an amateur.

"Are you ready to behave?" he asked with that same insufferable smile.

She leaned over and spat a wad of blood onto the carpet in response.

His eyes swirled in warning. "That is an antique."

She glared back at him. She was outmatched, but still, she couldn't release her defiance. "Fuck you."

He straightened, pointing to a large, velvet chair. "Sit there, answer my questions, and you will be released. I give my word."

"And what is your word worth, *monster*?"

"Everything," he said with a resonance that went straight through her bones.

Chapter Two

Kierse sat. What else could she do?

Monsters were real. He was a monster. He was well within his rights to kill her for invading his home. If he wanted to talk, then she'd talk. He wasn't the first monster she had dealt with, and she was determined that he wouldn't be her last, either.

Monster rights were still a new thing. It had only been three years since the war had ended and the Treaty had been signed. Before that, she never would have imagined that monsters and humans could come to an accord.

The war had started when Coraline LeMort was murdered in cold blood. She was a vampire visionary who led the charge on ending the feud between vampires and werewolves, and she'd had the support of her own army to back her words up. When a rogue werewolf publicly murdered her, it was the spark that lit the world on fire. Her death brought all of the monsters out of hiding and started the Monster War. Vampires and werewolves became even more divided, and the other monsters chose sides.

It got so bad that monsters and humans alike were starving. Then the Coraline Convention was called. Delegations from each monster race as well as the United Nations agreed to end the killing and restore order. The result was the signing of the Monster Treaty. It put limitations on all monsters, made laws for humans and monsters to live in this world together, and ensured lasting peace for humankind. They even built a statue of Coraline in front of the Metropolitan Museum of Art to commemorate the Treaty.

The world was finally beginning to recover from the decade-long reign of terror, but that didn't mean that every monster agreed with it.

And that didn't mean Kierse was going to survive this altercation.

"Now, let's start with your name," he said.

"Why don't we start with yours?"

"Surely you know the name of the man you are robbing." His smile said otherwise. As if he *knew* that she didn't know who he was. That he clearly wasn't the fake John Smith that owned the place.

"Man?" she asked.

"Your name," he repeated gruffly.

"Kierse," she spat out. "My name is Kierse."

"Is that short for Kirsten?"

She narrowed her eyes. "No," she snapped. "It's like Pierce but with a K."

"Ah." He hadn't taken a seat. He still stood a few feet away, lording over her with that impenetrable fire. "You may call me Graves."

"Graves?" she asked. "Like the thing you crawled out of?"

"Some do."

"You're not a human," she accused.

He stared straight through her. "No, I'm not."

She wanted to ask what kind of monster he was, but she wouldn't give him the satisfaction. He clearly wanted her to ask. To find out what side of the Treaty he was on and whether or not he was going to kill her.

"You don't look like much," he finally said when she didn't give in.

She gritted her teeth. "Appearances can be deceiving."

He leveled her with an imperious gaze. "So, who are you?"

"You already know that: the person here to rob you."

"Ah, perhaps."

He slid his hand out of his pocket and produced the ring she had just risked her life to retrieve. She stared at it agog. How had he gotten it off of her? It had been secured in a secret inner pocket in the left side of her jacket, and he hadn't frisked her. He hadn't even gone looking for it. But she only let surprise show on her face for an instant before returning to her cocky, disinterested veneer.

"A lot of trouble for one ring," he said, twirling it between his fingers like he would a coin.

"If you say so."

"How did you get inside my home?" Graves asked, pocketing the ring once more.

She watched carefully as he put the ring back so that she knew where to retrieve it later. "Through the window."

"Which window?"

"The one in the study."

He pursed his lips and glanced away. As if he were contemplating the study very closely. No, almost as if he could *see* to the study beyond and retrace her steps. But of course, he *couldn't* do that. No monster she knew of had *that* ability.

"How did you get past the security system?"

She nearly barked in laughter. "It was turned off."

Graves's head whipped toward her. "It certainly was not."

"Maybe you should check it again, then."

"*I'm* the security," he all but growled.

"Then you're shit at it."

He smirked again. "Says the girl I apprehended with no effort."

"Woman," she bit back.

He conceded the point. "How old are you exactly?"

"Don't you know it's rude to ask?"

He just arched an eyebrow as if to say *you agreed to answer my questions.*

She blew out a breath. "Twenty-five. Not much younger than you."

"Appearances can be deceiving," he said, throwing her words back at her as he strode casually to a wet bar and poured himself a drink.

He brought the drink back over and offered it to her. Drinking with the enemy was a bad, *bad* idea. But either way, she *couldn't* take it. Not with her shoulder in this condition.

"Oh, my apologies." He looked smug as he said it.

He set the drink down. And then with reflexes she could hardly comprehend, he grasped her shoulder and knocked it back into place. No warning. Just perfect precision and a hard *pop*. She doubled over as pain lanced down her arm. She barely kept herself from crying out again.

"Better?"

She cleared her throat. "Can we just finish this interrogation?"

"Is *that* what we're doing?" He held the drink out to her again and, when she still refused to take it, knocked back half of it. "Interrogations used to be a lot more fun." Her eyes widened. What did *that* mean? "Fine. Who sent you?"

"I don't give out names," she told him. "I can't answer questions that are going to ruin my career."

He leaned back against the table and crossed his arms. "Do you think that is the worst that will happen if you don't answer my questions?"

She swallowed. It was a threat. He'd probably kill her. He was capable of it. He could end her existence at his leisure. By the Monster Treaty terms, he'd even get away with it. The fact that he hadn't meant he needed something from her. Hence the line of questioning. She just didn't know what he needed.

She hated breaking her rules. She'd promised herself she'd never out a client. But if it was between her life and some dick billionaire who didn't care about her, self-preservation kicked in fast and hard.

"Gregory Amberdash."

Graves's eyebrows rose slightly. That wasn't the answer he had been expecting. "The wraith?" The ring magically reappeared in his hand. "Who is Amberdash working for?"

"That's above my paygrade."

He glanced back at her as if remembering that she was involved. "You will find out who he is working for."

Kierse huffed a laugh. "No, I won't. That wasn't part of our deal. And anyway, he'd never tell me. That's not how he works." She lifted herself off of the velvet chair in defiance of his other edict. She only wobbled slightly as she regained her balance. "I've answered your questions. I'm not going to do your dirty work. Ask Amberdash yourself."

Graves sighed and then shook his head once. He seemed frustrated that she wasn't groveling for her life and offering to do whatever he asked just because he hadn't killed her.

"You are going to make me do this the hard way, aren't you?"

"Just call the cops. We're on a first-name basis. Won't do a damn thing." There wasn't a jail in New York that could keep her locked away.

He grinned then. "I have no intention of alerting the authorities. My methods are much more...effective."

Her stomach twisted. "*Your* methods?"

Graves didn't respond. He just began to methodically remove his black gloves. He pulled each finger individually, slipping the material out of place before carefully tugging the leather forward. She caught a glimpse of the dark lines of a tattoo circling his wrists before he tugged the cuffs of his suit down. His hands were large, with long, slender fingers. She didn't know much about music, but the pianists she had seen in clubs had fingers just like that. Made to grace the keys and hypnotize a melody out of hidden strings. She had no idea why he covered them in gloves in his own home.

"Come here," he commanded with all the blunt force of a car crash.

But she refused to budge. She'd been on the receiving end of demanding men before in her life. She'd learned her lesson. She was no longer a sapling constantly moved by the next heavy breeze. She was a mountain, immovable.

He saw her defiance. The *no* that lingered in the air unsaid.

It infuriated him. This man—this monster—was used to incalculable respect. She could see it all over him. Power was the only way to test a person's character. She found him wanting.

He stepped forward then. Two quick strides that brought him directly before her. She tilted her head up to read the clouds roiling through those piercing gray eyes.

"Fine," he ground out.

He jerked the zipper of her jacket down, exposing her neck, and her heart sank. Fuck, he *was* a vampire—and about to drain her. She opened her mouth to protest but stopped when she got a look at his surprised face. He was staring at her necklace with bald interest.

"A wren." His gaze swept back up to hers. A cruel smile curled on his lips. "Interesting."

"Why?" she asked, protective of the necklace that was her most prized possession. The only thing she had left of her parents.

He didn't answer. Just slowly, ever so slowly, brought his hand up and pressed the tip of his index finger to the spot right behind her ear. With the grace of a predator toying with its food, he dragged the finger softly down the pulse in her throat. She refused to shiver, though her heartbeat had skyrocketed at the barest touch. Her body came alive.

She'd spent her entire life hating vampires, but suddenly she understood how some humans volunteered to be fed from. She was in pain and abjectly frightened of what was to come, but she couldn't move if she had wanted to.

His finger reached the hollow opening between her collarbones and trailed back up again. Then he wrapped his entire hand around her throat, caging her there. He had command. He had all the power. She could see the hunger in his features.

She swallowed back her own confusion and desire and fits of anger. As if he could touch her like this. As if he had her permission. How dare he! Yet, she didn't move away. Her body thrummed in response. Like met like. Power met power.

He leaned forward. And for one sharp moment, she thought he meant to kiss her. But he stilled, staring deep into her eyes. He shook his head once. Something like surprise hit his features.

"*What* are you?" he whispered.

Chapter Three

K ierse blinked. He was asking *her* what *she* was? On what plane of existence did that even make sense? He was the one who had moved across the room at lightning speed. She'd jumped out a window, and he'd hauled her back through it with one hand. He'd incapacitated her with ease.

"Tell me," he snarled.

"Name's Kierse McKenna," she said with lifted chin. "And I don't want to be fed off of. Now, get your hand off me."

He released her in a rush as if she'd burned him. She adjusted her stance, bending at the knees just in time to prevent herself from sprawling backward. She stood her ground, watching and waiting for some kind of explanation.

"You think me a vampire?" he asked with disgust, a flash of confusion on his lips.

Well, if he wasn't, then what the hell was he?

"You only gave me your name," he continued. "Explain the rest. Explain what you are."

"You haven't explained what *you* are," she shot back.

"We're talking in circles. It would be much easier if you'd give me a straight answer." He looked down at his hand, the one that had encircled her neck, as if he couldn't understand what had happened. "But you're *not* giving me a straight answer."

"I've answered all your questions. Just like you said. Are you going to let me go now?"

"No," he said at once. "I have more questions."

"Then ask them."

"How did you take the wards down?"

"Wards?" she asked slowly.

He ground his teeth. "Did the people you're working for take them down for you? Did they help you get inside?"

"I have literally no idea what you're talking about. I let myself in."

He assessed her again, as if looking for something—guile or malice, most likely—but there was none. She really had no idea what he was talking about. She'd heard the word "ward" in fairy tales before, but that couldn't be what he was referring to. Monsters *not* magic was the motto of the entire monster movement. Wards seemed to fit very clearly in the *magic* section. So, there had to be some other definition.

She was a thief—a very good thief—but *just* a thief, nonetheless. She knew how to take down security systems. She'd been taught how to break into any number of buildings. She could crack a six-pin lock in a matter of seconds. She'd even broken into a bank vault for Jason just to prove that she could do it and not get caught. She was damn good at her job, but she had no clue what kind of lock a *ward* was.

"You have no idea what I'm talking about," he said finally.

"You're quick on the uptake."

He took another step back, contemplative. "You truly believe you were sent here by Gregory Amberdash."

"He's paying me."

"And you know nothing else?"

"I know that you have the thing I'm supposed to bring him so that I can be paid."

He held his hand out then. "Give it here."

"You have it," she reminded him.

"Take it out of your pocket and give it to me." She hesitated, and he snapped, "Now."

She huffed and removed the giant ring from where she'd concealed it. She'd pilfered it off of him when he'd gotten close to her. She thought he'd been distracted with examining her neck like a crazed vampire, and she'd gotten to work.

Thieving rules numbers three and four: distraction and sleight of hand.

She dropped it back into his palm. "Worth a try."

He shook his head. "You're just a common thief. They insult me."

She straightened to her full height. "*Excuse* me?"

"I can't believe this is the level they're stooping to." He stuffed the ring away again. She barely caught a glimpse of where it disappeared this time. "I'll have to test it. Something they weren't prepared for."

"What are you testing?"

He turned away without answering. "Here we are."

He set a small, intricately carved wooden box down on the table. She recognized some of the whorls on it. The same holly design around the library doors. A language that buzzed just at her periphery shimmered in the vines but disappeared on closer inspection.

"Open it," he commanded.

She raised a brow. "Is this *interrogation* to go on much longer?"

He narrowed his eyes in warning. She sighed, tipping the lid of the box open. There was nothing inside. Even less interesting than the two-pin lock she'd picked earlier.

"Wow," she drawled. "I can open boxes."

Despite her nonchalance, he did seem impressed…and quickly it was replaced with what looked like scheming. "You appear to have interesting talents, Miss McKenna. The real question is…how have you been left unaware of them?"

"I am not unaware," she told him, tilting her chin up.

But there was something in his eyes. Something swirling and depthless that caught her interest. Something trancelike that spoke deep into her soul. That said…maybe he was right. Maybe there was more to her. Maybe she'd always known. It shuddered through her for an instant and then was gone.

Graves slowly closed the box again. "There are legends in our world," Graves began, slow and sure, his voice as thick as molasses and just as sweet. "Tales of beasts and beauties. Creatures and stories that would keep you up at night. Of monsters born."

She swallowed at the sensuous way the words fell off of his lips. "I know all about what goes bump in the night."

"There's much worse than the monsters you know of in this world," he said as if reading her thoughts. "All those stories you've heard. All the tales and legends come from a kernel of truth."

"Like what?"

"Like me," he said evenly. Then he tilted his head sideways. "And you."

"Me?" she blurted out. "I'm human."

"Are you?"

She snorted in disbelief. "Yes. Obviously. How could I be worse than a monster? Let alone a vampire? They feed on human blood." She made a disgusted face at him.

"Vampires are pathetic bottom feeders. We allowed them to live on the surface while we remained in the shadows so that they stayed out of our way with their pesky wars. You…are something altogether different." She swallowed and waited for him to say more. "If you're to be believed, you can take down my wards with no outside interference."

"You keep talking about wards, but I don't even know what they are. Or at least they can't be what I *think* they are."

He sighed heavily as if her ignorance affected him personally. "Wards are magical barriers."

"Okay," she said, disbelieving. "That is what I think they are. But... *magic*?" The word came out derisive.

"Yes, magic. Wards are the reason there's no standard mechanical security system necessary on my house. They keep out intruders and alert me to any interference." He slid his hands into his pockets. "You shouldn't have been able to get within five feet of my home without me knowing. Not without help or wardbreakers or some serious powers yourself."

Kierse stared at him blankly. Then a giggle burst out of her. Until she was laughing so hard, she couldn't keep it together. It had been a while since someone had brought her nearly to the point of tears. Ethan always tried, but it was usually Gen's dry wit that worked.

"What precisely is so funny?" he asked, cutting through her laughter.

"Magic isn't *real*."

He arched an eyebrow. "Is that so?"

"Monsters not magic," she said like a mantra. "That's what the monsters touted when they appeared. It's practically their motto—monsters *not* magic. They have supernatural abilities—strength, speed, agility—but they can't, like...move things with their minds. Or whatever wardbreaking is."

"And you believe them?"

She shot him a skeptical look. "Wouldn't I have seen magic being used before? Wouldn't someone have talked about it?"

"It's in every fairy tale in every culture in the entire world," he said. "There are reasons for our tales. It is a rare talent and usually snuffed out of children long before it can develop into something more useful. So no, I doubt you would have met someone who could do much of anything before."

"I just...don't believe you. Why would I believe you?"

He looked her over as if she were the most insufferable thing on the planet. "I'm not in the business of performing."

"Well, if you're not going to do *magic*," she said, putting air quotes around the word, "how else can I believe you?"

He inhaled sharply and then released it. Then he tipped the lid of the box back open and offered it to her. She looked inside and saw a thick gold coin the size of a silver dollar. He flipped it to her, and she caught it out of midair.

"So, you're a *magician*." She said the word sardonically as she dropped the coin back on the table. "I've seen a few of them on the streets. Good sleight of hand, though."

He scowled as he snapped the empty box closed again. "I'm not here to convince you, but why would I lie?"

"I can think of about a hundred reasons."

"Open the box," he snarled.

She took it from his hands. This time she popped it open with flair, tossing the lid back and smirking at him. And as she did so, hundreds of coins spilled out of the box. Her eyes widened in alarm. She lifted the box into her hands as more and more of the coins rained down to the floor. Once they slowed, she checked the box for a false bottom.

"What's the trick?" she asked. From every angle, the box appeared perfectly intact. And she had *seen* it empty. "It was…"

"Empty?" he finished for her. "What would be the point of warding an empty box?"

She gasped softly and tossed the box away from her like it could burn her. "What the fuck? Magic?"

He shot her an imperious look. "I told you."

Magic.

Holy fuck…*magic.*

All those years with monsters. They'd come out of the dark, killing humans and other monsters alike. Those days had been bleak. If she hadn't turned to thieving before the war, she would have been dead with all the others once it started.

In some way, Jason had saved her life by throwing her into his own dark world. Not that she hadn't suffered considerably at his hands over and over again. But even in all those years of death and destruction, she'd always known that it was monsters not magic. Monsters…*not* magic. And yet…

"Now do you believe me?" he asked.

She opened and closed her mouth. "Why are you telling me this?"

Nothing ever came for free. Not in her world. Not with all she had gone through. If magic was a rare and precious thing that had been hidden from the public even when monsters had come out of hiding and somehow, against all odds, she had some sort of the gift in her wretched veins, then what was the price of it all?

"Because I want to offer you a job."

Chapter Four

A job. There was the cost.

The last thing in the world she wanted to do was work for him. She hated the puffed-up, insipid billionaires she stole for, but they were predictable. They wanted knickknacks and baubles and artwork and other useless things. They paid her handsomely for them, though. So she worked for crime bosses and madams and anyone else who had the means to pay her to do the thing she enjoyed.

But with Graves, she knew, she just *knew* that getting involved with him would be the death of her. Anything he'd ask her to steal would be an entirely different kind of danger. Already he spoke of *magic*. So impossible and yet somehow…real. She had learned an important lesson growing up on the streets—what was and wasn't worth dying for.

Still, she pursed her lips and waited for the offer. This should be interesting.

"What kind of job?" she asked evenly.

"The kind you're clearly good at. I need you to steal something for me."

She eyed him up and down. Looked through the cool exterior he portrayed. He'd gone from wanting to kill her to offering her a job a little too fast. This was something he wanted badly. Something he'd cough up a lot of money for. She could read that on her mark already.

The part she didn't understand was *why her* and *what was in it for her*. Because money wasn't enough on a job like this. Even the security she so desperately wanted for her friends wasn't worth certain death.

She let her eyes go round, revealing the doe-eyed look that made men underestimate her. "Why would you need me?"

He smiled slowly. "Because I can't get *everything* I want myself, obviously."

So, she was valuable, then? Well, that gave her leverage.

If he couldn't get this item himself and another thief wouldn't do, then did that make her the *only* person he could work with? She wished she could read more off of him, but he was a closed book. Only revealing enough information to get her interested in the offer. Clever. It was her own favorite tactic.

"I can pay you handsomely," Graves said when she didn't respond. "I can make your life very, *very* comfortable."

"What? You think I need the money?" Her voice lowered to a rasp.

He dragged his gaze up and down her figure clad in black. Her clothes were enough to get by. Nothing fancy, but they worked. But she knew what he saw when he looked at her. He saw exactly what she wanted him to see. A torn collar from his roughhousing, scuffed boots, and gross overconfidence.

His smirk grew. "Come now. It's plain you need money. This bauble here," he said, extracting the ring. "It can probably fetch you several thousand. Enough to get by for a couple of months in this city."

She blatantly winced, giving him the impression that she had no idea how much a diamond of that size was actually worth.

"Not even that much?" he asked, noting her expression, walking right into her trap. "Pity."

Even though she'd been reaching for it, she still hated the word. Pity was a death kiss. When she'd been running in the slums, she'd despised the pitying looks. The stares that said she'd never amount to anything.

The looks from Jason's other protégés. At first envious that she was singled out and then…the torment for being his favorite. Worse, the pity when they found the bruises he tried so carefully to hide on her body.

But they all realized eventually what Graves soon would when she fleeced him out of everything.

"I don't need your pity," she snarled defensively.

"Fine. I can pay and pay well. Just say yes. Let me give you all that you desire."

Warning bells rang in her mind. He was too eager, and it felt wrong on him. As if he'd never really asked for something he wanted before. He just *took it*. And so far she had not been receptive to taking.

"You haven't even told me what the job is and who I'm stealing from."

"You didn't seem to care when you were stealing from me," he said coolly. The easy sidestep of someone who didn't want to give too much away before she agreed.

That was so far from the truth that he was on a different planet. She'd cared. She'd just needed the money to get through the month's rent with Colette. So, she'd walked inside the house without knowing if a monster lay in wait. She'd gambled, and she'd lost. She wouldn't lose this negotiation.

"No," she said simply just to see what he'd do.

He stared back at her in confusion as if she had just moved a chess piece that hadn't been on the board. "No?" he asked incredulously.

"I choose my jobs, and right now, I'm not choosing yours. So, if we're done here, I've answered all your questions and want to leave."

Something sparked in those dark eyes. "You can leave if you choose, but this is the adventure of a lifetime. An object so rare, so valuable, and so difficult to acquire, it will make breaking into vaults seem like child's play."

Breaking into vaults *was* child's play. Well, her childhood at least.

"What kind of object? The Holy Grail?" she asked with a mocking laugh.

But she shouldn't have shown interest, because he latched on to it. As if money didn't matter but the thrill of it all interested her. Perked up her ears.

"Of a sort. You could be the one to break it out of where it's kept deep under the city, guarded by an unbreakable security system and hidden by the vilest of monsters." He arched an eyebrow in her direction. "If you're good enough."

She narrowed her eyes. It was enticing. Stupidly so.

Jason had chosen her as a youth because she didn't pick pockets out of necessity. It had been clear on her little urchin face how much she *enjoyed* it. She shouldn't have. She'd learned over the years to hide her zeal. To mask the chase as something other. Normal people didn't feel like this. It terrified them that she enjoyed flouting the law so overtly. And yet, growing up on the streets had taught her that the law was a trifling thing meant to be bent and circumvented. Because of course, it was only against the law…if she were caught.

He leaned his hip into the table and reached for his drink, switching back into his aloof demeanor. All eagerness gone. His eyes tracked her all the while. Judging and weighing the calculations going through her mind.

"So, are we going to work together?"

She hesitated. It was enticing. It was meant to entice her. He offered what she really wanted now that he'd landed on it—adventure and ever-increasing stakes. A job that no one else could do. These were things much harder to find than money in this godforsaken city.

In fact, he'd offered things that he had no idea she wanted even more than adventure and money and security. If she was stealing from vile monsters under the city, she had an inkling of exactly what that meant. She'd seen firsthand what happened when you messed with the wrong monsters. The city opened its mouth and swallowed you whole. Any reason to hit back at those monsters was a win in her ledger.

And still…she hesitated. Not because she didn't want to say yes. She did. But she needed to get her ducks in a row before this one.

"Give me twenty-four hours," she said after a minute. "Then I'll have your answer."

He weighed her reply and then nodded. "Agreed. One last thing before you leave."

He produced a small leather book out of a drawer in the table. He flipped it open to a page near the middle and offered her a pen. She took it automatically, curiosity getting the better of her. It was a signature page. Four names ran across the top. Two of them were completely indistinguishable. Just chicken scratch on the page. The other two read *Uma Matthewson* and *Mateo Parrish*. She recognized neither of them.

"What's this?" she asked.

"Sign it."

"Why?"

He looked at her wryly. "Everyone signs it. If you want to leave, you'll add your signature."

"What does it do?"

"If my suspicions about you are correct, Miss McKenna," he said with a tilt of his head, "absolutely nothing."

Another game. She picked up the pen with her left hand and scrawled out her name. She dropped the book back on the table. "Are we through?"

Graves slid the book back into its drawer and then swept his hand toward the door. "After you."

He tugged his gloves back on as he escorted her out. It felt surreal that he was actually allowing her to leave, let alone escorting her out like a guest instead of an intruder. They left the library and headed down the massive staircase together. He clasped his hands behind his back as they walked in silence.

Unease bit into her, as if at any second, the rug would be pulled out. The police would show up to whisk her away to a place that couldn't keep her. Or something far worse.

But nothing happened. He just opened the front door.

Snow fell like a blanket over the front steps and sidewalk, transforming the landscape into a winter wonderland. Tomorrow it would all be a slushy mess, but right now it was breathtaking.

"I'll expect you promptly tomorrow," Graves said.

She tilted her chin up to look into those incredible gray eyes. They hadn't been this close, and she'd been so focused on retrieving the ring that she hadn't considered quite how tall he was. He towered over her frame. His heat burned through her like a brand. As if he could sear a piece of him onto her existence. Burn straight through her hardened exterior and reveal what could have been had she not been abandoned and used and abused.

She shuddered under that scrutiny. Seeing things in herself she'd rather keep hidden. "I keep my promises."

"If you don't, I'll come for your answer."

She didn't much like that idea.

"Fine," she said and then trotted down the snow-strewn steps.

"Miss McKenna," he called before she got too far away.

She whirled around, anticipating the catch. It had been too easy to just walk out. But instead, Graves tossed the giant ring toward her. She plucked it out of the air. Surprise hit her features as she looked at the robin's egg–size diamond. Why would he give this to her? He'd done everything he could to keep it.

"A show of good faith," he said.

Oh, he was going to be difficult to work with.

In that moment, she saw that he had as many tricks up his tailored sleeves as she did and more time and experience. She was going to have to be careful to survive him. Because standing there on the threshold of his mansion, holding the very thing she'd come for, with his handsome face half hidden in shadow, it was very hard to even think of anything in his presence.

And that scared her most of all.

Chapter Five

Ethan's brown eyes were wide with concern when he met her on street level. His hand ghosted over the black coils of his hair before dropping back down to his side in worry. "What the hell happened? You look like you got the shit beat out of you."

"I did," she grumbled.

"I kept radioing you and never heard back."

Kierse remembered the two-way radio crashing to the ground and skittering off into the shadows. She grimaced. "I lost it."

"You *lost* it?"

His hand dropped onto his face, running down the brown skin that always looked like it had been dipped in sepia. He was roughly the same height as Kierse but with long, lanky limbs that made him seem taller than he was. And right now, with him drawing up in exasperation, he gained a few inches.

"You were right," she said, trying to hide her limp. "It was a monster. A big monster."

Ethan made a noise of distress, putting an arm under her shoulders, and she leaned into his strength as the sting slowly eased in her ankle. "I never saw anyone come in or out. What was it? A vamp? Werewolf?"

"Fuck if I know."

He startled as they ambled down the street. "What do you mean you don't know?"

"I mean…I don't know, Ethan. It wasn't a man, but he wasn't any kind of monster I'd ever seen or heard of." She chewed on her bottom lip. "I'll tell you and Gen about it when I get back."

"Get back?"

She fingered the ring in her pocket and flashed it at him. "I'm going to just take this to Amberdash now."

His eyes rounded at the sight of the ring. "You got the ring still? Even after breaking the Treaty? What the hell?"

Her eyes darted around the seemingly empty street. "Later, Ethan."

He blanched as if realizing the severity of the situation. "You should come home now. See Amberdash in the morning."

She shook her head as they veered east on 75th Street toward Central Park, where they had planned to catch the bus. "I'll explain when I get home."

They always recounted the night's success with Gen. She was the center of their imperfect trio. She was the one who had saved them both from a fate worse than hell.

Ethan's grip on Kierse tightened. "I'll come with you."

She smirked at him. "Come on. I know you're still planning to see Corey tonight at the festival."

Ethan flushed in the dim light. "Not fair."

"He'll worry if you're not home. So will Gen. Tell them everything is fine. I'll be right behind you."

He scowled. "*Is* everything fine?"

Kierse didn't have an answer to that, but she put on her winning smile, the one that got her out of anything. "Now you're worrying."

"Kierse," he groaned.

But they'd reached the bus stop and the bus was already pulling to a stop in front of them.

"I'll see you later," Kierse said.

"Please be safe!" Ethan called back.

She waved goodbye, running past the M10 as it pulled into the uptown stop. She moved away from the wealthy brownstones that lined the well-lit street toward Central Park. She couldn't help but glower at the luxury that still existed as if it had never been touched by the wars. This part of New York City looked much the same as it always had here.

There were two worlds in her city—the wealthy and everyone else. The wealthy had integrated with monsters from the beginning. Some even suspected that they had already known of their existence and, when the Monster War started, had bought their way to freedom. They lived in their mansions as if the economy hadn't collapsed, monsters had never taken to the streets, and millions hadn't died. Nothing had changed for them from one day to the next except that they now coexisted with monsters. Well, at least the monsters with equal wealth. They ran businesses with them, went to galas with them, and sent their children to the same fancy private schools. It turned out money really could buy anything.

Then there was Kierse's part of the city. Once you left uptown behind, the world looked remarkably different. Ramshackle apartments that had tripled in price practically overnight. A police force that only cared for the ones lining their pockets. Gangs popped up on every corner. Women and men alike selling their bodies when all the other jobs had evaporated. The destruction hadn't only made the monsters appear; it had made monsters of everyone.

Since the Monster Treaty, shops were reopening, people went out after dark again, and prices were rebounding. More and more people were leaving the shadows to find the light, but the city hadn't completely changed. Gangs still ruled. Brothels lined the blocks of lower Manhattan and the surrounding boroughs. Monsters didn't kill openly for sport anymore, but everyone stayed out of their way. Maybe this was the new normal.

Kierse cut south until the lights grew brighter, then cut east. Midtown had recently begun to thrive again despite monsters still occupying Times Square, and she merged into the steady flow of sidewalk traffic. She angled out of the way of the bulky half troll trundling down the sidewalk and nearly ran into a wayward vampire. She sidestepped the vamp hastily, colliding with a tourist holding up her phone and snapping a photo of the troll. Kierse ducked her head to hide her distaste. Cell phones had been a necessity for many before the Monster War. The plans were sadly out of most people's budgets now…as was traveling. How and why wealthy tourists still wanted to come to New York City was beyond her. Let alone being clueless enough to take pictures of monsters on the street. Some people never found common sense.

She pushed past the tourists gawking at Rockefeller Center and angled toward the Amberdash building on Madison Avenue. Gregory Amberdash had used his skills as a wraith—advanced hearing, quick feet, and shrewd business sense—to get rich during the Monster War. And despite that, he was one of the few wealthy people she could stand. And though she didn't particularly care for working for monsters—after all, look at what they'd done during the war—she honestly preferred monsters to the rich, who had just sat by and let the world go to shit.

A doorman nodded at her as she entered. The interior had a sky-high ceiling, marble columns, and plush seating. Her high-end clients liked a high-end place to run their business. The Amberdash building was a perfect place to appease them. She strode straight past the concierge to the bank of elevators and entered the first that opened.

She tapped a keycard to take her straight to the top floor. Amberdash himself had given her the key to bypass his security and take her up to the penthouse. She had started working with Amberdash in Jason's thieving guild before things went sour. Their relationship had survived the fallout, and now he provided jobs for her when he had clients who needed a little under-the-table business. Amberdash as the middleman usually resulted in fewer people trying to kill her for their secrets.

The elevator dinged open, revealing the entrance that divided his office from his living quarters. She shivered as she headed for the office. No way did she ever want to be alone with a wraith in his own space. That was just asking for trouble. Like the loss of her soul.

She knocked twice, and a petite blonde opened the door. Her eyes were hollow and cheeks sallow, but there was a fever in her expression that Kierse had seen on Amberdash's other willing victims. Wraiths could feed off a soul for years if they were careful. Some even found it more enjoyable to watch the life slowly drain out of their victim one increment at a time. Like any other office job.

"Miss McKenna," she said, recognizing her at once. "I'll let Mr. Amberdash know you've arrived. Please come in and make yourself comfortable."

Kierse stepped over the threshold as the blonde moved languidly across the room to another closed door that led to the living quarters. Kierse crossed her arms and remained standing, waiting to get this thing over with.

Five minutes turned to ten, and she eyed the leather sofa with interest. She wasn't going to let her guard down, but she hated the mind games. Wraiths didn't sleep at night. In fact, she wasn't sure they slept at all when they were feeding regularly. The only reason he was making her wait was because he could.

Just when she was beginning to think that Ethan was right and she should have gotten rid of the ring tomorrow, a voice spoke into her left ear.

"So," Amberdash said.

She shivered and turned to face him. "Amberdash."

The wraith smiled, and she tried not to shudder. Wraiths could almost pass as human except for the general sense of death that emanated from them as they approached. They typically had distinctive sallow skin, grim expressions, and shadows clinging to them. Basically, no one wanted to be caught alone with one in a darkened room.

"Hello, Kierse." He slid past her, not quite walking, not quite gliding, behind his desk. "I assume you're here for a reason."

She fished the ring out of her pocket and dropped it onto the desk with a *thunk*.

Amberdash's face was recessed, and his clothes draped delicately on his tall, thin frame. "Your talents are, as ever, not exaggerated."

"I'll take that as a compliment."

"As you should," he said, reaching across the desk for the ring.

She dropped her hand over it and arched an eyebrow. "What exactly are you playing at, Amberdash?"

His eyes flashed at her audacity. His fingers were inches from her wrist. "Whatever do you mean?"

"You sent me to a monster's house without adequate information. I could have been killed."

"I am merely the middleman," he said, his hand brushing through shadows as if that were an answer. "You agreed to the job regardless. It is why I pay you so well. You get the job done. As you did tonight, I see."

She switched tactics, removing her hand from the ring and leaving it unattended. His eyes flickered down to it and then back up at her.

"You know I love the jobs that you give me. I want us to keep working together. I also want to live to see another day. I thought you valued the work that I did for you." She sighed and ran a nervous hand back through her hair, revealing the bruising from her tussle with Graves.

Amberdash tilted his head. "Don't often see you banged up."

"I'd really like to keep it that way." Her dark hair fell back over the cut. "I'm more valuable to you with all my limbs intact."

"Fine. I'll pay you for the expense, if that's what you're after." Amberdash pocketed the ring swiftly and then punched in a code on his desk that opened a drawer underneath. Kierse had broken the code lock once while she waited just to see if she could. She wasn't stupid enough to steal anything. Amberdash would hunt her down and kill her himself if she betrayed him.

"No more monsters without forewarning," she added as he doled out a stack of hundreds. When he was done, he pushed them across the desk, and she hid them in her right jacket pocket before turning to go. She debated telling him about taking another job, but she liked to keep her options open.

"I'd watch your back."

Kierse stilled at those words. When she faced him, he steepled his fingers in front of him.

"Is that a threat?"

"Certainly not from me."

Kierse forced herself not to react. "What do you know?"

"Only that talents like yours are in high demand," he said as he drifted back into the darkness of his office. "So...watch your back."

She shivered at the cautionary advice. Gregory Amberdash didn't issue them lightly. She waited until he was out of sight and then hastened from the Amberdash building, glad to be beyond his reach and that ominous warning.

Chapter Six

The bus dropped Kierse off a few blocks from home. Despite the night she'd had, she was still wired. Normally when she finished a mission, Ethan's comforting presence let her drift off no matter what manner of monster or human was nearby. The bus was one of the last vestiges of the old Manhattan. No one fucked with bus drivers.

She took a breath of relief when she stepped onto her home turf. Houston Street was bustling this late at night. The shops were all closed, including her favorite bagel joint in the entire city, but that didn't stop the Lower East Side from coming to life after hours. The local gang, the Roulettes, patrolled the neighborhood. Girls called out from windows as she headed south toward Delancey. She ended up on the corner between the Roulettes' headquarters, her go-to bodega, and Madame Colette's, a landmark brothel house and the place she called home.

She, Ethan, and Gen lived in the attic of the brothel. Gen was Colette's only daughter, and Kierse and Ethan were her two pet projects, then best friends, and now family. Everything that belonged to one of them belonged to all of them. That was how it had been since the first moment they met.

Kierse stalked up the front steps of the house, grinning at the Roulette standing guard at the main entrance, a casino chip on his lapel. "Hey, Corey. I thought you had plans with Ethan tonight."

Corey was Ethan's everything. Corey's parents had immigrated from the Philippines right before the monsters' appearance and the economic collapse. His parents had so many dreams for him, but after they'd died, he'd made his own way by joining the Roulettes. He fit right in with his broad shoulders, bulky muscles, and serious expressions. Kierse never would have guessed he and Ethan would be such a pair. But they'd met on one of the runs Ethan made to the Roulettes, and Corey had fallen instantly in love. It would have been disgusting if she wasn't so happy for Ethan.

Corey winked at her. "Plans are still on. I'm off soon. We're going to the festival in Little Italy. You and Gen coming, too?"

Kierse's heart panged at the thought of the festival. "It's still going on this late?"

Only a scant few years ago, nothing could have survived the monster brutality at night. Let alone a street festival. It really felt like they were coming to the other side of all of this.

"Yep," he said, tossing his glossy black hair. "Supposed to go all night, if the nymphs have anything to say about it."

She laughed. "Oh, I bet."

Nymphs were one of the few monsters that humans could tolerate. They were mischievous little things but good at a party.

"You should come. It'd be good for you."

She waved him off. "We'll see."

Corey let her pass without another word. The brothel during working hours was far from her favorite place in the world. Most nights, she took the fire escape to avoid the faux laughter of the sex workers and the prowling eyes and groping hands of their patrons. But rent was due, and she hated putting something off until tomorrow that could be done today.

When she stepped into the sitting area, she found a buxom redhead with all the grace and beauty of the leader of the home—Madame Colette. Beside her sat Carmine Garcia, her regular associate and the head of the Roulettes. Their frequent love affair was more than public knowledge. As well as the fact that she would never leave it all behind for him.

"You're late," she said from an antique armchair next to the flickering fireplace in the brothel house.

"Always, ma'am," Kierse said.

"Be useful. Make me another brandy."

Madame Colette never admitted that she waited up for Kierse when she was on a mission. The time Kierse had made the mistake of asking, she'd gotten her ears boxed for the stupidity of it—Colette had better things to do than stay up over some brat her daughter had taken into her attic—but Kierse knew the truth.

Still, she sloshed more brandy into Colette's crystal glass. The good stuff at that.

"Carmine, dear, I have business," she said, fluttering her red-lacquered nails at him.

He rose to his considerable height and dropped a bowler hat onto his gelled-back black hair. His light-brown skin was smooth and unblemished, but his onyx eyes were keen and calculating. They had to be, to rule one of the largest and most ruthless gangs in the city.

"Of course," Carmine said, adjusting his three-piece suit. The light glinted off of the silver casino chip pin on his tie. He brushed his lips against Colette's milky wrist. "I will see you later."

She waved him off, and it was only after he was gone that she said, "Why do you look like you got the shit beat out of you, girl?" Colette leaned back in her chair, tossing her bright-red bangs off of her fair and unlined forehead and out of her blue eyes.

Kierse rolled her aching shoulders. "I'm fit for a fight still, Colette."

"You'd be better off spreading your legs for money like a good girl. All this fighting makes you look like you strolled out of the dumpster. Doesn't befit my house or hospitality."

"Noted."

"Did you at least bring me something worthwhile?"

Kierse dropped the rent money down on the table, and Colette grinned. "Paid in full."

"Good girl."

The madame sloshed the brandy around in her glass. She'd had Gen when she was twenty and had still risen to be one of the most prominent madams in the city, taking over for her predecessor and growing the brothel house to its new form of glory.

"Anything else?"

"Tell my darling daughter, Genesis, that I'm going to need her in the tent tomorrow afternoon again, will you?"

"I'll tell her. Good night, Colette."

She strode out of the parlor and headed toward the magnificent staircase. The wide-open stairs were shiny with polish, bedecked with elaborate banisters. It was a remnant of a bygone era. Back before this four-story home was used as a brothel and instead for some wealthy socialites. Back when this part of the city had been used by someone other than the dregs of society.

Kierse gritted her teeth and climbed to the attic. Thankfully, no one disturbed her as she ascended the stairs that led to her refuge. The lights were dim as she entered, casting everything in different shades of midnight.

Gen was sprawled across her bed. Ethan had changed out of his gear and was curled up behind her, slowly working small braids into her rich copper hair. Kierse loved seeing them like this, without a care in the world. Gen, who had grown up in this brothel, always with the expectation that one day she would have to join it. And Ethan, who had been taken in by the church in his hometown of Hartford, Connecticut, and moved up the ranks before finally coming to Manhattan. Only to be abused and barely escape.

And Kierse—well, she loved an exit strategy, because Gen had been hers. Jason had found out she was trying to leave the guild. In his fit of rage, he'd beaten her to within an inch of her life and left her for dead. The one exit she'd never gotten to successfully take. And then Gen had found her and given her a home.

The world outside of this room was a horrifying place, but for just this moment, they had peace.

"Rough night?" Gen asked.

"I'm sure Ethan already told you," Kierse said as she padded across the creaky wooden floors.

She moved past the training facility at the center of the room and around the tattered orange sofa and colorful patterned chair that Gen had masterfully reupholstered herself. She was careful not to upend the small, round table, which held Gen's tarot-reading paraphernalia, and avoided the dozen plants that Ethan was currently nursing to health. He was infatuated with the stuff, and Colette might have pitched a fit if he didn't grow the herbs that Gen used to make her medicinal tonics.

"Colette wants you in the festival tent tomorrow."

Gen huffed. "Fine. But tell me about tonight. Ethan said that things went poorly. There was a monster."

"Yeah. You could say that." Kierse took a deep breath, flopping back on the adjacent bed. This was going to be fun. "It was a monster but not any that I've ever known before."

Gen made a sound of protest. She pushed Ethan off of her, tying her red hair into a knot on the top of her head. Normally so serene and calm, her face now showed a flicker of concern. She hated making Gen worry, but it was kind of an occupational hazard.

Ethan came to his feet between the beds. "I did tell you that."

"You did," Gen said. "I just didn't believe you."

She trailed off when she noticed Kierse's stillness. Gen had been slowly losing her vision due to early onset macular degeneration since she was seven. Most of her central vision was gone in both eyes, but she could still see out of her peripheral. The one time Colette had paid the ridiculous fee for a doctor to look at her, they'd diagnosed her with a rare illness, told her there was no cure or treatment, and sent her packing.

"What is it?" Ethan asked.

This was her world, her sanctuary. The only place she ever completely let her guard down. Gen was their beacon home. Together, the three of them had carved out this slice of the world for themselves. They'd needed Gen. They'd needed this home where a madame's daughter, an altar boy, and a thief could live free of expectations. And she was about to ruin it all.

"Two things: one, he offered me a job, and two, he has magic."

"Magic?" Gen said at the same time Ethan asked, "What job?"

"Yes, magic," Kierse said.

"And you believe him?" Ethan asked. Her eyes shifted to him. He was the youngest of the trio, long and lithe and beautiful. He could have raked in more money at the brothel than any of the workers on the floor below them if he'd wanted to. Even the ragged scar on one side of his face couldn't mar how stunning, striking, and alluring he was.

She shrugged. "I wouldn't have believed him if I hadn't seen it with my own two eyes."

"But then is he a kind of monster we don't know about?" Gen asked, stiffening as she considered this possibility. "Is he not subject to the Monster Treaty?"

"I don't know," Kierse said.

"But a representative from each breed of monster stepped forward and signed. It keeps them from killing us—it's the only thing that keeps us safe."

Kierse knew the terms of the Treaty. The monsters agreed with the humans that to have a better world, they all had to put their differences aside. The monsters would be subject to human laws, including murder. And humans were forbidden from interfering in monster business unless monsters were in violation of human law. Which meant that a human breaking and entering into a monster's home, like what Kierse did tonight, could be killed. No questions asked. It gave the monsters more autonomy than most humans were comfortable with, but it was a compromise.

"Honestly, that's the least of my concerns here." Kierse stood and paced away from her friends.

"What kind of job is this, Kierse?" Gen asked.

"The dangerous kind," Kierse said stiffly. "Stealing something very powerful from very bad monsters. The kind that have a following underground."

Gen gulped. "Oh, Kierse."

"And money isn't an object. We can have all the safety and security we need to get out of here after I finish it."

"Is this about Torra?" Ethan whispered. Gen grasped his hand, shushing him.

Kierse winced. She didn't talk about Torra, and she certainly wasn't about to right now.

"He might know more about where I come from," she said instead of touching the land mine that was her ex-girlfriend.

She knew so little of her past. Her mother had died in childbirth. She'd lived for a short time with her father, but he'd abandoned her at an early age. One day, she'd walked to school, and the next, he was gone. Hardship on the streets erased everything good that remained. She couldn't even remember his face or the sound of his voice. The memories were just blank.

All she had from them was her necklace.

She'd been left on the streets and learned to fend for herself. Only to be recruited by Jason when he'd found her happily pickpocketing. Then, she was in his thieving guild. She'd honed her talents with him, and she'd repaid his brutality with a knife in his gut. Good riddance.

It just proved that she had already been capable, and her time after her parents left had just honed her into the person she was today. Had her father taught her resilience? Had her mother given her her powers? She had no answers and never knew anyone who could teach her more about herself... until now. What happened to her before was lost to time.

But maybe now it wasn't. She'd just opened her mouth to say exactly that when she heard screams from downstairs.

Corey burst into the room, yelling, "Gang raid!"

"What the hell?" Ethan said in shock.

"Gang raid," he repeated. "We need to get you the hell out of here! I have to help the girls." He pressed a firm kiss to Ethan's lips. "Get out safe."

"We will," Ethan said, reaching for him even as Corey was already speeding back out of the attic.

Kierse jumped into action, ushering Ethan and Gen to the fire escape on the back of the building. The whole time, her mind was whirring. A *gang* attack? Which gang would be stupid enough to attack Colette's place? The Roulettes scared off most other activity in these parts. There were few gangs who could go up against them.

She didn't have time to think about it more than that. She needed to get her friends out of the brothel and somewhere safe.

Kierse checked that the coast was clear and then helped Gen out of the window.

"Go," Gen said irritably. "I can get down."

"Ethan?" Kierse called as she plunged down the fire escape.

"Coming up the rear."

She could hear gunshots in the distance and screams from within. She'd lived here for years, and while there had been scuffles with local gangs, disagreements with clientele, and disruptions with new workers, there had never been an actual attack. Her refuge had been raided, and she was furious.

Kierse checked that their escape route was clear before dropping the last few feet onto the sidewalk. Gen dangled her feet below, uncertainly reaching for the ladder. Luckily, she took the fire escape as often as Ethan to avoid seeing her mom. It didn't make Kierse worry about her any less in this situation as she landed uneasily on her feet. Ethan skipped half the ladder himself, landing with ease beside them.

Besides missions with Kierse, Ethan worked for Colette running errands, delivering messages, and dealing with the Roulettes. He spent most mornings working his body into a sweat, trying to bulk out those long, lean muscles. Kierse had never been as grateful to have him at her side as when they had Gen between them.

"Where to?" Ethan asked.

"The festival," Kierse answered at once. "People are cover."

Ethan nodded, taking Gen's hand as they all veered toward Little Italy.

They were rounding the corner when something suddenly felt off to her. Instincts took over as the hair on the back of her neck pricked and unease slithered into her belly. She leaned into that feeling. Whatever it was, whatever edge it gave her, she slid into it. Her focus centered on the next turn the second before a gun whipped around the edge and pointed directly in her face.

Gen screamed. Ethan gasped. Kierse returned to real time in that instant, stepping toward the intruder as he barreled toward them. She reached past the gun with only a second to spare and brought her hand down decisively against the delicate bones of his wrist. The man cursed as the gun clattered to the ground several feet away.

There was no time to ask questions. No time to wonder who the hell this man was. The gun was out of the picture, but in a contest of his strength against hers, it wasn't looking up. She *could* fight, but she wasn't built for it, and she didn't want to if she didn't have to. Stealth had always been her MO. Stay hidden, avoid notice, and if all else fails, run. One on one, this giant of a man would surely overpower her.

So Kierse dragged the man closer to her rather than trying to push him away. In the moment of confusion, she drove her knee up into his groin as quickly and efficiently as possible. He gasped and toppled to the ground.

No time to waste. Kierse whipped around to Gen and Ethan and yelled one word of direction. "Run!"

Chapter Seven

No one needed to be told twice.

Gen and Ethan hurtled past the man. Kierse was close on their heels. She glanced over her shoulder just once to see the man struggling to get back to his feet, barking orders as he did so. She seared the image of him into her mind. He was dressed completely in black with a beanie obscuring his hair. He was over six feet tall with red cheeks, eyes as green as an emerald, and a crooked smile. An oak tree pin was affixed to the lapel of his peacoat. Was that a Druid? What the hell did a Brooklyn-territory gang have against the Roulettes?

She had no intention of waiting for answers. She rushed out into the open night, getting ahead of her friends and taking off across Grand. No one spoke as they escaped the mayhem of the brothel and came to the outskirts of the festival. Here at least they could get lost in the thrum of the crowd.

Despite the snow, thousands of people danced and drank and caroused. They bought food and booze and sex and fortunes from the tents lining Mulberry Street in Little Italy. It was a carnival of old, complete with masks and costumes and revelry. Nymphs flitted about the gathering, their multicolored hair only partially blending in. They were a welcome sight at a party with both their ethereal beauty and muse-like inspiration, but they were still monsters, and the last thing a human wanted was to be on the bad side of a nymph, the mischievous little devils. But tonight, at least, it seemed that the Treaty held and all was well. Other dangers lurked in the dark tonight, though.

Grasping Gen's hand, Kierse shouldered her way through the crowd. It was hard to believe that on normal festival nights they'd be out here at the brothel's swirling pink, purple, and orange tent where Gen made money staring into a crystal ball and reading palms and tarot. People close to her knew that she only had luck with the tarot cards—and only when they spoke to her—but no one *else* knew that. It was her own form of stealing. And Gen had gotten enough correct for her to be respected in their community. Not just for being Colette's daughter but for being The Prophet Mistress Genesis.

A ridiculous title for half the truth.

The world had been plunged into darkness. Snowflakes fell on the revelers.

"What do we do?" Ethan gasped out.

Gen shivered against him. She looked so young and frail, standing there as snowflakes carpeted the streets as if a down pillow had exploded, releasing white feathers over everything. This was out of her depth. Her typical command had evaporated.

"Kierse?" Gen said.

"I don't think we were followed," Kierse said. She surveyed the vendors on the streets and saw no familiar faces. She was going to have a talk with the Roulettes about what the hell had happened when she got back. "Come on. Let's find a place to wait this out."

Kierse elbowed her way through the gyrating mix of people. It was dense enough to be difficult, but she found a path. She examined her surroundings, estimated the number of people between her and the nearest exit, and mapped out a route to the next empty stall. All while she clutched Gen's trembling hand and pulled her along with Ethan behind her. They darted around a couple kissing and a nymph twirling her blue-green hair around her finger.

They were nearly there when a brawny Black woman stepped in front of Kierse.

"Nowhere to go." Her accent was thick and unmistakably foreign. A rich Irish brogue. An oak tree was tattooed at her throat.

"Druid," Kierse hissed.

The woman flashed her teeth. "Boss says your time is up."

"Ethan," Kierse said low. "Protect Gen."

Kierse didn't wait to see if he would do it. She let time slow, anticipating what the woman would do next. If going around wouldn't work then she'd have to go through. Use all those techniques she'd practiced over and over again.

Kierse gritted her teeth, flicked a knife out of her sleeve, and sliced forward across the woman's chest. The woman jumped out of the reach of Kierse's knife and produced two of her own. This woman hadn't anticipated that Kierse knew how to fight. She was scrappy and fast but more of a sprinter than a marathon runner, so this needed to end quickly.

Kierse approached the woman, breathing shallowly and keeping her arms in. The woman struck first, thrusting one of her blades forward. Kierse turned sharply. She dodged the blow and pulled her own blade up toward the woman, slashing against her arm. The woman moved fluidly as she attempted again to take her down, but Kierse was ready for her. She hit her another time, dragging her knife against the woman's exposed thigh.

Kierse pressed her advantage. The woman whirled out of the way of Kierse's blade and then aimed her own knife toward Kierse's ribs.

"Your left!" Ethan cried.

Kierse jerked at the sound of his voice. She moved but not quite fast enough. The knife sliced outward across her left ribs, drawing blood.

She hissed as pain roared up her side. She couldn't lose. Not now.

It was shocking that no one paid them any mind. No matter that they were fighting in a public space and bleeding on the street. Maybe on the Upper East Side someone would have screamed and run away from the fight, but it was a common occurrence here—too many fights for people to be bothered. It was only when guns were drawn or fangs and claws came out that they knew to run.

Kierse's breathing intensified. She could feel her heart racing up out of her chest and into her throat. She tried to reach slow motion, but she was already drained. Too much adrenaline too fast. She needed a moment to think. A moment to breathe. But she didn't have it.

"It's over. Surrender and I promise to make it quick," the woman crooned.

Kierse refused to rise to her bait. She had people to protect. People who were counting on her. The woman wanted her to get mad and make a mistake. The only mistake was not finishing this sooner. She had to assume that other Druids had followed this woman here. And if the first attacker caught up with them, it would be at least two against one. She didn't like those odds.

Kierse sighed heavily as if she were giving up. She nodded her head once at the woman and let her knife drop slightly toward her side. Then she waited to see if she took the bait. Like clockwork, the woman rushed her, thinking that she was easy prey after all.

As soon as she was within reach, Kierse spun on a dime, grasping the woman's arm and popping the wrist. She dropped her knife with a strangled gasp. Kierse slammed her hand in the woman's kidney hard enough to drop her to a knee. And when she fell, Kierse smashed the hilt of her knife against the woman's temple. The woman swayed for a moment before collapsing like a sack of potatoes.

"Holy shit," Ethan cried.

"Kierse," Gen said with growing alarm.

"I don't know if there are more of them," Kierse said, turning to her friends. Everything had happened so fast, and yet the whole thing had taken too long. "We have to get moving." She grasped Gen's hand again and started to run.

"Why are they after us?" Ethan gasped.

Kierse had assumed this was a Roulette problem, but that woman had said the boss wanted her dead. Why the hell would the head of the Druids want her dead? Let alone want her dead enough to attack the brothel and the Roulettes in open warfare? Only one thing had changed—Graves.

"Fuck," she hissed. "Amberdash told me to watch my back when I left his building tonight."

"This is about the guy who offered you a job?" Ethan asked incredulously, dodging around three people laughing and dancing.

"Does he want you dead, or are these *his* enemies?" Gen asked between breaths as they continued to weave in and out of the crowd.

She had taken Amberdash at face value, but she hadn't thought that this would mean enemies would attack her safe house.

"Just…hurry."

Kierse didn't know what to do if there were more Druids after them, and based on that woman, she had to assume there were. She couldn't take on more people. She barely had the energy to run. And she didn't know what that meant for her friends. Did that make them collateral damage?

Something fierce and deadly opened up within her chest at that thought. *No*. They were her friends, her family, her home. She wouldn't make a mistake when it came to them. She'd *kill* before letting their attackers touch a hair on her friends' heads.

"I have an idea," Kierse rushed out, ignoring the sharp pain in her ankle as she darted between two more people. "Follow me. Just out of this mess."

With a renewed burst of energy, she careened through the mass of people north toward NoHo. Gen took heaving breaths behind her. While Kierse and Ethan had trained, Gen was soft and malleable. Her specialties lay in other areas. Kierse had never cared about that before today.

"I'm fine. Keep going," Gen said between pants.

So Kierse focused on the present and hurried past Prince and down the next left onto the mostly empty alleyway that connected to Lafayette. Kierse shoved Ethan and Gen in front of her. "Keep going!"

If she could get them out the other side, then she could face their attacker while they got away. She could see the opening like a beacon in the night beckoning to her as they raced toward the end of the street. Then, not twenty feet from the opening, the first man stepped into their pathway. And he had retrieved his gun.

The first gunshot ricocheted off the ground, barely missing Kierse. Gen cried out as Ethan flung them both sideways against the brick wall and out of the way.

"Get out of view," Kierse shouted at Ethan as he helped Gen into a closed doorway.

As Kierse found her own cover, she retrieved the gun from her boot and aimed at their attacker. With him silhouetted in the mouth of the street, she couldn't make out a single distinct thing about him.

"Put down your weapon," he growled.

"You first," she said.

"You've led us on a fun chase and took down Orla. Mighty impressive, if it wasn't a wee bit infuriating."

"Why are you here?" Kierse asked. "Why are you after us?"

"Not them. Just you," the man said with a grin that didn't sit right with her. "You're working with the enemy. That means you need to be eliminated. Business. You understand?"

Kierse's stomach twisted. So it *was* about Graves. Someone had found out that she had been at his house. She'd walked right out the front door.

A second man appeared at the mouth of the alley. "Got you cornered."

Kierse shifted her gun to the new man. "If I give myself up, you'll let my friends go?"

"No business with them. Only kill 'em if you continue to try to get away. Considering you're out of options, now would be the best time to do it."

"No, Kierse," Gen cried.

"Absolutely not!" Ethan said.

"Declan, you can't be serious," the second man said. "Lorcan will gut you from nose to navel if you let them go."

"Shut the feck up, Cormac," Declan snapped. He tilted his gun, telling Kierse to have her friends walk out.

Lorcan. She filed the name away for later, when Gen and Ethan were no longer in danger.

"Kierse," Ethan said, his voice barely above a whisper now.

The two Druids were arguing with each other. They thought that she'd chosen this building at random. She'd been putting on airs like she was beaten already. Like she'd actually give her friends up to them.

"Now," she said just as she sent a bullet toward the first man.

Ethan yanked the door open and barreled through with Gen's hand in his own. Kierse fell through after them. She took the extra second to relock the door and then was racing down the familiar apartment building. An ex-boyfriend had lived here for a few months before upgrading to a safer neighborhood. Kierse never forgot a layout.

The sound of shattering glass followed by boots on tile pounded after them as they raced toward the main entrance. A group of guys smoking weed backed into the mailboxes as they raced past them and out onto the much busier Houston Street.

Kierse stuck her hand out, flagging the first available taxi. She didn't have time to think about the exorbitant price before stuffing her friends into the backseat and falling in after them. She yanked the door closed just as Declan and Cormac landed empty-handed on the sidewalk and the taxi pulled away.

"Where to?" the man asked impatiently as if not realizing the danger the trio had just been in.

Ethan and Gen looked at Kierse in question. They couldn't go back to the brothel. It wasn't safe. That was obvious now. There was only one other option.

"Five Points," she said.

Chapter Eight

When the taxi finally came to a stop a block away from Five Points, she threw the fare down on the seat without preamble, jerked the door open, and jumped out. She held the door for Ethan and then Gen. Ethan clung to Gen, his eyes wide with barely suppressed terror. Gen was worse for wear from the chase, but otherwise the drive had returned her normal calm.

"We good?" Kierse asked.

Ethan and Gen exchanged a look before nodding. Gen took Kierse's hand. "Are you okay?"

Kierse shrugged. "Let's just move."

She fell into step between her friends.

"This whole thing is so messed up." Ethan's head hung forward, and he stuffed his hands into his pockets. "We can't go back to Colette's. We're going to have to find a way to tell her what happened to us. And Corey." Ethan looked panicked. "He's going to be worried."

"My mother is a formidable woman," Gen said. "And Corey knew he was sending us onto the streets. He won't worry too much tonight. It will be all right."

"But how will we contact them? We don't even have a phone."

Kierse blew out a breath and said the words that she hated saying. "Nate will know what to do."

Because Nate O'Connor had a solution to everything. She was certain he would have one for this newest dilemma. And she had more than just security and communication in mind.

"We're in good hands," Gen said.

"But that's home." Ethan whispered the thought they were all thinking.

"I know," Kierse said.

And they fell silent after that. Their home had been taken from them, but at least they had one another.

Kierse led the group around the corner and down 10th Street toward the giant warehouse that made up the ground floor of Five Points. The name was an homage to the famous Five Points neighborhood in lower Manhattan where the Five Points Gang dominated in the nineteenth century. It coincided rather well with the consolidation of the five wolf packs during the Monster War under notorious werewolf alpha Nate O'Connor. Monsters had mingled peacefully with humans on his property even before the Treaty went into place. It had long been a safe haven for those who saw a future for monsters and humans and continued to be so today.

The exterior was black with a large glowing blue sign and a line that wrapped around the building. They moved to the back, waiting their turn as Kierse watched the drug deals go on in the park across the street as she tapped her foot impatiently.

After a few minutes, they made it to the front. The bouncer looked the trio up and down and pointed at a sign that read "We abide by the Monster Treaty."

"You got a problem with that?"

"We're good," Kierse told him. "We're just here to see Nate. Is he in tonight?"

"Don't know," the man said. "Haven't seen him. You're good."

Kierse paid the cover charge and then stepped inside. It was a monstrosity of a building. What used to be a large warehouse had been converted into a pulsing nightclub full to the brim with people dancing. Ethan's face lit up at the extravagance of the place. He was more of a party boy than he liked to admit—young and beautiful and open to anything. Though he would have preferred to be here with Corey.

Kierse didn't understand how she and Ethan had gone through such similar things and he had turned out with his emotions on his sleeves and she had come out of it shut off and broken inside.

"This place has an energy," Gen said.

She wasn't wrong. Five Points was *the* nightclub. It used to be even more slammed than this, but the street festivals were new competition.

"Thank God it's not a full moon," Kierse grumbled. "The whole place goes on complete lockdown."

Ethan shuddered. "That would have been bad timing."

Werewolves could shift at will, but on the three nights surrounding the full moon, they had no choice. It was animalistic, and anything that crossed their paths was bound to wind up dead. She remembered when the streets used to go silent on those three days. Doors barred, no business, not a peep. With Nate as alpha, they locked themselves down to comply with the Monster Treaty.

"Come on. Let's find Nate."

They put Gen between them as they eased through the club. The crowds felt more oppressive than usual after their fun race across the festival. Kierse kept her chin tilted up and her eyes straight ahead.

When they reached the bar, she leaned over to speak to the blond bartender, who had a crescent moon with five stars—the symbol for the Dreadlords—pin attached to her low-cut bodice. "Hey, is Nate in?"

The woman poured two shots, pushed them to the couple in front of her, and took the cash before facing Kierse. "You want Nate? How do you know him?"

"We're friends."

"Nate is friends with everyone," she said with a laugh. "You'll need to be more specific."

"I'm his little sister."

The bartender checked her out. "Nate doesn't have any sisters. And thank the Lord for that. She'd be the most overprotected woman in the city. But if he's running around on Maura with you, I'll have his balls."

Kierse snorted and dropped a fifty on the bar. "I'd kill him myself if he ran around on Maura. We're more like colleagues. Tell him Kierse McKenna is here."

"Kierse McKenna," the woman said with appreciation as she pocketed the money. "I've heard about you."

"Have you now?" Kierse never knew if that was a good thing. She didn't recognize the woman, but it had been a year since she'd been with the wolves.

"Yeah, Finn's my boyfriend, and he said you two used to work together for the boss."

"That's a name I haven't heard in a while," Kierse said. Finn had been her point person back in the day. He and Ronan were in the upper echelon of Nate's circle.

"I'm Cara. Come on." She threw a rag down on the bar. "I'll see what the boss is up to."

Kierse dipped her head at her friends as Cara lifted a latch that let them come through to the back. They went through a servers' doorway and up a flight of stairs.

Cara knocked twice. "Boss, you're going to want to see this."

"I said I'm not to be disturbed," Nate yelled as he wrenched the door open with a feral scowl on his lips.

His eyes went from Cara to Kierse in a heartbeat, and his eyes widened. She shot him a rueful smile. "Hey, Nate."

"Fuck me! Kierse McKenna is in Five Points."

Kierse couldn't keep her smile from widening when she beheld him. Nathaniel O'Connor was in his early thirties, average height, and corded with muscle. He had a tawny complexion, like he'd stepped out of a harvest moon, and hazel eyes. His hair was chestnut brown, short, and coily, and he had a charismatic lilt to his tongue and that to-die-for characteristic O'Connor smirk. He was a handful and a half even before she'd found out he was a werewolf, with all of their possessive, predatory, and hot-tempered bullshit.

Nate's father's family had been powerful Irish mobsters going back generations, but then Nate had been turned during the war. The mob had fallen and Nate had come out alpha, uniting the Manhattan wolves around him into the Dreadlords. Kierse had worked with him on jobs for years until her own world had fallen apart. It had been more than a year since they'd gone their separate ways, but damn it was good to see him.

"I'm back."

He tried to pull her into a hug, but she stepped out of it.

"Okay. Okay," she said with a laugh.

"I know that you missed me." His eyes traveled down her body and gauged the state of her in a glance. He whistled low. "Looks like you've had a night."

"Tell me about it."

She hadn't spoken to Nate in a year, and seeing him again reminded her of the bonds that were knit between them. After Gen had saved Kierse, Colette had wanted to get her safely back into the thieving game. Amberdash was dangerous; tonight was proof of that. But she had a friend, a local alpha werewolf, who needed some jobs done on the side. Kierse had readily agreed. It'd been easy stuff, things she could do with her eyes closed, but it had changed her in ways she didn't know how to explain.

No longer did she anticipate Nate throwing her off a roof or leaving her for dead in the middle of a job. Suddenly, she'd realized...she could trust him. Then he had become a fixture in her world.

Until Torra.

Until it all fell apart.

"You remember Gen and Ethan?"

"Of course," Nate said, shaking Ethan's hand.

"Good to see you again, Nate," Ethan said.

"The Prophet Genesis," Nate said with a wolf smirk. He wrapped an arm around her affectionately.

"Hey Nate," Gen said shyly.

"Any friend of Kierse is a friend of mine," he announced.

"Any friend of Colette's, you mean," Ethan corrected.

"Hey, we're all family here."

Nate was so low-key that no one would have guessed he was the head of the Dreadlords. But Kierse knew that in his heart, he just wanted what was best for this city.

"Thanks, Cara," Nate said. "That'll be all."

"Sure thing. Nice meeting you, Kierse," Cara said and then disappeared.

He put a finger to the injury at her side. "Let's get a look at that. I assume you're in trouble if you're here to see me. It's been what, a year?"

Kierse nodded, wincing as he touched the wound. "It's fine."

"Maura is on her way here. You'll let her patch it up."

"All right," she conceded.

"So, this trouble?" Nate asked. He tipped his head at her.

"I took a job. I was caught." Nate's eyebrows rose. "I know. Unusual. Anyway, the guy let me go, but he apparently has powerful enemies."

"How powerful?" he asked.

"Druids."

Nate growled low. "Fucking perfect."

"Yeah, they attacked the brothel while the Roulettes were there and tailed us to the street festival in Little Italy tonight. We barely got away."

"You're in a world of shit."

"I know it's an imposition, but could we stay here? Just until I figure out how to get these fuckers off our backs."

Nate looked at her more closely with a head tilt that said she had left out a great deal of the truth. Still he nodded. "Of course. You all look like you've seen a ghost. Why don't I show you to some rooms? And then Kierse, I'll have Maura look at that." He turned to Gen and Ethan. "Either of you have injuries?"

They both shook their heads. Nate cracked the door back open and led them up a staircase into living quarters.

"This going to be all right?" Nate asked, gesturing to a set of rooms.

"That would be perfect," Kierse said. "I know you want to know more, but I need to talk to them first. Can we talk after Maura gets back?"

Nate nodded to the door. "If you're not bleeding out, I think it can wait a few minutes. Looks like they need you."

"Yeah," she said. "It's been a long night. And could you do me a favor and reach out to Corey in the Roulettes? He's Ethan's boyfriend. He's going to be freaking out."

"Of course." Before she could walk into the room, he said, "Hey, it's really good to see you again."

Something panged in her chest. The reason that she'd stopped coming by. The heart that had broken in her chest when everything had fallen apart with her girlfriend and even Nate hadn't been able to fix the problem. She'd stopped going to anyone for help after that. Stopped seeing anyone who reminded her of the old days. Only her family could even get away with mentioning what had happened...could even say Torra's name.

"You too, Nate."

Then she stepped into the room to figure this all out.

Ethan had his long legs spread out across the bed on the far side of the room. Gen had taken a seat beside him, staring down at her hands. Kierse knew exactly how they were both feeling. They had been driven from their home. Their world narrowed to this blank room and an uncertain future.

A twinge of guilt hit her. This was all her fault. She closed her eyes around the pain of that thought. No, this had started because of Graves. She placed the blame at his feet.

"How are your ribs?" Gen asked, glancing up at the sound of Kierse's boots.

Kierse pushed her jacket back and looked at the gash. "It's shallow. Maura will wrap it."

"I wish I had my herbs. I could at least dull the sting."

Even though Gen read futures in her tarot cards, her real gifts were more medicinal. She had a knack for the perfect hangover cure, collected herbs that Ethan had a green thumb for growing to help with Kierse's many scrapes and bruises, and had even worked out a form of birth control. Since modern medicine was so expensive, Gen's skills were unreasonably valuable.

"It'll be fine," Kierse said as she sank onto the bed opposite her friends. "It's been a long night, but we need to talk about what happened."

"Which part?" Ethan asked. "The almost-getting-murdered part or the audacity they had to attack the brothel?"

"The job," she said. "The job and the magic."

"You can't still be considering this?" Ethan demanded. "He just almost got you killed."

"Look, I'm not jumping up and down that entangling myself with this guy has these results. I knew as soon as I saw him that he could kill me on the spot and that there's only one reason he needs me alive. I can use that."

"And that's because he wants you to steal something for him?" Gen asked. "Why you?"

Kierse glanced down at her fingers. This was the unreal part. Him having magic was bizarre enough. "Because he thinks I have magic, too."

Gen and Ethan were silent a beat too long. She glanced up to gauge their reactions. Ethan seemed incredulous, but Gen looked interested.

"What makes him think that?"

"Because his house wasn't barred by modern security systems like the regular billionaire pricks I steal from. He had a ward system. That's what he called it. He used magic to protect the house, and I walked right through the wards. He tested me while I was there, and it's true. I can break them."

Ethan gaped. "Magic? Seriously? But I thought the whole point was monsters *not* magic."

"I said that, too," Kierse acknowledged. "But I can't deny what I saw, either."

"So you're the only one who can do this job," Gen intuited.

Ethan whistled. "That means you could charge anything."

"I don't think he cares about the money, and I intend to collect so that we can have a safe place when this is all over," she told them, brushing a hand back through her dark hair. "But he's also the only one who can give me more information about if I actually have magic."

"So what are you going to do?" Ethan asked.

"What I do best," she said, throwing on a smile of overconfidence. "Swindle information and money out of unsuspecting assholes."

Gen sighed. "I hope it's that easy, Kierse."

"When have I ever been wrong before?" she asked with bravado for her friends' sakes. Gen and Ethan needed to believe in her skills as much as Kierse did. They needed the reassurance that she would get out of all of this alive. After tonight, Kierse needed that, too.

Chapter Nine

"Maura's five minutes out," Nate said when he peeked his head back into the bedroom a few minutes later.

Kierse said goodbye to her friends and followed Nate down the stairs to a small infirmary. He pulled out supplies for Maura. She was a nurse at one of the lingering hospitals that took patients who couldn't afford treatment. She'd patched Kierse up one too many times when she'd still been working for Nate. It was lucky to have someone on staff, considering how difficult and expensive healthcare was.

"So, you ready to tell me what actually happened?" Nate asked.

"I guess I left out a bit of the truth." Kierse sank into the open seat with a sigh.

Nate guffawed. "A bit? You left out everything, I'd wager."

"Look, I don't mean to intrude on you."

"Kierse, it's not intruding when you're in need."

"I'm not charity, Nate," she said.

"No one said you were charity. You have Druids after you," Nate said, slamming down the bottle of antiseptic and turning to face her. "What I don't understand is the last year. Where the hell have you been?"

Kierse frowned. "I don't know…"

"No, don't do that. We're friends. We can talk about what happened with Torra. You didn't have to leave."

"I don't *want* to talk about it," she bit right back. She swallowed around the sound of Torra's name. "We tried to save her. We *failed*. There's nothing more to say."

"There's a hell of a lot more to say. You weren't responsible for her kidnapping, Kierse," he said with a frustrated growl. "It's not your fault that she got caught up with the wrong people."

"I should have been there," Kierse said through gritted teeth.

"You weren't even a couple when it went down," Nate argued.

"Like that matters."

"She was my friend, too, you know?" Nate said. "She was working for *me* as my bartender when you two met. She wasn't pack, but she might as well have been. She was my people, and they took her anyway."

"Don't you think I know that?"

"Then you never should have disappeared."

Kierse jumped to her feet. "You have no idea what I was going through. You have no right…"

"We all miss Torra."

"Nate!"

He lost all of his anger as soon as hers was unleashed. He dropped his gaze. "You're right. That was shitty." He crossed an arm over his muscled torso. "I don't blame you for what happened. I hope you don't blame yourself, either. We did everything we could." His hazel eyes were earnest when they met hers again. "A day, a week, a year, Kierse. I'm here. You being here proves that."

Kierse deflated. "Thank you."

"Now, tell me the truth this time. Start from the beginning and don't leave out all the good bits."

So, she started from the beginning. Nate had a shockingly blank look the entire time he listened to her story. It wasn't until the end of the tale that he breathed out and said rather forcefully, "Fuck."

Kierse chuckled. "Yeah. It's been a *fuck* couple of hours."

"And you're sure he said Lorcan?"

"Certain. Do you know him?"

"Know him?" Nate said with a sardonic laugh. "Course I know him. He's the head of the Druids and one terrifying bastard."

"Human?"

"As far as I know. When the mob fell on Manhattan and we consolidated the wolves into Five Points during the war, we reached out to him and offered an alliance. He had enough clout at the time to join up. He laughed in my face and said wolves were beneath him."

"Graves said much the same about vampires," she admitted.

He pursed his lips and crossed his beefy arms. "Well, the thing I can't figure is what his angle is. Lorcan is not someone I want to fuck with, but I've never heard of him chasing down innocents to kill them in the streets."

"Well, apparently Graves is his enemy."

"And now yours," Nate added.

"Great," she grumbled.

"If someone had asked, I would have put Lorcan firmly on the good side of the fight," he said with a shrug. "His territory has always been safer for humans than the Manhattan streets. I don't know what he does in Brooklyn, but he keeps people alive."

"Yeah, well, he tried to kill us. So I don't know if he's good or bad. Just that he's against us."

Nate nodded but was held from saying anything by a tall Desi girl striding into the infirmary. Her lush brown hair fell in careful waves to the middle of her back, and the dim light played along her golden-brown skin. "Nathaniel O'Connor, what have you done this time?"

"Maura," he said like a man ready to pounce. "Look at you."

She stripped out of her jacket, revealing maroon nursing scrubs. "The sexiest I've ever looked."

He grinned as he stepped toward his girlfriend. "Don't have to tell me twice."

As he came in for a kiss, Maura pushed her hand into his face. "Patient first."

Nate growled in the back of his throat. "Always patient first."

Maura laughed at him and went straight to Kierse. "Hello, darling. It's been a while. What have you done to yourself to end up in my infirmary?"

"Hi, Maura," Kierse said. She'd never get used to someone being able to handle Nate the way that Maura did. "Knife to the ribs."

"Of course." Maura got to work, cutting Kierse's shirt open and cleaning the wound.

Maura had left Jersey City to become a wartime nurse in Manhattan. She was still close to her parents and brothers back home, and they were proud that she'd done something so selfless. She'd met Nate one of the many times he'd needed to be stitched up, and he'd convinced her to get on his payroll. He'd charmed his way into her life, her bed, and her heart ever since.

"This will need a few stitches. It's going to suck. Nate, give her the whiskey."

"I'm good."

"I have tequila," Maura offered.

Kierse shook her head. "Nah."

"Your call."

Kierse gritted her teeth while Maura sewed up the wound and expertly tied it off. It hurt like a bitch. But afterward, Maura provided her with a change of clothes, and she felt more human once she pulled her jacket back on.

"Now, to the topic at hand," Maura said with a smile. "What brings you to our doorstep?"

"She met him, Mar," Nate said.

"Him?"

"That scary motherfucker I told you about."

"Oh," Maura whispered.

"Wait," Kierse said with growing alarm, "you know him?"

"I know *of* him. A lot of people know of him," Nate confirmed. "He's the guy who can get you anything you want for a price."

"Well, he's hiring *me* to get something for *him*," Kierse said.

"I heard he makes people sign their name into his black book so that you're bound to your deal with him and sworn to keep his name secret."

Kierse froze. Was *that* what he'd meant when he said that it wouldn't do anything to her? She'd signed that book, but she'd been able to say his name clear as day. She'd only held his secrets, but that was because she didn't want to endanger her friends, not because she *had* to hold them. More proof that she had magic he couldn't control. No wonder he was after her.

"Oh, and he helped get the Treaty signed."

Kierse stared at him, speechless. "Are you saying he's…a good guy?"

"No," Nate said carefully but then shrugged. "I'm sure he did it for his own benefit. But I wouldn't say he's all bad, either."

Kierse chewed on her lip at the news. Well, she hadn't expected *that*. Not that it changed her calculus. Not when he was also this dangerous.

"What do you think I should do?" Kierse asked.

"He's terrifying," Nate said. "He can control the flow of politics and shit. But he also helped humanity. I wouldn't want to be on his bad side."

"So, I should take the job?"

"If he wants you to do it, he's the kind of person who gets what he wants. It'd be better to do it on your terms."

Kierse breathed out. That was the truth at least. She didn't think it was ever going to be that simple. Get in and get out. But she didn't think Graves was going to stop, either. Not when he saw his prize in reach. It'd be better to do it her way.

"Plus, think about what this could mean for the cause," Nate continued.

Kierse arched an eyebrow. "You and the cause."

He smirked. "Look, we all know that the Treaty didn't solve all the problems. There are still monsters out there who want it to be like the old days. They don't want any interference from the humans. If you steal this prize from them, it could only help us going forward, right?"

That was a take that she hadn't considered in all of this. She hated the monsters for all they had done to her and her city. For everything they had taken. Not all humans were saints by any means—Jason was proof enough that men could just as easily be monsters—but any blow to monsters who wanted to wreck her city again was a good one.

"True. I'll have to be careful, though," she said. "I don't think he's going to be an easy mark."

"Yeah, but he's never sparred with our Kierse, has he?" Nate asked.

Maura laughed at them both. "Lord help the man or monster who goes up against Kierse McKenna."

"Thanks," Kierse told her sincerely.

"But I'm coming off a twelve-hour shift and need to sleep," she said with a yawn. She ran a hand down her pallid face, and Kierse could see the strain of her job in that look. "Be safe and check in. It's been too long."

"Good night," Kierse said.

Maura kissed Nate once on the lips before leaving the pair of them alone.

Nate touched her hand, and she didn't pull away. "Whatever you decide about this job, I'll be here for you if you need anything. I have contacts and the pack. You don't have to disappear again. We're family."

She hadn't known how much she needed to hear that. That someone believed her and would help her figure it out. "Thank you. I'm regretting the last year."

"Well, when Torra left, I knew it would be bad."

"Left," she repeated on a harsh whisper.

Torra hadn't left. She'd been taken. Sure, they'd been on rough times and would have probably broken up anyway, but then she'd just vanished.

"I know," he said with a tip of his head. "Either way, it's good to have you back."

Exhaustion pressed heavy on her, and she left Nate behind in the infirmary. She'd been downstairs longer than she thought, because when she came back to the room, the lights were still on and Corey was seated in one bed with Ethan. Gen sat on the other.

Gen patted the empty space on the bed next to her. Kierse slid her jacket off her shoulders and climbed into bed beside her friend.

"When do you leave?" Gen asked.

Corey and Ethan whipped their heads to her.

"Leave?" Ethan asked.

"You knew I was going to go?"

"Of course. I know you like I know myself, Kierse. You're the closest thing I've ever had to a sister."

Kierse swallowed back the knot in her throat. "I feel the same."

"Wait, you can't leave tonight," Ethan argued.

"It's almost morning," she said. "And I think you two need to hole up here until I can figure out how much danger you're in."

Gen pursed her lips. "I had a feeling you might say that."

"Live here?" Ethan asked in shock. He was on his feet, crossing his arms. "We can't live here."

"You should stay under Dreadlord protection until I can figure out if you're still in danger."

"That's ridiculous," Corey said, putting a hand on Ethan's shoulder. "Roulettes can protect Gen and Ethan just fine."

"They didn't tonight," Gen said quietly.

Ethan scowled at them. "We can't just stay here. All of our stuff is back home. Our entire lives. Who is going to water the plants?"

"My mother can have someone take care of them," Gen tried to assure him, but he seemed unconvinced. Kierse was, too. Colette had many talents, but making things grow was not one of them.

"You won't have to stay long," Kierse insisted. "Once I finish this job, we'll get our own place with its own security, okay? Until then, I just want you to be safe."

Corey sighed when he realized she wasn't budging. "Kierse is right. You'll be safe here. I can bring stuff over from the attic. Some of your favorite plants, too."

Ethan gaped at his boyfriend. "You're okay with this?"

"I'm sorry, Ethan," Kierse said. "I wish there was another way."

"I'll be around. Don't worry," Corey said as he pressed a kiss to Ethan's cheek. "It won't be all bad."

"I bet Nate would even give you access to the roof for new planting," Gen said. "You know how he is. He'd want you to be comfortable."

Ethan sighed. "Fine. Fine, we'll stay."

"We'll see you soon." Gen pulled her into a hug.

Even after years of being friends with all of Gen's warmth and good nature, Kierse still froze. It wasn't really the touch that was the problem. Not as casual as her friends usually were. It was the intimacy of the touch. This wasn't just a hug. It was a hug goodbye. It was a hug that said *I love you*.

But she needed this hug. So, she let the tension pass and hugged her friend back.

"I won't tell you to be careful," Ethan said.

Kierse shot him a confident smile. "I'm always careful."

He snorted. "We all know that you won't be."

"For real," Corey said.

Kierse crossed the room. "At least you know me."

Ethan sighed. "We'll be careful enough for you, okay? Just come back soon."

She nodded because words wouldn't suffice. She could stand here forever with her friends, her family, and never be ready to leave them behind.

Gen pulled her into one more hug and whispered so Ethan couldn't hear, "Just promise *to* come back."

Some part of her knew that she couldn't promise anything, but she said the words anyway. Even though they both knew they were a lie.

Interlude

"Lorcan is not going to like this," Cormac said as he strode up to his side.

"Fuck off," Declan spat.

Of course Lorcan wasn't going to be happy. They'd had one job, and here they were. Orla was down, Kierse had gotten away with both of her friends, and Graves hadn't even needed to stroll in and save the day.

"You're going to have to tell him."

Declan glared at Cormac. "Go find Orla and bring her back to the house."

"I shouldn't go with you?"

Declan stared at him. "Do I need to repeat myself?"

"No," Cormac said hastily. "No, I'll go find Orla."

Cormac went in search of the missing member of their team, and Declan ran a hand over his face, trying to figure out what the hell he was going to do. He hadn't worked his way up to Lorcan's second in command by making this kind of mistake. He was quick and efficient, qualities Lorcan admired in him. He got shit done.

Well, not tonight.

So, Declan walked until he reached an SUV that they'd abandoned earlier while stalking the girl. He hopped into the passenger seat and told the driver to move, and luckily he didn't ask questions about the others. He was smarter than that.

Declan was not looking forward to this meeting. If only Graves hadn't stuck his nose in where it didn't belong. Like always.

He remembered the first time he met Graves some twenty years ago. Declan had been fresh into the city from his small hometown in Ireland. Half of the people couldn't understand a word out of his mouth. He'd been working in the dregs of Lorcan's mob for about three months when the order came through. Lorcan had a special mission just for him.

He'd thought it was a reward for coming over and leaving everything behind. Maybe the bathrooms he'd cleaned looked exemplary. He'd had stars in his eyes, but he should have known better. They offered the worst jobs to the new recruits, and Declan was as green as they came.

Declan had taken an SUV much like the one he was in right now and driven it across the bridge and through the glittering city. It had been different back then. Brighter, more vibrant, with cars covering the streets. There had been less fear before the collapse, before the monsters came into the daylight. It had taken him a half hour to figure out where the hell to park. That problem was all but obsolete now.

With the box from Lorcan in hand, Declan had stridden right up to the bastard's door. Just a faint trickle of fear had licked through him. He'd heard from the others about Graves. They made him out to be the boogeyman. Declan had doubted it until the moment he met him.

Graves had a butler who had gone to get him, and when he'd appeared at the door, he'd looked like any other wealthy feck Declan had met. Except for the eyes and the fire. Something was off about him. Declan caught it on first sight.

The box was innocuous. He'd had no idea what was in it when he handed it over to Graves. But he'd smiled like he did and told him, "Lorcan sends his regards."

Graves had stiffened as he took the box. He'd popped open the top, and inside lay a bouquet of Irish wildflowers. They were the sort that bloomed in the fields behind his ma's cottage in yellows, purples, and dark blues. They made Declan think of home. He hadn't even known he was homesick until that moment.

But Graves had looked up at him, and something had flashed in his eyes. Death incarnate. He tossed the bouquet onto the floor, where the glass vase shattered and the flowers scattered across the entranceway. Then he came toward Declan.

Declan wished he could say that he'd been brave and held his ground against the boogeyman, but he'd known Graves meant to kill him. He had gone wild over a box of flowers. Declan had tucked his tail and run. Run as fast as his legs could take him. And he'd hated the bastard every day since. The flowers from Lorcan had been a threat, but for feck's sake, you didn't shoot the messenger.

Declan hopped out of the SUV when it reached their headquarters in Brooklyn and took the elevator up to Lorcan's office. At his entrance, a robin fluttered in a cage nearby.

"Well?" Lorcan asked. "Are they dead?"

"They got away."

Lorcan lifted his gaze from the paperwork on his desk. His blue eyes held menace. "What?"

"Hopped into a cab. We lost them in Dreadlords territory."

Lorcan pushed away from his desk and paced toward the window. "And Graves?"

"No sign of him."

"Hmm," Lorcan said, staring out at the Brooklyn streets beyond. "And you're certain that this was the same girl who walked out of his house?"

"Absolutely." Declan cleared his throat. "Her evading us should show her value to him. That's never happened before."

"Did she know of the agreement?"

"She didn't seem to know who you were at all," Declan admitted.

His mouth lifted into a curve. "Well, that will change, won't it?"

Declan feared that smile. "Do you want me to go after them?"

Lorcan held up his hand without looking at him. "You've done enough. I'll take it from here."

Declan knew a dismissal when he saw one. He hustled out of Lorcan's office, cursing Graves's name all over again. Bastard.

PART II

THE WREN

Chapter Ten

Kierse headed out of Five Points and back onto the Manhattan streets. She needed to be out of the West Village and back uptown, but knowing the bus and subway routes wasn't enough anymore.

Even though New York was beginning to turn around, transportation was a luxury. She was still regretting her hasty taxi last night. If there had been any other option, she would have taken it. The buses ran semi-regularly, if you were lucky enough to be on their route, but the subway was the better bet. It hadn't always been safe before the collapse, back when police cared to patrol the city. Now, it was a world of its own. Dangerous and deadly and full of gangs…and monsters. The subway was half the reason she left the house every night with a gun.

Kierse would have loved to choose the bus, but Nate had recommended Dreadlord-controlled subway entrances. She could have taken the 1 to the Upper West Side, but she needed a minute to figure out her move before she went back to Graves. Instead, she headed north to 6th and 14th to catch the more familiar F train, straight up to Midtown.

She tensed her shoulders as she descended into the subway. Lights flickered overhead, barely illuminating the gloom. Another consequence of monsters in the public eye were the trolls who managed the subway entrances. They associated with certain gangs and forced tolls on unsuspecting victims. In a way, it was paying to cross a bridge.

"Thad," she said with a head nod as she approached the troll at this stop.

He grunted. She forced herself not to shiver at the sight of a full-size troll. He was almost double her height, with meaty shoulders and clubs for arms. His bulky head rested nearly flat on his shoulders, and his eyes were small and beady. The cruel twist of his lips and the shine in his black eyes said he'd rather crush her than allow her access. But with the Treaty in place, so long as she paid her toll, all would be well. She hoped.

"Nate said to let me pass," Kierse told him, revealing the pin of a crescent moon with five stars that revealed her association with the Dreadlords.

He stood to his considerable height. "You still have to pay the price."

She hated the ritual, hated having to pay a toll to use a facility that already charged for usage. But it was easier than shooting her way through, which she had done before when she'd stumbled into the wrong station run by the wrong monsters in the East Village.

Nate had assured her that she wouldn't have to pay, but she wasn't about to fight a troll to find out if he was right. She fished out a five and passed it to him. She'd paid way more at other stops and hoped that he wouldn't ask for more.

He took a minute to make sure it was what he wanted. Trolls weren't that intelligent. The payments were more about power than the money itself. Finally, Thad pocketed the cash and nodded her into the depths below. She already had a MetroCard handy and hopped on the next F train north. She took the first available seat, carefully bolstered on either side by other humans who wanted nothing to do with her. At the last second, a shifter entered with a goblin. They were both packing and almost rippled with malice. Everyone immediately turned their attention elsewhere, and Kierse followed suit. She had enough problems as it was.

The reason she loved the F train was that it was the most direct route to Midtown without any of the more…unsavory stops. It was an unwritten rule to avoid the Times Square stop on the 1. Tourists were still stupid enough to do it, but Kierse always took another stop over and hoofed it if she had to go nearby. She equally rejected the 4, 5, or 6 north even though they were sometimes faster. Stopping at Grand Central was just asking for trouble. She shivered even thinking of it.

No, the F was the safest. And when she reemerged into the first rays of daylight on 57th Street a half hour later, she was glad to leave the subway behind her. Though she had been uptown last night, the contrast was worse during the day. The entire world was bright and vibrant, with skyscrapers of glass, open restaurants without bars on the windows, mothers pushing their babies in strollers, businesses with bright signs beckoning pedestrians inside, and not a seedy character in sight. Money could buy happiness.

Kierse had to stuff her hands in her jacket pockets to keep her thieving habit at bay. It was hard to ignore the naive little lambs wandering the streets wide-eyed who were just begging to be pickpocketed. But cops actually patrolled these streets, and she'd had enough trouble for one day.

Instead, she headed into the Upper East Side and straight to her favorite Jewish bakery. It had been a staple in its prime Madison Avenue location for decades. Even during the Monster War, it had only closed for a few months.

After paying for her treats, she took the paper package filled with black-and-white cookies, rugelach, and cinnamon babka and headed out onto the busy streets. She rolled her eyes at the tea shop full of monsters reminiscing about the good old days. Wealthy women had been fond of this tea shop with little finger sandwiches and desserts before the war. That was when they'd found out that a succubus had used it as a feeding ground. Kierse pulled out a cookie and bit into it as she crossed to the Met.

She dropped onto the Met steps and stared up at the famed statue of Coraline LeMort as she ate her breakfast. Coraline stood on a pedestal with her shoulders pushed back and chin in the air. Her eyes were clear as day, looking toward a future she never was able to see but had visualized as she fought for monster unity even before humans knew about their existence. Kierse had always wondered what Coraline would have thought of her death starting the Monster War. Would she be disappointed? Or just unsurprised?

She'd never know, of course, because they'd killed her—and everything had changed.

The beautiful Met steps could fool anyone into thinking that the world was back to how it had been before the war. That Coraline's death hadn't been in vain. But Kierse had a map of the city in her mind, and it didn't just show buildings—it showed territories. The human gangs that had survived the war by banding together. Roulettes on the Lower East buttressed against their biggest competition, the Jackals in Nolita. There were half a dozen other gangs spanning the city. And then there were bigger players: the Gents in the East Village, the Italian mafia in Little Italy, and the Druids in Brooklyn.

Worse yet was monster territory, which had mostly been shored up since the war but was sometimes still disputed and could be catastrophic for humans. The largest vampire clan on the Upper East and Nate's competing wolf pack on the West Village, to name a few. Not to mention the disputed territories like Times Square.

But at least those entities abided by the Monster Treaty. There were other monsters who didn't believe that they should be subjected to the humans they fed off of. Some factions were vocal, some just silently continued as if the Treaty had never been signed, and the worst of them had organized—the Men of Valor.

Kierse had heard whispers of the Men of Valor for years before they took Torra. The only positive thing she could say about the bloodthirsty and deranged organization was that despite the word "men" in the title, they didn't limit their members solely to that gender. Just…terrible monsters who wanted to kill all humans. Delightful.

She swallowed as she stared up at Coraline LeMort and wondered if this all would have been different. If she had survived and the war had never started, would Kierse still have her girlfriend?

She tossed her bag into a trash can, still reminiscing about Torra, as she strode into Central Park. As snow gently fell, she moved down the leaf-strewn walkways and passed the green-roofed Boathouse until she came upon Bethesda Fountain. The angel at the center of the famous fountain looked down upon her subjects. Kierse had always imagined her judging them for their humanity.

Kierse wouldn't blame her. The only person Kierse really held responsible for Torra's fate was herself. Just over a year ago, the Men of Valor had snatched her up for a debt that Kierse had never even known Torra had. One day, she was home, and the next, she was gone without a trace. Kierse should have been there that day. But they'd had a huge fight the night before. She'd said some horrible things. Torra had told her to leave, and she'd left. Then she never saw her again.

She dropped down onto a snow-crusted step in front of the Lake, sinking into her melancholy as she watched the mer bathe from a distance. Few dared the waters now, and Kierse wasn't stupid enough to do so, either. The mer could walk on two feet when it pleased them, which was how they had ended up in the Lake, but no one wanted to be in their path when they did. They lured sailors to their deaths, had voices like songbirds, and teeth like sharks.

One was staring at her now. "Hello, pretty."

Kierse smiled, not drawn in by the mer's sweet voice. The mer was pure innocence, if you could look past the fact that she likely wanted to drown Kierse at the bottom of the Lake and leave her there for a snack.

"Not today," she told the mer, who splashed water at her in a huff and swam away.

Kierse considered her plight as she headed through Bethesda Terrace and across the Mall, slowly veering west toward Graves's brownstone.

Monsters had taken everything from her. And now even her sanctuary wasn't safe.

Graves wasn't a safe option, either. Not that she had ever considered him one. But he was the one who was going to fix what she'd broken, and he'd never even see her coming.

Chapter Eleven

Kierse stood outside of Graves's mansion. Every entrance and exit was mapped out in her mind. The best places of shadow as the sun moved across the property. The movements of those who came in and out…except, apparently, the owner. She had done her homework, and still he'd caught her. Standing here now felt like she had given up a piece of her battle strategy to become someone else's pawn. But she was no one's pawn.

With a deep inhale of the frigid air, she cloaked herself in a shroud of overconfidence and climbed the stoop to the devil's mansion. Only a day earlier, she had worried about the snow and how it would leave footprints behind. Now, she purposely left them against the front walkway, announcing her arrival to all who were watching.

She shivered. Not from the cold this time.

The iron knocker was ancient: a slithering dragon shaped into a figure eight with its serpentine tale whipping around at the end and a crown of holly floating atop its head. Perhaps it was his mark. He certainly had holly all over the property. Either way, it left a weighty impression when she lifted the giant thing and banged it three times against the stately door.

The door creaked inward, and the butler appeared in the entranceway. He was a graying man of average height with sturdy steps and a kind blue gaze. She'd guessed him to be in his fifties, but up close she could tell that he was more fit than she'd assumed. As if his fifty years had hardened his body. To what purpose, she had no idea.

"Hello. Miss McKenna, I presume?" he said with a cheery disposition and slight British accent.

"Yes. That's me."

"Excellent. Come in out of the cold. It is wonderful to have you in residence."

"Umm, thanks," Kierse replied.

"Allow me to take your coat," he said, helping her out of her leather jacket.

"And you are?"

He smiled. "I am Edgar."

"Nice to meet you, Edgar."

"The pleasure is all mine, Miss McKenna."

"Kierse. You can call me Kierse," she said with her doe-eyed smile.

"As you wish."

"How long have you worked for Graves?"

Edgar just gestured her forward. "Follow me and we'll get you warmed up. The snow is really coming down."

Kierse appreciated the dodge. She hadn't expected him to give up his master's secret, but it was worth a shot. She let him lead her through the house. It was as grossly opulent as ever, with Persian rugs and tapestries and priceless paintings. She was a thief. She could put a price on every item she passed, knowing exactly how much she could fence it for. But Graves's house was something else altogether. A firedrake's hoard. The dragon on the knocker was certainly fitting.

His assets seemed to be limitless. And yet the one thing he wanted and couldn't get, he needed *her* for.

Edgar led her into a cozy sitting room, complete with a fire burning in a fireplace the size of a small child. No other light came from the room. No electricity at all. Just the soft glow from the fire revealing the velvet-lined chairs, luxurious fur throws, and carved wooden tables. A large matching wooden bookshelf was adorned with the kind of knickknacks she collected for her clients. Somehow the vases and carved figurines and candles didn't look out of place. They brought the rest of the room together.

He couldn't be a wraith. They loved their opulence as much as the vampires, but she couldn't imagine a wraith enjoying a roaring fire. Not to mention he'd touched her and she hadn't lost a part of her soul. She checked that off her list, too.

She'd told Gen and Ethan that he didn't seem like any other monster she'd met, but until she knew, she couldn't help but wonder.

"Well, have a seat, dear," a woman said, bustling in after her with a silver tray laden with a teapot, cups, and saucers as well as a few biscuits and tiny little delicacies. She had a thicker British accent than Edgar. As if he'd tried to train it out of himself but she reveled in it.

Kierse followed her to the most inviting chair and took a seat.

"I'm Isolde. Don't mind Edgar. He's not used to guests," she said with a warm smile. Everything was warm about her, from her brown hair up in a bun at the top of her head, to her black-and-white serving dress, to the softness in her lined face. "We are delighted to have you in residence. How do you like your tea?"

"Um...hot?"

Isolde chuckled. "We're British, dear. Tea should only be hot."

"Right. Of course. Earl Grey with honey is my preference, but however you like it is fine."

"I'll make a note of that," Isolde said easily. "But for now, milk and sugar it is."

Kierse watched her serve the tea with fascination. This was nothing like how Gen made tea in the attic. It was more like the fashionable ladies uptown with their little cups and saucers and finger sandwiches.

Isolde passed her the cup of tea, and Kierse brought it to her lips.

Her eyes widened. "This is excellent."

"We can make a Brit out of you yet," Isolde said, beaming. "Now, have a scone with some jam and cream. I'll be back if you need anything else."

Kierse tried to drink the tea as daintily as the cup and saucer suggested. She glanced at the tray to take a scone but saw that there were only biscuits. After slathering one with cream and strawberry jam, she bit into the biscuit. Then hastily devoured two of them. This food was...incredible. As if extra flavor was baked into every portion.

"I'm glad that you appear to enjoy my refreshments," Graves said from the doorway.

Kierse jostled some tea onto the saucer, setting it down as she came swiftly to her feet at the sound of his voice. She hadn't heard him approach.

But he held his gloved hand out. "Please, stay seated." Graves leaned against the doorframe.

When she did no such thing, he stepped into the room and drew the door closed behind him. He took the seat across from her, and then finally she eased back down.

"You know, once it was commonplace to drink from the saucer. It's gauche now, of course."

A new thought bubbled to the surface. She shot him a shrewd look. "Is it magicked?"

His lip quirked up on one side. "The food? No. Isolde is just the best cook I've ever encountered. I also devour her scones with a sick fascination."

Her eyes flickered to his lips as she imagined a man like this devouring anything.

"You've decided to take the job." It was said as a statement, not a question, and she bristled.

"We'll get to that," she said, leaning back and forcing calm into her expression. The negotiations had already begun. She couldn't back out now. "I have a few questions first."

His own face was blank, but he held his hand out to allow her to proceed.

"What's your association with the Druids?"

If he was surprised by this line of questioning, he didn't show it.

"'Association' is the incorrect word," he said, crossing one leg at the knee and leaning against an arm of the chair.

"Enemy?" she suggested. "Is that what they are? Are you going to tell me that the Irish are the bad guys and the British are the good guys? Because it's a bad look."

"Not everything is as it seems." His face was passive as he added, "There are no good guys or bad guys. This isn't a fairy tale."

"No, I'm not chased down at gunpoint in a fairy tale."

"Depends on what story you're reading." He arched an eyebrow as if daring her to argue. "And once you are in my employ, you'll be under my protection. The Druids will not be a concern."

"Lorcan suddenly won't want me dead?"

Graves frowned at that name. "Lorcan and I are under an…agreement. I won't go after his if he doesn't go after mine."

"A cease-fire with the enemy. That's convenient but does nothing to assure the safety of my friends, who he also tried to kill."

Graves raised one gloved hand. "They seem safe enough with your Dreadlord friends."

Kierse didn't balk at that. Of course he already knew what had happened and where exactly Gen and Ethan were. And she had to take him at face value. Gen and Ethan were safe with Nate. She wasn't going to get more out of him about it without giving something in return. She needed to change tactics if she was going to get through these negotiations.

"Are you the reason we have the Treaty?"

"I was involved," he said all nonchalant as if it hadn't changed the entire world.

"And did you sign it?"

He looked amused. "Did you?"

"I wasn't involved," she reminded him. "But you were."

"I assure you that I did it for my own aims."

"I'm sure you did," she said dryly.

She waited to see if he would say more, but he didn't. Normally, leading people to the point got them to start talking. Most people wanted to talk about themselves. But Graves seemed content with the silence.

Well, it had been worth a shot. She'd gotten at least a handful of reassurances from him, if not explicitly. Gen and Ethan would be safe. Lorcan wouldn't bother her. Graves had helped with the Monster Treaty, but he hadn't signed it. He must agree with it if he'd been involved. So he probably wasn't going to kill her for no reason. Probably.

"I accept your job offer with some conditions."

"Oh?" He leaned backward, dropping his foot back to the floor. His hands were still in those slim black leather gloves. His cheekbones were razor-sharp in the firelight.

She gritted her teeth, holding his gaze. She nearly choked on the words that came out of her mouth. "I want ten million dollars."

Graves didn't blink. "Three million."

"I am not negotiating my salary. If you won't pay me, I'll walk."

"Five million."

She narrowed her eyes at him. "I'm the only person who can do this for you, which means I know my worth. Ten million. And half up front."

"Fine," he growled, clearly upset that he was giving in to her demands. "But I will only pay the full amount upon completion of the task. Your expenses will come through me."

"Done."

She kept her smile to herself. Holy shit. She hadn't expected him to go over three mil.

She'd already gotten the main things she wanted: money and safety. She didn't expect him to guarantee hers. She could die in this job. She'd known that from the start. Her real concern was her friends.

Because she was going to fucking make it out of here if she could help it, but in the event that she couldn't, they were all that mattered. Her chosen family had to survive.

She lifted her chin. "And if I die, the money goes to Gen and Ethan."

He nodded once.

"I need you to say you agree," she demanded. "They are what matters here. I do the job. They get the money. They remain safe."

Something like surprise shone in his eyes at the demand, but all he said was, "Done."

"Good."

"Anything else?" he pressed.

The only other thing she really wanted was information. But Graves hardly seemed like the kind of person who was going to tell her everything she wanted to know. She actually doubted he'd tell her everything she even needed.

It was sort of how she operated anyway. Need-to-know basis. She couldn't flat-out ask him to give her the info she wanted, but she wasn't doing this without hoping to find out more about herself, too.

"I'm not going to ask for a guarantee of my safety, but I think we both know the real currency in this city is information. I can't be the valuable asset you need me to be without knowing what I can do."

"You'll be trained," he said flatly.

"On my magic?" She nearly choked on the word but managed to keep her head up and meet his mercurial gaze.

"Your magic, your mind, your body."

Her eyes widened at those words. "Explain what that means."

"If you're going to be working with me, then you'll have educational assignments and weapons training."

"Trust me, I'm pretty handy with weapons."

"Not spears."

She shot him a skeptical look. "Why would I need to know how to wield a *spear*?"

"Because, Miss McKenna," he said gravely, "that's what you're stealing."

"Oh," she whispered. Well, now she had more questions. "Why are you stealing a spear?"

"I'm a collector. I collect rare objects. As you might have noticed when you cased my house."

No use denying it. "I did notice that. And you need this for your collection? For ten million dollars?"

He didn't even blink. "It's worth it to me."

"Okay." She ground her teeth together. "Fine. Weapons training. But educational assignments? What kind of assignments?"

"I don't deal with the uncultured," he told her flatly. "I'll provide you books to read, and we'll discuss them."

"Uncultured," she said with narrowed eyes. He just stared her down as if willing her to disagree with him. She was a thief; she hadn't the luxury of *culture*. "So, reading, weapons, and magic lessons."

"When you're ready for them, yes."

"And will I learn about your magic?" she asked.

Those gray eyes seemed almost impressed with her audacity. "You have spirit, I'll give you that."

"So, is that a no?"

He rose to his feet, buttoning the front of his dark suit. "If information is what you're after, I applaud you for trying. I am a man of many secrets. No one person knows all of them. Very few know *any* of them. Most people don't even know my name or my likeness. You're going to have to take what I will offer."

"And what is that?"

"I will train you the way I know how. You may or may not enjoy that. What you discover about yourself in the process is at your disposal, but all else…" He waved his hand as if to say that was beyond him. "My secrets are my own."

Kierse stood and held his gaze, despite feeling like she should shrink under it. He'd seen right through her line of questioning. This was going to be more difficult than she'd thought.

"I understand," she said, offering her hand.

He didn't take it but instead said, "Then I will provide my terms."

She let her hand drop and waited for his side of the negotiations. Other than the money, hers hadn't gone as well as planned. She didn't want to make it easy for him, either.

"Which are?"

"You must stay in my residence." She opened her mouth to reject—no way was she staying here—but he barreled on. "It is mandatory. You cannot stay with your friends and hope to keep them safe. You stay *here*." He waited for her to argue, but she could hardly do so.

"Their safety is my first priority."

She hated that he knew that information about her. But they were allies now, however tenuous. Hopefully that meant they would stay safe.

"Understood," he said. "The next requirement is that you keep a cell phone on you."

"I don't have a cell phone." Which he probably knew. So many of the towers had come down during the Monster War, and after they'd finally gotten people to work on them, the plans were outrageously priced. Kierse couldn't manage the expense.

Graves shrugged. "I can provide one."

"Two. So I can give one to Gen and Ethan."

"No. They are precious to you, which means they can be used against you. It will be best for you, and them, if you cease seeing them entirely."

"That's out of the question."

"Do you want to get them killed?" he asked sharply. "Would you like to see Lorcan put a bullet in them? Have one of his lackeys follow you around until you give up their location and they're murdered in cold blood?"

She swallowed back the bile rising in her throat, hating that he was right. She would never sacrifice Gen and Ethan. She was taking this job for their safety. But she couldn't just let them think she was never coming back.

"You can't forbid contact until I let them know I'm staying. They'll do something stupid, like try to find me," she told him.

"Contact your Dreadlord and let him know. After that, you work for *me*. That means you live here and you no longer risk their lives."

Her jaw flexed in frustration, but she nodded. How would she survive all this time without them? But then, wasn't it more important that *they* survive without *her*?

When he saw that she had agreed, he continued. "The last is the most important—you don't tell anyone else my secrets."

"What secrets?" she asked coyly.

His gaze cut straight through her. "I cannot bind you to your promise. And this *partnership* requires a level of trust that I have not given in years. Give me a reason to trust you with this."

Good. She was glad that he couldn't bind her to her promises. He'd just admitted to another benefit of his magic not working on her. She was not just valuable. She was a liability. He wasn't keeping her close to train her. He wanted to keep an eye on her. So much was slotting into place now.

"Your secrets are your own." She threw his words back at him.

But she made no promises. And she could see that he despised not being able to force her to keep her word. She just met that steely gaze with a smile. Negotiations worked both ways.

He waited for her to say more, but she held her tongue. Flames danced in his irises. "That will have to be enough." He held his hand out. "Deal?"

She was making a deal with the devil, but still, she placed her hand in his. An old sort of magic, this bond between them.

"Deal."

Chapter Twelve

Graves withdrew his hand. "The bargain is struck."

"Then we'll begin today." Now that the hard part was over, she was eager to learn all that she could. What exactly were all of her interesting talents? Why could she walk through wards? What did it all mean?

Graves just slid his hands back into his pockets. "You can begin after you've slept."

She was tired. Yesterday had been…impossible. Between the heist that had gone all wrong, the chase, and fleeing to Nate, she was a wreck. It had been a full thirty-six hours since she'd had a second of shut-eye. But still… she wanted answers.

"Still kind of keyed up, to be honest," she told him. "I could start right now."

"Perhaps," he said, eyeing her up and down as if he didn't believe her. "But I need you to be clearheaded to begin your spear training. Take a few hours, and then meet Edgar in my training facility."

"And when will we begin magic training?"

"I have other business to attend to this day. I will show you to your living quarters. We can talk when I return." Graves pulled the door open for her.

She strode purposely toward it. "You already have a room set up for me?"

"Isolde prepared it while you were sitting on the Met steps."

She arched an eyebrow. "Am I supposed to be impressed that you tailed me?"

"You should be more cognizant of your surroundings."

The truth was that she'd felt eyes on her the second she left his place the night before. She wasn't sure if they had been him or the Druids or both. She'd felt them all but hadn't quite known what they meant until it was too late.

"Is this my first lesson?" she teased. "I know how to drop a tail."

"Not well enough, it seems." His eyes roamed her face as if he couldn't quite guess the game she was playing. He gestured to the hallway beyond.

"Ouch," she said, placing her hand on her heart. "Come on. You seem like the kind of guy where every interaction is a lesson." She backed out of the room as he strode toward her. "You could start with the obvious: What am I? What can I do?"

He didn't answer. Just began to walk down the hallway. "You know, you never once asked about the job."

"We're stealing a spear," she said. "You told me that."

"But nothing else."

She shrugged. "It doesn't matter."

She could steal anything from anyone. Even Graves, if she had to. The specifics of the job were unimportant. The least of her concerns. She suspected someone like Graves had a plan for what she was about to do. It would be like any other job. Just more likely to kill her.

"I wouldn't be overly confident," Graves said.

"I'm not. Overconfidence gets you killed. I'm as confident as I need to be. I'm a thief. Most people see it as a poor excuse for a talent, but I'm good at it. It's what you need. Why else would you hire me?"

Graves had no answer to that. His eyes slipped to hers again, assessing, maybe approving.

She matched his long strides as he led her to the giant staircase at the center of the home. They walked up two flights of stairs. She could have gotten lost, the house was so enormous. She was used to Colette's brothel. It was smaller than Graves's mansion by far but large enough to accommodate the women she housed within. All those bedrooms. All the workers. But this… No one else *lived* here. It was excess for the sake of excess.

"I have a few house ground rules."

"We already made our deal."

"This is for living in my home. My rooms are off-limits. Even from a little thief who knows how to break into them." He added explicitly, "Don't go into locked rooms."

Kierse's fingers itched to do just that. Telling a thief not to use their skills was tantamount to encouraging them to do so. Especially because now it made her wonder—what exactly did he have to hide?

He seemed to realize that as soon as it was said. "I've lived alone for a *very* long time, Miss McKenna. I value my privacy more than my possessions. I will give you privacy so long as you extend it to me as well."

"You ruin all my fun."

"Is that a yes?"

"Yes," she agreed.

He kept his eyes on her face as if trying to judge the weight of her conviction.

"Promise," she said with what she hoped sounded like sincerity.

"Good." Satisfied, he walked to the end of a hallway on the third floor. "This is your room."

"Truly, I'm not tired," she told him. It had been a long night, and she was weary but also hyped up from all that had happened. "Is the library available to me?"

"The library?" he asked, then nodded once. "You are free to read anything on the shelves."

"Maybe we could go there, then."

"Another time. If you're so eager to get started on your studies, then I will have books for you after training."

He reached for the doorknob, and she touched it at the same time. Their hands brushed, and even with his gloves on, she could feel the heat from him. He was much taller than her, and she looked up at him from under her eyelashes. Their bodies were close together, she realized, and she swallowed. She'd been playing up her wiles but somehow was ensnared in his gaze.

He retreated first. "You were chased and shot at and forced to leave your friends and family, your home. You are in shock. Though you hide it rather well. You need to sleep."

"Honestly, I'd rather you tell me more about myself."

"No new shocks."

"I'm not a delicate flower that you should fear crushing in your palm."

"No, you're delicate like a bomb."

She grinned like a wild creature. She liked that.

He took another step back as if she ruffled his carefully controlled exterior.

"Just one thing," she teased, arching an eyebrow.

"I see you won't be dissuaded. I will start with the most basic. Satisfactory?"

She nodded. She was surprised she had gotten him to bend when she'd been certain he was a mountain not to be swayed. Not that she wouldn't *try*.

"What you *are* is up for debate. We'll have to figure it out together. Though I have my suspicions. But what you can do is far more fascinating. As far as I have observed, you can nullify magic."

"What does that mean?"

"It appears that you have some sort of natural immunity. It's why you can walk through my wards like water. How deep or wide that goes is for us to discover."

"Immunity," she whispered as if overcome by a potent drug. "I am immune to magic."

"That is what I believe."

The words seared through her. She'd spent over a decade thinking monsters *not* magic, but now that she knew it existed—that against all odds, *she* had powers—well, immunity sounded *incredibly* useful. Especially if it had the implications she was considering.

"Am I immune to you?"

He stilled. His face was blank. "Yes."

Oh, he didn't like that. Walking through his wards and entering his residence without him knowing was one thing. A thing that he already didn't like. But *his* magic didn't work on her? That was life-altering.

He clicked the door to her new room open and gestured for her to enter. She did on a wave of shock and something like euphoria.

"How much magic is there in this world?"

"Why do you ask?"

"Have I been interacting with it my entire life and never known?"

"That is entirely possible," he admitted, his accent crisp. "Something we will discover together. Good day, Miss McKenna."

She watched him walk away, his hands clasped tightly behind his back. She should have let him go. But somehow, like there was a string between them, she felt a tug to stop him. Just once before he left again.

"Graves," she called.

He stilled in the darkened hallway and then faced her once more.

"Are there others who can do what I can do?" she asked, the only hopefully hopeless question she could. Maybe she had family. Maybe they were out there. They just didn't know about her.

"I have never met one in all my years," he said solemnly, almost…kindly.

She recoiled from the tenderness in his expression. As if she were naked before him.

She locked her jaw and returned her expression to neutral, refusing to let him see how affected she was. "And how long is that?"

Graves shook his head, walking away again, but she still heard his barely uttered, "A very, very long time."

Chapter Thirteen

Kierse awoke with a start, reaching for a knife that wasn't there. She was instantly alert. Her breaths came out heavy as she inspected her surroundings in confusion and horror. Then it dawned on her. It all came crashing back. Everything that had happened in vivid detail.

The Druids. Five Points. Taking Graves's job.

She checked the time and saw that it was early afternoon, then flopped back down onto the decadent four-poster bed. She had been so exhausted that she hadn't even bothered to look at her surroundings. Just went from the door to the bed and collapsed. Now, in the absence of her adrenaline-fueled rush, she was drained. Her ribs were tender. She winced as she felt along the careful stitches Maura had administered. She'd have to see if Graves had anything for the pain.

Probably best to wash up first. With sunlight streaming through the windows, she gaped at the room as she slid out of bed. The room was elegant, with light-blue paint and cream-and-gray wood furniture. The bed had almost been too soft to sleep in compared to what she was used to back at Colette's. The navy duvet was fluffy with goose feathers and a dozen throw pillows that she'd haphazardly strewn onto the floor.

She headed into what she assumed was an adjoining bathing chamber. It was bigger than Colette's entire bedroom, with a full sunken tub with jets and trays of oils, petals, and salts. The shower was a large, open stone room with three heads and another waterfall that fell from the ceiling. The chamber also had two sinks, a vanity, and a separate room just for the toilet.

Then she found the closet. It was easily twice the size of the bathroom and, as far as she could tell, completely empty. Empty space was the epitome of wealth. A whole room of *nothing*. Was he planning to fill it? Had it originally belonged to someone else? Just…why?

But she didn't have those answers, and she had more important ones to get today.

First, a shower. If the rest of the house was any indication, this would be nothing like showering at the brothel or Five Points. She removed her clothes and her prized wren necklace before stepping into the stream of water. She thrilled at the instant heat on her skin and luxuriated in the fanciest bottles of shampoo and conditioner. She scrubbed herself with a lavender-and-honey-scented soap, careful with her injured ribs. She even opened a razor and shaved just for good measure. The water never got cold or ran out. She could have stayed in there for *hours*. She might have if her stomach hadn't started rumbling loudly. Those biscuits from this morning hadn't been enough to replace all the energy she'd burned through.

Kierse turned off the shower, which she was convinced was her favorite part of the house, and exited the bathroom in a fluffy white towel. Her dark hair was wrapped up beneath another towel. Maura's clothes were still scattered across the floor of the room, but she didn't exactly want to get back into dirty clothes. So, she headed into the closet and opened drawers. Empty, empty, empty. There really wasn't a scrap of clothing in here. Not a thing. Then she heard a knock on the door.

Kierse rushed back out and gently pulled the door open an inch. "Yes?"

Isolde smiled at her cheerily. "Oh good, you're already up. I thought you might want these."

She held up a bundle of clothes.

"You're a lifesaver," Kierse said, taking them from her.

"Food will be served in the parlor whenever you come downstairs."

Kierse's stomach grumbled again noisily, and she shot Isolde a wry smile. "I'll be right down."

She closed the door and dropped the towel to the ground. She pulled apart the bundle to find a pair of the nicest pants she had ever seen. They weren't quite leggings. More like athletic pants. A soft cotton but somehow functional. She could run in them if she had to. The top was the same material and came with an insulated athletic jacket. Lightweight but warm and nicer than all of her own clothing combined. A pair of wool socks and tennis shoes finished it off.

Efficient, practical clothing. Nothing frilly or sophisticated. It fit. It did the job. She hung her trusty leather jacket on a hanger and left the closet.

She reattached her necklace on a breath of relief. Now she was ready.

Kierse retraced her steps from this morning, letting muscle memory guide her. She emerged into the main hallway and then followed her nose to the kitchen. The smell was warm and cinnamony with a touch of maple and oh god, bacon!

Isolde turned around at her audible groan. She laughed with a wide smile. Kierse had dismissed the older woman as insignificant when she was casing the place. Now, Kierse could see that she was the key to the house.

Isolde wore a black dress with a white apron over it. Black stockings and practical black shoes finished the ensemble. She wore her hair up and off of her lined forehead. She was still striking, and it terrified Kierse to think what she must have looked like in her twenties. Perhaps she was a siren but with food. Was that a thing?

"The parlor is through that door, dear," Isolde said, pointing toward it.

"Is he already in there?"

"The master? Not yet. He's still out."

Kierse stepped up to the island and pulled out a heavy iron chair with a blue cushion. "I can eat in here."

Isolde waved a hand. "Suit yourself. I'm not used to having anyone else in my kitchen, though."

"I won't interrupt."

Isolde started piling enough food to feed a small army onto trays. "It's breakfast, since you slept through the day."

"It all looks amazing," she told Isolde.

And it really did. Her stomach growled noisily as she looked on. Pancakes, scrambled eggs, over-easy eggs, bacon, and sausage. Plus hashbrowns, fresh fruit, bread for toast, bagels, and half a dozen types of cream cheese. Still more juice, coffee, and tea were set out for her.

Kierse must have held her mouth open too long, because Isolde said, "I didn't know what you liked. So I made a little bit of everything."

"Just…just for me?" she all but gasped.

"The master will eat some if he didn't dine out."

Kierse stared at the spread in awe. She'd never known anything like it. A chef at her disposal. Someone who seemed anxious for her to put it all on her plate and devour it whole.

"You didn't have to do all of this," Kierse told her. "There's no way I'll finish it all. What do you do with the rest of it?"

"We donate what we can and help charities for those in food deserts."

"Which is everyone," Kierse added softly.

Isolde smiled at her warmly. "If it concerns you, you let me know what you like and we can set up a schedule. I won't make as much next time, but I work best on a schedule."

Kierse just blinked. "Uh…okay. Thank you so much."

Isolde beamed. "Your enjoyment is all the thanks I need. Now, eat up.

You look like you could eat a whole horse and still be hungry."

She wasn't that far off. Kierse filled her plate not once but twice. Everything tasted so good. So rich. It was a struggle to stop eating. To listen to her ever-expanding stomach that strained at the edges to contain all that she'd taken in. She didn't go hungry at Colette's, hadn't gone hungry in many years, but the need to clean her plate never really left.

"What is that delicious smell?" Graves asked as he strode into the kitchen.

Isolde blushed furiously. "Nothing new, sir."

"Bacon," Kierse said around her final mouthful.

"You outdid yourself," Graves complimented.

"Shall I fix you a plate?" Isolde asked.

"Unfortunately, no. I ate already. I won't make the mistake again."

Isolde grinned like a schoolgirl, clearly taken with her boss's praise. "Never a mistake where you choose to dine."

"No one cooks like you, and I do believe Miss McKenna agrees."

"Yes," Kierse said instantly. "I do."

"Hoping to put some meat on her bones. She's half starved," Isolde said.

Kierse raised her eyebrows. "This is *not* me half starved."

"Could have fooled me."

Graves nodded as if he agreed with Isolde. The traitor.

Kierse knew what she looked like half starved. She thought she looked pretty healthy, actually.

"Are you ready to answer all of my questions now?" Kierse asked with a wink.

Graves shook his head with a slight tilt to his lips. "How about over dinner tonight?"

"I thought lessons were starting after I woke up."

"We'll talk over dinner."

Her eyes moved up to meet his—dark, swirling gray. There was something in those eyes. Something she just could not decipher. "Fine. Dinner it is."

"Isolde will prepare a menu. It will be late. Nine o'clock?"

"I'm a night owl. The later the better," she said. "I'll have to head back to my place to get clothes."

Graves shook his head. "Give your preferences to Isolde, and she can buy you new clothes. Whatever you need. You'll begin spear training with Edgar immediately after this."

"Yeah, I wanted to ask about that, too. Why would I need to learn how to wield a spear?" she asked askance. "I'm stealing it, not fighting with it."

"It will be the best weapon with which to fight your way out if something goes wrong."

She didn't like that sentiment one bit. "I prefer stealth to fighting, but guns and knives if I must."

"I'd rather account for all possibilities."

"All right." She'd already agreed to do it in negotiations, so she'd train with this spear, but she sure hoped that it didn't come down to needing to use it.

"I also got you some other things while I was out," he said.

He stepped out for a minute and then returned with a light, stealthy backpack. "Everything you need. I retrieved some cash for you as a small advance. Half of our agreed-upon sum has been deposited into a bank account for you, card included," he said, offering her a black card, "and the rest will go to the same place at the end of the job."

She took the bag and unzipped the top. Inside was the promised hoard of cash, two brand-spanking-new, top-of-the-line handguns with built-in silencers and extra ammo, and a sleek cell phone with a giant screen display that turned on at her touch. Only one number was programmed into the thing.

"This is you, I'm guessing?"

"That's me. Answer when I call."

"Will you be calling often?" she asked.

He slid his hands into his pockets. "Let's hope not. For the both of us."

Then he nodded at Isolde and disappeared without another word.

Kierse turned back around in her seat. "Is he always that cryptic?"

Isolde smiled. "You have no idea."

Kierse laughed and then went in search of the training facility. Edgar was waiting when she arrived, and from the very moment she had a spear in her hand, she didn't like it. Not compared to a knife or a gun. One for close range and one for distance. This spear felt all wrong. It was meant for thrusting and throwing, but she couldn't get the hang of either. They worked methodically on thrusting motions, trying to get her knife reflexes to take the bulkier spear. The weapon was steel-tipped and fire-hardened, attached to the tough ash end with a charcoal iron, making the whole thing nearly impossible to break. The force it would take would have to be incredible. Thankfully, they were working with practice spears, so no one accidentally got gutted.

Edgar was an unrelentingly impressive teacher and made her do the same maneuver over and over again, until her hand blistered and broke and her muscles ached for release. She knew the training method. He wanted her to have so much muscle memory built up that she wouldn't freeze in a combat situation. Didn't make it suck any less.

When she finished, she wandered the halls of the house as her cooldown. Most of the rooms were locked, which led her to the one room completely open to her—the library.

She walked up and down the holly-lined shelves, admiring the endless books and looking for all the hidden treasures within. One day, she was going to be able to look at a place and not calculate how much it cost or whether there was something inside worth stealing. One day.

A soft noise came from the stacks. It didn't sound human. She froze, wondering what else lived in this library.

Just as she was sure her imagination had gotten the best of her, a small black cat appeared at the end of her aisle. Kierse laughed. She'd been about to bolt all because of a *cat*.

"Here, kitty," she called gently. She dropped to one knee and held her hand out in front of her.

Of course the cat ignored her. Stared blankly at her with its uncanny gold eyes.

"You trapped in these walls, too?"

The cat made a disconcerting sound and flicked its tail.

"Well, we can be friends," she suggested. A cat was better than loneliness.

So, she did what she knew from the streets worked best with cats. She ignored the thing and went back to her perusing. Within ten minutes, the cat had strolled forward as if it owned the library and wrapped itself around Kierse's legs, purring.

"Oh, I see how it is. Only want me when I don't want you," she said with a smile. "Story of my life."

Kierse reached down and stroked the cat's back. The tiny thing hissed, batting at her with one of its clawed paws and then bounding up the stacks to watch her from the top of the shelf.

"We'll be friends, you and I," Kierse declared.

Isolde found her among the stacks at one point later when she was trying to coax the cat back out.

"Oh, I see you met Anne," she said, holding a little brown book and a plate with a grilled cheese sandwich.

"Anne," Kierse said. "So that's your name."

Anne retreated a few more steps.

Isolde just chuckled before setting the food down. She offered Kierse the book. "The master said to give this to you when you finished training. He'll expect you to read it before dinner."

She eyed the thing apprehensively.

"All right. I'll do my best." She sat down with the sandwich in hand and thumbed through the pages until she found a story that caught her interest.

It was about a redheaded child who had been waylaid by a will-o-the-wisp. She'd seen the blue light flickering in her awareness and followed it, unaware, into the woods, away from her parents. The girl had to get through a series of tests to prove her mettle, including getting past an evil witch and outwitting a warlock. Kierse had flipped through all the trials of the girl, anxious to see her happy return to her family.

But the redheaded girl never made it home. The will-o-the-wisp kept dragging her deeper and deeper into the forest until she came upon a bear and it consumed her. What was the moral of that story? That no matter how much you try, you can't escape your fate? That the temptation that led you off your course will also lead you to your death? *Beware!*

But there must be something to this, or else why would he suggest she read it?

Anne jumped up, and Kierse followed the cat's golden gaze as she folded into the space beside her.

All the tales and legends come from a kernel of truth. That was what Graves had said. Could *these* tales also have a kernel of truth? Did he want her to reflect on the moral story of wandering off her path? Or was it about the being-consumed-by-a-monster part? She was already *well* aware she was off her path and ready to be consumed.

Still, she had enjoyed the volume and finished with plenty of time to get ready for dinner.

At quarter to eight, she returned to her rooms to get ready for dinner, anticipating another nice, *long* shower. But she was shocked as she stepped into the room to find the closet bursting with new apparel—ball gowns, business attire, cocktail dresses, club wear, a dozen pairs of pants and T-shirts, workout clothes, sports bras, sleeping clothes, and even little lacy unmentionables. Kierse quickly closed that drawer. She seemed as likely to wear those scraps of fabric as the ball gown.

After a luxurious shower, a blowout from the fanciest blow dryer she had ever seen that made her long, dark hair shine and fall in waves over her shoulders, and even a collection of makeup that Isolde must have picked up as well—the woman thought of everything—Kierse felt like a whole new person.

She slid a black cocktail dress on. The material was formfitting, hugging her like a glove to her knees. It wasn't what she'd normally go with, but somehow it was better. Money, probably. The quality was top-notch. Then she grabbed a pair of heels off of a rack and looked at herself in the full-length mirror. Her wren necklace was on full display with the plunging neckline of the dress.

This was good enough. It was just dinner. A business dinner at that. It wasn't a *date*. There was nothing at all to be nervous about. It had nothing to do with her intimacy issues. And how she hadn't had dinner with anyone since Torra and had decided wooing just wasn't for her. The physical stuff, she could get behind. After all, sex was just sex. It was the other stuff that was too hard.

Now her palms were sweating. Which was ridiculous.

This wasn't even that kind of dinner. Yes, she found Graves attractive. She'd have to be blind not to see how hot he was. But besides the fact that mixing business with pleasure was a bad idea, it just wasn't even that kind of dinner. Why did her body have to react like this? She could face down Declan with a gun pointed at her chest without blinking. Yet, *this* unnerved her?

She straightened her spine and let the anger carry her downstairs. She made it to the dining room and found Edgar waiting at the entrance.

"Miss McKenna, you look charming tonight."

"Better than when you last saw me. That's for sure."

"Not better, just different."

She nodded. "Thank you."

Edgar opened the door, and though she had known what to expect, it didn't prepare her for seeing the dining room in all its splendor. The table was a deep, rich mahogany fit for twelve, though only two seats had place settings: one at the head of the table, where a dark, smoldering Graves sat reading a brown leather book, and the other to his left. Candelabras encircled the table, illuminating the space, while gorgeous floral arrangements ran down the center. She had no idea where he'd found the intricate bouquets in the city at this time of year.

Edgar cleared his throat. "Sir, your guest has arrived."

She steeled her nerves and stepped inside to meet her own dark captor from a fairy tale. The warlock who had led her off her path.

Chapter Fourteen

Graves's eyes flickered up from his book as if he'd been so engrossed that he hadn't heard anyone come in. Then those gray eyes found Kierse across the room. They darkened considerably as he took her in. Down the formfitting dress to her exposed legs and then back up to meet her gaze. She shivered at the attention. He remained unreadable, and yet she knew what it meant when someone looked at her as he just had. He found her attractive, too.

But "Ah" was all he said before returning to his book.

Edgar pulled out her chair, and she sank down, her back stiff against the delicate cushion.

She tried to ignore Graves seated next to her, but he had a certain presence, as if he filled the entire room. And though he was lethal, she couldn't help but admire him in kind. He was dressed in an all-black suit with a crisp white shirt and black tie. His stormy eyes moved swiftly across the words, turning the pages with a black-gloved finger. He'd exchanged his normal black leather for fine evening gloves. But still…gloves.

She cleared her throat. "Do you always wear those?"

Graves looked up briefly. "Hmm?"

"The gloves. Do you always wear them?"

But then his eyes dropped down to the necklace at her throat.

"Do you always wear that?" he countered.

She brushed her finger against the wren. "Yes." He'd seemed surprised by the necklace on their first meeting. "It caught your attention before."

He nodded and held his hand out. "May I see it?"

The last thing she wanted was to take the necklace off and let him touch it. "You're dodging my question about the gloves."

"I prefer gloves," he answered, giving just a little. He made a beckoning gesture, and with a sigh, she took the necklace off and placed it reluctantly into his palm.

He studied the delicate artwork of the wren. The way her wingspan extended to the edges of the circle pendant. The faint filigree around the edges that led to the metal backing. It was her most prized possession, and just seeing it in his hands made her feel sick.

"Do you know the symbolism behind wrens, Miss McKenna?"

She shook her head. "No."

"In some cultures, the wren is a symbol of spring and rebirth. To see a wren in the winter is a sign that spring is forthcoming, that winter will not last forever. It is a positive sign. The day after Christmas is called Wren Day. Wrens are hunted down and slain. They are put on pikes and carried through the town. It's thought to help banish the winter god."

Her eyes widened in alarm. "Wow. I've never heard of that before. So, you thought it meant something when I wore it?"

"I believed you to be a good omen in winter." His eyes flicked up to hers. "Where did you say you got this?"

He removed one glove, and she caught a peek of that tattoo once more. Her eyes lingered on it, trying to make out what was hidden beneath that impeccable suit. More vines and a glimpse of thorns, but that was all she could manage in the dim light. Then her eyes were drawn away from the ink to Graves's finger running over the face of the pendant. He dragged it down slowly and decisively. It was almost obscene.

"It belonged to my mother."

"And where did she get it?"

Kierse turned her face away from him. She didn't like talking about the mom she'd never known. "I never got the chance to ask her."

Graves's eyes flicked up to hers, abandoning the pendant at the harsh quality to her voice. "She passed?"

"She died in childbirth."

Now there was interest in his look. "My apologies for your loss."

Kierse shrugged.

"And you've always had the necklace?" She nodded. "Well, it might be a key to learning why you are immune to magic. Have you worn it every time we've been together?"

"I wear it everywhere."

Without preamble, he grasped her wrist. She gasped at his bare skin against hers. At the heat of him and the unexpected physical contact. He sent a chill up her back, and goose bumps exploded on her arms. He looked deep into her eyes as if willing her to reveal herself. She inhaled at the heat of him. His concentration was focused on her. Direct. She hovered in anticipation as she waited.

Then he blew out his breath in a huff and released her.

She rocked back in her seat at the loss of him and covered it by reaching out for her glass of water and taking a long sip.

"Just a trinket," he said as he handed her the necklace.

She tied the wren into place, contemplating how he could possibly know that from one touch. "You can…tell that by touching me?"

"Yes."

Which meant that his magic had something to do with touch. Was that the reason for the mystery gloves? She watched him slip his glove back on, more curious than ever.

At that moment, Isolde and Edgar entered from the kitchen with trays laden with food. Once the food was on the table, they removed the silver covers and served them. Kierse's mouth watered as food was added to her plate. Some sort of beef on a bed of rice, a side of steaming creamy corn, glossy dinner rolls, a leafy salad, and even out-of-season berries. God, she loved berries. It all looked delectable, but she reached for a raspberry first, popping it into her mouth. It was even better than she remembered.

Graves stared at her with open interest.

"What?" she asked, grabbing for another berry. "They're out of season."

For a moment, he said nothing. Then, as if it was against his better judgment, he said, "I don't remember ever enjoying something that much."

"When you live on the streets, you learn to appreciate what's in front of you. Guess you probably don't know what that's like."

"I did not always have what you see before you. I was once discarded as you were."

She covered her wince by cutting into her beef. *Discarded.* He wasn't wrong. It just sounded like she was the trash that had been tossed out.

"How could someone get rid of someone like you? Someone with magic?"

"Easily. And without remorse."

She had no response to that. She didn't know why she had been *discarded*, either. She had no memory of before. The earliest thing she remembered was standing on the street, starving. She'd had no other option than to turn to theft. Stealing was better than dying of hunger, and she'd gotten really good at it fast. Jason found her a short while later. She'd all but given up hope of discovering who she was…until Graves happened.

She went back to her food. She ate the beef so quickly that she barely tasted it. The meat was so rich and tender in some sort of cranberry sauce. She'd never had anything like it.

"Before we begin, tell me about the book I lent you."

"It's a bit dark," she confessed. "Everyone dies in all the tales. I thought the will-o-the-wisp would have some happy moral ending at least."

"Why? That's a product of modern storytelling."

Kierse paused at this conclusion. When she met those storm-cloud eyes, she saw interest in them. She decided to meet him with her own interest. "I felt like I understood the little girl who was led astray by a will-o-the-wisp. It was a common theme in the city during the war."

"Ah," he said as understanding narrowed his eyes. "And you wanted a happy ending for the girl when there wasn't one for you."

She refused to recoil from his assessment. "I didn't need a savior. I saved myself. But others weren't as lucky as I was."

"That's the way of the world."

"It is. I assume you wanted me to see that I could be consumed by the monster that was waylaying me. Was that a metaphor?"

"She isn't consumed by the monster at the end. She's consumed by the bear."

"Fine," she acknowledged. "Then the only real monster in the story is the bear." A natural monster, like the very human monsters Kierse knew all too well.

"Well, the bear and the monster that pulled her off her path—the wisp. They both led to her death."

"She never stood a chance."

"No, she did not."

"But you still haven't told me anything about *me*."

He cleared his throat. "Well, we know that your pendant isn't controlling your immunity. Which likely means you're like me."

She leaned in eagerly. "Like you how? A monster?"

"We're all monsters. But for simplicity, yes. I'm a type of monster you've never encountered. Though with your immunity you might not have ever known what you were experiencing."

"And what do they call you?" she asked. Labels didn't always matter, but putting a word on what she was felt important. Solid.

"There are several words for what I am. The others who are like me choose which word they prefer to be called. It usually depends on when they were born or how they were raised. Though most of us choose one word over others—a warlock."

"A warlock." Her mouth went dry. This was real. This was her life. "And there are others?"

"Yes. Not many. Unlike the other monsters, who have come into the light, we chose not to. We're rare and *very* territorial." He looked strikingly possessive in that moment. "Most cities have no more than one master warlock at any given time. We prefer our privacy."

"Okay, but what does it actually mean to be a warlock?"

"Traditionally, we were called wizards or sorcerers or warlocks. The word 'warlock' actually came first—around 900. It was generally believed to mean 'oathbreaker' or 'devil.' Most people of the time were superstitious." He cut his meat into pieces with deliberate precision, not bothering to look up as he continued. "They believed that the magic they perceived was a negative force. That it went against God and nature. It wasn't until around the fourteenth century that other words developed to discuss magic in a positive light—wizard, mage, even astrologer."

"Why don't you call yourself one of those, then?"

His stare was dangerous, and she knew before he answered why he'd chosen "warlock." Because he was the darkness.

He shrugged. "I choose to claim what I am."

Kierse gulped down her wine. "I see."

He finished off his glass and poured another. "As for you, the signs point to you being a warlock as well, but I don't want to say for certain. It's surprising that you survived this long with magic in your veins without your knowledge. Though perhaps, since your power is negative, passive, it didn't try to burn through you."

"Burn through me?" she asked in alarm.

"When warlocks come into their power without their knowledge, it's likely to kill the person. Even trained warlocks can use their magic too quickly and burn through it, destroying us from the inside out. I don't know why yours never manifested in that way. Warlock powers vary widely. Some can do one thing incredibly well. Some have a wide variety of base powers. Perhaps you just got lucky."

"And you? What can you do?"

He smiled tightly. "We're not talking about my powers."

A sidestep if she'd ever seen one. But already her mind was reeling with all this new information. With how reticent Graves had been up to this point, she was surprised that he'd even dished out this much.

Edgar entered then to clear the plates while Isolde set down a tiny, delicate white dessert. It was a small rectangle with layers of pastry and cream with chocolate feathered on top. It looked like she could pick it up and eat it all in one delicious mouthful.

Kierse took one bite of the dessert and decided it was her new favorite.

"A mille-feuille," Graves answered before she could ask. "It's a French delicacy."

"I approve."

Graves offered her his portion, and she didn't even feel guilty taking it off of him. His grin as she bit into it said that maybe he was enjoying her enjoyment as well.

"Shall we discuss the job? As that's why you're here," Graves asked while she ate.

"Yes. Tell me everything I need to know." She polished off the last bite of mille-feuille and leaned forward against the table. The dinner had been nice and all, but she wasn't here for fancy dinners or cute banter. It was time to get down to business.

"As I told you before, you're stealing a spear."

"Got that much already."

"How did training go?"

She grimaced. "Like bleeding blisters all over my hands."

"That's normal when you start a new weapon. You'll get there. We don't have much time. So you'll have to train daily to get accustomed to it."

"That's fine. But tell me more about this spear. Where is it? What do I have to do to steal it?"

"Have you heard of Third Floor?"

Her blood turned to ice. "I've heard of it," she said. Torra had disappeared down there and never resurfaced. It was basically a black hole. A place where people like Torra went to die.

"The spear is locked away in the heart of Third Floor, in the residence of the leader of the Men of Valor."

Kierse's smile tipped up. Finally, a chance for some revenge.

"You've heard of them as well, I presume?"

"A group of all different kinds of monsters working together against the Treaty? Yeah. That's something I think most people have heard of. Even if they haven't come across them."

"And have you?" Graves asked.

Kierse had no interest in telling him about how they'd taken Torra. So she just smiled deviously.

"I work with billionaire clientele. I've seen the gold wings-and-arrow pendants before."

"Indeed. Third Floor itself is warded, and the spear is in a warded residence."

"But I can get through the wards."

He nodded. "That you can. But you can't just stroll in and take it and expect to get out alive without a plan. To get you in and out with the spear, we'll only have one opportunity. On the winter solstice, the Men of Valor are throwing a party inside the leader's residence. The doors will open, and hundreds will flock inside. That's when we strike."

Kierse blinked at him as she realized that he was actually serious. "The winter solstice?"

He arched an eyebrow. "Will that be a problem?"

"It's only a few weeks away."

"So, you won't do it?" he asked flatly.

Graves's gaze roamed her face, as if he was waiting for her to reject him. She would be up against the worst sort of monsters in their own stronghold with a ticking clock. But she hadn't thought she was stealing from just anyone. Not with ten million at stake.

"Oh, I'll fucking do it," she said simply. "There's too much riding on it to not do it, but I sure hope that your training is good enough to get me out of this alive."

"You'll do it, knowing that you could die?"

"I knew I could die when I walked into your house," she said. "I would do anything for my family. Anything to keep them safe."

Something flashed across his face that she couldn't quite place. Remorse or pain. But neither seemed to fit with Graves.

She couldn't resist raising her glass. "To the winter solstice, then."

Finally, he smiled slow and genuine, raising his glass to clink against hers. "To the winter solstice."

Chapter Fifteen

N ow that Kierse knew they only had mere *weeks* to do the most impossible heist of her entire life, she needed to put some of her own contingencies in place.

She had agreed not to see her friends, and she would hold to that. Even though it killed her on the inside. Graves had suggested she call Nate, but the things she needed to tell him couldn't be said over the phone. Let alone one Graves likely had access to.

But she had one other place to go before her meeting with Nate.

She changed out of her cocktail dress and back into the sleek workout clothes, then snuck out of the brownstone with her hood up against the chill and backpack tight against her. She hated the subway at night, but her time was limited. After paying the troll standing guard at the subway entrance off 8th Avenue, she slunk through the shadows, ignoring the catcalls from the goblins around a small trashcan fire and the similar catcalls from the *human* men who were just as slimy. She kept her backpack angled away from any of the other unsavory travelers when she stepped on the B train. A gun was cocked in her pocket, the new grip a reassurance in her palm. The other gun was in a holster under her jacket. It didn't even look bulky against her close-fit clothing.

Thankfully, there was no trouble when she hopped off a stop before her usual exit. She'd been tracked from Graves's place before. She didn't want to encounter any Druids tonight. She'd recognized one guy who she had evaded easily leaving Graves's place. And there were currently two patrols around Colette's. Not close enough to rub up against the Roulettes, but not far enough away to be anything but a patrol. Luckily, she'd lived in the brothel house for years. She knew every in and out on the property and all the surrounding streets like the back of her hand.

Bypassing the patrols was a cakewalk. She slipped in a side entrance to Colette's brothel. No alarms went up. No one burst in after her. No one had even seen. Kierse inwardly smiled. Lorcan's men had gotten the jump on her, but they weren't better than her. They'd had the element of surprise. That was all. Maybe the infamous Lorcan was of a higher caliber, but not his crew.

Kierse stalked through the backside of the house. It was still quiet within. She could hear the kitchens firing up for the girls and footsteps overhead as they prepared for the evening work. Business would pick up after dinner, which meant that she didn't have long. She swept through her home, taking the back way into Colette's chambers. The house had been built to have serving quarters and a network to allow servants to go about unseen. It was helpful now. Kierse headed up the back staircase and into Colette's bedroom.

A figure shifted near the window. "If you're here to kill me, then you will have to try harder than that."

Kierse found Colette with a pistol hanging lazily from her hand. A tingle went up Kierse's spine but not from Colette's appearance. She sensed the man before he reached for her. Kierse darted out of the way, dodging the first attack and blocking the second.

"It's me," she gasped out. She recognized the man coming after her as Carmine, the leader of the Roulettes. Which was not good for her, since he had been a prize fighter in his youth.

She tried to dart out of his way again, but he got his arms around her. He was as strong as a tree trunk, and there was no breaking free. Not unless she wanted to hurt him, which she did not.

"Wait," Kierse cried.

"Carmine, no," Colette said, jerking away from the window. "It's Kierse."

Carmine released her immediately, though he looked put out by it. He straightened his suit vest and took a step backward as he ran a hand across his dark gelled hair, cursing under his breath in Spanish.

"What are you doing here, girl?" Colette dropped her gun on the nearby table.

Kierse shifted her attention between Colette and Carmine, not comfortable disclosing information in front of him.

Colette read it immediately. "Carmine, check the entrance Kierse came through. See if anyone followed her in." She glanced at Kierse one more time and then added, "And grab Corey while you're at it."

Carmine grunted and then sketched a small, mocking bow. "At your service, madame."

When he disappeared through the door, Colette marched across the room and dragged her into a stiff hug. Kierse froze in shock and then loosened. When Colette stepped back, she slapped Kierse across the face. Kierse actually laughed a little as she held her cheek.

"Don't ever scare me like that again."

"The great Colette can feel fear?"

"Don't test me," she said, but lightly, as if she wasn't quite used to being this vulnerable.

"I didn't come to test you. I came for this." Kierse removed the small backpack Graves had given her and unzipped it.

Colette's eyes widened when she saw the pile of cash. "Where did you get that?"

She took out half of the money and left it on the side table.

"The less you know, the better." Kierse waved her away. "This is for you. Keep it safe. Use it in emergencies or if…if things go bad."

Colette didn't even touch the money. She just stared past it to Kierse. "What have you gotten yourself into?"

"A job. For a very dangerous man." Kierse removed what she'd used her own money to buy after getting off the subway—a burner phone. "Here."

Colette took the thing in her hand. "What's this for?"

"I won't be able to check in again. It's not safe."

"Of course I know it's not safe, Kierse. When a Dreadlord shows up in my brothel with a letter from Nathaniel O'Connor, I know to pay attention." She pursed her lips. "Nate and I go back a long way. I sent you to him, after all. Are you going to tell me what's going on?"

"The less you know, the better," Kierse told her. "This phone is how you reach me if things get really bad. Don't let anyone know you have it."

Colette sank into the chair next to the window. The small phone was still clutched in her hand. "You don't think you'll come back." It must have been written on her face. "Is there anything I can do?"

Kierse shook her head. She zipped the backpack closed and slung it over her shoulder again. "I'm going to take this to Gen and Ethan."

"So you're working with the Dreadlords again?" Colette asked. "Nate missed you."

"I'm working for myself." Kierse shot her a challenging smile. "Always myself."

Colette nodded in understanding. "And my daughter?"

"Gen and Ethan are safe with the Dreadlords."

"And they're not coming back?" she asked as Corey entered the room.

"No," Corey said. "Dreadlord security is tighter than any I've ever seen."

Colette looked mildly offended by that. "*You're* part of my security."

"Which is why I can admit that I'd rather my boyfriend stay there if he's in trouble." Corey glanced at Kierse then. "He's in trouble, right?"

Kierse nodded once. "You've been discreet when going to see him?"

"Who do you think I am? I don't fuck with Ethan's protection. But is he going to be okay?"

Colette cleared her throat. "Of course he is. Who is going to cross the Dreadlords?"

Corey locked his gaze with Kierse's and waited. She swallowed. She didn't want to lie. "Gen and Ethan are okay for now, but this is my contingency plan in case it all goes south."

He nodded reluctantly. "I hate this."

So did she.

She hated this part, too, and knew he wasn't going to like it, either.

"Maybe you should go stay there with them. If they're in trouble, all the Druids have to do is track you to get to them."

Corey cursed under his breath. "Carmine will never let me…"

"Leave Carmine to me," Colette said.

"You think it's that bad?" Corey asked.

"I'd rather be safe than sorry."

She flicked her eyes back to Colette's. She was worried that she might have to convince the madame as well. But Colette just lifted her chin. "Be safe, girl," she said low and solemn. "There is darkness in your future."

Chapter Sixteen

K ierse took Colette's warning for what it was—truth. She could hardly deny that it felt real. And it was a darkness she was walking swiftly into. At least her eyes were open.

She backtracked out of the brothel, narrowly avoiding another Druid patrol. Bastards were everywhere. She skipped the subway for a chilly walk to Houston Street, where she hopped on a bus just before it pulled away. She headed off the bus again in Greenwich Village, walking the last few blocks to her meetup point with Nate. Varying her routes was another sure way to keep anyone from tailing her, and by the time she hit the late-night coffee shop, she was certain she was alone.

But Nate hadn't come alone. Wolves lurked in the shadows. The bartender from Five Points, Cara, was on the corner, her blond hair slicked back into a tight ponytail. Her stance was predatory and ready to pounce at any moment. A taller brunette with a pointed nose hung to her left. Farther out were more wolves she didn't recognize. But one she did. Slim Ronan, with his black hair parted down the middle and his beige skin almost completely covered by the black pack attire, had a cigarette dangling between his lips. He'd joined the Dreadlords to get his family protection during the war, but they always threatened to move back to Korea. Not that anyone could afford it.

If Ronan was here, that meant his brother-in-arms was nearby.

Finn stood at the entrance to the coffee shop as she approached. He had onyx skin and a muscular physique, but while Ronan was the intimidating one, Finn was all love with full golden-retriever energy. His smile brightened at the sight of her.

"Hey there."

She tipped her head at him. "Finn."

"Good to have you back, McKenna." He pulled the door open for her.

"Can safely say the same," she said as she entered.

Nate was already waiting at the empty coffee shop at their regular booth. She slipped into the seat across from him.

"Fancy meeting you here," Nate said.

This had been their favorite place to meet back when she'd worked for the Dreadlords. Money and stolen goods had changed hands over burned coffee and from-scratch pie.

"Cute," she muttered.

"It's nice that you could just text this time," Nate said with his easy laugh.

He wasn't wrong. She hadn't had a cell phone to communicate with him back then. She'd left coded messages on the chalkboard out front when she wanted to meet. A text message sure would have been easier than hoping they didn't erase the board early.

"My, how times have changed."

He nodded. "Like your outfit. I see he can afford quality."

"He could afford the moon if he wanted," Kierse said. "But that's not why we're here."

"Suppose not. You took the job? Why the cryptic message?"

"I took the job with the condition that I won't see Gen and Ethan again."

Nate scowled. "Why the fuck was that a condition?"

"I want to keep them safe. There are Druid patrols everywhere. The last thing I want is for them to hurt the people I love trying to get to me."

"Their increased attention is nothing we can't handle."

Kierse didn't doubt it. If she could evade patrols, so could Nathaniel O'Connor. Didn't mean she'd risk Gen or Ethan.

"They can stay with you?" she asked. She shoved the backpack under the table, and Nate took it from her. He pulled the zipper and looked inside. He arched one eyebrow at her. "Should that suffice?"

"Sure," Nate said, yanking the zipper closed.

She had a feeling he would have done it for free, but she didn't work on debts. Their relationship had always been on equal footing, and she wanted to keep it that way.

"There's a burner in there. Use that to reach me. I looked over the phone he gave me, but I don't trust him farther than I can throw him."

"Is there anyone you trust farther than that?"

She just tilted her head. Of course she trusted her friends more than the *warlock* who was certainly going to get her killed.

"So, what's the job?" he asked, knowing to change the subject.

"The heist is taking place inside Third Floor on the winter solstice."

Nate's eyes bugged at those words. "Third Floor. Kierse…"

"I know, but he can get me in."

"Torra isn't still down there," he said, his voice going soft. "It's been a year."

"I know that," she snapped and then forced herself calm. "I know she's gone. This is about justice. And I want to know that you'll back me up if I can get you inside."

Nate pursed his lips. "The solstice? That's the twenty-first?"

"Yeah."

"Fuck," he said. "That's a full moon."

"You have to be fucking kidding me," she grumbled. "You'll be locked down."

"The whole pack," he said. "At least you won't have to worry about Gen and Ethan. No one goes in or out of Five Points during the full moon."

"Yeah." She didn't know why she'd gotten her hopes up. Of course she had to do this on her own. She'd agreed to it with Graves. "At least they're safe."

"I got them, Kierse."

She shook off the disappointment. She could only rely on herself after all.

"I am also forbidden from revealing his secrets," she told him, waggling her eyebrows.

"Uh-huh," he said. "Did you cross your fingers?"

She shrugged. "I'll see what he tells me first."

Nate's expression went pensive. "You sure you can handle this?"

Kierse slid out of the booth. "Don't ask stupid questions."

"Just looking out for you. Someone has to."

"I look out for myself."

Nate came to his feet and gripped her wrist before she could bust out of there. "This isn't like our other missions, Kierse." She held her ground as she was caught in the wolf's claws. The feral side of Nate that had made him the undisputed leader of the Manhattan wolves was something that he usually kept covered in her presence. His heat was always there, but the fire radiated with energy as their eyes met. "One wrong step and you're dead."

"You don't have to go all alpha on me," she teased, moving from a challenge to a coy smile and lowered lashes in an instant, her training kicking in the second it encountered a threat.

"Kierse," he groaned. "You don't have to do that with me."

So, she twisted her wrist, breaking his grip with ease. "Then don't treat me like I'm a liability and not an asset. I know exactly what the mission is,

Nate. Just keep my friends safe and let me do the hard work."

He nodded once, appreciation in his irises, before she brushed past him and left the coffee shop behind. She took the subway to the Upper West Side, sneaking back in the way she'd come, with no one the wiser. A smile touched her features as she slid into her satin sheets.

She'd put her plans in place. Now the real work began.

Chapter Seventeen

When Kierse came downstairs the next morning, Graves stood in the entranceway in an impeccable three-piece suit with his face buried in a different book than what he'd been reading at dinner last night. She tilted her head to try to make out the title, but when he sensed her approach, he snapped it closed and tucked it under his arm.

"Just some light reading?" she asked.

"Something like that." He eyed her workout attire. "We're going out."

"I thought I had weapons training. We only have a few weeks," she reminded him.

"I'm well aware of the timeline. You will train when we return. This is more pressing."

She sighed. "Where are we going?"

"I'll tell you on the way." He gestured toward the entrance to what she presumed was the garage.

Before they could enter, Edgar appeared, offering her a long, black woolen jacket. "For the chill."

"Thanks," she said, sliding her arms into it. Compared to Graves, she was grossly underdressed, but he seemed unconcerned.

Edgar swung the door wide for them, and she followed Graves into an elevator. Graves pressed the button for the bottom floor. It opened again on a darkened room big enough to hold a dozen cars. A limo idled silently on a circular underground driveway. The driver, a gruff-looking man in his fifties, stood at attention, clad in an all-black suit and hat. A third employee that she had never seen in her stakeouts. What the fuck?

"George," Graves said in greeting.

"Sir," George said as he whisked the door open at their approach. "Miss McKenna."

"Thank you, George," she said with a polite smile before getting into the limo.

Graves settled into the backseat next to her as George closed the door and walked around to the driver's side.

"Does George always drive for you?" Kierse asked.

"He does."

"Does he know what you are?" She had to assume that Edgar and Isolde did. They couldn't serve him day in and day out and not know there was something else, something *more* to him.

"George has been in my employ for many years."

Which seemed to be answer enough because he returned to the book he'd been reading.

"Is he magic, too?"

Graves sighed heavily, as if unused to someone interrupting his reading time. "He is not a warlock, if that is what you are inquiring."

"But there are other beings with magic," she pressed.

George sank into the driver's seat and closed the door heavily behind him. "Ready, sir?"

"Yes, George. You know the way," Graves told him, then returned to Kierse's question. "There is other magic in this world. But those of my employ are just good workers who I pay handsomely for their time."

"And silence," Kierse guessed.

George coughed under his breath at her impertinence as he pulled away from their spot and into an underground tunnel that led away from the property.

"Silence is preferable, yes," he said pointedly.

Kierse bit her lip as she watched the limo climb toward the surface. An automatic garage door lifted, and they pulled out onto the New York City street. She craned her neck at the cross street, surprised to find they were several blocks away from Graves's house. It was clever. No one would ever suspect that a mansion lay half a mile on the other side of the garage they'd just exited. No wonder she hadn't ever seen him coming or going.

"You seem fascinated by my garage," Graves said.

"I like exits. A thief's first resource is their surroundings," she told him, slouching back into the seat. "Stealing is as much or more where things are kept as what you need to get."

He listened as if interested in learning her trade. "How so?"

"Well, it's in the architecture. Front doors aren't for stealth. They're guarded. You have to look at the place as a blueprint. Entrances and exits, visible or made."

"Made?"

"Sometimes it's easier to cut through the ceiling or break through hinges

than pick a lock. It depends on if you want anyone to know you were there."
Kierse lifted her hands and held them about a foot apart. "Think of it like a
rat. Rats don't come in through the front door. They climb through the walls,
rip apart insulation, bite holes into surfaces. They're agile little thieves. You
don't even know they're there if they don't want you to. Mimic what they
do. Use the house to your advantage."

"Hmm." He considered what she said. "Blueprints and rats. It's like
you're an architect. You have to build the property in your mind to gain
the advantage."

"That's a good analogy."

"I'll have to think on that. We can use that mapping to our advantage
when we infiltrate the Men of Valor."

"That's where my favorite part comes in: reconnaissance."

"Indeed," he said thoughtfully. He was silent another moment before
changing the subject. "We're going to a hospital."

"I'm not sick."

"While everything I've told you has been rather…mythical thus far, there
is a science to it. Warlocks over the years have tried to map what makes us
unique. Covertly, of course. We still don't know exactly why we can do the
things that we can. But we do know that there is a gene for it."

"A warlock gene?" she asked.

It sounded as silly as the magic. And yet, based on her rudimentary
biology lessons, she knew that gene mutations happened in humans as well
as monsters. Despite the monsters not wanting the information disseminated,
recent research said there was a biological component to why vampires
needed to drink blood or why wraiths lived off of human essence or even
what caused werewolves to shift at the full moon. It made sense, then, that
warlocks would have scientists or *become* scientists to look into the source
of their magic, too.

"Not exactly," he said. "I'll let Emmaline explain it when we get to The
Covenant."

"The Covenant?"

He just grinned wickedly. "You'll see."

Forty-five minutes later, they veered off the parkway in Queens and
pulled to the entrance to a stunning two-story building. In big, bold letters,
The Covenant was written on the front with a symbol underneath it of a
circle and two opposite-facing crescent moons. She hadn't been inside a
hospital like this since before the war. Most of them had been taken over by

private for-profit companies. Many people resorted to back-alley medicine, or if you were in good with a gang, they usually had a medic on the payroll, like Maura. People either went into debt or—more often—just died. And no one cared. It made her ache for a past she could hardly remember yet felt viscerally.

Graves buzzed them into a side entrance to the building. She shook snowflakes out of her hair and off the shoulders of her jacket as she looked around. The small waiting area was empty, save for a woman in a white frock with a name tag that read *Harper*, who Graves approached.

"Hello," Harper said pleasantly. "Welcome to The Covenant. How can I help you?"

"We have an appointment with Dr. Mafi," Graves said brusquely.

"Excellent. Name?"

"Under Kierse McKenna."

"Ah, Kierse," Harper said with a smile, turning to Kierse. "Have you ever been here before, dear?"

Kierse shook her head. Who could afford a hospital?

"I need you to fill this out." Harper slid a clipboard across the counter. "Answer the questions on the first two pages and sign the last one."

Kierse plopped into a chair and filled out the paperwork. So much of it she didn't know how to answer. Like her current address. She couldn't put Graves's house down, but she couldn't put Colette's, either. She decided to leave it blank. It got worse as they asked about family history. She had no clue if her mother had had breast cancer or her father's side had a history of high blood pressure. She eventually gave up, flipped to the back page, and scribbled her signature.

She took it back up to Harper. "Here you go."

"Thank you, dear. It'll just be a few minutes."

Kierse shot her a small smile before returning to her seat. Just as she'd dropped her butt into the uncomfortable cushion, a door opened and a woman said, "Kierse."

She was in a dark-purple frock that matched Harper's. The color emphasized her black hair and wide-set eyes. Kierse liked her on sight.

"That's me," Kierse said, stepping forward. Graves was close on her heels.

"Friends wait out here," the woman said quickly. Graves shot her a look of pure wrath. The woman hardly blinked.

"He can come with me," Kierse insisted.

"Are you sure?"

Kierse nodded. "Promise. It's fine."

Plus, Graves would probably kill someone before he let her go in there alone. Not when he had planned all of this and knew the doctor. Everything else felt like a formality. Bureaucratic nonsense, to be honest. She would have thought Graves would have a doctor make house calls. Not put her through this.

"All right. Well, I'm Jesy," she said, holding the door so they could step inside. "Welcome to The Covenant."

They went through basic measurements—height, weight, blood pressure, temperature, et cetera. Then Jesy brought them back to a room. Kierse sat awkwardly on a bed with paper that crinkled under her weight. Graves looked completely out of place, standing next to a small teal chair that wouldn't have held all of him. The light was harsh against his midnight-blue hair yet somehow softened his sharp features. He looked more human here.

A few minutes later, another woman, who Kierse guessed was in her late thirties, walked in. This one was wearing a black frock, with beautiful, sun-kissed brown skin and a stylish red hijab. She had a small stud in her nose and eyelashes for days.

"Ah, hello, Kierse." She held her hand out. Kierse was unnerved by the woman's enthusiasm as she shook her hand. "I'm Dr. Mafi. It's great to have you at The Covenant today."

Graves cleared his throat. Dr. Mafi took him in with a sniff. "Emmaline."

"Graves."

The tension was palpable between them. They were either natural-born enemies or lovers. There was no in-between in their expressions.

"It's been a while," Dr. Mafi said. "I didn't think I'd see you in here again. Not after last time."

Graves shrugged, seemingly unconcerned. "I'm here for Miss McKenna. As we discussed."

Dr. Mafi huffed. "Yes. For Miss McKenna."

"Well, then let's begin."

"I'm going to request that you wait outside while I talk to my patient for a moment."

"No."

"Then I cannot help you and you will need to find someone else to keep your secrets," Dr. Mafi said with bite in her voice.

Graves looked like he wanted to argue. He didn't like his wishes disrespected. Kierse had seen that he expected—no, demanded—respect.

Beyond respect. He was a god to his underlings. How he tolerated Kierse, she didn't know. But this thing with Dr. Mafi seemed to go beyond that. She was challenging him, giving him an ultimatum.

Graves tipped his head. "I'll remember this."

"I'm sure you will," Dr. Mafi said with an actual eye roll.

As soon as Graves walked out of the room, Dr. Mafi faced Kierse. "Well, I don't know how long we have, but I thought I'd cut to the point. Do you have any idea what you've gotten yourself into?"

"I'm going to guess the answer is no?"

"You do not want to work for him. And this testing…you don't want it."

"Why not?" she asked. "I thought we were just looking for a gene mutation."

"You are. That and a physical and a blood test and a drug test and a pregnancy test and…"

"Wait, a pregnancy test?" she asked in confusion. "Whatever for?"

"Standard procedure," Dr. Mafi said automatically.

"That doesn't feel standard."

"Have you had sex?" she asked blithely.

"Ever?"

"Recently?" Dr. Mafi corrected herself. "In the last month?"

"No?"

"Then we could probably skip it, but it's completely standard." She shook her head. "But that's not what matters. What matters is that he'll have access. You can try to keep it private, but if you know him at all, as I once did, then you know privacy is a lie. He has his hands in everything."

Kierse apparently didn't know him as well as this doctor. "Why should I trust you?"

Dr. Mafi let out a breathless laugh. "You probably shouldn't. But you shouldn't trust him, either."

"I trust myself."

The doctor looked unconvinced. "I don't know what he told you about our hospital. The Covenant was started by a coven of witches."

Kierse eyed her skeptically. "Witches?"

"Not like what you're thinking. We mostly specialize in herbs and remedies."

"No magic?" she asked, her eyes darting to the door, where another magical being stood out of sight.

"There's some magic. Nothing like warlocks," she assured her. "We started the hospital as a cover. We work with much of the supernatural community. We help them, heal them, hide them," she said, meeting Kierse's gaze with her own. "So if you ever need any of those services, you know where to find us."

Kierse held her hand up in disbelief. "You're helping *monsters*?"

"I'm working with Graves right now," she said in frustration.

"But, like…other monsters. Wolves and vamps and wraiths and such?"

Dr. Mafi raised an eyebrow in question. "Why shouldn't we? Humans have their places for healing. Why shouldn't monsters?"

Kierse knew it was a valid question. But she couldn't help thinking about what monsters had done to her world. Shattering New York City into a million pieces and making every interaction ten times more difficult. Sure, she had monster friends now, and monsters she worked with. They weren't all the same. It was just hard to shake the burning *hatred* she felt toward the monsters that had stolen Torra.

"You're helping the very things that ruined our healthcare system. Not to mention killed millions."

"Since you are working for a monster currently, I will assume that you are not naive enough to believe that it's entirely black and white."

"No," Kierse said tersely. "There are just as many bad humans as there are good."

"And just as many bad monsters as good." Dr. Mafi's pointed look toward the door said much of what side she thought Graves belonged on.

But before she could say anything else, Graves barged back into the room. "All through?"

"All through," Dr. Mafi said with a wide, unassuming smile. "Girl talk out of the way, right, Kierse?" She winked at her.

Kierse managed a smile. "Indeed."

"Okay. Then let's get started," Dr. Mafi said.

Kierse was there for another hour, giving samples to Dr. Mafi. It ended up being a whole lot more than a cheek swab to run her DNA. Apparently, warlock DNA sequencing was notoriously wily. Something about the changes in proteins or amino acids. She wasn't entirely sure. Something to do with the genetic mutation, and her basic knowledge of biology hadn't helped the matter.

"We'll have results in a week or two," Dr. Mafi said. "I'll call to let you know what I find out."

She and Graves were silent as they stalked back to the waiting limo.

Kierse had a million questions rushing through her mind. Despite Dr. Mafi's warning still ringing in her ears, she couldn't keep quiet.

"So, how do you know Dr. Mafi?"

He sighed, waiting to respond until they were seated in the limo. "We were involved before she completed her medical degree."

"Oh," she said. "What happened?"

"She left." He cracked open his book, going frigid. "They always leave."

Chapter Eighteen

"I'm off to training," Kierse said as they pulled back through to the tunnel that led to his house. "What's your plan?"

Graves remained entrenched in his book. "I need to get to work."

She tried to read over his shoulder, but he tugged the book away.

"What exactly do you do for a living? Why do you need to work?"

"I trade in the most powerful resource of all."

She shot him a skeptical look. "Money?"

"Knowledge," he said, gesturing to the book. "And there are things I need to learn tonight."

"You're a spy?"

He laughed, and it was with genuine surprise. "Not for many years." He closed the book and met her expression as he continued. "I make it my business to know everything that I can about everyone of importance. I use that knowledge to get the things that I want and to sway the course of history."

She met his gaze. "You make it sound like blackmail."

"Sometimes," he said without mirth.

"Oh." She nodded as if that made sense.

He weighed her reaction. "You don't seem surprised."

"Should I? I make my living as a thief. You use people and information to get what you want."

"Are you saying we're much the same?"

She laughed. "Hardly."

"Perhaps we're more alike than you think."

She waited for him to say more, but he said nothing. They were just walking around in circles. Every time she felt like she was cracking the surface of who he was, he switched up just as easily as she did.

Dr. Mafi's warning still rang through her mind. It wouldn't change anything about Kierse's plan. She had one objective, one job. She would complete it. But the interaction had made her restless. This was the longest she had gone in years without seeing her friends, and already she missed them. She missed having Gen and Ethan and Corey around. She missed returning to a chastising Colette. She missed home.

When George finally stopped the car, she didn't wait for him to come around to the back and release her. She just opened the door and stepped out.

"Good luck with work," she told Graves as she made for the elevator.

She trekked up to the training facility and headed inside to find Edgar waiting for her. When he finished kicking her ass, she barely had enough time to read a story in the new book Graves had left for her while she scarfed down dinner impeccably prepared by Isolde before face-planting into bed.

The next day was the same—train, read, eat, repeat. Until her muscles ached and her head hurt and she wondered if Graves was torturing her.

On the fourth day of training, she stepped, bleary-eyed, into the training facility and froze.

Graves stood facing the weapons rack. His suit coat was discarded against the bench. The crisp white button-up's sleeves had been rolled to three-quarters, revealing stretches of ivy-tattooed forearms. The corded muscles that the slivers of skin revealed made her swallow. His face was in profile, and the proud jut of his chin and sharp lines of his cheekbones caught the light. He was a Renaissance sculpture come to life.

Her stomach twisted with something akin to desire. She didn't like that she needed to remind herself that this was *business*.

"What are you doing here?" she asked, dropping her own jacket before striding across the mat.

Graves's eyes tracked her. "Your weapons training thus far has been… unsatisfactory."

She blinked. "Edgar said I was improving."

"I feel like his methods haven't been to my standards with the timeline we're on." He smirked, and she knew to be afraid. "So, I thought *I* would take over today."

"I see," she said.

She had very *real* memories of him dislocating her shoulder and tossing her on her ass the first time they ever met. He hadn't broken a sweat, nor did he even need to change out of his suit.

Graves hefted a training spear in his hand and tossed it to her. She caught it with ease, the weight already beginning to feel more normal in her hand.

"I thought you could use some motivation." He picked up another spear and tossed it back and forth between his palms. "Every time you get a successful hit in on me, I'll give you an answer."

She blinked. Well, that *was* sufficiently motivating. "To any question?"

"To this," he said, producing a thick white envelope.

The kind of envelope that was meant for weddings and funerals. The face of the envelope was blank. No address or name or return label. She turned it over, noticing that a seal of a bird looking backward had been pressed into bright-red wax. It dripped down like blood pouring out of a wound.

"What's that?" she asked.

"That is a question," he said with a smirk as he stepped onto the mat.

She could strangle him. It was just like him to make it a game. But she had to train anyway. Might as well get something out of it.

"Ready?" he asked with a beckoning motion.

Fuck.

"Let's go."

"After you, Miss McKenna," he taunted.

Kierse lunged with the spear in hand. Graves sidestepped her as if she had barely moved. He tapped her on the shoulder with the blade.

"Going to need to do better than that."

She gritted her teeth and tried to work on her focus. She had spent only three days working on this. There was no way she was going to be as good as Graves. But if she could just quiet her mind, slip into that place like slow motion, she could get a hit on him. She knew it.

With renewed fervor, she moved forward with her honed instincts. Graves blocked the first blow, and then he stepped forward, thrusting his spear toward her. The practice tip blazed in her line of sight. Her eyes widened, and then she pushed her body to the breaking point, shifting into slo-mo and dodging the blow. The tip of her spear barely caught the sleeve of his white button-up.

Graves's expression was appreciative. "You already look better than yesterday." He scooped up the envelope and passed it to her. "As to your question…"

She took the envelope in her hand and opened it, removing heavy cardstock festooned with gold embossing that read:

Montrell and Imani Cato cordially invite you to their residence for a black-tie affair to celebrate their union.

Then it listed a date and time, as well as *one additional guest welcome*.

"A test for you," he said simply.

"A test of what?"

He gestured to the mat again. "Shall we?"

She breathed out heavily. This was going to be laborious. But he wasn't wrong—she was getting better.

Kierse hefted the spear in her hand, then practiced the thrust that she and Edgar had been working on yesterday. The first one was sloppy, all arms. He narrowed his eyes at her as he got the first hit with ease. And the second hit. She missed the third on a razor's edge and nearly tossed the thing down in frustration. Maybe that first hit had been just damn lucky.

But she wouldn't give up.

And the next time he came at her, she used her old knife reflexes to switch thrusts and catch him off guard by half a second. Just long enough to get a hit in.

She put her hands on her knees and glanced up at him for answers. "A test?"

"Of your magic." He offered her water, which she gulped down as he continued, unfazed. "I already know that you can walk through wards. You're walking through mine every day." Was that bitterness in his tone? "I also know that you're a good thief. You got into my house undetected. I've looked into your past."

Her eyes narrowed. "What about my past?"

"Do you want me to answer that?" he asked.

She ground her teeth together. She had more important questions to ask. "No."

"Sources confirmed you're good at what you do."

"Great. So what is this test?"

He lifted his spear, and she nearly groaned. This was going to take all day. But maybe that was the point. Maybe he wanted her training to take longer so he could tire her out and extend the answers as long as he could. It was a good strategy. No, an excellent strategy. Because now she was fucking invested.

And when she finally landed the next hit, she thought she'd pass out from the effort it took to get back into that zone. Equally frustrating knowing that he barely looked affected.

"It's threefold," he began as she rested her already aching body. "First, to test if you have limits to your powers. Second, to see how you react to a large amount of magic. And third, to see how you work under pressure at another monster's house before I send you into Third Floor alone."

Her mind spun at that answer. There were more questions in there than the answers she could possibly get from this one training session. But he *had* given her more than she'd thought. The place they were going had monsters and magic. So likely other warlocks? She didn't know what to think about the possibility of discovering that her powers had limits, but it seemed like a good thing to know.

So, she needed to get the information he hadn't already provided.

"Are we stealing from them? Because this is tomorrow night," she said.

He hefted his spear once more. "Again?"

"Fine," she grumbled.

Before she could get started, though, Graves moved behind her. The heat of him seared through her as his body came nearly flush against hers. He put one hand on the spear and the other on her arm. Her breathing hitched as her body betrayed her. It was impossible not to react when his hands were on her and his breath was brushing against the skin of her neck. No matter how much she told her mind that it meant nothing, her reaction said otherwise.

"Use your body weight, rather than just your arms, to guide the thing forward." Graves directed her through the movement. She was jerky at first, unaccustomed to him at her back. Then she relaxed and tried again. "Like that."

When he released her, she exhaled softly and shook her arms out to try to get her head back in the fight.

He didn't wait for her approval this time, just moved forward. She met the hit with her own, exactly as he'd shown her, and followed it up with a second. Graves blocked it, but something lit in his eyes. She was getting better.

Her arms felt a hundred pounds each as she pushed through the next few thrusts and parries. The tip of Graves's spear came within inches of dragging across her cheek, but she blocked it at the last second, whirled, and got another hit in.

"Better," he said with a nod. "Yes, we're stealing from them tomorrow night."

"Fuck, Graves, that's not enough time," she said. "An impossible heist inside Third Floor in a few weeks and I'm supposed to do *another* one tomorrow? That's not possible."

He didn't seem concerned. "I'm acquainted with the place. You'll have everything you need. But to get inside, you can't go as a thief. You have to go as my…" He trailed off, his eyes devouring hers. "Pet."

She stayed perfectly still as that word heated her through. "And…what does that entail?"

He made a come-hither motion as he raised his eyebrows, the *wouldn't you like to know* painted on his face.

Her hands shook on the spear. Yes, yes she very much *would* like to know what being Graves's pet would be like…

He made the first move, and she countered. Thrust, parry, thrust, parry. She wasn't as fast as him and was flagging quickly. She'd had momentum when they'd started, but she didn't know if she could keep it up. She needed that answer, though. She *needed* it.

Her next thrust went wide, and Graves moved at full speed. Her mind could barely comprehend it. His movements were precise and calculated. Then he tucked his shoulder and tossed her easily over his back and onto the mat. All the air released from her lungs in a gush and left her gasping.

Graves carried through on the roll, landing on his knees with his body over hers. Her lungs were burning, and she could barely catch a breath as she stared up into those gray eyes. And for a second, his gaze swept downward, to her lips, before pulling back up again. As if he, too, was thinking about the precarious nature of the position they were in…and what exactly they could be doing instead with him on top of her.

"You'd be at my beck and call." Graves answered the question even though she'd failed. And her core tightened at the words. "Letting everyone assume we're in a," he began, his voice a caress, "physical relationship."

She accessed all those years in Colette's house and let the charm ooze out of every pore. "I can do that."

For a second, the balance of power in the room shifted. As if, in that one moment, he was caught in *her* snare. She used his lapse in concentration to flip their positions and toss him onto his back.

"I used to live in a brothel," she reminded him.

"Good." He cleared his throat and came swiftly to his feet. "You'll have to put on a good act, because we cannot let them know that you are immune to magic. And you'll have to do it without weapons."

He collected the practice spears from where they'd been discarded and replaced them on the rack.

Her stomach was still fluttering as she said, "Gowns can hide knives just fine."

Then his eyes were on her again, and she felt trapped all over. "The gown you'll wear won't have enough material to hide even a single knife."

Kierse's eyes widened as he headed to the door without a dismissal.

Another challenge.

She'd be so fucking good at it she'd wipe that smug smirk right off of Graves's face.

Interlude

Emmaline Mafi sighed and pushed back into her chair at the end of her long shift at The Covenant. She pulled off the blue-light glasses she wore for long hours in front of the computer and stared blankly at the samples of blood nearby.

She had a headache. She'd taken herbs for it earlier and pain medication when it hadn't gone away after that. The herbs usually did the trick, but this was different. A different sort of headache. Not one from staring too long at the screen or impatient patients or twelve-hour days. This had started behind her eyes and burned through her scalp. It had started when Graves had called and scheduled his appointment for his new…well, whatever she was. Girlfriend. Lover. Apprentice. Emmaline really didn't know. Nor, she tried to convince herself, did she care. She had too many other things to worry about than Graves.

And yet, he was the crux of her problem. As he so often was.

The air had been balmy and bright the first time they met. A mere fraction of weeks before the economy collapsed and the entire world went to hell in a handbasket. He'd been handsome then. He was handsome now. All hard edges and insufferable quirks. She'd known he was dangerous. Dangerous and powerful. Just the way she liked them.

When they'd gone to bed that first time, she thought she would be able to handle him. That she'd be in control. She hadn't been. She never was. Graves didn't relinquish control. Not to anyone. And she had learned the hard way that she was hardly a speck in his stormy eyes.

He'd released her as he did all the others and given her enough money to weather the worst of the storm that blew in. Luckily, she was only a year from completing her medical degree, and that money put her into practice here at The Covenant.

Her headache bloomed. She needed to get out of the hospital. Her shift was over. Well past over. And yet she couldn't stop staring at Kierse's blood and *wondering*.

She'd chewed her nails down to the quick. An old habit she thought she'd rid herself of. But old habits die hard.

Especially when she knew what she had to do.

Her hands trembled as she reached for her phone and pulled up the number that she'd programmed there almost precisely two years ago. *King Louis.* A fake name, of course. Just a moniker for a new tyrant. She'd known it was a fake name when she met the vampire, the leader of the Men of Valor. She'd been trying to protect the community when he'd swaggered into her life, all cut suits and immeasurable power. Always with that damn gold pin at his throat—wings with an arrow through them. The Men of Valor's symbol that was as absurd as their mission statement. The whole thing boiled down to putting monsters back on top.

And she'd gotten on his bad side. In one meeting, he'd bound her to him with blackmail and fear. She didn't think that he'd ever let her escape his clutches. Certainly not today.

She typed out a text message…and waited.

I think I found something.

The response was nearly instantaneous. *A match?*

She shook her head. She didn't think so. She didn't know what she had, and she hated herself for even sending the message. Kierse was no more than a pawn in this game. Just as Emmaline herself was. But Graves had brought her in for a reason. Whether or not the girl was a warlock meant little to her. She was special in some way. Graves only dealt in special.

Emmaline had tried to talk Kierse out of it. She'd tried to tell her that she didn't want these tests done. "Privacy," she'd said. Yes, Graves would see them. But so would Emmaline, and she owed King Louis too much not to spill her secrets now. She didn't want to do it, but when did she ever have a choice?

Possibly. I'll need some time to determine if it is fit for you.

She swallowed. He was nothing if not impatient.

I'll send someone for what you have now. Keep enough to do your research. I'm counting on you, Emmaline.

Emmaline shivered. She considered destroying the blood and everything else she had on the girl. It would be safer. But it would end in Emmaline's death, and she didn't want to die.

It made her a coward, but she packaged up the blood, setting it in a cooler for safekeeping, and then, with her conscience weighing heavy on her that night, she got back to work.

PART III

THE IMMUNITY

Chapter Nineteen

Kierse could have forgone the makeover, but Isolde had insisted that appearances were everything. After all, it must be important if Graves had hired an entire team of people to pluck, wax, and prod her skin into shape. By the end of it, she was as soft and supple as a newborn baby. Even her hands, which she'd destroyed sparring, were smoothed over and made new, like magic. Her hair was parted severely down the middle and smoothed back into a low bun. The makeup was mesmerizing. Layer after layer after contouring layer until her features were both amplified and obscured. She was just a canvas for the artists.

At the end of it all, Isolde appeared with the dress. If you could call that thing a dress. No wonder Graves had said no weapons.

Still, she put it on along with a thick jacket. To complete her outfit, she had a bejeweled black clutch and four-inch heels that she was already cursing as she headed down the stairs. She was just missing her wren necklace, which Isolde had insisted she leave behind. She already felt lost without its comfortable weight against her chest.

Kierse huddled into the warmth of the fur-lined jacket. Thank god for Isolde's forethought. The snow had finally let up, but it was still below freezing out there.

As she reached the landing on the second floor, she noticed a light on in a room down the hall. When she had done her perusal of the residence, she'd guessed by the way Edgar and Isolde carefully avoided the area that these were Graves's quarters. Though she was incredibly curious about what lay beyond those doors, she'd respected his privacy.

Without another thought, she walked toward the light and knocked on the door. There was a stillness on the other side. As if Graves had even stopped breathing at that knock.

She cleared her throat. "Graves? Are we leaving soon?"

A second passed and then another before suddenly, the door opened. Her heart stuttered in her chest at the first sight of him. She'd known he was attractive underneath the hardened exterior, but in the all-black suit, he was something to behold. She could see the outline of a tattoo forming around his wrist as he slipped gloves over his long, strong fingers.

He cleared his throat, and she jerked her eyes back up to his, heat flushing her cheeks.

"Miss McKenna," he said. She barely got a glimpse inside of an office before he pulled the door firmly shut behind him. "I was just about to come fetch you. George was on an errand. He should be back any minute to escort us to the airport."

Kierse stumbled back to reality at those words. "The airport?"

He reached into his suit coat for his buzzing phone. "That's him now."

He held his arm out for her. A gesture of good faith, but her stomach was roiling. He hadn't mentioned that they'd have to fly to the party. She'd never been on a plane.

Right before the Monster War, the three major airlines had consolidated into a monopoly that the government hadn't even blinked at. They controlled the prices of transportation, weeding out the competition that tried to stay afloat. Then planes had been all but entirely grounded during the ten years of conflict. Transportation between cities was greatly reduced. National, let alone international, travel had been off the radar. Only in the last three years had any travel become common again, and the rich tourists had begun to flock back into New York. There was a whole world out there, and now…it all seemed to be possible.

She slid her hand into the crook of his elbow and allowed him to escort her to the garage, where George was indeed waiting. He'd traded out the limousine for a more practical black SUV with heavily tinted windows.

"Here," he said.

She pulled her attention back to him and found him holding out a worn copy of a small, brown leather book.

"I brought this for you."

"A new assignment?" She took the book from him with relief.

"You finished the last one."

She flicked through the pages. All the edges were worn thin and almost crumbling from use. The binding barely held the shoddy thing together. "Why did you choose it?"

"You have an affinity for wrens. The best story of the wren can be found in that book."

The book dropped open where the spine was creased as if that particular story had been read over and over and over again. "The Oak and the Holly King."

Graves said nothing. Wrens were one thing. She had always loved her wren necklace. The last thing she had from her mother. But *holly* was Graves's symbol. It was everywhere on his property, in his warding, in the library that took it as its namesake.

Her eyes lifted to his with a small smile. "Thank you."

"And when you're finished, you'll have to tell me your thoughts on the subject."

Kierse nodded, dropping into the story. George drove them smoothly to JFK International Airport. He pulled the SUV right out onto the tarmac and stopped in front of one of the planes.

"Are you sure we have to fly?" she asked, staring up at the mammoth thing.

Graves's attention shifted to her. "We're on a time crunch. How else are we going to get to Chicago?"

She had no response to that and hated that he got to see a flicker of fear creep into her.

"You've never flown," he said in understanding.

"No," she said with an exasperated expression. "When would I have flown?"

He shrugged. "Pre-monsters." His hand came to the small of her back, his warmth seeping in through the fur-lined coat. It was more reassuring than she wanted to let on, having him touch her like that. "It will be fine. I've kept the pilot on since before the collapse. It's safer than riding in a car, I assure you."

Stairs were wheeled out for them.

"What about the snow?" she asked, reaching for any excuse.

"They cleared the runway. The snow is letting up, but they can fly in snow regardless. Would I take you into the skies if I thought that we would be harmed?"

She wasn't sure about her safety, but he definitely wouldn't risk his. "No."

"You're right. I wouldn't."

"But…"

"It will be fine, Wren," he said softly but with perfect resonance, and the word held her in thrall.

She met his steely gaze. There was command in his eyes, and she took strength from it. He had never called her "wren" before, and she found that she liked it. Maybe a little too much. He'd never even called her by her first name. Only ever "Miss McKenna." But now…wren. It was all just fairy tales and myth, but when he called her wren like that, her nerves settled.

He must have been able to tell, because he nodded. "Good. Let's go."

They exited the SUV together. She was glad for the hood and high collar to protect her from the brisk cold as Graves ushered her up the steps first. She took each one carefully in her heels and delighted in the warmth once inside the plane. She'd only ever seen pictures of commercial planes with seas of small seats, but this was a private jet complete with luxurious couches and a wet bar. It was beautiful, modern, and incredibly inviting.

"Have a seat wherever you like while they prepare for takeoff," Graves said after he boarded behind her.

She settled onto one of the couches and jostled her foot nervously. "No attendant?"

"I don't particularly like people. If you haven't noticed."

"I have," she admitted.

Graves sank comfortably into the seat next to her. "We have some last-minute things to discuss about this heist."

"What last-minute things?"

"Things we didn't get to during our training session." Their eyes met, and she remembered exactly how close they'd gotten in that session.

"You couldn't have given them to me at that time?"

"I could have, but you asked different questions."

She huffed. "Fine. Tell me."

"Imani and Montrell are fellow warlocks."

"I guessed that," she admitted. "Based on the other information you gave me."

His answering smile was genuinely warm. As if her piecing together context clues from his words made him like her more.

"Good. You chose your questions carefully, then."

"Yes, and now that I don't have to fight for them, why are we breaking into monsters' property to steal from them?"

"One, you're not breaking in. We were invited. And two, you broke into my home."

"I thought you might be human," she argued.

He smirked. "Did you?"

As if he couldn't fathom that.

"Well, I can see now that you're all monster." He pursed his lips and said nothing. But she just prodded him to continue. "Start at the beginning. If I'm breaking the Monster Treaty…"

"Again," he quipped.

"Then I need more information."

"I've been acquainted with Imani and Montrell for a long time."

"What can you tell me about their powers?"

"Imani grants wishes. She's tailored her abilities so that she can imbue substances with her wish-granting powers, usually very specific wishes. They call it wish powder."

"That sounds powerful and mildly terrifying."

"It's not scary—at least, not the way she uses it…anymore."

His eyes went distant as if he remembered a time when her powers weren't used in such a benign way.

"She mostly focuses on wishes of the…sexual nature. The wish powder isn't dangerous. It's not like a drug, even though it has effects like getting high. You can't overdose on sexual desire."

"So, she grants sexual wishes. Isn't that…assault?"

Her stomach clenched at that word. It certainly sounded like it could get problematic fast. As with most things.

"Not at all. She is very specific in what she will grant. You can't just ask for anything that will harm someone else and she'll do it. The wishes don't work like that."

"Okay. I don't know how the magic works. If I'm going to meet her, I want to feel prepared."

"There are rules to her magic. Everyone who attends the party does so with their consent, and wishes can only be fulfilled by a willing participant. If a person wants a certain sexual act, then someone who wants to do that act would fulfill that wish. It's not a free-for-all."

It took her considerable training not to break eye contact. "Got it. So, I won't be in any trouble. And if I just don't wish anything, then nothing will happen."

His eyes flickered to her mouth and then away. "You will be immune to her magic. You will have nothing to worry about."

"As long as it's not past the limits of my powers," she argued.

"I'll be there," he assured her.

"And her husband?"

Graves clenched his fist for a beat at that question before saying, "Montrell has several smaller base powers. Mostly, perfect recall."

"So, he's not as powerful as you?"

Graves huffed, his ego filling the cabin. "No one is as powerful as I am."

The words weren't boastful; they were fact.

She glanced down at the book still in her lap. "How much do you know about what we're stealing?"

"A great deal. We're collecting a packet of letters. I have blueprints of the house, and I can show you where I expect the letters to be located."

That sounded more than satisfactory. She'd gone off of less and succeeded. She just hoped it was as easy as Graves made it seem. She would be stealing from monsters again, and the last time hadn't exactly gone to plan. If this didn't work, she'd be subject to the Monster Treaty. Graves might be all-powerful, but that wouldn't stop the Catos from killing her.

"What is in these letters?" she asked. "Will they help us get to the spear?"

"Once we complete the mission, I'll have a much better understanding of how to proceed with the spear."

"Okay," she answered. Something about what he said sounded off, but at the same time, it made perfect sense to test her. If that helped them get to the spear, all the better. "Show me the maps."

By the time they were high over the world below, she was engrossed in the new information. It put her at ease, but it didn't make her completely forget her fears—or the persistent thought at the back of her mind that she was walking into enemy territory in a gown as thin as vellum with two predators at her front and one at her back.

Chapter Twenty

T wo hours and one jittery-as-hell landing later, they touched down in Chicago on the western banks of Lake Michigan. Graves had spent the flight reading a fiction novel. Kierse had the book he'd given her in her lap. Now that they were on the ground and driving north in another SUV, adrenaline pumped through her veins.

It was another twenty minutes before they pulled off onto a long, wooded lane. They wound ever upward until an enormous glass house appeared on the ridge. It was mesmerizing and completely impractical. She'd *known* what it was going to look like, thanks to prep for the job, but it didn't compare to the magnitude of seeing the house in person.

On top of that hill, the mansion appeared to be twice as large as Graves's house, with a perfect view into many of the living spaces. She could see people milling around inside, dancing, consorting. If she didn't know about the obscured paneling in many of the rooms, she would have wondered about privacy. But only the living spaces were completely open for anyone to see, which was good for what she was about to do.

The SUV parked in the large circular drive. Graves exited first and then held his hand out for her to follow. He tugged her in close. His hand slid to her waist. Alluring and possessive.

She shivered as his lips dipped to her earlobe. "Remember your role."

She hadn't forgotten. "I know."

Graves said nothing else as they reached the door. There was nothing more to say. Not with eyes and ears likely tracking their every move.

A man greeted them at the door before they had a chance to knock. "Invitation, please."

Graves slid it out of his pocket and passed it to the man.

"Name?"

Graves just smiled. It was a dangerous thing. The man took one look at him and made some small, unintelligible sound. He took a step backward and returned the invitation.

"Right this way," he said shakily, holding open the door.

And then they were inside. A large oak tree soared to the ceiling at the back of the room, while chandeliers cast dizzying lights across the packed partygoers. Couples writhed against each other as if caught under some fae magic from the stories, dancing for the pleasure of their hosts. Montrell and Imani stood directly before the tree, observing the party like a king and queen of old.

Montrell had a shaved head, full lips, and skin as radiant and rare as the Hawaiian black sand beaches. He was bare from the waist up, wearing only loose, white linen pants. Imani's head was shaved close as well. Her light-brown skin dusted in gold powder that made her shimmer in the lights. She was rail thin, with small breasts and narrow hips concealed by a long, gauzy white gown. She held herself like a goddess, and it made Kierse wonder if she *was* in the presence of royalty.

"You're staring," Graves said.

"It's hard not to stare. You didn't warn me that they'd both be so beautiful."

"Both?"

She nodded. "Don't you think so?"

His gaze was hot on hers. "I did once as well."

Secrets, secrets.

"May I take your coat?" a woman asked, appearing before them.

Graves held up his hand. "I'll keep mine."

But this was her moment. She took a shallow breath, careful not to draw attention to her own discomfort, and then shed the fur-lined jacket.

For a moment, it was as if the entire world slowed. A breath was drawn from the room, and eyes drifted to her. Her and every inch of her exposed skin.

The dress was one piece of sheer black gossamer. The neckline plunged between her breasts, where a series of shimmering diamonds obscured her nipples from view. The same diamond pattern ran low across her stomach and then down to cover her…but just barely. She wore no bra but a tiny scrap of black lace that hardly covered more than the diamonds. There were no sleeves, leaving her arms bare. Though the fabric fell to the floor like a ball gown, nearly every part of her was exposed.

She heard another small intake of breath, and this time she turned away from Montrell and Imani, who were clearly enjoying the show, and faced Graves. There was a stillness about him that went beyond his usual demeanor. The stillness of a stalking predator right before the lunge. His pupils were blown out, his sensuous mouth parted, and one eyebrow slightly quirked. It didn't just say interest; it was as if he wanted to reach out and claim her as his own.

A chill ran down her spine, and goose bumps erupted on her bare skin. That look unmade her. To be the center of that focus and know that she was here, like this, for him. She had been tiptoeing around her own interest in Graves. It had been nearly impossible to hide with his hand on her and his breath against her neck and his body covering her in training. But still, he'd stepped away quickly. Here, he did not pull away, and seeing the desire painted so plainly on his face made her entire body flush with want. She wondered if her own need was so apparent. She didn't have any interest in intimacy, but she'd be more than happy to be his...pet.

She swallowed, letting her throat bob as the heat drew taut between them. Then she let her dark-red lips part erotically. His arm slid around her waist again. His hand drifted lower, so low, cupping her ass. A whimper escaped her lips.

His breath hitched.

"Ready?" she purred, using the sultriest voice she could dredge up.

He squeezed her ass and dragged her flush against him. "Very."

The line between acting and reality blurred.

"Shall I introduce you?" he asked.

"By all means."

Chapter Twenty-One

Montrell and Imani waited for them before the great oak tree. "I never thought I'd see your face again," Imani declared.

"Imani," Graves said with a swift nod before turning to her husband. "Montrell."

Montrell's eyes were tight and his lips pursed. "It's been a long time."

"Fifty years," Imani said. "And we haven't been civil in a hundred and fifty."

Kierse startled. A hundred and fifty? Graves was that old? He'd said that he had been alive a long time, but she hadn't considered what that could mean. That he could look mid-twenties and actually be hundreds of years old.

"Indeed," Graves said. "Long enough for us to reconcile. I did, after all, introduce you two."

"Reconcile?" Montrell ground out. "After you…"

"Darling," Imani cooed. "Leave it."

Montrell took a step back and lifted his chin. "Who's your date?"

A flat question as if from a jilted lover. That would certainly explain all the body language. Graves really *had* left out all the important parts of this party.

"Allow me to introduce you to Wren," Graves said, tugging her closer.

She swallowed at the name. They had agreed not to use her real name with the other warlocks, but she hadn't chosen…this.

Montrell's eyes widened. "Wren, really?"

Graves nodded, and understanding seemed to pass between the two. Something that Kierse didn't comprehend.

"So, she is yours, then," Montrell said through gritted teeth.

"She is mine," Graves confirmed. And it sounded like sealing a bargain.

"Girlfriend?" Imani asked.

Graves laughed slightly. "And I thought you knew me."

Montrell snorted. "That's not his style. She's a lover."

"A little doll," Imani amended. "Pretty and breakable."

"Still acting out the same story," Montrell said derisively.

Imani tsked. "Good for a few fucks?"

Kierse tried not to bare her teeth at the woman. That was exactly what she was supposed to appear to be to these people, but it didn't mean that she liked to hear it on their lips.

"Maybe he's only good for that many," Kierse blurted out.

Graves squeezed her waist, hard. A warning.

Montrell laughed. "A little fight in her. Good. She'll last longer that way."

"I'm surprised you let her speak out like that at all," Imani said. She sauntered down a step, off her dais.

She felt that heat from Imani as she drew nearer. As if she was burning from the inside out. If she got closer, would she feel it from Montrell, too? That heat she associated with the warlock holding her close at this very minute. While it was a similar feeling to Graves's, it wasn't as intense or all-consuming.

"She's new," Graves said with a shrug as if that explained it.

"What does she read like?" Imani asked with an arched eyebrow.

Read like? What did that mean?

"You know that I don't kiss and tell, Imani," Graves said carefully.

"Come on, darling. Remove those gloves and let me in a bit."

Graves leveled her with a bored look. "You aren't getting everything you need from the party and your wonderful husband?"

Imani's eyes shifted back to Montrell and then hastily forward as if Graves had put her off-balance. "Of course I am."

So those gloves *did* serve a purpose, as she'd suspected. Not that she knew what that purpose was.

"Why are you really here?" Montrell demanded from where he stood above them all. "It's clearly not because you wanted to parade your new toy in front of us."

"I received an invitation," Graves said coolly.

"It's a formality," Montrell said. "And you know it."

"I can't want to see you two?"

"You don't like people," Imani said. "You must have known we'd ask."

He sighed. "Well, I do have some business for you."

Montrell barked a laugh. "And there it is. Business. Why am I not surprised?"

Graves turned his attention away from the formidable pair and to Kierse. His eyes lingered on her breasts before gliding up her body to stare into her dark eyes. She bit her lip as her heart rate jumped.

"Why don't you go get us some punch?" he suggested.

She was immune to Imani's magic, but Graves had warned her not to drink the punch under any circumstances. It was laced with Imani's magic, but he couldn't guarantee that was the only thing in her drink. She'd taken ecstasy at Five Points once, and Nate had saved her from herself. She had no interest in repeating the experience.

She pouted. "I don't want to leave you."

Graves narrowed his eyes. "The grown-ups have things to discuss right now."

Fire flared in her gaze. Anger and indignation at the comment. But then coherent thought fled as he leaned down toward her as if he was going to kiss her. She'd prepared for this, but somehow she wasn't prepared at all.

At the last second, he moved to her neck, letting his lips linger on the very spot where her heartbeat thrummed. She leaned into him. The kiss was soft. It was nothing. And yet, it was so much more.

His nose brushed her earlobe, and she shivered against him. "Punch."

She swallowed hard and nodded. "Right. Punch."

She took a step backward as if it were physically painful to walk away from him. She could hear Imani snicker as she staggered away, but Kierse couldn't even care what she thought. It was as if her only thought was punch. She needed punch to douse the flames in her.

But as soon as she was out of the warlocks' view, she shook her head to brush away the spell Graves's touch seemed to ignite in her. She was immune to magic but not *him*, apparently.

As she crossed into the next room, she dropped her little act. Her favorite thief smile crossed her face.

"Time to get to work," she whispered under her breath.

Chapter Twenty-Two

The mission was at hand. She needed to steal the packet and get out of here. Everything else was secondary.

Bypassing the bar, she recalled the map of the house to guide her around. Graves wouldn't be expecting her back right away. He would occupy Imani and Montrell, giving her time to work the job. That old familiar feeling radiated through her limbs. She tried to keep the smile from her lips. She still had to pretend to be Graves's plaything if anyone saw her. But it was so good to be using her talents. What could she say? She liked stealing things.

Kierse navigated the glass rooms carefully. Thankfully, the rest of the party had already had the punch. Everyone swayed drunkenly. She passed a couple having sex in a not-so-discreet corner and peeked into a room in which there was a full-on orgy. She wasn't a prude, and yet it still made her blush. The wish powder in that punch must be potent.

Finally, she came to Montrell and Imani's main quarters. The bedroom was at the farthest end of the hallway, but there were rooms on either side that she knew from the blueprints were their offices. With a careful glance at the drunks at the end of the hall, she removed a bobby pin from her hair and made quick work of the tumblers in the lock on the door to the left. She pushed the door open and startled when she saw what was inside.

Crates.

Floor-to-ceiling crates.

What the hell was all of this? Regardless, it wasn't what she was looking for. Kierse double-checked that the coast was clear and then carefully locked the strange room behind her. Time was ticking. She stepped across the hall, wondering if she was going to find the same thing in the next one. But as soon as she'd picked the lock, the crowd surged toward her. She couldn't discreetly check what was in this room without everyone now seeing her. She couldn't even lock it back up without drawing attention.

So she pretended like she was one of them and let herself get swept up in the crowd. When she reached the bar, she grabbed two glasses of the house punch and sauntered back to Graves's side.

He stood before Imani and Montrell, though they had moved closer to him. Drawn like moths to a flame, no doubt. None of them noticed when she slipped back to his side.

"But what about Kingston?" Montrell asked, bristling.

"Leave Kingston to me," Graves said.

"You're sure that you can get this past him?" Imani asked.

"If anyone can, Graves can," Montrell said. His eyes were wide with lust.

Kierse leaned forward, sloshing punch as if she'd been drinking the poison. She giggled. "Dance with me."

Imani smirked up at Graves. "And how can you deny her?"

Graves took the drinks out of her hands and set them on a nearby table. "I can't deny her a thing."

He took Kierse's hand and pulled her away from business discussions. She wondered if it had something to do with the crates. She was anxious to tell him about them, but not with all these people around and Imani and Montrell suspicious of their appearance. They had to act the part. So, she let him pull her into his arms at the periphery of the crowd. She wasn't sure Graves would even dance. He didn't seem like the type. He always stood so stiffly, with a book in his hands. Yet here he was, surprising her.

She rolled her hips to the tempo of the music. His hands slipped down her exposed arms, the leather of his gloves smooth on her skin. Then he took one of her hands and twirled her around away from him. She kept moving as if they were always this close. His gaze roamed from her waist and down over her hips, appreciating every curve in her diaphanous dress.

It was an act. A clever, cruel act. And yet, as he tugged her hard against his own hips, the evidence of what she was doing to him was very real. She gasped. Her core tightened. He was turned on by her. And oh god, she was turned on by him. She raised her hands up over her head, swirling provocatively, unabashedly against him. Someone who was sleeping with him wouldn't be surprised that he was hard against her ass. She'd revel in it.

"Wren," he growled into her ear.

"Mmm," she hummed, the sound of that one syllable steadying her.

"Did you drink the punch?"

She slowly turned back to face him, keeping their bodies pressed together. Her hand looped around his neck, and she fingered the ends of his midnight-blue hair. "I did everything you told me to."

It was a seductive sentence. As if she frequently took orders.

His eyes searched hers, looking for signs of intoxication in her. But she was clearheaded.

"And would you do *everything* I told you?"

She nearly froze but remembered where they were and how important this was. She was in his arms. He was teasing her. She could tease back. She dragged her bloodred nails down his neck and over his chest. She snagged his tie, pulling his face down closer to hers. Those beautiful thundercloud eyes combed for answers he couldn't seem to find.

"Everything and more," she teased with a wink.

He cleared his throat, and she felt him press against her almost involuntarily. "Then perhaps we should see where that leads."

He took her hand in his and looked nowhere but at her as they disappeared from the main room. Her heart pounded as he guided her away from Imani and Montrell. She was his plaything. This was normal. But it wasn't a game. Not entirely. Not with the tiny scrap of underwear hardly concealing her desire.

He slipped down the hallway to the study, and his breath came against her ear. "Which door?"

She returned to herself all at once. A job. Just a job. They were here to steal something.

"Right," she said. "I already unlocked it. Left was just full of crates."

He nodded and stopped before it. "We have an audience," he whispered under his breath.

Then he rocked her back against the wall, his body covering hers. A sharp exhale escaped her. She could feel the hard lines of his body, feel his fire leeching into her.

An audience. Which meant there had to be no reason to suspect that they were going into that room for any other purpose but a hookup. Graves's head dipped into her neck. His breath was hot against her skin. Her hands gripped the front of his suit as she tipped her head back seductively, wanton.

"What are you?" he growled low. He wrapped an arm around her waist. "Are you a siren, luring me to my death?"

She was stunned by the words. The real words there. "Are you lured?"

His response was to turn the handle and push the door open. He tilted his head to the side, and she entered the darkened depths. The door clicked closed behind them.

"This is it."

Graves nodded. They were in a study—Imani's study—which was exactly what they were looking for. "Get started. I'll guard the door."

Kierse swallowed down the feelings rushing through her and got to work. She rifled through Imani's belongings. She was careful and meticulous, and after a minute, she asked, "Can you sense anything? Any magic in the room that would indicate where the letters would be kept?"

"No. The whole house is flush with magic. It's everywhere."

She grumbled, "That's helpful."

Kierse had moved to the bookshelf and was pulling at the books in hopes of finding a hollow one when Graves cursed softly under his breath. In the span of a heartbeat, he was before her. She faced him in confusion, but he just tugged her back against him. Her lips parted at the sudden change in his demeanor. Time slowed in the way she had only experienced when she was fighting. And then Graves descended on her.

At the first touch of his lips on hers, she was lost. It was neither gentle nor comforting. It wasn't even intimate, exactly. It was possessive, demanding, and achingly alpha. It said *mine, mine, mine*. The kiss was an awakening. Like every kiss before ceased to exist. There was no moment before or after this. Here was eternity.

He leaned her back against the bookshelf, heedless of the books digging into her spine. His hands cupped her face like she was one of his prized possessions. And his mouth owned her, parting her lush lips and brushing his tongue across her own.

That was the moment the door creaked open.

Chapter Twenty-Three

A throat cleared. "I don't mean to interrupt."

Graves kissed Kierse for another moment before retreating. He brushed his thumb over Kierse's swollen bottom lip. The gesture was almost tender. Then he faced Imani in the doorway. "Do you mind?"

Imani looked as if this was exactly what she'd expected to find. "Might I offer a bedroom on the second floor?"

"You know how I like my books."

Something dark passed across her features. "That I do. But this is my personal study. No guests allowed."

"Well, come along then, Wren," Graves said, offering her his hand.

She let him guide her out of the room. Imani watched them the entire time, even as they played up their parts. It didn't seem to matter. Imani closed and locked the door again behind her. They weren't going to be able to get back in there while anyone was still coherent.

She could see on Imani's face that she didn't trust Graves. If they had more time, Kierse would suggest staying in the city for a few weeks, gaining their trust. But she only had tonight.

Instead, they spent the remainder of the night dancing and enjoying the party. But that kiss had brought her too close to reality. She was too cognizant of everything going on around her. She almost wished that she was drunk just so she wouldn't have to be so aware of everywhere Graves touched her.

There was a point in the middle of the night when everything seemed to hit a fever pitch. As if the magic in the punch had reached its apex. Kierse didn't understand it. Imani and Montrell didn't seem affected. They watched on high and occasionally touched each other provocatively, to the delight of the party.

It was now or never.

"I'm going to find a bathroom," she said, pressing her lips to Graves's ear.

"Do you need an escort?"

She shook her head. "Entertain the hosts."

He arched an eyebrow and then nodded. "Be quick."

Kierse blew him a kiss as she walked away. But before she could go, he said her name: "Wren?"

She turned to face him in confusion, and then his lips found hers. The only thought in her mind was of him against her.

"Very quick," he said firmly against her lips.

Her head went fuzzy all over again. She was going to need to masturbate after all of this. She bit her lip to keep it from showing on her face and then took a step back. She needed to find her business sense. She and Graves couldn't work in any capacity. But all she felt were coals that he was fanning with his tongue. Maybe she'd find that reality again after she wasn't so damn turned on.

Kierse swept across the room without a backward glance. She didn't dally in the hallways. She went straight for that study door. Imani had made it clear that this was where the information must be. Why else would she have forced them out of it in such haste? Maybe there was even some ward on it that Graves had triggered. Well, if that was the case, she could slip by unnoticed.

She used her handy-dandy bobby pin to pop the lock. Graves had said that magic was everywhere in the house. Though she couldn't sense it like he could, Imani's eyes had drifted to the bookshelf behind them not once but twice. Kierse was good at reading people, and that meant that what they wanted was here. Right here.

After closing and locking the door again, Kierse headed straight for the bookshelf and ran her hand along all the edges of every volume. Nothing seemed out of place. No hollow books. No reason to think that the information they needed was here. Except that Imani had made it clear that it was.

Then Kierse felt it.

A smaller book that she'd skipped over. It was pressed farther back than the rest. Purposely so.

She reached for it, but when she tugged on it, there was a click. A hidden door opened behind the bookshelf.

Her jaw dropped. Imani hadn't been looking at the bookshelf because what they wanted was hidden there. It was because what they wanted was hidden *behind* it. Kierse had stolen from a lot of places before. She'd broken into museums and carved her way through warehouse concrete and climbed across ceiling tiles, but she'd never seen a secret passage.

And she was about to venture into one.

Chapter Twenty-Four

A giddy bubble of laughter surfaced as she pushed aside the bookshelf and stepped into the darkened room. She closed the door behind her, running her hand along the wall until she found the catch that released it. She'd need a quick escape, and she couldn't use the precious time on the way out. Light bulbs glowed faintly, revealing a set of stone stairs. Apparently, this glass house had been built on top of something already in existence. Pre-monster housing, likely. Nothing glass like this could have survived those tumultuous times.

There was only one option—down.

Kierse descended into the warlock's lair. The steps were smooth as if feet had trod on them for centuries, wearing them away in the middle. She could hear noises ahead. Not voices, exactly, but something out of place. She steeled her nerve, loving every minute of unease that swept through her as she reached the bottom of the steps. She entered a hallway that split into diverging paths. The noises were coming from off to the left. Silence to the right. Knowing what was happening would be to her advantage, even if it likely meant going deeper into the lion's den.

Her feet were silent on the stone floors as she veered to the left. It wasn't long before she saw a wooden door at the end of the hallway. Her heart thudded in her chest. All sounds from the party above were gone. It was just Kierse and whatever awaited her. She turned the knob and opened the door a fraction of an inch. Enough so that she could peer into whatever lay ahead.

Her eyes rounded when she took in the enormous underground chamber. Crates that matched the ones upstairs were neatly stacked along the perimeter, and the interior was full of six-foot-long metal autopsy tables. Thankfully, they weren't being used for their practical purpose, but instead for the hundred people inside cutting, packaging, and crating a fine red powder.

Kierse had one guess for what that was—wish powder. This was not some small operation. This was...a whole business. Did Graves already know about this? Was this the "business matters" he was talking to Imani and Montrell about? Was this what they needed to keep from Kingston? Whoever he was...

More questions. No answers. Graves had said that the powder wasn't dangerous. It was just an extension of Imani's magic. But it was clearly a bigger operation than he'd let on.

But this wasn't what she was here for. Kierse retraced her steps and headed down the other side of the tunnel. She walked for what felt like ages, counting her steps along the way to make sure she knew how far she had gone. Maybe her objective wasn't even here. It was just their business they were protecting.

Then she took the next turn and came upon a large, round bank vault door. The enormous thing was built into the stone. Likely, the entire structure of the house had been built around this beautiful, gilded door.

Kierse smiled. Showtime.

She didn't have any tools with her save a hairpin, but she didn't need them to break into this vault. It was old. It must have been here for at least a hundred years. They didn't even *make* these anymore. Which was good for her. Getting into an old, abandoned bank vault was going to be a piece of cake compared to the kind of situations Jason had forced her to break into and out of. At least this one wouldn't end up with her breaking her arm when she didn't crack a vault fast enough.

The warlocks must have figured the carved whorls and swirls in a language she couldn't quite read would keep anyone out. Wards. They were different than the ones on the Holly Library. Graves's warding was threaded through with holly vines, but this had little birds in the pattern: a long-necked bird facing backward with feet facing forward. She'd seen the symbol on the wax seal of the invitation. If she had to guess, this was Imani's warding. She was more powerful than Montrell. She'd want to protect the contents. Which meant that the holly was specific to Graves. Interesting.

Luckily, wards didn't work on her. And Imani and Montrell hadn't thought that they'd need increased security. They hadn't anticipated *her*. Just like Graves. No security systems. Nothing to disable. No heat sensors or alarms or motion detection. Sloppy. Though clearly effective. Graves had said there was no one else like her. Normally, wards would be enough, but not tonight.

Kierse lowered herself before the locking mechanism, placing her ear to the gears behind it. Though she was well trained, vaults by their nature were not supposed to be easy to break into, unlike those little fireproof safes that she could sometimes just hit right or drop from the top of a building and *click*, they'd bust open.

The fastest, most effective way to get into a bank vault was to drill through until she could see the pins and gears beyond. Then she would be able to reverse engineer the combination and turn it over. The problem was that not everyone knew exactly where to drill. Most vaults had a relock function. If damaged they would shut down so that the person would have to completely dismantle the vault over the course of *hours* to get to it. By then, security would be there to arrest her. And they had.

Kierse shuddered. It was a memory. A bad one. Jason had left her for the cops. He'd said jail was just another vault to break out of and that she'd need the practice. She had never again reengaged a locking mechanism in a vault. Not after he'd put his fist through her face.

But of course, tonight, she didn't even *have* a drill. Nor had they anticipated the Catos having a vault in the first place.

That left her with one option—breaking the vault code.

And while she had been trained for it, it did take time. Her most valuable resource. She was going to need to break her own personal record tonight to not be noticed.

Kierse turned the dial, listening for the small variation in rhythm that said she had hit an internal disc movement. She noted the placement and then kept on, moving the dial back and forth and back and forth, trying to get the vault to tell her all its secrets. Jason had been fast at this, but she was always faster. As if the vault spoke directly to her and she was the only one who knew how to listen.

Her shivering kept her alert. The basement was freezing. It had none of the artificial heat that blasted through the warlocks' main room, which was made worse by the fact that she was in next to nothing. Her hands trembled as she worked. She was thankful for whatever immunity powers she had, but right now, in the deepest parts of winter, she wished that she had some fire in her veins.

Time passed slowly. With each ticking moment, she waited for someone to venture down the dark corridor. She had no idea how long she'd been there when she turned the handle one final time and a hissing noise came from the door as it popped open.

She coughed as a cloud of white smoke burst into her face. Kierse waved it away, swiping at her eyes to try to keep them from burning. So there *had* been one last defense mechanism, and still, it had been magical. Kierse was certain that whatever she had just ingested was wish powder, but it was a different color than everything she had seen in the crates. Magic didn't work on her, but she had no desire to find out if this stuff did.

The white smoke was a hanging question mark. She needed to hurry.

Kierse tucked her clutch under her arm, hauled the vault open, and stepped into the space. The vault was roughly a large rectangle, big enough for her to walk into, and it held enough money to weather a lifetime or ten. Cash was wrapped and stacked in staggering amounts. Gold bars lined the floor like bricks on a city street. Jewelry and gemstones sat like Ali Baba's treasure trove. It was dazzling.

Her palms began to sweat as she stared down at them in confusion. She was frigid and yet…sweating. She placed her hand on her forehead, and she was hot. Unnaturally hot. She staggered forward, knowing that if she was found here, they would kill her.

Kierse searched faster, looking past the luxury for just one innocuous envelope. She rummaged through boxes full of jewels, and as she weakened, she stopped caring if she left them scattered on the ground. She moved past the African masks on display, the bags of what appeared to be seeds, and some sort of water machine. And then…there it was, nestled on top of a container.

Sweat trailed down her spine and over her breasts, carving crevices in her skin. She swallowed hard again. She wished she had some water. Anything to quench this eternal heat. She had wished for heat, and now she was ablaze. Maybe magic *did* work on her.

Kierse collected the envelope. Graves had described it to her perfectly. A small square stuffed to the brim and sealed with a holly leaf pressed into black wax.

This was it.

She needed to get out of here or she might literally turn to ash right where she stood.

Chapter Twenty-Five

K ierse stashed the envelope in her clutch and then hauled the vault door closed behind her. She turned the dial on the vault and then headed back the way she had come. Her feet were slow, slow, slowing. She trailed her hand along the wall to keep herself upright. She stumbled another step, landing hard on her hands and knees. She cursed softly when she righted herself and saw that her left knee was bleeding and her hands were scraped up. She had tripped over her own feet, which was odd, since she wasn't clumsy.

After what felt like an eternity, she reached the stairs. And it was only her heightened sense of awareness that made her stop before ascending.

There were voices coming from directly above her.

Kierse scrambled backward and around the corner, pressing her body against the wall as hard as she could. She prayed that she hadn't tripped some alarm. That they weren't coming for her, because she was in no state to fight. She could hardly stand.

"He was the one who said he wanted to sell?" a voice she didn't recognize inquired.

"Yeah. It's not like him." This was definitely Montrell's baritone.

"Are you suspicious?"

"Of Graves?" Montrell asked with an easy laugh. "Of everything he's ever done in his life."

"And yet, you're going to send crates of wish powder with him?"

Montrell sighed. "We are. Just the red powder. And we'll watch him. See how it goes from there."

The pair had reached the bottom of the stairs. Kierse held her breath. Sweat gleamed on her forehead, and she felt fatigued and malnourished all at the same time. She could barely concentrate on what they were saying.

"Seems risky."

"Everything with Graves is a risk. After what he did to me..."

But Kierse didn't get to find out what that was. Montrell and the other man had turned left and were heading toward the underground chamber full of wish powder. This was her opening. She hurried to the stairs and raced up them as fast as she could. Which ended up not being very fast. She stumbled twice, her hand slipping against the stone wall and causing her to fall *up* the stairs.

To her relief, no one was guarding the upstairs door. She found the latch after a few swipes at the release and entered the study.

Her fever spiked, and she moaned as it ate at her. She needed to get to Graves.

Kierse ignored the bookshelf. She hardly had the strength to get it back into place. And why bother at this point? Hopefully they would think that Montrell hadn't closed it all the way.

Kierse exited the study. Coming back into the light of the party was like entering a different world. Everyone was sweating from dancing, so her heat didn't even look out of place. She staggered like the rest of the partygoers. Her heels barely held her up. She should have left them behind. They were just a hindrance.

A man stepped up to her. "You want to have a little fun?"

She blinked at him, finding him fuzzy around the edges. "Graves," she gasped out.

"Call me whatever you like, sweetheart."

"No," she said, pushing him away.

But her strength was gone. It was an illusion. All of her many ways of taking down a grown man had evaporated. She was nothing but a small, pathetic, human girl. And this man wouldn't listen to her. He kept pushing her backward. It made no sense. Everyone else in the party was a willing participant. They wanted this. Why her?

Her brain shut down. Retreated to that horrible little place she had made for herself. The place where she could go and live alone and away. Compartmentalize her pain until she didn't feel it…didn't remember its brutality.

Then a hand clamped down on the man's shoulder. "She said *no*." The voice was brutal and ancient. "You should learn to respect a woman's answer."

"Ah, we were just having fun. And dressed like that…"

"If you say that she was asking for it," Graves said, low and gravelly, "I will rip out your throat with my bare hands."

The guy backed away and held his hands up. "Sure. Sure, dude. No problem. I didn't mean any harm."

"This is in clear violation of the rules of the party. This will get back to the goddess."

The man paled. "I didn't mean…"

Graves was already turning away from him, his focus on Kierse. The man glanced between them and then scampered away.

"Wren?" Graves said. That voice was different somehow. Softer. Concerned, even. "My wren, are you okay? What happened?"

"Hot," she whispered. "I just wanted to be hot, and now…I am."

"Fuck," he spat.

Then, without a thought, Graves lifted Kierse into his arms. His heat mingled with her own. Called to it.

Her mind drifted now that she was safe. Drifted far, far away. She saw a winged lion roaring from a dais made of stone. A crowned dragon breathing fire in answer to the lion. A group of sheep for the slaughter. Everything erupted into death, and she closed her eyes against the hallucination.

Then she saw black.

And then she saw nothing.

Chapter Twenty-Six

A loud whirring sound filled Kierse's head. It drowned out everything except how awful she felt. She was going to throw up. Puke her entire guts up. She groaned as she shifted and suddenly felt a hand on her shoulder. She tried to block it but found she hardly had the strength. Instead, she leaned over the side of wherever she was lying and vomited onto the floor.

Cursing followed, but she couldn't find the will to care. Not as she puked until she had nothing left in her stomach and then dry heaved for a solid minute after that.

"Ugh," she groaned as she rolled back over.

"I am regretting my decision not to bring on staff," Graves said distantly.

She squeezed her eyes shut and tried not to be sick again. "What... happened?"

Graves said nothing for a few minutes as he cleaned. A fact in which she would surely find mortification later. Once he was done, she felt his weight rest on the cushion next to her. "You must have ingested *a lot* of wish powder."

"Right," she said, her memories coming back to her in a rush. Or at least some of them. Vague outlines of memories. It all felt very disjointed, as if she was looking at something that happened a few years ago rather than a few hours. "Where are we?"

"In the airplane."

"Good."

"Drink this," Graves said.

She slowly opened her eyes to find him holding a glass of cloudy water over her face. Just the thought made her want to vomit again.

"What is it?"

"An antidote. It will help," he told her.

Kierse rose to an elbow, fighting nausea, and took the drink in her shaking left hand. She forced herself to drink the whole thing. She didn't even ask why it tasted disgustingly like sulfur. Then she collapsed back onto the plane cushion.

She felt less like she might die from vomiting, but still she ached everywhere. Her eyes burned. Sweat clung to her skin. Fire coursed through her veins, though its heat was thankfully fading.

For another moment, Graves was silent. His eyes focused solely on her face. If she didn't feel so addled, she might say there was *concern* there.

"How are you feeling?" he asked.

"That helped." She closed her eyes. "Thank you."

"When you were incapacitated..." He trailed off and cleared his throat. "That should *never* have occurred."

She swallowed hard. "Yeah."

"Can you tell me how this happened?" Graves asked.

"It wasn't in the study. The study led to a secret passage into a basement. They were crating wish powder. I broke into their bank vault and retrieved the envelope. It's in my clutch."

"Good," Graves said but frowned. "They had a bank vault?"

She nodded. "It was warded, but that wasn't a problem. Once I broke in, a cloud of white smoke erupted out of the opening. It coated my skin, and I inhaled it."

"White powder," he said, his face going pale. "I didn't think she made that anymore."

"I thought I was *immune* to magic."

"I thought so as well." He shook his head, a shadow crossing his face. "Imani is the living embodiment of 'be careful what you wish for.' She's a powerful warlock, but the powder enhances her reach. Before Imani perfected her powder down enough to be sold, she experimented with some dangerous varieties. The red powder that she uses at her parties—what was in the crates you saw in the study—that is her desire wish powder. It's her most useful and the best business she's invented. But to get to a safe powder, she'd overwhelmed enough of her participants with dangerous wishes. White powder usually kills people. Sometimes instantly. I thought she had given up making it."

"But how does this work on me? I didn't think it was possible."

"When you wanted to be warmer, it set you on fire. I knew she was capable of such things, but I was certain your own abilities would counteract that. They seemed to be working fine before the vault."

Kierse was slipping again already. Felt like she was being pulled under. "So, am I or am I not immune to magic?"

"You must be," he said with a frown. "Or you'd be dead."

"Then how did it affect me like this?"

"My working theory is either you ingested an amount so great that it penetrated your immunity or you aren't immune to ingested magic."

"Okay," she said, dragging the word out. "So you have no idea."

"This is why it was a test."

Kierse shook her head, the weight of the last twenty-four hours heavy on her. "Do *you* have powers like that?"

"No," he said flatly.

"Well, small mercies," she muttered. She dropped back onto the cushion and closed her eyes. It was all too much to take in right now. Not like this, when she couldn't concentrate or move or breathe without aching.

"You should get some more sleep," Graves said.

He stroked her hair gently out of her face. Her eyes fluttered closed at his suggestion, her body responding to his soothing touch.

"We'll be back in the city soon. You can recover at home."

"That's not my home," she murmured as she slipped toward oblivion.

His next words were faint, so she wasn't even sure she heard him say, "It could be."

Interlude

I mani left her supplicants to their debauchery.

The wish powder had stealthily wound its way through their system. It drained her to imbue the powder with her abilities, but once the wishes were granted, she was full to the brim with power. Beyond reason. Beyond care.

No wonder Graves had fled her mansion with his intoxicated plaything. Imani could have challenged him in that moment. Flush with her own power with hundreds of people fueling her. He wouldn't have stood a chance. Her mood dampened a little as she thought of him. Perhaps…he still would have stood a chance. He was Graves, after all.

Better to have him gone. Gone for good.

She would stop sending him invitations. Insist that Montrell not send them, either. It had always been a formality. They sent them to Kingston as well, and he didn't pop into their little soirées and ruin all her fun.

But that was Graves. A fun ruiner.

She brushed imaginary lint off of her virginal-white dress and headed through the crowd. Fingers brushed her brown skin, aching for her pleasure. She liked it that way. The easiness of the parties and the fornication. The wishes were simple here. Just sex and drink and ecstasy. All things she had always been adept at providing.

"Please, goddess," a woman gasped, falling to her knees. "Bless me!"

Imani watched the half-naked woman. Her white skin gleamed with oils. Her pupils were dilated to infinity. Her cheeks were rosy, and her chest heaved and trembled in her sight. She could tell this woman to slit her own throat, and she would. It was pure, unbridled power.

She resisted the urge and set her palm upon the woman's head. "There. Now go and be ripe with my blessing."

The woman shivered. Tears came to her dark eyes. She babbled her thanks and fell back into an awaiting woman's arms. They kissed, and Imani moved on.

When she first met Graves, she'd thought she could trap him with her wishes. She had been young and foolish. She saw him as her ticket out of dirty Victorian England and into adventure. The adventure she had always longed for. She had been right and wrong. Graves had seen her potential as a warlock. He had wanted to cultivate it like a garden.

At first, she had resisted. For so long, she had wanted to return to her home in Ghana and learn from her people. But Graves was a world traveler. He'd learned from magic users all over the world. She didn't regret going with him to his residence in Paris, but her life would have been forever altered if she hadn't said yes.

Paris felt like the height of the modern world at the time. Writers, painters, and artists of all kinds filled their evenings. She became a personal friend of Alexandre Dumas as he penned incredible novels. When the world's fair came in 1900, they watched the colossal structure of the Eiffel Tower be built.

With it came Montrell.

This poet with perfect recall of everything he had ever read. He had left Nigeria to start over in Paris during the fair, using his magic to gain passage on a vessel. She met him at W. E. B. Du Bois's sensational exhibit featuring photographs of the lives of African Americans. And from the first moment she looked at Montrell, it was like his magic sang to her. His mere presence seemed to settle the frustration at her core that she had felt during the last fifteen years at Graves's side.

She should have been content that Graves was deftly honing her powers to make her a master in her own right. But he had always rejected her as a lover and hid his dalliances from her. They were as close as any two people could be, and still he would not let his guard down. And when she discovered he had a lover—one she had never seen before, who was *not* her—she had to know who this woman was.

So, she conspired to find out. And what did she find?

Him in bed with a man.

Montrell.

Her Montrell. Who made her magic come alive. Who knew her suffering as his own.

Some part of her knew that joining them would be the end of everything. Still, she hadn't been able to resist. And it *had* ruined everything.

Before Graves's eyes…they had fallen in love. But a part of Montrell still loved Graves. Loved and hated him for letting him go to Imani so easily. For letting them both go…as if he had known that they would one day leave him anyway. They had just proven him right.

It was why she had stolen his letters in the first place. As leverage. No one let two of his best go that easily without a plan. And Graves *always* had a plan. The bastard.

She sighed as she stepped into her study. It was best he was gone. Best for Montrell and her, their marriage, and the world at large. Nothing good could come from their coexistence.

She paused in the doorway. Something was wrong. The door to the powder operations was ajar. Not fully open but not closed, either. Montrell had gone downstairs to prepare the crates to ship to Graves, but he wouldn't be so foolish as to leave access open.

Imani moved forward with grace that did nothing to hide her growing fear. She raced down the stairs. She could sense it before she even hit the steps. Her wish powder. The white smoke she had engineered herself to recreate a person's nightmares, to wish them to death. The smell of it coated the tunnel. Its sweet tang suffused the air. She didn't sell these kinds of wishes. She only unleashed them on her enemies. Her eyes widened in horror. The *vault*.

She picked up her skirts and *ran*. No, no, no, no, no. But there it was. White powder littered the floor. Enough to kill a person. To overpower their senses and make their last wish literally eat them alive. It hung in the air, taunting her.

She knew what this meant. Knew it before she opened the vault and crossed the threshold. Before she looked into the box. Before she saw that the letters were gone.

Graves had *stolen* from her.

She sank to her knees, coating herself in her own powder, and screamed and screamed and screamed.

He would pay for this.

Oh, he would pay.

PART IV

THE OAK AND THE HOLLY KING

Chapter Twenty-Seven

K ierse had no reference for how long she'd been out when she woke up again in her bed in Graves's brownstone. Her mouth tasted like she'd eaten cotton balls, and her throat was just as dry. She was no longer burning up. She just felt a general malaise.

It was exactly how she'd felt the time she contracted influenza. She'd gotten it right after the war started, when the worst strain in recent history had been running rampant. She was working with Jason, and he'd told her he didn't care if she was sick—they had a huge job lined up, and she couldn't pull out of it. And she'd done it, because she'd weighed that the consequences of saying no to Jason were worse than the illness.

Her fever had topped out at a hundred and five for a whole day, and she'd seen stars. The next three weeks, she had been laid up in bed. Normally, she healed so quickly. She should have died from it. A lot of people did during the Monster War, but even after she'd officially gotten over the illness, it had clung to her like a dryer sheet unable to shake off.

The aftermath of the wish powder felt much the same.

She needed to figure out how long she had been unconscious. They were short on time, and any loss would directly impact the mission. Fuck.

Kierse kicked off her covers and found thermal sweats in her closet. She tugged on a pair of Sherpa slippers, then snatched her wren necklace off the counter and put it back around her neck where it belonged. She grabbed the book Graves had given her and padded downstairs.

Early-morning light from the windows outside her room made her squint. She held her hood tight over her brow and walked like a specter to the kitchen. It felt like dragging her body over hot coals and then dry ice by the time she made it. Two flights of stairs were two too many.

The kitchen was empty. So, Kierse padded to the sink, poured herself a glass of water, and downed it in two seconds flat. Then she poured herself a second glass. She shivered as she held the cold liquid in her hands and headed to the open sitting room door. Secretly, she was hoping it would just be Anne curled up in front of a lit fire, but what she found instead was Graves.

He was seated in the armchair closest to the fire with the packet of letters open in the lap of his black slacks. His gray sweater was fitted, exceedingly expensive and high-quality, but it was disarming to see him look almost…normal. That blue-black hair fell into his eyes. It was still wet, as if he'd come straight from the shower. Her cheeks heated at the thought of him in a shower. She was most surprised to find that he wasn't wearing his gloves. He always wore them, even in the house.

Kierse took a step forward as if drawn to him. His head snapped up. Their eyes met, and the memory of their kiss slithered through her mind. The way he'd slammed her back against the wall. The moment he'd called her a siren. It flooded her, heating her through.

Because she had liked it. And the look on his face said he had liked it, too.

Graves jumped to his feet. "Wren, you're awake."

The nickname brought a ghost of a smile to her face. "How long have I been out?"

"Just over a day," he said.

"Fuck," she whispered. "We can't afford to lose a day. I should be in training." Even though it felt like the last thing she could do.

"Forget about training," he said. "You could have died. Take a seat."

She accepted his offer. The warmth of the fire licked at her, and she leaned into it, remembering that this was what his body felt like against hers.

"Thank you."

He sat across from her, dropping the letters onto the side table. "It's good to see you up and about again."

"Yeah. I haven't felt that bad in ages." Her eyes lingered on the letters, and she wondered what he'd found in their contents. If it was the last bit of information they needed to get the spear. She could do this job and then…leave. Because that was what she wanted. As her eyes slid over his handsome face, it was hard to make those words form in her mind.

She was saved from having to think more about that when Anne slunk into the room from the door Kierse had left open.

Her yellow eyes glanced between both of them before she jumped up onto a pile of books and made herself comfortable.

"Hello, kitty," Kierse said. She stroked the cat's back once, and when Anne only glowered at her, she did it again.

"I see you met Anne Boleyn," he said fondly. "She's as tempestuous as her namesake."

Kierse blinked. "Wasn't she the queen of something?"

"Indeed. She was Henry VIII's second wife. Famous for beguiling the king and turning the world upside down from the force of his affection."

"Sounds like my kind of woman."

Graves grinned. "And then he cut her head off for it."

Kierse couldn't help the short bark of a laugh that escaped her. "Of course he did." She glanced to the ceiling and back. "Sex and danger. The best kind of stories."

"Such an interesting perspective," Graves said as he shook his head at her and returned his attention to the pile of letters. Kierse had her sights set on the cat.

"We are going to be fast friends," she insisted.

"I don't know that Anne has friends."

"So, she *is* your cat," Kierse said, meeting his gaze.

"She is," he said softly. The one thing he seemed to soften for. And then he added, "I've been checking on you."

"Personally?"

Maybe she was wrong. Maybe he was starting to soften for *her*, too.

"Yes, personally," he said, his eyes boring into hers. "The magic burn is hard on your system. I gave you an antidote, but it didn't seem to be speeding up your recovery. Or at least not fast enough for my liking. How are you feeling?"

"Not great," she admitted. "I still don't understand how I wasn't immune. I know you told me on the plane, but it's fuzzy. Actually, a lot after the wish powder is fuzzy."

He frowned. "I believed that you were immune to Imani's wish granting, because it was in the ventilation system. So you would have been breathing it in all night and you didn't appear to be addled."

Hadn't she, though? But it certainly hadn't felt like being set on fire from the inside out. It had just felt like lust. Plain and simple desire.

"Did you know beforehand that it would be pumped in through the ventilation system?"

He was silent a moment too long before saying, "I needed to test your immunity to it, and I had the antidote with me."

So, he had known, and he'd risked her anyway. He had told her it was a test. He'd informed her from the beginning, but that didn't stop it from riling her. Not after what happened underground.

"I could have died in that vault."

"I believed it to be a controlled test," he told her. Then his eyes hardened. "Things got out of hand."

"No job ever goes exactly to plan."

"No, but I never intended to risk your health or safety as mine were when my limits were tested," he admitted, then frowned at that admission like he hadn't quite anticipated saying it. "I did not like to see you hurting."

Her heart hammered at those words. Because her brain told her that a man like this could not want that. Jason had never considered her health and safety. In fact, he had been the one to purposely put her in harm's way. It had been his hands doing the dirty work.

Yet Graves looked sincere. And in that moment, she believed him. He hadn't thought that she would get hurt. He didn't want to see her hurt. The last piece of that train of thought slotted into place: he had been upset by her sickness.

"I'm okay," she told him softly. "I'm already feeling better. With a meal, I can probably start training tomorrow."

Tension released from his shoulders. "Good."

"Well, did we even get the information we were looking for?"

His stormy eyes were dark, but he looked away from her as he casually cast one of the letters into the flames.

She gaped. "What are you doing?"

He still didn't look at her as he said, "What information did you think was in these letters?"

"You said it held information to get the spear."

"Did I?" he asked, tossing another into the fire.

She racked her brain. Had he said that? He'd definitely implied it.

No, he hadn't said it. She was the one who had implied it, and he'd agreed. She'd walked right into his plans. So eager to prove herself, to get this test over with, she hadn't even considered that he was sparing the truth for his own aims.

"So...what's in the letters?"

"They're of a personal nature. I've wanted them back for a hundred and fifty years."

She nodded her head, understanding winking into existence. A dangerous smile crossed her lips. "You used me to strike back at your enemies."

Oh, how clever he was. She'd hate him if she didn't appreciate the brilliant machinations under his dark exterior.

"Something like that."

"And if I'd failed?"

This time, he smiled, that lethal calm washing over him. "You assured me that you didn't fail."

"Of course."

"This is how things are done. I wasn't going to let you attempt to steal the spear before you even knew if you could access it."

She felt the truth in his statement. "Well, at least we are one step closer to the spear."

He stilled at the sardonic tone in her voice. Like for a moment, he wasn't sure if he'd actually gotten away with his own subterfuge or if she was going to bellow at him. They watched each other across the sitting room, his eyes considering her thoughtfully.

"We are."

"But when we go after the spear, maybe I should know all parts of the plan."

"As you say," he said simply.

She wouldn't have believed him if she hadn't seen his momentary break about her being sick. He hadn't wanted her to fall ill. And maybe he had kept the truth from her about the packet, but would it have changed anything? Looking at him right now, she really doubted it.

"Why did you call me Wren?"

"Ah." He tilted his head to the side. "I wanted them to know you are mine."

"Wasn't that the point of me playing your pet?"

"This felt…more succinct."

"Why?"

"Did you read the book that I gave you?"

"This one?" She had started it, but then he had distracted her with information about the heist.

"That one," he confirmed.

The book flopped open all on its own to the story she'd been reading— The Oak and the Holly King.

In the tale, summer and winter were gods who fought for their claim on this world. The Oak King was the conquering hero, the spring and summer champion that brought forth sunlight and joy. The Holly King was the dark, elusive winter god. He was as feared as he was praised. Twice a year, on the nights of the solstices, the two kings would battle. With the Holly King's loss, the Oak King shepherded in spring, and with the Oak King's loss, the Holly King brought forth fall.

She loved the story, the turning of the seasons explained in this fantastical way. But she didn't know how this was supposed to help her understand Graves. He was a warlock, not a winter god.

Yes, the wren was an important representation of the Holly King, just as the robin was for the Oak King. But she just wore a wren pendant. Had Graves chosen holly as his symbol because of this story? Was he calling her Wren because he saw her as a symbol of rebirth? A muse? It was so convoluted. Answers wrapped up in fairy tales.

She didn't have the words to spar with him about this today. Not with the magic burn. Not with him purposely playing her.

He smirked and slipped his hands into his pockets. "Read the book."

They breathed the same space for a tense moment. Neither of them willing to back down or move forward.

"Is that all you're going to say?"

"Now that I know where you stand, we can begin. I have to be away on business today to look for the final thing I need for the heist. You should train with Edgar when you feel well enough. We'll meet once I have what I need." He turned his eyes to the letters, dismissing her.

She stared a hole through his skull, but he never looked up. "That's it?"

"You need to regain your strength. We can do nothing until then," he said, casually tossing another letter in the fire.

She nodded, gritting her teeth. Fine. She would read the book. She would train. And she wouldn't forget that he could play her as well as she could play him.

Chapter Twenty-Eight

Kierse trained until she thought she would literally collapse. Then she trained some more. She'd lost a day to her magic burn, and she couldn't afford to lose another. But by the time night fell, Graves still hadn't returned.

She had just considered crawling into bed when she dug out her burner phone and saw that she had a message from Nate, asking to meet. Now that she was well enough to move again, she needed to get out of the house and hear how her friends were doing.

She changed into all black, slunk from her room—careful to evade the new cameras Graves had installed—and slipped out of the house without anyone the wiser.

Kierse headed toward the subway entrance on Amsterdam, but within a few blocks, she was flagging. There was no way she was going to be able to make it very far, let alone brave the subway in her condition. Between magic burn and training, she was shot.

It was an outrageous expense, but she flagged down a cab, directing it toward Greenwich Village. She paid the cab when he dropped her off and was back out into the cold night with a sigh. Nate had agreed to meet at the coffee shop, but all she wanted to do was say *fuck it* and walk straight into the Dreadlords' headquarters. She missed her friends so much. Her friends and the attic and Colette.

Maybe if she hadn't still been recovering, she would have noticed the Druids before they closed in.

"Hello, Kierse," Declan said with a feral grin.

Declan and a half dozen Druids materialized out of the darkness. In the state she was in now, they'd kill her before she could move a muscle.

She reached for bravado as she faced him fully. "Declan. What can I do for you?"

"Funny you should ask," Declan said. "Lorcan wants to talk to you."

"It's not a good time. Maybe we could set up a meeting. I can pencil him in." She felt like laughing at him, but he looked so goddamn serious. She just didn't have the energy for it.

"Lorcan won't be kept waiting."

Kierse rolled her eyes. "Do you hear yourself? You sound ridiculous."

"We either take you willingly or by force." He crossed his arms over his beefy chest. "It's up to you."

"You can't touch me. You know Graves and Lorcan have an arrangement."

"We're not going to break any parts of that arrangement as long as you come quietly."

"'Quietly' isn't really my style."

Declan narrowed his eyes. "We've been following you since you left his place. You can barely walk. You couldn't stand a chance against me right now. Let alone the rest of us."

She ignored his comment. "What does he want? And why didn't he come himself if he is so interested in talking to me?"

"You'll find out when you meet him."

"Do I have your word that you'll let me leave after I hear him out?"

"It's not my word you need. It's Lorcan's. But if you want to leave after you've spoken to Lorcan, then we cannot keep you, per the arrangement."

She paused, letting them see her deliberating. Her eyes cast around the shadows, searching for any wolves that lingered in them. She didn't want the Druids to think she was giving in too easily, but based on their patrols of Graves's house, she'd known this was a possibility.

"Fine. Then let's go."

Declan looked startled by her acceptance. He must have thought that he'd have to wrangle her, probably knock her out to get her to comply. She would go meet the infamous Lorcan. It was overdue, anyway.

"Are we going? Or are we just going to stand here?"

"You're not going to try anything?"

"It's amazing what you can accomplish when you don't point a gun at a person."

Declan roared with laughter. He stepped forward and clapped Kierse on the back. She stumbled at the force of it. "Spritely thing, you are. Come on, then."

She didn't feel spritely as she jogged to catch up to him. Declan led her to a series of large, black SUVs. She piled into one of the cars after him, and they rode in silence away from the familiar streets. Kierse was surprised that they didn't blindfold her. She knew their territory was in Brooklyn, but she didn't think they would be comfortable with her knowing where their headquarters was located. They crossed the Williamsburg Bridge in silence, and she watched the island fall away behind her as they drove into Brooklyn.

Eventually, they parked in front of a brick building with towering oak trees lining the walkway, their leaves long gone from their branches. Across the street was the large, white-domed edifice of the former Williamsburgh Savings Bank Building on Broadway. Declan hustled her outside again, and she wrenched herself away from him.

"I can walk," she ground out.

"Fine. This way."

He strode through the entrance of a first-floor restaurant with black-and-white-tiled floors and hard wooden booths. Declan barreled through the place as if he owned it, and they ended up in a hallway with an elevator. One of the Druid underlings pressed the button, and when the doors opened, she followed them in. Declan slid a keycard into a slot, and that allowed access to the top floor, which just read EQUINOX.

The doors opened to a stunningly elegant restaurant. Crystal chandeliers hung from the high ceiling. The floors were solid wood, waxed and polished to perfection. Candlelight flickered from an array of circular tables about the room. Long, forest-green drapes were pulled back from windows that showcased the view of a lifetime—the entire Manhattan skyline lit up.

Kierse had been living with Graves for weeks, and still the luxury astounded her. Here, tucked away in this borough, was this magnificent restaurant—Equinox. Her brow furrowed as a memory of that name teetered on the brink of recollection. But before she could pluck it out, a man appeared.

He moved with the grace of a dancer—light and effortless. Kierse understood feet like that. She'd had to learn to be that quiet, and it had taken years. Yet he was neither slight nor burly, either. He appeared to be in his mid-thirties and was perfectly muscled beneath the clean three-piece suit. Not bulky or showy but…stylish, elegant, self-assured.

As he drew closer, she marked all the intricacies of him. The gold watch gleaming on his wrist; the trimmed, dark-brown beard; the smooth gait; the cerulean-blue eyes that reminded her of a crystal-clear day in Central Park. But most of all, his smile. The way it reached his eyes without effort. As if he had never known true pain.

He stopped before her. "Hello, Kierse. It's a pleasure to make your acquaintance. I'm Lorcan Flynn."

Chapter Twenty-Nine

Lorcan held his hand out like a proper gentleman, and Kierse stared down at it in question. Did he think that they were somehow friends here? He and Graves might be in a cease-fire, but she wasn't about to forget that he had tried to kill her and her friends and had just kidnapped her.

He dropped his hand. "All right. No handshakes. It's good to finally meet you."

"Is it?" she asked.

"For me at least. Not for you?"

She shrugged. "It's nice to put a face with a name."

"My apologies about the circumstances, but it was imperative that we meet." He had a light Irish accent. Not as thick as Declan's but just enough to make him sound foreign.

"Why is that?"

Lorcan just smiled, gesturing to a back table that was set with beautiful silver dishes. A bottle of wine was already open, with a generous pour of the red in each glass like blood set before a vampire's feast.

"I'm not exactly dressed for dinner." In fact, she was wearing workout clothes and sneakers. Her hair was in a ponytail. She barely had on a lick of makeup. This place was a five-star location, probably Michelin-starred in the times before. She hardly fit in.

"Ah. Luckily, the owner won't mind," he said cheekily. Then he saw that she was still staring blankly at him. "I think we…got off on the wrong foot."

"You *think*?" she asked. "You tried to kill me."

"A miscalculation. You're perfectly safe with me."

Why did men always say that? As if they thought that women would believe them. "You have a funny way of showing 'safe' after kidnapping me."

"An invitation," he amended.

"With armed guards," she said. "An invitation you could have delivered yourself."

"Graves's reach extends through much of Manhattan. It was better for us to speak in Brooklyn, on my property. This way, I can guarantee we won't be interrupted. But after we have dinner, I will have my people return you safely wherever you choose." He pressed his hand to his heart. "I give you my word."

Kierse wavered at the threshold of the restaurant. She didn't want to have this meal with Lorcan, but she was curious about him and all the reasons he and Graves hated each other. He appeared earnest in his resolve to return her when he was done, but she wasn't pleased with the circumstances.

"I realize that your word is valuable." It was a guess based on the arrangement he had with Graves. Lorcan nodded. "So if you go against it, I will kill you."

He laughed, loud and effortless. A man accustomed to laughing. So unlike her. So unlike Graves.

"I would expect little else," Lorcan said.

She nodded. "So, I'll eat, but don't ever do this again."

He bowed his head once. "Next time, I'll come myself."

She rolled her eyes but followed him to the table. Lorcan helped her into a chair and took the seat across from her. That was when the memory hit her. "Gregory Amberdash frequents this place."

Lorcan tucked his chair in. "Ah yes, he is a client of mine."

"He mentioned it in passing once."

"That sounds like him." He whipped out his napkin. "He loves the lamb, which is, coincidentally, what is on the menu tonight."

"Amberdash is a wraith. He doesn't eat lamb."

"Wraiths can eat human food. It just doesn't nourish them," Lorcan countered.

Kierse grimaced. She did *not* want to think about that.

"And he worked with you?"

Lorcan gestured to her. "He was the one who gave me your name."

"Wonderful." Well, that explained the cryptic warning. Part of her should have anticipated Amberdash double-crossing her, but they'd known each other for so long that it still hurt. "So, why me?"

"I was looking for someone who could break into Graves's house. Amberdash offered me a few unsuccessful candidates before we decided on you. If it makes you feel better, he seemed unwilling to offer you until all other options ran out."

It didn't.

"Doesn't that go against your arrangement with Graves?"

"It toes a line," he conceded.

"And why would you try to kill me *after* I got into the house? Doesn't that seem counterintuitive to your plans?"

"You walked out the front door. I believed you were compromised."

"But you don't now, when you know I'm living there?"

"Oh, you certainly are," he said with a wide smile, giving away nothing. "Do you like cabernet sauvignon?"

He swirled his wine around the glass and took a sip. He gestured for her to try her own, but she'd barely eaten anything since the party. She wasn't sure wine was the right choice to start with.

She reached for the water instead. Fresh green salads and a basket of bread were placed before them. He picked up his fork.

"Not wine, then," he said. "Hopefully the salad is to your liking."

She stabbed her fork into the salad with relish but didn't eat.

Lorcan sighed and set his fork down. "This is the point." His tone softened. "I'm making conversation. I want to get to know you."

She leaned her elbows against the table, bucking etiquette. "Why?"

"I was wrong about you. When I saw you walk out the front door of Graves's house, I believed that he had gotten to you, that you were working together, or even that Amberdash had set me up. I didn't want Graves to have a new pawn. I admit that I'm sometimes rash when it comes to Graves. But you and I are not enemies."

She wanted to ask him why he was so rash with Graves. She had so many questions. Things that Graves had merely scooted around nimbly, like a too-clever fox. And here was Lorcan, willing to feed her information. But at what price? She needed to tread carefully. Lorcan may seem like an easy mark, but anyone who went head-to-head with Graves must be able to play the game.

"If you say so," she said instead, leaning over and taking a bite of the salad.

Her necklace hung forward over her meal. Lorcan made a small noise in the back of his throat. "What bird is that on your necklace?"

She glanced up at him and was certain he already knew the answer. "A wren."

His answering smile was all teeth. "Really? Wrens are such beautiful birds."

She shot him an exasperated look. "Are you going to tell me about how they're all killed the day after Christmas, too?"

"I see Graves has been feeding you information," he said with a knowing look in his eye. "Wrens are a sign that spring is near. The end of winter. The seasons are turning and all that."

"And then they kill them for sport."

"Well, not anymore. It's mostly just a party now," he said, taking another sip of his wine. "But I bet Graves found that necklace very interesting. As do I, little songbird."

She kept her hands carefully at her sides, when all she wanted to do was tuck the necklace away.

"Now, eat. You look like you haven't had a meal in weeks."

Which was absurd because, before the wish-powder hangover from hell, she'd been eating better than she ever had in her life. She chalked it up to the sickness and decided to eat. She took a bite and then another and another. What was with the food with these men? How did they make a salad taste this good?

"It's goat cheese from my home farm and fresh raspberries."

"How did you get raspberries in the dead of winter?" she asked, plucking another one from the salad and indulging. Both he *and* Graves had them. Money was the answer.

"We all have our secrets," he said with a gleam in his eyes.

When they finished their salads and Kierse had gorged herself on the warmest, crustiest bread in existence, the main course arrived. As promised, it was a lamb shank in a fragrant sauce with brown-butter mashed potatoes on the side.

"Tell me about yourself," Lorcan went on. "What do you like to do for fun? Your hobbies? Your taste in music?"

She considered his play. She'd thought he'd be gruff and arrogant. That he'd dismiss her, attempt to recruit her, and then try to kill her if it didn't work. Or at the very least warn her that Graves was a bad, bad man, wagging a finger and all. Except…he wasn't doing that.

"Why do you want to know about me?"

"I can't find a beautiful woman interesting?" Lorcan asked.

She leaned forward and fluttered her eyelashes. "You think I'm beautiful?"

"You know you're beautiful. And beyond interesting to have survived this long on the streets with your level of skill."

"You're a charmer," she teased.

He laughed again. He made it look so easy. "If you find me charming now, wait until dessert. I won't ruin the surprise, but it's my favorite." Lorcan took another bite of his lamb and finished chewing before speaking again. "Well? Your interests?"

"You first," she said, taking a bite of the most succulent meat she'd ever tried.

"I enjoy long hikes through the woods and across the moors. I love sailing and fishing on clear days and, when it rains, huddling in a gazebo with nothing but my guitar. I enjoy festival days and rituals and farmers markets. I confess that I'm easy to please," he said, setting his fork down. Those blue eyes looked straight through her. "What about you? Are you easy to please?"

The question was loaded. He wanted to know about her. Yes. But he wanted more. He wanted to know if she was poachable. If he could convert her to his side with kind eyes and warm smiles and delicious food. She decided to go along with it and see where it landed her.

"I like…training," she said with a shrug.

"That's work," he said, waving her off. "What do you do for fun?"

"For fun," she said softly. "I admit there hasn't been much fun to be had."

"Surely you enjoy something other than thieving and training."

She looked down, playing up the role of the innocent victim. "I guess I like babka from a Jewish bakery across from the Met."

"Babka?" he asked excitedly.

A small smile came to her face. "Cinnamon babka. It's the best I've ever tasted."

"You must give me the name. I will become a patron of their establishment." He leaned in. "What else?"

"Well, I like spending time with my friends." She frowned as if just remembering where she sat. "The ones you tried to kill."

"Again. I was wrong. I'm sorry about the misunderstanding." He held up his hands. "Can you forgive me?"

Fat chance.

"You're going to leave them alone?"

"My interest rests solely with you, my dear."

That wasn't a promise, and they both knew it.

"Please continue," he encouraged.

"I like brandy," she confessed. "I got a taste of it at sixteen, and it feels like the thing to drink when you've accomplished something."

"I have an impressive brandy collection. We'll have it over dessert," he assured her. "Tell me more."

"Well, really, I just like pickpocketing unsuspecting rich people."

He snorted. "You should get out more. If pickpocketing the wealthy is your idea of fun, I could show you a really good time."

And though they were both playing parts, she believed him. He didn't act like the villain that she had painted in her head. He didn't feel bad at all. She was sure it was a ruse to get her to let down her guard, but he just… didn't even seem dangerous. Yes, she knew he *was* dangerous. He'd tried to kill her. He was in a feud with Graves. He was a gang leader, controlling the entirety of Brooklyn. All of those things should have read like a giant warning sign: *Danger. Keep Out!* Except she didn't feel that way.

Their empty plates were whisked away, and dessert was revealed to be a stunning cinnamon bread pudding with a creamy vanilla-bourbon sauce to pour on top with the promised brandy as its accompaniment. She'd only taken a sip before deciding it was the nicest brandy she'd ever tasted.

"Thank you for a delightful dinner. Open invitation to Equinox whenever you like. On the house," Lorcan said.

"Why? What even is this place?"

"It's my restaurant. 'Equinox' means balance, and balance is an important concept for me. I try to apply it to my life, the seasons, my food. So, three days a week, I open the restaurant to the poor and hungry. Free hot dinners for whoever shows up. And the next three days, I open it for the wealthy and privileged of our society. Those who want to run their businesses and have their meetings outside of the prying eyes of their peers." He smiled at her, completely guileless. "I provide a much-needed service. All above the books. Balance."

How often had she so desperately needed that hot meal? How many times had she gone hungry without anything in her stomach at all? Too many to count, but it didn't change the fact that he was likely playing her, telling her exactly what she wanted to hear. He might do some good deeds, but they didn't erase his hand in all of this.

"Why do you hate Graves?"

His lips lifted. "He didn't tell you?"

"I want to hear your side."

He considered her for a second, draining his last bit of brandy from his glass.

"We should leave that until next time," he said finally. "You will come back, won't you?"

"I don't know," she answered with a raised brow. What more could he tell her? How much could she get out of him in all of this?

His smile grew, and those cerulean eyes lit up. "How about you give me a call when you're ready? That way I don't have to send Declan."

Lorcan retrieved a business card from his suit pocket and slid it across the table. Kierse took the card in her hand. The heavy off-white cardstock was embossed with his name and number in shiny gold. A small acorn was the only other adornment. She stuck it in her pocket. Could come in handy.

"Maybe," she said. Then she stood.

He promptly stood, too, stepping closer to her as if drawn to her in some way. "I'll have Declan drive you back into the city."

"Perfect." She glanced up at him again, ready to judge his response to what she said next. "I'm going to tell Graves about this."

Lorcan nodded. "Well, I'd expect nothing less. Though it doesn't impinge on our arrangement. Would you say you were harmed?"

"Kidnapped," she suggested, not backing down. Their bodies were so close together. She met his gaze, using sleight of hand to filch his watch while he remained transfixed by her face.

"I'm releasing you." His smile faltered, and he looked down at her with something genuine in his eyes. "Though, I admit, unwillingly."

"You're a shameless flirt," she said, stepping back to diffuse whatever tension he was attempting to create. She slid her hand into her pocket. Such an easy mark.

"A character flaw, I assure you." But he reached out and grasped her arm. "That isn't nice." Lorcan turned her palm up, opening her fingers to reveal the watch she'd stripped off of his wrist. "I think I'll take that back."

That was the second time someone had figured out she was stealing from them. Graves and now Lorcan. Either she needed to sharpen her skills or her opponents were getting more terrifying by the day.

"What gave me away?" she asked curiously.

"I'll tell you next time," he said with a wink as he refastened the watch.

Another trap she had no intention of walking into. The next time would be on her own terms. "I'm leaving now."

Lorcan seemed as if he couldn't quite let her go. "Come back again, Kierse."

She gave him one last look that suggested she just might like that. "Maybe."

Chapter Thirty

Declan didn't even bother to take her to Graves's place. He set her down right where he'd found her with another laugh when she tipped him a middle-finger salute. She'd have to find her own way back to Graves's house that night. Lorcan might have promised her a safe return, but it didn't seem like his second-in-command cared exactly how *safe* it would be.

She waited until his black SUV was out of sight before blowing out a breath of relief.

Good riddance.

"Quite a night you've had," Nate said from behind her.

Kierse turned then to face Nate. "Yeah, yeah," she grumbled.

Wolves lingered in the shadows across the street. She caught Cara and Finn huddled together. Finn had his arm slung around Cara's waist, and she was grinning at something he said. Ronan's gaze slipped to them in obvious annoyance before returning to scouting.

"Waters." Ronan snapped his fingers in a brunette's direction. The woman nodded at Ronan. "Lopez, Keller." He gestured at a short man with brown skin and a redhead with light, freckled skin across the street. They loped out of the shadows as humans approached their meetup. They worked so effortlessly together to clear the area, moving as one body rather than individual wolves.

"Could have warned us it'd be tonight," Nate said, drawing her attention away from his pack.

"But you are always so very prepared," she teased.

She sidled up to him, falling into step as they continued down the street toward the twenty-four-hour coffee shop.

"How did the meeting go? I didn't think it was going to happen tonight. You seemed pretty banged up when they picked you up on the street."

"Well, it wasn't exactly to plan, Nate, but when opportunity arises…"

"You mean they were going to kidnap you either way."

"Yes. I wasn't really in any shape to say no. I was glad we'd already planned this," Kierse told him. "Even if it happened when I wasn't expecting it."

She'd spotted the patrol casing the house multiple times since she'd moved in with Graves. She'd suggested to Nate that she get Lorcan's attention, though of course she hadn't planned for it to be *tonight*. And now she'd blown her chance to see Gen and Ethan, but it was better to find out what Lorcan's play was.

"So?" Nate asked. "A success?"

She shot him her own wolfish grin. "He gave me everything."

He snorted. "I've missed you."

He yanked open the door to the deserted coffee shop and signaled to his people. They fanned out around the perimeter. Nate strode to the beleaguered barista as Kierse took a seat in their normal booth. Nate made cheerful conversation before returning with their drinks.

Kierse blew on the steaming liquid. "You were right, too," she conceded.

"Yeah?" he asked.

"No need to be afraid of the Druids when there are Dreadlords in the shadows, eh?"

Nate assessed her and then nodded. "That's true. I'm glad I had my men watching out for you. Though I didn't feel too comfortable when you went into his headquarters."

"They brought a fox into their chicken coop. They should be more worried than you were."

He chuckled. "You got me there. So, tell me everything."

She gave Nate a rundown of the conversation with Lorcan. He nodded along as she told him and rolled his eyes at all the attempts to charm her.

"Well, he's an arrogant prick."

She laughed. "Pot, meet kettle?"

"At least I own it. I wish we'd gotten more information about Graves out of him."

"He'll give it to me eventually," she said with a shrug. "Didn't you see how desperate he was?"

"He seemed into you."

"Oddly so. I'm not sure how much of it was an act, but he sure puts on airs like he's the hero in this story."

"He probably thinks he is."

"Yeah," she said. Though it was so unlike Graves, who clearly believed he was the monster in the tale. "What do you think he and Graves have against each other?"

Nate sighed. "I have no idea. But I wouldn't trust either of them."

"I don't trust anyone."

Nate flashed her a winning grin. "Except me, of course. That's why you're spilling all the goods."

Kierse shook her head at him. Even if this was her plan from the start.

Step one: get close to all the big players in the city and learn their secrets, objectives, and future moves. It wasn't a secret that monsters chafed under the Monster Treaty. The Men of Valor were just the loudest players in the game. She wouldn't stand on the sidelines of the battle this time. Not when she had this new advantage. Not when those bastards had stolen Torra. Now it was personal.

Step two: work with Nate and his Dreadlords to consolidate that information into action they could eventually use against the monsters. If and when that anger spilled over, they would be prepared. And Nate was the best option. He was her ally and an ally of humans. She would take him over the alternative.

Step three: steal the spear. Landing a blow against her enemy, those who killed Torra, was the ultimate goal. Anything that kept them from having the advantage was the most important.

And while she had planned all of this to begin with, she hadn't planned for Graves. Whatever was going on between them since their training session and Imani's party. He'd told her not to divulge his secrets, but she knew him well enough now to know that if he found out that she'd double-crossed him to work with the Dreadlords, he would go absolutely ballistic.

"We're allies," she said.

"Friends," Nate countered.

"Fine. Friends," she said as if that word meant nothing to her. Nate was her friend, but all the players in this game made her uncomfortable in some way. They all had power over her if they needed it. Even Nate. Maybe most of all Nate. He knew the most about her, after all.

"We'll wait Lorcan out, then. If you're certain he'll come after you again."

"He will," she said with assurance. "He can't help himself. He thinks that he can play me to get to Graves."

"The way you're playing him," Nate said with a laugh.

"It's amazing how many people will give up and not look at the truth when they see a pretty smile." She shot him that same pretty smile, and he snorted.

"So, what the hell happened to you the last couple of days, anyway? You went radio silent."

"I was doing my job."

"As long as you're safe."

She scoffed. "I wasn't safe the moment I took this job."

Nate frowned as if he didn't like that assessment, but he just said, "This meeting has gone on long enough. We probably need to get you back to his house before he realizes that you're gone. Anything else on Graves that I should know about?"

Kierse shifted once uncomfortably. It wasn't that she didn't want to give information about Graves to Nate and the Dreadlords. She didn't trust Graves. He didn't trust her, either. He'd made that abundantly clear from the beginning. But she'd given him her word she wouldn't spill his secrets, and for some unknown reason, she wanted to keep that promise. At least for now.

When she hesitated, Nate raised an eyebrow. "Don't tell me you're going soft on me."

Kierse rolled her eyes at the werewolf. "I'm hardly going soft." She stood from the booth. "I'll contact you when I have more information."

Nate shot her a shrewd look as if trying to see whether or not she was playing *him*. "We're on the same side, Kierse."

"I know," she said.

And as much as she wanted that to be true, in this, at least, she was only ever on her own side.

Chapter Thirty-One

The house was eerily silent when she snuck back into her room at the brownstone, and its warmth felt reassuringly safe. She closed the door quietly behind her and padded toward the bed, stripping out of her jacket as she went. She didn't know what alerted her, but when she looked up, Graves was seated in a chair in her room.

She gasped slightly. He wasn't supposed to be home yet. Nate would have told her. "Graves," she whispered. "What are you doing in here?"

He rose slowly to his feet, a menacing figure in every regard. She shivered at the force of his presence as he loomed over her. "You went out."

"Yes."

"You evaded the cameras."

"I thought you put them up as a challenge."

He took a step toward her, closing the gap easily. "Do you take everything as a challenge?"

She tilted her head up to look into his too-intense eyes. "Isn't that the fun of life?"

He breathed out sharply. "Surely you can understand why this was a bad idea."

"I'm not confined to the premises," she reminded him flippantly.

Graves's entire body tensed at her tone, and something seemed to shatter within him all at once. "You were still recovering," he growled low.

Concern was laced into his swirling eyes, and tension flexed in his jaw. And for the first time, she realized that maybe he wasn't upset with her… maybe he was *worried* about her.

Something in her eased at the gesture. She'd believed he was made of stone. Even when he had saved her life, she hadn't truly seen him unsettled.

"I'm okay," she assured him.

"You should not have gone without a clean bill of health."

"You're right," she conceded. Her body relaxed, her voice going with it. "I shouldn't have gone out. The Druids tracked me. They brought me to Lorcan at Equinox. We had dinner."

"What?" he asked in utter disbelief. "Tonight?"

"Yes, I've just returned."

"That goes expressly against the terms of our arrangement." He looked like a dragon ready to unfurl his wings and breathe fire. "Lorcan will pay for this."

Kierse stepped into his path. "I am safe and hale, as you can presently see. We just talked."

"You do not know Lorcan the way that I do. He does nothing without purpose. And if he brought you to Equinox, then he's encroaching. I can assume he recruited you?" he asked, going very still as he waited for her answer.

"Something like that." She looked up at him through her lashes, feeling the vulnerability in the moment. "I told him that I would tell you about what he did. I think he expects you to react."

"Are you suggesting that I am playing into his hands?"

Kierse held her own hands up. "I don't know. I just can't think of another reason he'd kidnap me and then set me loose if it wasn't to dangle me before you."

Graves's jaw tightened farther as if he saw the wisdom in her words. "What did he tell you?"

"Nothing really," she lied. He'd given her enough to chew on, but it wasn't really what Graves was asking, anyway. "He just wanted to know more about me. I think he was testing me more than divulging anything."

"He said nothing about our relationship?"

She shook her head. "No. I don't know what's between you two. He wouldn't tell me, and I hardly expect you to if he wouldn't," she said with a sigh.

Graves's gray eyes smoldered. He looked torn between two worlds in that moment. As if he were standing at the mouth of a canyon, wondering if he could jump to the other side but only seeing deep into the abyss. Finally, ever so slowly, he met her gaze. She could see shadows dancing in those dark irises. Shadows of his past and whatever had happened there.

"Many years ago, long before you were born, Lorcan and I were...family, of a sort," he said, his eyes drifting to the closed window as if he couldn't bear to speak the words while looking at her. She held her breath, unable to believe he was giving in even a little and frightened that he would spook like an alley cat if he remembered her existence. "We were an unlikely pair, but for a time, he was the other half of my coin, my brother in all but name.

When tragedy struck, it fractured what was between us. He blamed me."

He was silent a moment, and Kierse thought that may be the end of his story.

"Perhaps his blame was placed correctly," he finally said. "But no amends were sufficient. They never could be. And thus, we have been enemies ever since."

The ache in his voice struck her plainly in the chest. She didn't want to feel for him, and yet she couldn't help but feel anything else. He told the story so succinctly and with such pain that it was clear that no matter how long ago the events had unfolded, they would always hurt him. Whatever the supposed tragedy was and even if Lorcan had in turn become his enemy with a score to settle, the beginning, when Lorcan had been his found family, would always remain. No one could hurt you like family.

"Graves," she whispered.

He came back to himself then, almost startled, as if he hadn't planned to tell her that much. "Let's go to the library. I found what I was looking for."

She wanted to go back to that moment of vulnerability, but it had passed. So, she just nodded and followed him out of her room and to the Holly Library. Anne was curled up on a cushion of the couch. Kierse took a seat across from her, and the fiery thing got up in offense before trotting over to another empty spot.

"I see how it is," she told Anne.

She thumbed through the book on the side table with half a mind as Graves poured himself a drink. She declined one for herself. And though she was trying to focus on the reading at hand, she couldn't seem to stop thinking about Anne Boleyn. The cat, of course.

It seemed uncharacteristic for him to have a cat. After all, cats *chose* people. Not the other way around.

She had met *many* an alley cat that loved her and just as many that hated her on sight. She'd befriended them and fed them when she could manage and watched Gen try to sneak a tabby past Colette.

So, why had Anne chosen Graves, of all people? Of all *monsters*?

Graves took his own seat beside her, breaking her from her thoughts.

"What are you reading?" she asked. She hadn't noticed that he'd been carrying a book all this time. A little green thing that he held out to her. She took it from him and looked at the cover, which had three spirals connected to a small triangle on the front.

"I thought you'd like it, actually. Did you finish the other?"

"I did."

"And what did you think?"

She brushed her thumb across her bottom lip contemplatively. "I like the story of the Oak and Holly King battles."

"Of course you do."

"What is that supposed to mean?"

Graves's face was a mask. "You couldn't like the tale of the High Priestesses and their healing arts."

She had read that one, too. She wrinkled her nose. "Please. Virgins who live on a separate island from men to help them control the weather for their vessels. No thanks."

Graves shrugged. "It was a different time. Tell me what you like about the Oak and Holly Kings."

She bit her lip and wondered what he wanted her to see in this story. She couldn't deny that there were seeds of it that rang true. Even if she couldn't put the pieces together. "Well, I like the idea that twice a year there's a battle for whether winter or summer will dominate. The Oak King is always trying to bring back the light, and the Holly King is always trying to bring back the dark. It's harmony. Could you imagine if it didn't work? If the Oak King lost at the winter solstice and we had darkness and winter forever? Or at least until they battled again?"

"You start with harmony and end with chaos," he said, amused. "I'm not sure I know anything else that perfectly sums you up."

"I've lived much of my life in chaos. I don't know that I'd know where to start with harmony. Why do you like the story?"

He tapped his fingers against the armrest. "It's about life. About something real."

She was aware of his gaze on her. "It's just mythology."

"Some would say so. Others would say that it's as true as any other religion. It only becomes mythology after it has fallen out of favor."

"That's one way of looking at it." The book was just as worn as the other she'd borrowed. He must have truly enjoyed it, considering he had such an enormous library yet had read this one book so much.

"Do we not still see the seasons turning year over year?"

"Yes, but we have science that explains that. The planets moving around the sun," she said, trailing off.

"And yet we have monsters and magic," he said, "that science still does not understand."

"True." She stared down at the little green book for a second longer, wondering about his connection with holly and the love of the story. "Holly is your symbol. It's in your library and threaded through your wards. Is it because of this story?"

His eyes went distant. "Holly is a symbol of eternal life because they stay green in the winter, and the berries are poisonous. I recognized myself in that."

Graves stood and retrieved some papers. He laid them out on the table, revealing several blueprints stacked haphazardly on top of one another, the corner of what looked like another invitation, and drawings of various *computer components*?

"What is all of this?"

"*This* is the business I've been working on. As soon as I had a wardbreaker, I set into motion all the plays I've been holding on to."

She nodded her approval. This was the sort of work she did alone or with Ethan's help. It was actually nice to have someone else who was competent to have so many of the pieces she required in one place.

"Tell me everything."

"Have you heard of the vampire King Louis?"

"The name sounds familiar," she admitted. "He runs the underground or something?"

"Indeed," Graves said. "It's a moniker after King Louis XIV of France, the Sun King, who was the longest reigning French monarch. The vampire King Louis was cast out after the Monster Treaty and has since risen up as the rightful king of the monster underworld. He runs the Men of Valor. He is not quiet about his distaste for what he considers to be monster suppression and believes he should rule this world. In fact, he was the Monster Treaty's most vocal dissenter. But a man...a vampire like that isn't going to stop because of a treaty."

"And he has the spear," she said.

"Yes. I believe his predecessor was in possession of it. When he was killed, an informant told me that it had transferred to King Louis."

"So, you haven't seen it yourself?"

"No," he admitted. "Not since I lost access to the underworld."

He pushed one of the hand-drawn pictures toward her. It revealed a vault door with a security system. She squinted at it to try to see if they'd gotten anything she could go off of. "This is where the spear is being kept. The wards will be easy, but you'll still have to break through the vault without raising an alarm."

"That's fine. I think I can break down something like this. It'd be more helpful if we got a make or model on it. Anything like that will help me get through it faster."

"I'll see what I can do. In the meantime," Graves said, handing her a picture. "This is King Louis."

The resolution was grainy. He was broad and large yet healthy. His hair was thick and dark, and his alabaster hands clasped a cane. He looked as if he was going for refined but in the end didn't quite make it there. His eyes were wild even in the poor quality. And there was a twist to his mouth as if life had been cruel to him and he intended to deal it back tenfold.

"He looks like there's something wrong with him." She knew at once that having *this* monster leading anyone was a bad idea.

"There is. Many, many things," Graves said solemnly.

"But he's not the reason you haven't been able to get to the spear. He's just a vampire. Vampires can't make wards, right? So what's the problem?"

Graves reached into his folder and passed her another image. When she reached for it, their hands brushed. Fire curled up her arm at the barest contact. She shuddered slightly and tried to hide it with a change in position and carefully looking down at the photo.

This one was of a gangly youth with wide, black-rimmed glasses. He had medium-brown skin with a thatch of curly brown hair and an overly eager expression.

"He is the problem," Graves said.

Kierse looked skeptical. "*This* guy?"

"That is Walter Rodriguez. A base warlock who is causing a lot of trouble."

"Wait. I thought you were the only warlock in the city."

"I never said that. Simply that we're territorial. I allow lesser warlocks to live within my boundaries as long as they know their place."

"'Lesser'?"

"Yes, there are three levels of warlocks—base, apprentice, and master."

"And you are…" He stared straight through her. "Right. That's obvious." He had to be a master if he controlled who lived in his territory. She cleared her throat. "So, how is someone who is the lowest level causing trouble?"

"I met Walter several years ago. I approached him about training to be an apprentice. We worked together to attune his abilities. Some apprentices go on to become masters of their craft, like Imani. Others reveal that their promise was a flame in the night but will never grow, like Montrell. Walter's flame burned out magnificently."

Kierse soaked in all of the new information. She wanted to ask where that put her, but she didn't want to derail the conversation. "So, how is he a problem?"

"He held on to one of his powers—force fields—and became nigh untouchable. Any warlock can use warding. It's a base ability."

"Really? Even I could do it?"

Graves nodded. "Yes."

She buzzed with that new information. "Do all the wards look different? Will Walter's look different than yours?"

"What do you mean?" he asked, leaning forward with curiosity.

"All the wards have symbols in them. Yours is holly and Imani's is that bird?"

His expression was startled. "Yes, all magic is individual. And Imani's symbol is a sankofa," he explained. "It's a West African symbol that means 'look to the past to build a better future.'"

"Would my symbol be the wren?"

His smile was sharp and knowing. "I guess we'll find out."

Kierse couldn't wait.

"But back to Walter," Graves said. "Wards are strengthened by imbuing them with your power. Thus, my wards would be stronger than Imani's, whose are stronger than Walter's. Except that Walter discovered how to push his force fields into wards in the way Imani can put her wishes into powder. And now I cannot break his wards."

"Unbreakable wards," she said. "No wonder you need me."

"Yes, I need a wardbreaker."

"How did he learn to make these wards?"

He shrugged one shoulder. "I still don't know. I didn't teach him. He must have figured it out on his own. He was a bit of a math genius and a tech guy when I first met him. He thought that he could program his magic like a computer."

"Smart." Kierse suddenly saw where this was heading. "He saw a way to be valuable, and he's working with King Louis."

"Protecting the Third Floor and, by extension, the spear."

"That makes sense."

"This is the plan, as I see it: You enter the Men of Valor's winter solstice party with access through this invitation. You escape the festivities, break into the vault, retrieve the spear, and escape. If it goes south, this is where your training comes in. You can fight your way out with the spear."

"That sounds simple enough."

"And about a thousand ways it could go wrong." His eyes moved back to all the paperwork on the table. "We have just over one week to acquire everything else that we need to pull it off."

A week. Fuck.

"That's close. What *else* do we need?"

Graves withdrew a small notebook from his suit pocket and began reading off of a list. "The easiest route to get you through the security system and wards into Third Floor—the invitation will get you into the party itself. The information on the vault so that you can break into it. A suitable ball gown. And an exit."

"Oh, my favorite," she crooned.

"Yes. The exit will be our most difficult element. I've not found a way in or out of Third Floor without passing through a checkpoint. That would not be ideal with you carrying the spear."

"Well, the best part, then—reconnaissance," she said with a grin. "When do we start?"

She didn't realize how close she had drawn to him as her excitement had mounted. Her shoulder was pressed tight against his. His heat melted into hers. She looked up into his eyes, wondering if he was about to break the tension and acknowledge whatever was happening here. Her stomach twisted, and she recognized it as yearning.

He opened his mouth as if he were going to say something about what had happened. But in that moment, a banging came from downstairs.

Kierse followed Graves out of the library and down the main set of stairs just as Edgar answered the door.

A booming British voice rang out. "Edgar, my old chap, just look at you!"

The breath went out of Graves as if he had been expecting the worst.

A figure strode inside. "There you are, Graves. What in the bloody hell have you gotten yourself into this time?"

Graves laughed at the man. "Hello, Kingston."

So *this* was the infamous Kingston.

Chapter Thirty-Two

Kingston was half a head shorter than Graves, with jowls and a belly protruding under his waistcoat. He looked like a proper gentleman out of the nineteenth century in a long, black suit complete with a cravat, a top hat, and a cane. He flipped his hat off and tucked it under his arm.

Kingston vigorously shook Graves's hand. "You came all the way from England to berate me?" Graves asked.

Kingston chortled. "Wouldn't have to if you'd be sensible and come home."

"When have I ever been sensible?" Graves asked dryly.

"Ah, right you are. Not as long as I've known you." Then Kingston looked past Graves to where Kierse stood awkwardly apart from it all. Kingston pointed his cane, which appeared to only be used for fashion and not as a walking stick, at Kierse. "Is this her?"

"Her?" Graves asked. His gaze swept to Kierse. "Ah, Kingston, allow me to introduce you to my apprentice, Miss McKenna."

Kingston's eyebrows rose sharply. "You took on another one?"

"It passes the time," he said evenly. "This is my mentor, Kingston Darby."

Graves gestured for Kierse to step forward, but she was still shaken by that word. *Apprentice.* She was Graves's apprentice? He'd conveniently left that part out when they'd been talking about the warlock levels. Did that mean she had apprentice-level magic and that he was going to train her as a warlock?

She stepped toward Kingston and held out her hand. "Pleasure to meet you. You can call me Kierse."

Kingston took her hand in his, but instead of shaking, he bent dramatically at the waist and brushed his lips against her knuckles. "The pleasure is mine, my dear."

Kierse's eyes rose to Graves's in dismay. Was he always this outrageous?

"Mentor?" she asked instead.

Kingston straightened and looked put out. "What have you been teaching this girl, if she doesn't know that I took you on as an apprentice and raised you up to be what you are today?"

Kierse tried to keep the smile off her lips and failed. "It's hard to imagine Graves as an apprentice."

"You say that now. But he once was a young scrap of a thing, falling into trouble wherever he stepped."

"Not much has changed, then," Kierse said.

Graves slid his hands into his pockets, letting his mentor and his apprentice take jabs at him without comment.

Kingston, on the other hand, burst into laughter and put a hand on her shoulder. "Right you are. Right you are. Now, where is your bourbon collection, Graves? I traveled a considerable distance. And if I'm going to be in this traitor of a country, I might as well imbibe the good stuff."

"Edgar will show you the way," Graves said with a shake of his head as Kingston ambled after Edgar toward the Holly Library.

Kierse stepped up to Graves's side and watched the man. "Apprentice?"

"Are you not?" he asked.

"Am I? I haven't learned a lick of magic."

Graves straightened to his considerable height. His eyes were almost soft when he looked at her. The light shifted on his midnight-blue hair. She ached to brush it out of his dark eyes but chided herself for the response.

"Haven't you?"

"Would it kill you to answer a question with something other than a question?"

A smirk touched his lips. "Would it kill you to do the same?"

Kierse tipped her head at him. "Touché."

"I'll let you know that Kingston's gift is persuasion. In the way that Imani is wish granting and Walter is force fields. It will be interesting to see how much of his magic you will be immune to and how much of it is just the force of his personality."

"And what are *you*?"

His eyes lingered on hers. "Knowledge."

That was what he'd claimed his business was. Not what he *was*. But didn't it make sense, with what he did for business and the way he'd acquired information for their plan without her having to lift a finger? "Well, that explains the library," she said at last.

Something flashed in his eyes, dark and hungry. A look she'd seen right before he'd devoured her mouth at the Catos' party. Her lips parted, a bubble of anticipation rising in her throat.

"Well, are you coming or not?" Kingston asked from the top of the stairs.

Kierse startled, pulling away from Graves. Though he didn't appear to be flustered at all. He just strode toward Kingston without a word.

Kierse's heart raced as she followed them. She needed that drink right about now.

Edgar exited right after she entered with a portfolio in his hand that had to contain the contents of their mission, as the table was now empty. Perhaps even Graves's mentor didn't know they were going to steal the spear. Interesting.

Kingston had already settled into one of the velvet armchairs, flicking a vine of holly away from the seat. He'd produced a pipe out of a pocket and added tobacco to it. Graves had gone to the bar. Kierse teetered between the two before taking a seat on the couch that had nearly given her a concussion that first night here and tucked her legs up underneath her. She watched as a container of matches materialized out of another of Kingston's pockets. He puffed on the pipe a few times and then nodded approvingly.

"So, Kierse," Kingston said, assessing her more closely, "Graves is always so reticent with information. I wasn't even aware he'd taken on an apprentice. What ability have you manifested? How are you restoring your reserves?"

"Well," she started, then glanced to Graves to see if he would interrupt the conversation, if he wouldn't want her to tell Kingston, but he didn't seem to mind. Perhaps he trusted this man. "I have immunity."

Kingston pointed to the ceiling. "Ah ha! No wonder he's keeping you here all to himself."

"It's not like that," Graves said, stepping over with a drink for Kingston.

"Thank you, kind sir," Kingston said.

Graves passed one to Kierse, who took a nice, comfortable gulp. Graves returned to the wet bar for his own drink, then sat on the opposite end of the couch with an ankle crossed over the opposite knee. He looked almost pleasant. None of his edges visible at all despite the flickering dim light.

"Immunity," Kingston mused. "That is quite rare. Passive, though. Perhaps you don't have to recharge."

"No, she does," Graves said.

Kierse's head swung to his. He hadn't said any of this to her. "What are you talking about?"

"Graves, honestly. Should I take over the girl's education?" Kingston asked with a wide smile. He turned back to Kierse when Graves said nothing. "All warlocks have at least one main ability. Immunity for you. For me, persuasion. But I also have a lesser power—portaling. It's how I arrived here, in fact. I stepped out of my home and straight onto Graves's doorstep."

Kierse couldn't help herself. Her mouth hung open. "You...have the ability to step between one city and another?"

"Indeed. Very handy power. But it's my lesser ability. Lesser powers take more energy to achieve properly. But *all* magic comes with a price. You will feel weaker after you've used your abilities, and then you will need to recharge them. Discovering your limitations, boundaries, and weaknesses comes first in training. That way, no one else can catch you unaware."

Kierse looked to Graves in all but shock. He *had* been...training her this whole time. He'd nearly gotten her killed stealing those letters, but she could see now that it was part of his training regimen.

"You could have told me," she hissed at him.

"I did tell you it was a test."

"Ah, did he almost kill you?" Kingston asked with a boisterous laugh as he sucked on his pipe. "Classic weakness tactics."

"Did you almost kill him?" Kierse blurted.

Kingston tipped his drink at Graves. "Naturally."

Kierse shook her head. These people were ridiculous.

"Now, simultaneously with your other training, you should be discovering how you regenerate your abilities. Sleeping and eating help," he said, patting his belly, "but using those alone takes much longer than a proper recharge."

"Then how do I do it?"

Graves sighed. "It's something different for everyone. Sometimes it has something to do with your past. A thing you did when you were a child that brought you peace, or something that gave you back a sense of your life as an adult." His eyes went distant. "For Kingston, it's art. He looks at, analyzes, critiques, and makes art, and his powers rejuvenate. He has a mild obsession with art museums."

"We should make reservations for tomorrow, while we're discussing it," Kingston said.

"And you?" Kierse asked.

"I read," Graves said simply.

Ah. Well, that explained why he was *always* reading. Always regenerating his powers.

"And me?"

"I'm still working on that," he admitted. "You recovered slower than I would have liked after the wish powder, because I didn't know how you recharged before we broke into Imani and Montrell's."

"Sloppy," Kingston said.

So many of the pieces were falling into place. The reason it had taken so long to recover from the wish powder was because she had to recharge.

"Speaking of Imani and Montrell," Kingston said darkly. He rattled the loose ice in the bottom of his empty cup. Kierse realized her drink was gone, too.

Graves grabbed the bottle off of the bar and brought it to the table, refilling everyone's glasses. "Must we discuss them?"

"They were the ones who let me know about your little project. Though... you didn't inform *them* she was a new apprentice. In fact, you gave them an entirely different name. Wren?" His expression was knowing. "Montrell had a fit."

"That's not my problem."

"Is she a wren?" His gaze swept back to her. "Are you?"

Kierse's hand went to the pendant at her throat. "Last I checked, I wasn't a bird."

Kingston laughed.

But she didn't know what was funny. Graves had called her "Wren," and it had gotten a reaction out of them, but she hadn't realized at the time that it meant more. Was she not the first wren in his employ, then? Something like disappointment was there for a beat, and then she pushed it away.

"It was a name I used to get their attention, and it worked," Graves snapped at Kingston.

"That it did. And it kept them from looking too carefully for her own magic."

"Was I required to inform them?" he asked, his voice dripping in bridled anger. He was not one to take orders, and he would not be told how to run his empire.

Kingston just threw back more of the bourbon and laughed. "Of course not, but there's a balance to things, you know."

"Yes, and *they* were disrupting the balance. I put it back in order by reclaiming what was taken from me."

"They'll want retribution," Kingston said.

Graves's voice turned dark. "Let them try."

"You are more powerful than both of them. Bloody hell, son, you're more powerful than every warlock I've met, save myself. But you are not invincible."

"I am well aware," he said evenly.

"Well, anyway, I came at their behest. My warning has been delivered. I have officially put you back in line," Kingston said with a chuckle as if he knew that was impossible.

"Did they tell you about their little operation?" Graves asked so low and casual that Kierse could only assume it was a bomb waiting to go off.

"Of course. Of course," Kingston said, waving his hand. "I know all about the new version of wish powder. Very clever, actually."

"And that she's selling it."

"In Chicago, she is queen."

"What about outside of Chicago?" Graves asked. "What about here? What about in London?"

Kingston stilled. "She wouldn't dare."

"She didn't want me to tell you about it, but since they *sent you to me* as reprimand, I see no reason to hold their secrets."

"What's wrong with selling it elsewhere?" Kierse asked.

"Magic is more volatile the farther from its owner. And volatile magic threatens all magic users," Kingston said furiously. "You are one of us now, Kierse, so listen well. Your greatest objective is to keep magic hidden. We are not like the other monsters. The revelation of the magical world can only doom our way of life."

Everyone was silent a moment as that answer soaked in. There was a reason "monsters not magic" was the motto. Magic was dangerous in its own way. She'd seen it as soon as she entered this strange world.

"Perhaps you should remind Imani of that," Graves said.

"Believe you me, I will," Kingston grumbled. Then he waved his glass at Graves again. "Enough business. Tell me everything since I've seen you. It's been too long, and I plan to finish this bottle yet."

Graves visibly relaxed at the change in topic.

Kierse leaned back in her seat. Maybe having Kingston here was a blessing in disguise, because she was content to sit in the library all night to have him reveal more of Graves's many secrets.

Chapter Thirty-Three

Kierse might have had one or two too many. She startled awake as a blanket was being draped across her shoulders, not having remembered falling asleep on the couch. Graves was still seated, polishing off the last of the bottle of bourbon. Kingston was long gone. The top of her head brushed against Graves's thigh, the fur of the blanket and his body heating her.

"I didn't mean to wake you," he said, still staring straight ahead.

"It's fine. I should probably get into my own bed if I don't want to wake up with a crick in my neck."

"Sensible."

Kierse sat up, stretching out her neck. Then she looked at Graves. So somber, so angry, so much like her. They'd reacted to circumstances differently. But like called to like. And right now, she could feel him draw her in.

"You never brought up the spear," Kierse said.

"No, I did not."

"I would think you would want your mentor involved."

"Would you want your mentor involved?"

Kierse recoiled at that thought. Jason was not a welcome thought in this conversation. He'd taught her everything she knew. He'd been her mentor and her worst nightmare. She was glad that he was gone and she never had to see him again.

"No," she said stiffly.

"Kingston and I have a rare relationship among warlocks," he continued. "We're still something like friends with separate territories. I don't always approve of his methods, and he doesn't always approve of mine. He would not approve of this."

"Why not?" she prodded.

"The spear may be valuable, but it is also dangerous to possess. He thinks it's a waste of effort. And I wouldn't put it past him to intercede. He likes to collect things as I do."

She nodded in understanding. She would keep her silence around him. They didn't need another complication to add to the mission. But at least it explained why Edgar had packed up everything before Kingston gotten to the library.

She decided to change topics. "You were training me this whole time?"

"Yes. I've assumed you were a warlock from the start. We have to wait for proof, but I like to go ahead as planned anyway. My methods are…unique."

"They appear to be exactly what you were taught."

"Similar, but what happened to you was not part of my plan."

"Which part?"

"Your illness," he said, his eyes skimming down her body. "I did not like to see you hurting."

"I recovered."

"You did, but not as fast as I would have liked. Nor did you see yourself when you passed out." He tipped his head. "You were so…delicate. So fragile."

She nearly laughed. "That doesn't sound like me."

"No, that is why I didn't like it. You were hurt, and there was nothing I could do about it."

His eyes bored through her, letting her see into the depths of him. Something she was certain he very rarely let anyone see.

"I do not like to be out of control."

She swallowed. She knew that about him. And about herself as well. Control was what held her life together. It had been predictable even in its villainous qualities. She had grown to expect them. Here, she was not in control. She had carved a small corner into his world and pried at every instance where she could grapple more power from him, but that was as much control as she could have with Graves. He was the apex predator.

A part of her shivered at the thought. She had never been with someone before where she was not the highest on the food chain. It made heat pool in her core, and she shifted her legs. Her head was still woozy from the alcohol. She had no idea how much she had consumed. Only that it was enough to loosen her tongue and her body.

The simple fact was: she wanted him.

Why *shouldn't* she have him?

Kierse pushed the fur blanket off of her lap as she came to her feet. Graves's eyes landed on her, carefully neutral.

"Going to bed?"

"Not yet." She took the glass out of his hand. There was a knuckle's worth left, and she tipped it back into her mouth like a shot.

His eyes tracked the bob of her throat as she swallowed the liquid courage. Heat flared as their gazes met once more, and he leaned back on the couch, spreading his arms wide, abandoning his book.

"I was going to drink that."

She set the glass down on the coffee table and grasped the bourbon bottle. She shook it back and forth, the dregs sloshing around in the bottom. "Just enough for one more."

He reached for it, but she grinned and tipped back the bottle, letting the last bit slosh into her mouth. He growled in the back of his throat. Something primal. Something uncharacteristic of Graves. Perhaps he was also a little drunk from good conversation with his mentor, from the booze, and from the ounce of relaxation in this maddening timeline.

"That's coming out of your expenses." He leaned back in his seat once more, watching her with those calculating gray eyes.

"I think I can afford it." She dropped the bottle back onto the table. "Though it's not what I want."

His answering gambit was to tip his head up and raise his eyebrows. He must have known what she wanted. Sensed it. How could he not? It had been circling between them since the night of the party.

"What is it that you want, Wren?" he responded with that edge of desire on the final syllable.

The echo of the conversation hung on that word. *Is she a wren? Are you?* She didn't know what it meant. But she'd done enough research now to know that holly and wrens were intertwined. One a symbol for the other. The end of winter. The beginning of spring. They belonged together.

Then by all rights, she was his.

She straddled his tall frame, settling herself onto his lap. Her hands came up around his neck. He was searing. Hot as fire, but not in the way the wish powder had burned through her. In the way she wanted *him* to burn through *her*. She could see in the quirk of his mouth and the storms in his eyes and the tilt of his head that he was intrigued.

"What are you doing?"

"What we should have done the night you kissed me."

Then she dropped her mouth onto his. His hot, perfect mouth that tasted like every deadly sin. His lips were decadent, soft and smooth, unlike the hard lines of his personality. He tasted like bourbon and cinnamon. A potent combination that made her head spin. She knew his magic didn't work on her, that she was immune to him, but for a moment there, she could also taste his magic on her tongue. She shivered at the contact, wanting nothing more than to be devoured whole.

He pulled back roughly, breaking the kiss with a disgruntled noise. "I can't give you what you need."

"Oh, I think you can," she said coyly.

"Deserve," he corrected.

She scoffed. "That word is meaningless."

His hand brushed a lock of her hair out of her face. "Little wren, I am a monster. A monster in a suit, but one with claws nonetheless."

"I don't care," she told him. "That's what I want."

"You don't want…"

"Don't tell me what I want. *I'll* tell you what I want. I want you." Her hand came to the tie on his suit, dragging him in closer to her. Their mouths were a hairsbreadth apart as she commanded, "Let the monster off its leash."

He groaned. He had been contained for so long—had held back nearly every bit of what made him *him*—that at her word, he erupted.

Their lips crashed back together, hungry and wanting. It was nothing like that kiss at the party and yet, somehow, *exactly* like it. Maybe he hadn't been pretending any more than she had. That night had been an awakening, and here they were, reaching for completion.

Graves's hands landed on her ass. That night at Imani's, he hadn't been able to keep his hands off of her ass at the party. And now he was getting his fill. He gripped her hard. Hard enough to bruise. And fuck, she liked it. She couldn't hold back the groan against his lips. Because it had been a long time since she'd felt like this. A long time since she'd been comfortable enough to let go of control and just exist in the moment. She never would have thought it would be with Graves, but fuck, he felt so good.

This was what she'd asked for, what she wanted. Sex. Plain and simple. None of those pesky emotions or complications. This was the easy part, and she wanted it all. All of him.

"Wren," he growled as his lips ran across her jaw.

"Yes," she gasped.

He pressed a kiss to the pulse at her neck, the very point that was beating furiously. It was where he'd first touched her when she thought he might be a vampire and want to drain her dry. She'd considered then that she just might let him. And now, she was putty in his hands. Willing, very willing to do whatever he requested.

When his tongue found her collarbone, his hands slid up and under her top. Those gloved hands weren't enough. She wanted to feel his *hands* on her, and yet the heat coming from him was hot enough to burn. Would she even survive his hands on her?

She rolled her hips against him with an urgency she could hardly suppress. She didn't *want* to suppress it. Not anymore.

"Fuck," he snarled.

He hoisted her into the air and crashed her back down onto the couch, putting him in the dominant position. Her eyes flared wide at the abrupt change. She should have been afraid with him over her like this, but when had he ever not been in control? Never. And even this sliver of release, the sensuous word *fuck* out of his lips, was a more powerful aphrodisiac than wish powder.

He thrust forward, and her eyes rolled into the back of her head at the hard length of him against the thin material of her pants. She arched backward, meeting his rhythm beat for beat. Her body tightened and went loose all at the same time. Her legs wrapped around his hips, and she just wanted him to shred her clothing. Tear it to pieces with his hands and own her.

"Graves," she gasped, his name a plea on her lips.

He broke her grip around his waist, and his face drop to the hem of her shirt. He slid the material out of the way and kissed along the edge of her pants. She squirmed as he tortured her with his lips and tongue on her bare skin. She would never have thought that this was the way Graves would torture her.

"Please." The word slipped out before she could stop it.

A flash of his pearly whites sent heat straight through her. Oh, he liked that. A little shameless begging. It certainly wasn't something she had ever done, but if he didn't get inside her soon she was certainly not above it.

He gripped her shirt and pulled it up and over her head. Then his mouth buried into her breasts. She'd gone without a bra and was thanking everything in the universe that she didn't have another article of clothing between them. He tugged a nipple into his mouth, rolling the bead between his teeth and massaging it with his tongue. She writhed beneath him, reaching for the strands of his midnight-blue hair. Wanting him to keep going and to maybe go a little lower and all of it at once. When he nipped at the nipple, pain flickered through her, hot and needy. He rolled his tongue over the other nipple, taking his time with it as he had the first one. And no amount of arcing or grasping at him or trying to bring him closer would stop him from the methodical seduction of her body.

Her poor scrap of underwear never stood a chance.

"I can't…" she muttered incoherently.

He smirked. "Oh?"

A finger slid up the seam of her pants, and she nearly exploded all at once. She saw a flash of light. A burst of wings. The beginning of spring. Her world narrowed to that finger as it traveled over her clit, circled once, and then disappeared.

Her moan was met with a satisfied chuckle. Then he delved lower, lower, lower. His kisses lingered over her stomach and circled around her belly button. Then he grabbed her legs, hauling them up around his shoulders. She didn't even have a moment to tense before he buried his head between her legs. Even with her damn pants between them, she felt her body surrender to his desire.

"You smell so good," he grunted. "Let's find out what you taste like."

She nodded. Yes, fucking finally.

He slipped her pants and underwear over her hips, tossing them backward over his shoulder. Then in one swift motion, he returned to her awaiting body.

"What a pretty pussy," he said, his breath hot on her.

"Graves," she said, shifting and trying to get him closer.

His tongue darted out, slipping against the sensitive bud. "Is this what you want?"

"Fuck," she gasped.

"Where are your manners?" he teased.

She was going to kill him.

"Please," she whispered.

"You can do better than that, Wren."

"Graves," she said around a strangled moan. "Fuck me with your mouth, your lips, your tongue. I need you…" His nose brushed against her clit, and she choked. "Fuck me or I'll die."

"Well, we can't have that."

Then, he bent down and brought his lips to her pussy. At the first brush of his tongue all the way up the seam to the awaiting bundle of nerves, she thought she was going to combust. If she had been on fire at the party, it didn't hold a candle to this moment.

She was already holding on to a precipice, ready to jump over the edge. So when he spread her legs wider for his access and swirled his tongue around her clit, her entire body was shaking with barely contained control. He licked up her center, tasting her heat and desire. When his mouth clamped over her core, she saw stars.

"God yes," she groaned.

Her hands fisted in that blue-black hair, feeling the silken threads as he drove her on. Begging had been fucking worth it, because the man *knew* what to do with his tongue. She only regretted that he hadn't removed those damn gloves. Because she desperately wanted to know what his fingers felt like.

"Gloves," she muttered incoherently.

But he didn't even break to respond to her. As if to prove that he didn't need his hands to bring her to orgasm. And fuck, he was right. His tongue was a relentless pressure against her clit, hitting her in the exact place to drive her completely and inextricably over the edge. She held his head down, pulsing against his lips, and cried out to the room beyond. She didn't care who else heard. It didn't matter in that moment.

Her body dropped back limp against the couch. She met his swirling gray eyes as he lifted himself from between her legs. She could see the shape of his cock, hard and long, straining against his suit pants. His eyes were hungry, and she was desperate to give him his fill.

"I'm not finished with you."

"Thank fuck."

He hefted her up and guided her toward the bookshelves. The holly vines tangled down the expanse, red berries visible in the thorny branches. Books lined the shelves for what felt like miles. He turned her and slammed her back into the shelf. Thorns dug into her back, and berries crushed under her spine. The entire shelf shuddered behind her.

She reached for him, dragging their lips together and getting a taste of her own arousal on his tongue. Fucking hell, it was hot.

She fumbled for his suit pants, unwilling to break the kiss but needing him in fewer clothes. She slid the belt loose, snapped the button on his pants, and then dragged the zipper low. When they hung loose on his hips, she slipped her hand in and brushed her fingers against his cock.

A guttural noise left his lips as she wrapped her hand around him. But fuck, she could barely close her fingers around him. She broke away long enough to get a look at the full rigid length. Her body trembled with need at the sight. As she stroked him, her eyes widened with appreciation.

"Like the view?" he asked.

She licked her lips and met his gaze. "I'd like it better inside of me."

His answer was to grasp her thighs and wrap them around his legs. She reached overhead and wound the vines around her wrists, clutching them firmly for support. They bit into her skin, and she couldn't even care, because with one easy stroke Graves buried himself deep inside of her.

Her head dropped back, and she tightened her grip on the vines. She had been thinking about this since they danced that first time, and he did *not* disappoint. He stretched her to fullness, her body enveloping his cock. He held her up like she weighed nothing with his hands on her ass. And she didn't care, didn't think of the magic that likely allowed it or any of the other things that could complicate this. Just him, all of him. Then he started to move. An easy slide out and a hard thrust back in. She had no words, no pleas left on her tongue, just satisfaction in every movement. And she wondered if he was no beast or monster at all. But a god. A fucking god.

He slammed her against the bookshelf as he did exactly what she wanted—he let loose. The tightly controlled Graves was gone. The man, the beast, the god was here. And he showed no mercy.

His hard thrusts were as relentless as the beating sun. All she could do and all she wanted to do was take it as the sun shone on her in all its glory. She might get burned, but it was worth it.

She'd been with other lovers. But nothing, not a single other person could compare to him. Not even if she managed another lifetime of lovers.

Her heart galloped ahead of her as her climax rose deep and intense within her. "I'm so close."

"With me," he commanded, and she could do nothing else.

It wasn't magic that held her. It was him. A command that needed no magic to have power. She held on and on as he drove into her. Then she could hold on no longer. She opened her mouth to tell him, but all that came out was a cry as she released around his cock.

He followed immediately, roaring as he emptied deep inside of her. His hands tightened on her ass, and she could feel every ridge and pulse and flex inside of her body. She shook as he pumped into her a few more times, hitting her at all-new heights, before he finally finished.

Her own cries turned to whimpers and groans as she came down from her high. She released her hands from their bruised and aching grasp on the vines and dropped them onto his shoulders. Her head fell forward against his chest. Their heartbeats united as their chests heaved from the exertion. He slowly slid out of her and dropped her gently to her feet. She stumbled, her legs turning to jelly, and he kept a steadying arm around her waist.

"I..." she whispered, looking up at him with bedroom eyes.

His answering kiss stole her breath from her lungs. As if he, too, needed one more kiss after all of that. When they broke apart, she just stared up at him, perplexed.

What had he done to her? Had he ruined her for all other sex?

Only a glimmer in the back of her mind said she didn't care.

She didn't care one bit.

Chapter Thirty-Four

Kingston smiled at her as cheery and bright-eyed as ever when she came downstairs for breakfast the next morning. Was that a glimmer in his eye? Did he know what had happened?

Isolde just hummed to herself over the griddle. Graves was nowhere to be seen.

Kierse had rarely woken up in the same house as the person she'd had sex with the night before, and she certainly hadn't had breakfast with them. But here she was…still in Graves's house. Waiting and wondering if he was going to be changed by what had occurred.

"Have a good time last night?" Kingston asked.

Kierse startled as she took a seat across from him at the breakfast bar. Did he know about her and Graves's hookup? She reached for the pancakes and bacon on the bar to keep her hands busy.

"Uh, yes."

"Excellent. Graves has always been unconventional, but he gets the job done."

Kierse coughed around her first bite of pancake. "He does."

"Such a power play, to not inform you of the start of your training," he said with a guffaw. "Isolde, darling, more coffee, hmm?"

Isolde bustled over. Her cheeks were rosy and flushed as she came up to Kingston's side. "Of course, Master Kingston. Enjoying your breakfast?"

"Best food this side of the pond, my dear."

She blushed a deeper red and dipped her chin as she darted away.

"You should concentrate on how to replenish your powers once you're depleted," Kingston said with a wink. "Once you figure that out, you'll be a lot safer."

"How did you figure it out?"

He took another sip of coffee and considered. "My father was an artist. He was a gentleman first, of course. In the peerage and all that."

Kierse raised an eyebrow. "Peerage?"

"Ah, he was an earl of some importance during the Hundred Years' War."

He noticed her blank look. "It was a very important war between Britain and France that began in the fourteenth century."

Kierse should not have been taking a sip of her juice at the time he said it. She sputtered, the juice running down her chin. She swiped at it with a napkin. "How old *are* you?"

Kingston just laughed. "*Old.*"

Kierse's eyes widened.

"Back to the subject matter at hand—my father was an earl, but his true passion lay in the arts. An uncommon thing at the time, but he painted and sculpted and set about making a legacy that was more than just war. I was part of that legacy. I was raised to take his place, which meant I grew up at his side while he painted and at his side while he rode and at his side while he went to war." Kingston took another drink from his coffee. "Art was always what rejuvenated me. It is not surprising that it also helps my magic."

"You speak so freely about your powers."

"Unlike Graves, you mean? I had a much different upbringing. I have no shame from my abilities. My conscience is clear." He tapped his head. "Much of what we do is mental. And while I saw many warlocks hanged and witches burned in my day, they never came to my door. Graves was not so lucky."

Kingston turned surprisingly quiet after that. Contemplative.

Kierse finished her breakfast. Thinking about what Kingston said brought her mind back to Graves. She had seen terrors in her time, and she had been the subject of them. She knew that shame and how it wrecked a person.

Graves appeared in the kitchen a moment later, freshly showered, in a crisp black suit and black gloves. "Morning."

Kierse looked up from her plate. Her eyes found Graves, and he met her stare. She thought that he'd look away or make it awkward. But…he didn't. He just tipped his head at her, a small quirk of his lips, same as always. She sighed slightly in relief. She was glad that things could go on as they had been. Wasn't she?

Kingston finished his plate and stood to clasp Graves's hand. "Morning, indeed. Are we all set to go?"

"Yes," Graves said. "We have reservations."

Kierse pushed her plate away from her. "Do I have to go to the museum?"

"Of course," Kingston boomed. "I have so much to teach you."

"Was he regaling you with British history?"

Kierse nodded. "He was."

"He tends to do that," Graves said, a look of exasperation on his face.

"I still relish when the sun never set on the British Empire," Kingston said.

Graves pulled a disgusted face. Like he couldn't believe Kingston would admit that out loud. Kierse was starting to realize why he didn't invite his old mentor around more often.

Kierse frowned. "I don't know as much history as you two, but wasn't the British Empire actually terrible?"

Kingston looked at her askance. "Depends on who you ask."

Graves narrowed his eyes at Kingston. "Yes, like if you ask all the colonized countries, they would agree that it was terrible."

"So progressive," Kingston grumbled.

"Kingston," Graves said with an irritated scowl. "You cannot still believe that is true."

"The British have done much good in the world," he said, all bluster. "We were good to *you*."

Graves's face went sharp at all edges. If it had been Kierse he was looking at that way, she would have known to run the other direction, but Kingston seemed unaffected. "I would hardly say '*good*' was the correct word."

"If you say so," Kingston said, dismissing the conversation.

Graves and Kierse exchanged a look, reading each other in the span of a second.

"Let's go before he starts up again," Graves said with a tip of his head.

Kierse followed Graves and Kingston to the elevator. George was idling with the limo, and Kingston swept inside. Graves stepped up to her before she could follow him into the car. "Try not to filch the entire museum."

She scoffed. "As if I'd let you see what treasures I nicked."

And was pleased to see his amusement.

The drive to the Met was quick in Graves's limo. Kingston prattled on the whole time, and Kierse watched Graves evade Kingston as deftly as he did her. Then George parked out front and opened the door for them.

Kierse had stood outside of the Met hundreds of times, staring up at Coraline LeMort's all-seeing statue. She'd eaten from her favorite bakery right around the corner. She had stolen from wealthy patrons off these steps.

But never had she imagined that she'd be allowed in through the front door.

The museum used to permit everyone within its walls. But after monsters appeared, several prized paintings had been stolen during the looting, so they'd closed their doors to the public. Admittance was by reservation only, and the price for entry had become steep. Nearly impossible for most people. Another elite club that she never thought she'd have access to.

Entering through the high white columns in her dress and heels made her feel like a fraud. The only thing from her old life was the wren at her neck. Did they know they were letting a thief on their grounds? But Graves and Kingston held their own esteem, and no one even looked at her as hands were shaken and pleasantries made.

Graves seemed to have no taste for the museum itself, but Kingston came alive inside it. This was his area of expertise, after all. Kierse's eyes bounced along the white marble walls and the intricate entrance that gave way to galleries upon galleries of artwork.

"Do you think it's wrong that they hide all this art from the rest of the population?" she mused aloud.

Graves tilted his head, his gray eyes considering her, though he was clearly surprised by her question. "Art has always been collected, catalogued, and coveted by the wealthy. It is no surprise they do so here."

"Everything is like that with the wealthy."

"True," he conceded, coming to her side as they walked. She could almost brush his arm. Her stomach flipped at the brief contact. "They closed the museum, thinking they were protecting the art, but all they did was close it off. Art flourishes in the dark times, in the pain and heartbreak. I feel many of those not admitted would understand these paintings in a way that the wealthy never can."

"Yes," she breathed. "If you've always had a full belly, how can you understand hunger?"

"Precisely."

She leaned in closer to him. "I feel as if we're wasting this day with Kingston. Shouldn't we be doing reconnaissance?"

His eyes met hers, darting to her lips only briefly. She could feel his warmth intensify. "Sometimes there's information to be found when you're not looking for it," he said mysteriously.

She believed him, but the winter solstice was a ticking bomb in the back of her mind. Their time was running thin.

"Now, now," Kingston said, wagging a finger at them. "None of that. I can feel the heat from over here."

Graves pulled back, taking his warmth with him. His face turned perfectly neutral. "I have no idea what you mean."

Kingston shook his head at them both, and she blushed. "Come along. I want to see the new exhibit first. It's Egyptian."

"Haven't you been to Egypt?" Graves asked as they fell into step.

"Naturally."

Kierse listened to their easy banter as they moseyed through the museum. After only an hour, she wondered why she had ever wanted to be in this place so badly. Of course, the answer was because it was forbidden. And forbidden things tended to be the things that she liked best.

But otherwise, it was insanely *boring*. Kingston must have been getting something from all this aimless wandering, but all Kierse got was sore feet. Why had she sprung for heels when she had perfectly good sneakers?

Kierse forced down a yawn as they left the Egyptian wing and headed into an exhibit filled with portraits. She needed the conversation to turn or she'd never make it.

"I know that look in your eye," Graves said.

She stuffed her hands into the pockets of her jacket. "What look in my eye?"

He raised an eyebrow. "You're going to rob us all blind."

"Who says I haven't already?"

Kingston laughed. "We surely would have noticed."

"Where is your pocket watch?"

Kingston reached into his jacket to take it out and show her. But then he froze. It wasn't there. "By god, I must have misplaced it."

Graves held his hand out to Kierse. "I did tell you not to steal anything."

"I thought you meant from the museum," she said with a dainty laugh as she slapped the watch into his hand.

She didn't mention the bills she'd taken out of Kingston's pocket earlier. He wouldn't miss them. Not that she had any use for British pounds with the current royal's face on the front. She quickly changed the subject so he didn't start to wonder what other mischief she had gotten into. "How did you and Graves meet?"

Graves sighed, rolling his eyes. "Oh, this story."

But Kingston beamed. "It's a good one."

"If you say so."

"And I do!" Kingston cheered. He directed them past the portraits and into some seriously strange room of abstract paintings. Kierse didn't understand how a circle and a line on a canvas was art. "Graves had recently arrived in London after getting into a spot of trouble."

"What sort of trouble?"

"The sort that doesn't need explaining," Graves said, low and unapologetic.

Kingston tipped his hat at him. "It doesn't matter, but it was not pleasant. He arrived with nothing but the clothes on his back and a knife wound that split his belly. It was shallow but long. Here to here," Kingston said, motioning to one side of his stomach and then the other. "People died from worse all the time, especially then."

Kierse wondered *when* exactly this had all taken place. If Kingston was from the 1300s and Graves had known Imani a hundred and fifty years ago, there was a lot of time in between. But she didn't push. Graves didn't like to talk about his past any more than she did. She could see he was already uncomfortable with this line of conversation.

"I found Graves near dead outside of an inn. He was pleading with the innkeeper for dinner while he all but bled out on the steps. I made to intervene, but then he used his powers. All magic has a sense or a taste or a feeling attached to it. You can get better at masking it, but for the trained individual, it never fully goes away."

"And you helped him?" she asked. Though she wanted to ask what Graves's power felt and tasted like. Every time she was with him, she just felt heat.

"No," Graves said curtly, stuffing his gloved hands into his pockets. "He didn't."

"Well, of course not," Kingston said as if it were the most natural thing in the world. "I thought he was a street urchin near death."

"You left him to die?"

Kingston snorted. "Does he look dead?"

"He left me to the innkeeper," Graves said.

"And bless her poor soul, she felt sorry for you. Nursed you back to health and tried to marry you off to her daughter."

"That was…an unfortunate side effect. Thank you for reminding me of that, Kingston."

"Anytime. Jolly good." Kingston laughed. "Well, I didn't see all of that. But when I came back to the inn a few months later, Graves was all but running the place. He'd even come into some money and was in negotiations to buy out the tavern next door."

"Yes, yes, we all love a feel-good story," Graves said grimly.

"He made something of himself, and I decided then to offer him an apprenticeship. Bastard didn't think he needed it."

Graves shrugged one shoulder. A confident smirk graced his features. "I didn't."

Kingston grinned at Kierse. "He needed it."

Kierse couldn't help but snicker as she filched the watch back out of Kingston's pocket.

Chapter Thirty-Five

They spent hours meandering the halls and hardly encountered anyone else. At one point, Kierse gave up and took her shoes off, walking barefoot across the polished floors. It wasn't professional, but she just didn't care. As soon as Kingston left, they had to start running reconnaissance on King Louis and deal with Walter's wards, and she couldn't have blisters on her feet.

"One more gallery," Kingston encouraged.

"I can't do it. I'm going to go sit on the steps. You keep on."

"Kingston needs to finish up soon," Graves told him with a pointed look. He also sounded almost eager to leave. She raised an eyebrow. Apparently, he didn't love long walks through museums, either.

Kingston sighed. "All right. This will be the end. I'll look through one more and then we can go."

Kierse felt such relief even as she put her horrid shoes back on her feet and stepped out into the brisk winter chill.

"So you found it as boring as I did?" she asked Graves.

"Or I found exactly what I was looking for," he said with a knowing smirk.

She wanted to ask what *that* meant, but he just turned his gaze from her.

She hugged her jacket tighter around her as they headed down the Met steps and stopped before Coraline LeMort's statue.

Graves came to her side, his arm brushing against hers. She shivered but not from the cold. His gaze slipped to hers, and without a word, he removed his own overcoat and wrapped it around her shoulders.

"Better?"

She met his usually mercurial eyes and found only warmth there. Maybe last night *had* changed things. But the way her stomach was flipping said she wasn't sure that she minded.

"Did you know her?" Kierse asked, gesturing to the statue of the revolutionary whose death started the Monster War.

"I heard her speak once," he told her.

"What was she like?"

Graves shrugged. "Too young to understand she was doing nothing but putting a target on her back."

Kierse frowned at that assessment. "Everyone talks about her like she was going to change the world."

"She did, but not for the better."

Well, that was the damn truth. "If she hadn't died, would the world be where it is now?"

"I guess we'll never know." Graves gestured to his phone. "I have to take this."

She waved him off, tugging his jacket tighter around her body and breathing in his purely masculine scent as she leaned back against the base of Coraline's statue. There was no use wondering about the past. They couldn't change it anyway. Only move forward to make sure it didn't happen again.

Right now, her thoughts were trapped by the warlock at her back. The one who had surprisingly given her his coat. She tried to keep the smile from tugging at her lips, but she didn't quite succeed. She just turned her body to face the sun, closing her eyes and soaking up the last of the dying rays.

"Kierse McKenna?" said a voice she didn't recognize.

She opened her eyes and found a frail older white gentleman wearing a kippah standing before her. She squinted as she tried to place him. "Do I know you?"

He nodded. "I work at the bakery around the corner. You used to come in regularly."

"Oh, yes." Confusion and slight panic shot through her. Why was he here? How did he know she'd be here? "Can I help you?"

"This is for you," he said. She saw his hands were shaking with fear as he passed her a small, white paper bag.

She took it in her hands before she could think better of it. "What is it?"

"Your favorite. He…he said it was your favorite," the man said and then hastened away.

Kierse frowned deeply in confusion. Her favorite? Her favorite *what*?

She opened the bag and found an entire loaf of cinnamon babka. Her mouth watered at the same second she recoiled. She had a feeling she knew exactly who would send her babka from her favorite bakery.

"What's that?" Graves asked, returning from his phone call.

"A man just delivered this to me," she told him.

Graves immediately scanned the crowd. "What man? How did he know you'd be here?"

"I'm not sure."

Graves frowned at that, his gray eyes going dark and stormy. "Point him out to me. We need to question him."

"I knew him. He works at a bakery I used to frequent all the time." She showed him the loaf of sweet bread. "It's babka."

"Doesn't matter. That means you had a measure of trust. We need to know who did this. Throw it out. You don't know who sent it."

"Actually…I think I do." Kierse swallowed. "Lorcan sent it."

Graves went still as night and dark as shadows. His jaw set tight, eyes hard and uncompromising. He was silent for a tense second before saying anything. "How do you know?"

"Well, I told him this was my favorite food."

Graves clenched his hands into fists. He looked ready to snatch the babka from her and toss it himself. "It seems he has an…interest in you."

"Yes. It seems that way."

"I don't like it," he said, meeting her eyes.

"That's probably why he did it," she said.

He straightened, scanning the area. "I'm sure it is."

And yet, he still looked furious.

No, not just fury. He looked *jealous*.

But that couldn't be possible. Not Graves. She had no idea why he would even feel that way. Was this part of his feud with Lorcan? Or was this about her? Was this about last night?

Kingston traipsed down the steps to meet them at the base of the statue. "Well, well, that was invigorating." Then he seemed to sense tension between them. "What's going on?"

"Lorcan sent Kierse a present," Graves bit out.

Kingston sighed. "Well, he does like to addle you. You know how he is. It's like the wildflowers he used to send."

Graves glared at his mentor for the suggestion but then slowly released the coils of tension in his shoulders. His face returned to its neutral blankness. No anger, no displeasure, no…jealousy. He'd been angry…angry at the thought of Lorcan giving this to her? Or Lorcan putting his own power on display?

Kierse didn't know. But it certainly felt like both.

"Let's just go," Graves said, striding toward the limo.

Kierse followed in his wake, considering Graves's masked fury. Lorcan had done this to get to him. To get to her. She didn't like being caught in his little game. She was supposed to be the player, not the other way around.

When they passed a trash can on the way back to his limo, she dumped the babka inside. She didn't want to think at all about where that left her loyalties. Or why her stomach flipped when Graves looked back at her with approval.

She slid into the seat beside him in the limo, and he leaned in close until his mouth was nearly against her ear. Her heart leaped at the nearness. Memories from last night flooded her mind. "You didn't tell me you like babka."

She blinked. "You didn't ask."

He nodded. "Well, now I know."

He pulled away as Kingston dropped into the backseat beside them and said cheerfully, "Time to go, Georgie-boy!"

They made it back to the brownstone later that evening. Kingston stretched, hemming and hawing about getting the portal just right.

"Maybe I should do it tomorrow," Kingston said. "Just to be sure."

"You're getting cautious in your old age," Graves said with an arched eyebrow.

Kingston's nostrils flared. "I can do it just fine. No need to be belligerent."

"Of course," Graves said, but his glance cut to Kierse, and she stifled a smile.

Clearly, he was ready for Kingston to be gone. Urging him along in his own way.

"I won't wait another year," he promised Graves. He held out his hand, and they shook.

"I'll believe it when I see it," Graves replied.

Kingston tipped his hat at Kierse. "Good luck with your training."

"Thank you," she said.

Then he sketched a doorway of his own making. One second, he was on the sidewalk outside of Graves's house, and the next, she could see that he was on a different continent. The doorway winked back out of existence behind him.

"That must be the most useful ability ever," she breathed.

Graves shrugged. "It makes things too convenient."

"*Too* convenient?"

"All magic comes with a price. Every power is as much weakness as strength. I have become immune to how humans interact. You will become immune to the dangers of magic. Kingston is immune to consequences."

"You were certainly ready for him to go," she said.

"I usually am," he said with a shrug at the empty space where Kingston had been standing. "I had a thought about Lorcan."

"That I should stay away from him?"

"Maybe we can use his interest in you to see what he knows about you, the mission, your friends."

Her smile turned lethal. "I like how your mind works."

"The feeling is mutual," he admitted.

High praise from her reticent warlock.

"But we'll have to discuss it at a later time. Emmaline called while we were at the museum. She found something interesting in your blood."

Her heart soared. "Really?"

"Yes. And the last thing I wanted was for Kingston to look too closely at you."

She bristled. "What does that mean?"

"He has a history of killing things that he doesn't understand and asking questions later."

"Oh," she whispered.

"Now that he's out of the way, we're leaving."

Chapter Thirty-Six

Kierse followed Graves out of the house. The streets were empty as they navigated down 75th Street toward Amsterdam. Instead of fear, excitement pricked her. This was her favorite time of day.

"We should take witching-hour strolls more often." She stuffed her hands into the pockets of his jacket, glad that she hadn't given it back to him.

He quirked an eyebrow. "Witching hour? At least I know you're reading the assigned books."

"They're good," she admitted. "I love the stories in them."

"What story are you reading right now?"

She considered what she'd last read. "The gods, the Tuatha Dé Danann."

A smile cracked his features. "It's pronounced Tew-ha day dahn-en."

"Oh. Well, have you ever tried to pronounce Irish words out loud? There are a lot of vowels."

"Gaelic was my second language," he said smugly.

"Of course it was," she said with a pointed eye roll. "Anyway, I like The Morrigan."

He directed her into an underground parking garage. "I should have known."

"What woman in a modern world wouldn't want to have the amount of power The Morrigan had? She was a ruler, a goddess of war, and foretold the future. Granted, it was mostly doom, but still."

"Indeed." They took the stairs.

"Plus, she's depicted as three sisters. I kind of like the idea that one person can also be a trio. Like Gen, Ethan, and I are stronger together."

"That's an astute observation. Three is sacred to the Irish—life, death, and rebirth."

"All the better."

Two levels down, he patted a slick black car. "Here we are."

"Why do you have a car in a parking garage when you have your *own* underground garage?"

"For emergencies."

She didn't even question it. Why bother? It was Graves.

He revved the engine, and they were off, zipping out of the garage and through the empty NYC streets. Graves handled himself behind the wheel with the confidence that he did everything else in life.

"Is that all that you got out of the last book?" Graves asked once they were heading toward Queens. "There was a lot more than the gods in there."

"I read about the Druids."

Graves's fingers flexed on the steering wheel. "Oh yeah?"

"They have magic, too."

"They are the warlocks of their people," he said with a shrug.

"But like actual *priests*," she said. "And there are some stories of them being healers and prophets."

"Sure," he said easily. "Who told those stories?"

"I don't know. You're the one who assigned me the book."

"Well, as with most things," he said gravely, "history is told by the victors."

She knew that to be true. They were still writing the history of the Monster War, and already some people forgot how bad it had gotten. She couldn't imagine what it would say in books thousands of years from now.

"The rest of the book was pretty dense. *Lots* of history. Names and dates and stuff really go over my head."

"Nothing jumped out at you?"

"Well," she said softly, "I was interested in the festival days."

He snorted. "Why does this not surprise me?"

"I mean, it sounded like a good time," she said with a smirk. "Sounds a lot like Imani's parties."

"Indeed." Graves's eyes flicked to hers. Heat traveled through her. She'd had one taste. That should have satisfied her. And yet, she couldn't help but admit that she wanted more.

She cleared her throat and glanced away. "But otherwise it was a lot of this deity here and that deity there. Oh, and fairies. Can't forget the fairies."

"*Sídhe*," Graves corrected again. "Or just Fae."

"And four magical artifacts. A sword of something, a cauldron, the Spear of Lug…"

"Lugh," Graves corrected, looking at her sideways. "Like the name Hugh."

"Right, okay. Definitely was pronouncing that wrong." She squinted, trying to remember the last.

"The Stone of Fal," Graves supplied. "The four treasures of the Tuatha Dé Danann."

"That," Kierse said. Then she froze. "Wait, a spear." She pointed at Graves. "You said all this shit is real."

"I did."

"Okay," she whispered, sobering. "So, are the magical objects, fairies—sorry, *sídhe*—and gods real, too?"

"All the tales come from somewhere."

Which meant yes.

She ruminated on that as they breezed through Queens and to the back entrance of The Covenant. The building was dark. It was way past its hours of operation. But Graves had said they had to make their window.

Graves cocked his head to the side, and they entered The Covenant. He directed her down a hallway until they reached a lab. Dr. Mafi was seated at a computer, typing furiously. Tonight, she wore a mustard-yellow hijab, but it looked hastily thrown up rather than perfectly put together like last time. Bags hung heavy under her eyes, and her brown skin was sallow as if she had been working sunup to sundown. She didn't even notice them enter.

"Emmaline," Graves said.

Dr. Mafi startled. She closed out of whatever she was working on. "Graves, you made it."

"We did," Graves said.

She looked Kierse up and down. "Nice jacket."

Kierse met her steely gaze with one of her own. "Hello, Dr. Mafi."

"I see you don't take advice well."

Graves cleared his throat. "Emmaline, you were vague on the phone." His eyes shot momentarily to Kierse, and she saw something like concern flicker through their depths before they returned to Mafi. "You need another sample?"

Dr. Mafi stood, brushing imaginary lint from her clothes. "Yes. Come sit over here, Kierse."

Kierse looked to Graves, and he nodded. Mafi seemed…rattled. As if something had scared her. Kierse did as she was told, and Mafi quickly went to work hooking her up and drawing more blood from her arm.

"What's going on, Emmaline?" Graves asked. He crossed his arms, his face stern. "I can read you. Something is off."

"*Don't* read me," she bit out.

"It's all over your face."

Dr. Mafi settled at that. "Yes. I suppose it is. I'm just…" She looked down at Kierse. "I'm not sure what to make of the samples she gave me. I have some answers, but I need more time to analyze what is going on. I've never seen it before."

"Explain," Graves commanded.

She ground her teeth together. "Well, she's not a warlock."

Kierse nearly jumped out of her seat. Her eyes went wide, and her jaw dropped. "What? But I have magic!"

Graves didn't look surprised. Or at least it didn't show on his face.

"I have magic, and I'm not a warlock," Dr. Mafi said.

"So I'm a witch?" Kierse asked, sitting back in the chair in defeat.

"No." Dr. Mafi hurried to her desk and retrieved a piece of paper. She passed it to Graves and pointed at something on it. "That is warlock DNA sequencing. The few that have been mapped. That is the gene that has been isolated that is attributed to your abilities. There are a few other protein variations. A DNA and RNA combination difference, but *this* is what it should look like. You don't have to sequence for everything else if you find this."

"Okay," Graves said.

Dr. Mafi settled another piece of paper onto the first. "This is what a human genome looks like." Then another paper. "And this is what hers looks like."

Graves frowned, his eyes zipping across the page. "So, she's not human, either."

Emmaline shrugged. "No. Which we already guessed, but she's not any of the other known monsters I've mapped." She looked to Kierse apologetically. "Sorry. I'm not sure *what* she is."

"I don't understand," Kierse said.

"You look pale. Hold on." Dr. Mafi reached into a nearby refrigerator and brought her a juice box. "Drink this."

Kierse dutifully put it to her lips, sucking down the grape juice.

"What did you learn from the other samples?" Graves asked.

"Not much," she admitted. "For almost all metrics, she looks human. I mean, look at her. She looks human."

"So do you," Graves pointed out. "So do I."

"Right. Yeah. I mean…besides her DNA, nothing really looked different except one other metric." Dr. Mafi retrieved one last piece of paper. "It probably won't make sense. It doesn't make sense to me."

Graves looked at the paper. Kierse craned her neck, hoping to catch a glimpse of it. Dr. Mafi was showing all of this to Graves and not to her, after being all cryptic about her privacy. She must have been really flustered.

"What am I looking at?"

"Elevated white blood cell counts," Dr. Mafi said, pointing at a number.

"So, she's fighting off an infection?"

"I'm not sick," Kierse told them.

"No, you're not," Dr. Mafi agreed. "In fact, you're one of the most fit people I have ever seen in my lab. Have you ever been sick?"

She nodded. "I got the flu once. Right after the collapse."

"Were you tested positive for influenza? Do you know the strain?"

"Well, no. I was young. No one could afford to go to the doctor, but I had all the symptoms. I was working with my mentor on a big job. It was a few days away, and I couldn't back out. So I did it anyway, and then, I don't know, I was in bed for like three weeks."

"But what did the flu look like?"

Kierse shrugged. "The flu. I had an outrageously high fever. So high that I was seeing things, hallucinating. Then I blacked out in the middle of a recon mission. Once I finished the job, I was so weak. Weaker than I'd ever been. As weak as… Wait."

Something like realization flickered onto his face. "As weak as you were after the powder?"

She nodded. The whole thing was dawning on her. "Yeah. Just like that, actually."

He turned to face Dr. Mafi. "You have an explanation?"

"Her body eats magic," Dr. Mafi said.

"Excuse me?" Kierse blurted.

"*Eats* magic?" Graves asked in disbelief. She'd never seen him look so confused. "Explain what you mean by that."

"This is a supernatural facility. It's common practice to use magic to make things easier or to make them faster. I was using some of those techniques on the blood while I was testing it, and it gobbled the magic right up. The white blood cell count is higher because it's breaking it down in some way. I didn't have enough blood. I'm still figuring it out."

"I don't eat magic," Kierse muttered. "Wouldn't I know if I was doing that?"

"Her body's not eating it," Graves said slowly. He tapped a gloved finger to his lips. Then, when he looked back up at her, a light was in his eyes. He knew. He'd figured it out. "It's absorption."

"*Absorption.* You've heard of this before?" Dr. Mafi asked in awe.

"I've heard of someone who had this ability. The magic doesn't go up against a barrier. It absorbs into the body."

Dr. Mafi tapped her fingers together. "Huh. Yeah. Yes, okay, that's a great thought, Graves." She immediately went back to her computer and began typing away. "I'll analyze what we have here and get back to you if I see anything else."

Then she strode back over and unhooked Kierse. She removed the bag of blood and transferred it to a cooler.

"Have you told anyone else about this?" Graves asked immediately, his voice suspicious.

Dr. Mafi looked affronted. "No. Of course not."

Graves glowered at her, and she stared resolutely back. Kierse didn't know if she believed her. It was a big hospital. Anyone could have seen what Dr. Mafi was doing. Not that she had any idea what it would be if she could absorb magic. But if she was valuable enough for her immunity, she couldn't imagine what it would mean if she could draw other people's magic into her body.

"Emmaline," he said, his voice on the verge of threatening. "No one can know about her."

"Patient confidentiality, Graves," she reminded him.

Graves's eyes cast back to Kierse with something like worry in them. No, it was *definitely* worry. She was starting to recognize the stoic looks he cast her way. And he didn't like that she was something unexplained. More importantly, he didn't like that Dr. Mafi knew about it, either.

"She's not going to tell anyone," Kierse told him. She looked to Dr. Mafi. "Right?"

Dr. Mafi glanced between them in surprise. As if Kierse and Graves were windows and she was peering through to whatever feelings were growing beneath. But all she said was, "Right."

"Keep it that way," Graves said. "I'll call in a few days, and I expect an update."

She nodded, her hands shaking slightly. "I'll work on it. Thanks for coming in."

Graves tipped his head at her, tucking the papers under his arm, and gestured for Kierse to precede him out.

"I can't believe this," Kierse said, her voice trembling. "What does this mean for me?"

"Nothing changes," he said at once. He put a steadying hand on her back, and she leaned into it. "You're not a warlock, but you have magic. Magic has laws and rules. You would still be ruled by them, and we'll train you like you are."

"Does this mean I'm something new?" she asked softly.

He was silent a moment before saying, "Or something very old."

Chapter Thirty-Seven

Graves stayed on the phone while Kierse stepped in the house ahead of him. Her head spun. She was something new or old or different, but she wasn't a human and she wasn't a warlock. Her heart sank a little. She didn't realize she had been putting so much stock in that idea until she found out the truth. Being a warlock meant that Graves could train her magic, which would help her escape this job alive.

He'd been shaken when she was hurt at Imani's. Would he still send her in without magic training? She didn't know how she was going to make it out otherwise.

She needed to get herself under control. Whatever she was hadn't mattered before, and it hadn't mattered all those years on the streets. She'd survive this like she had everything else. And if she didn't, at least Gen and Ethan would be set up for life.

She pushed her shoulders back and tipped her chin up. They still had a spear to steal. Her plans didn't stop rolling forward just because they had taken two steps backward.

"Let's go into the library," Graves said, sneaking up behind her.

She jumped. "How do you do that?"

"Do what?" he asked. His eyes twinkled and were full of humor. One day, she would figure him out.

She slunk into the Holly Library, settling into her favorite seat.

"Drink?"

"No thanks."

Graves poured himself a glass of bourbon and then came to sit across from her. "Ask me your questions."

She skipped the ones that would make her sound weak. She needed facts, not reassurances. "What is absorption exactly? I mean, I know what it means to absorb something, but I don't understand how it works."

"Well, what we have been assuming thus far is that when you were bypassing my wards, you were immune to their touch. So the magic couldn't touch you or was even repelled by you. A passive ability that you couldn't control," he explained. "With absorption, instead of repelling the magic, you would take it into your body. Every time you stepped over my ward threshold, the magic to keep you out would be brought in through the skin. It's unclear at this point if you store the magic and can use it later. You've never mentioned any other abilities that would suggest that."

"I don't have any other abilities." She pursed her lips and then sat up straighter. "Wait…"

He raised his eyebrows. "Yes?"

"I never thought of this as an ability. I just thought that this was who I was, but I'm fast. Not as fast as you, of course, but when I would spar with Ethan, he always said that I had an advantage because I could go so fast. It wasn't actual speed, though. I could kind of…slow things down. That way I could see him coming at me and react. I called it my slow motion."

"Interesting," Graves said. "How long can you do this for?"

She shook her head. "Not long. I usually burn through it so fast. And once it's gone, I become sluggish and feel sick."

"You were using your abilities this entire time, and you didn't even know it."

"It didn't feel like magic. It felt natural."

He nodded, understanding lighting his features. "I understand. Mine does as well." He poured the rest of his drink down his throat. "We will figure out the rest of your abilities, Wren."

She shivered at that word. "How can we if I'm not a warlock?"

"I know you're concerned, but I am not. I've lived a long time. We can figure this out."

She wanted to have his faith, but she hadn't lived a long time, and magic looked daunting.

Graves took the seat beside her. She could feel his bright fire against her leg—searing and delicious. A part of her froze at his nearness—old habits—before she relaxed again.

Graves held his hands out in front of him. Then he removed his gloves. Her heart galloped. His hands. Those long, beautiful fingers and commanding, powerful hands. The ones she had so rarely seen. Beyond that to the vines that laced his wrists and disappeared up his sleeves in black ink. She hadn't gotten to see them when they'd had sex. He hadn't even taken his gloves off then. Her face flushed as the very vivid image of him stripping out of his suit coat and shirt to reveal just how much of his body that ink washed over assaulted her senses.

He cleared his throat, and her eyes snapped back up to his. She carefully schooled her features so that he couldn't see what she had just been thinking.

"I am a master of my craft. I have mastery over more than one key ability and several smaller ones." He placed the gloves to the side. "First, I have noise distortion. I can make a room soundproof or close off conversations from prying ears." His eyes met hers. "Or moans."

Her mouth opened slightly. She'd thought he was just going to ignore what had happened, but here it was on his lips. She tried not to squirm. "Well, at least Kingston didn't hear," she said. "Though he seemed to guess anyway."

"Indeed," he said. "As I told you before, I *am* knowledge, but I didn't explain further. My main ability is reading."

She frowned. "Everyone keeps saying that. What does it mean?"

"My body is a weapon." He held his hands up between them. "When I touch someone, I can read them. I can skim the surface of their mind. I read their memories and whatever is loudest. Usually, their deepest desires and all the pleasure they want. It can happen in an instant or, for those trained against it, it can take hours."

"Oh," Kierse said, flustered. She remembered his hand around her throat that first night. The shock in his eyes as he held her in place. Obviously checking to see if he could read her. So deliberate. He hadn't known what to make of her. "But...you couldn't read me?"

"No," he admitted. "I couldn't read you. There were so many times I have wanted to know what was going on in your head."

"That must have been frustrating."

"You have no idea. I have spent much of my life learning exactly what and who people are based on a bare touch on the street."

She bit her lip. "Is that why you always seemed so confused by me?"

He nodded. His eyes, usually so blank, were open to her now. "You make little sense. I have no context. I admit that I had gotten a bit complacent with the ability. I had to learn your body language, the shape of your face, all the things you said and didn't say."

He told her about that like he hated it, but something about it seemed backward. Like he'd enjoyed getting to know her. Like not being able to glean information had made him appreciate every new thing he had to learn from her the old-fashioned way.

"Well, I'm glad that you can't read me. It feels invasive."

"Hence the gloves," he said, reaching for them.

Kierse didn't know what compelled her, but she put her hand on his.

"Don't." His swirling gray eyes met hers. "You don't need them with me."

"Habit," he admitted, looking uncertain.

"You can go without." She withdrew her hand.

"All right." He put the gloves on the table. "I should let you know, since I am telling you my powers…that I actually *have* read you."

"What? You read my mind?"

"I don't read minds," he said with a shake of his head. "That isn't how it works. I mostly read memories. Sometimes very close thoughts. Things that people are yelling at me. In my business dealings, I use it by drawing the answers to the surface through questioning and then scanning what their memory brings to the surface. It's not an exact science, but it is how I have become this successful."

"Using your powers in business dealings is how you've gotten the information on Third Floor and the vault."

"Yes."

"And I thought you were torturing people."

His stare was flat when he asked, "Who said I wasn't?"

She nearly choked. She would put nothing past him.

"And what memory did you read from me?" she whispered, suddenly terrified of what he might have seen.

"When you were in my arms after the wish powder, I had no idea how to help you. I had the medicine, but you couldn't drink it. You'd drown. So, I tried to read you, and I can only assume what I saw were hallucinations from the wish powder. It was all a jumble from the drugs. You had bruises on your throat and face. You were bleeding from your mouth." His face darkened. "You were in a gutter."

"Oh," she said with a gulp.

She knew exactly what memory he had seen from her. The night that Jason had tried to kill her when she'd tried to leave him. But she didn't want *Graves* to know that. If she told Graves about her past, it would have to be on her terms.

"Like I said, it must have been a hallucination," he continued when she said nothing else. "And I haven't tried since. More to the point, the absorption powers make sense, considering what happened that day with the wish powder. You must have absorbed more magic than you could process. So the magic took hold and did its job to try to kill you. That was why I could read you as well. You had so much magic in your system that you couldn't absorb mine fast enough."

Kierse ran her thumb across her bottom lip as she processed that information. It made sense. All of it made way more sense than immunity.

"We really had to test my limits, then. We would have been blind to that."

"Precisely. What we need to figure out now is how to restore your magic. That way, we can train them safely."

"How did you figure out that reading restored your magic?"

He considered for a moment, his eyes going distant. "After Kingston took me on as an apprentice, I threw myself into my education. I'd always wanted to read everything at my disposal long before I had access to Kingston's library, but there was only so much a poor boy could read at the time. The green book that I lent to you was actually a translation of a book I read in my youth."

No wonder it was dear to him.

"During training with Kingston, I would routinely return to my books weakened and in pain, and I would leave them stronger and sustained. It is like with Kingston's art—the process of doing something that always brought me energy in the past now brings me energy in my magic as well."

She considered his explanation. Something that energized her in her past. That made her feel stronger and more whole. That sustained her when she felt her weakest.

"Stealing," she realized. "Stealing is what recharges my magic. It's the only thing that makes sense. It's the only thing I've done my entire life that made me feel better. And that time I thought I had the flu, I couldn't go out and steal for weeks. It was the first time in my life that I wasn't out casually picking pockets. Except the day after Imani and Montrell."

He actually laughed. "Of course it is. The thief *would* think that picking pockets would energize her magic."

"A thief is who I am. Just like you specialize in knowledge and Kingston swears that art is its own form of persuasion."

"Stealing it is, then," he said, coming to his feet.

He returned a moment later with a plain box much the same as the one she had opened her first day here.

"What's that for? Another magic trick?"

"I'll get to it in a minute. I think that we need to change our strategy to get the spear."

"This late in the game?"

"Before, I was under the impression that you were a warlock and that you were immune to magic. Absorption is something else entirely. It's *not* passive, which means it opens a whole new level of powers that I can train you to use. And more to the point, you can be trained to absorb wards so that *I* can come with you to the solstice party."

Her eyes widened. "You think I can do that?"

"I think you can if we train. You're already passable with the spear. We can work on this instead."

Kierse could hardly believe it. Not just about her magic, because she had been certain that finding out she wasn't a warlock meant certain death on this job. But if Graves was going to train her anyway *and* he was coming with her, then she might actually have a much better shot of getting *out*. Something she hadn't let herself consider.

"When do we start?"

"As to that…" He passed her the box on his lap. "We'll begin with you making wards and then move on to removing them."

She tingled with excitement. "I'm going to practice magic."

"You probably won't get it on the first try," he warned. "But I'll start with the basics."

"Okay," she whispered in reverence, staring down at the little wooden box.

"Warding is like all other magic, but it requires barely any energy. You can have multiple active wardings at all times and hardly ever run out of power." That explained his house, if he was always maintaining the wards. "Most magic starts off with a sense, but I'm going to leave that for another day, another lesson. All you need to know right now is that magic is intent."

"Intent?" she asked.

"You have to tell the magic what you want it to do, and then it does it."

"That easy, huh?"

"Not at all. But warding is the easiest, at least. If I wanted to ward this box, all I would have to do is think about wanting it and then use my magic to make it so."

"Would that put the ward language all over the box?"

He grinned. "Not unless my intent was for it to be there. It can be masked so only I could see it, but it would be weaker. A ward is stronger the more it's seared into something. The library has the strongest wards, as they're carved into the frame. This is a temporary ward. It doesn't need to last two or three hundred years."

"I see," she said, eyes wide.

"So, I want you to focus your intent on the box. And I want you to reach out to it and seal it shut."

She looked at him dubiously. "That's it?"

"If you don't think you can do it, then you're right."

Well, she wouldn't have that. She *could* do this.

Kierse focused all her intent on the box. The little wooden square. The metal clasp. The slick edges. This was her box, and no one else could get inside it. She would stop anyone who sought access. She pushed her will toward it, but nothing happened.

She sighed. "I don't think it worked."

"No. You would have felt it, but I hardly expected for it to work on the first try."

She nodded and returned her concentration to the box. She would exert her will on the thing. And so she tried again and again and again. Nothing happened. No matter how much she focused, she couldn't seem to get to the point of exerting her will on the box. It was just a box. She wasn't even warding anything within it.

She slumped backward. "Ugh. I don't have it."

"Keep the box," he said with a nod. "And keep practicing."

"Okay," she said, disappointed in herself.

"This isn't the only thing we have to work on. You're going to like this part."

Her eyes perked up. "Oh?"

"Reconnaissance," he said with a feral grin. "Tonight, we go to the underworld."

Interlude

E dgar had many functions for his boss.
Cleanup was his favorite.

He knew that it was supposed to be his least favorite. Despite its name, it was a messy business. But he enjoyed it nonetheless.

He strode to the door of the hospital, The Covenant sign shining bright on the side of the back entrance. He'd disabled the video footage before he'd arrived. No one needed to see what came next. He wasted no time with subtleties. Edgar slammed a brick down onto the door handle and felt it rattle loose. He hauled the door open and stepped into the freshly sterile environment.

Personally, he wasn't fond of hospitals. Too many bad memories. He'd had seizures as a child and still had them on occasion now. But when he was young, his parents hadn't wanted to hear the word "epilepsy." The townsfolk whispered that he had demons in him. His parents were particularly religious, and he'd gone through a few exorcisms before he'd taken matters into his own hands and gone to a doctor. His parents believed something was wrong with him until the day they died.

Maybe there was, but it had nothing to do with his epilepsy.

When he first met Graves, he'd run away from home. He was tired of the constant attention to his illness with little attention to him. He thought he was meant for more. So, he'd left his small town behind and hitchhiked into the big city.

He had been there not even two weeks before his apartment was ransacked, all of his money stolen, and he'd been held at gunpoint for even the shoes on his feet. Stupid small-town boy. Worse, he had started seizing as they ran off with his clothes. He hadn't had a seizure in nearly a year by then. Bad timing.

Graves had been coming out of a theater when he saw Edgar seizing on the ground. One hand on him, and his life had changed. Graves had gotten him cleaned up and given him something he never knew he'd always been craving—purpose.

Edgar was an eager student. He learned everything Graves would teach him and beyond. He had no magic of his own, but he could do everything else that Graves required. Now, he was an invaluable asset. Something Graves had honed over the last thirty-five years. It didn't bother Edgar that he got older while Graves stayed the same age. Edgar didn't *feel* like he was older. He just looked it. And Graves didn't *look* older, but he felt it.

He was someone worth dedicating his life to.

Including cleaning up his messes.

Edgar stepped into Dr. Mafi's lab. He felt no remorse for what he was about to do. He wanted to feel bad for the good doctor, but she was just in the wrong place at the wrong time.

He surveyed the equipment. Large white machines that did who knew what. It was beyond his own expertise, but they were expensive and important. He wasn't here to ruin the place doing good just to fix an error. Graves didn't make many.

He found Kierse's file. He rifled through the notes and located every piece of information on Kierse McKenna. Saliva swab, urine sample, blood sample, physical information, temperature, blood pressure, and all the other tests that were done to her. He destroyed each of them individually, reducing the evidence to ash. He couldn't leave a speck of her behind.

Then he went to the computers and hacked into the doctor's email. He sighed when he saw what she had done.

Well, that complicated things.

He'd thought he could just destroy the lab. Now, he might have to destroy her, too. She was working for King Louis. From the look of their exchange, he'd had her in his pocket for many years and it hadn't been entirely her fault. She owed him a substantial amount of money. She'd been paying it back with blood samples from her supernatural clients, looking for a specific blood match for the vampire king. Dr. Mafi wasn't a bad person; she was just in a bad situation. What to do with that information was up to Graves.

He forwarded the emails to Graves. He'd await instructions, though he already suspected what Graves would say. It wouldn't be the first time he'd killed someone on his orders. The doctor might be a problem with her witch abilities, but he'd figure it out, like he always did with time and patience.

Finished with the emails and server, Edgar removed the hard drives and drilled holes into each of them. It'd be more fun to smash each of the monitors successively, but all the information was on these babies. It didn't appear that she had taken Kierse's info off the server, but he'd go to her home just in case. He had a feeling she wasn't there. She was scared Graves was onto her. Well, she was right about that.

His phone buzzed. "Report," Graves demanded.

"It's what you suspected. Want me to terminate her?"

"No," he said at once. "She's more valuable alive. Just find her. Bring her here if you can. I bet she's already on the run."

"I thought as much, sir."

"You got everything else?"

"The only thing missing is the blood from tonight."

Graves cursed. "I bet we know exactly where that will be."

"Yes, sir."

Edgar smiled as he ended the call and looked around at the hospital. He didn't have time to play. He hoisted the bag on his shoulder. He had a hunt in front of him, and his quarry had a head start.

PART V

THE THIRD FLOOR

Chapter Thirty-Eight

Graves insisted on arming her to the teeth.

To which she did not object one bit.

She opted for all black from head to toe. She'd even removed her wren necklace, much to her dismay and possibly Graves's as well. She strapped on the two beautiful guns that Graves had given her when she'd first taken the job. Plus, he offered her two for her boots and extra magazines for the inside of her jacket. She slipped knives up her sleeves, down her boots, and in her jacket. She'd added pins to her hair just in case—never know when a bobby pin would save her life. She felt like she was going into battle.

"Stop looking like that," Graves said.

"Like what?"

"So happy."

"I will temper my energy when I'm in the underworld. But come on. We're finally going out into the field. I've been waiting for this."

"If I'd known you would get this excited, I would have considered bringing you to my business meetings."

Kierse went very still, surprised that he would even suggest it. "No, you wouldn't."

Graves smirked. "Are you sure?"

And the look on his face told her that she wasn't. He actually *had* considered bringing her. She couldn't imagine Graves letting anyone in on his secrets.

"Don't forget the mission for today. We're finding a way to get you inside and make sure you can pass through Walter's wards."

She blew out a breath and refocused. Reconnaissance, after all, was more fun than failing at magic training, which she had been working on since Graves showed her the box to ward. Walter might have been one of Graves's warlock trainees before he let him go, but his wards were reinforced with force-field magic. They were pretty sure she could get past his warding with her absorption, but today would be the test of that.

"He's not as strong as Imani," Graves continued. "We just want to get you inside Third Floor."

"I'm armed to the teeth. What do you think I'll find there?"

"It's a dark market stories beneath the subway. Monsters congregate there to feast on their darkest desires, organize illegal weapons deals, and so on. It's not a place where the Monster Treaty holds any sway."

That much she *did* know.

"Remember, I can't get inside. I've had no access to Third Floor since Walter joined forces with King Louis. I won't be able to protect you."

"I won't need protection," Kierse said. "I can handle myself."

Graves leveled her with a look. "It's a monster market, and the currency is humans. You may not be human, but they don't know that. Weapons are only going to get you so far."

"All right. I hear you."

"So, if we can get you safely inside, the next important step will be to get the lay of the land without being noticed. Then you can start looking for another exit from Third Floor."

"This is the part that I'm good at," she assured him. "I know how to play this."

He looked dubious but acquiesced. They set out on foot, taking the back entrance out of the property through the garage tunnel that deposited them a few blocks southwest on Amsterdam. They trekked down to the 72nd Street subway entrance and took the stairs two at a time. A subway troll snoozed in a chair at the bottom. Kierse was thankful that she didn't have to deal with him today.

"Monsters," Graves muttered with disdain as if he weren't one himself.

They bypassed the troll and headed toward the turnstiles. Graves touched the reader with his bare hand and then gestured for her to go ahead.

She listened for the satisfying click as she passed through. "How'd you do that?"

"Magic," he said casually.

"I didn't think you took the subway."

"I don't." He started off across the dingy platform. "This way."

"Where are we going, exactly?"

"Times Square."

She blinked at him. "Really?"

"Unfortunately, yes."

Times Square was one of the last places that she wanted to be in the city. The once glamorous locale had been demolished in the first wave of the

Monster War. A major battle between two factions had rendered it useless. There was a push to restore it to its former glory, but monsters had claimed the area and it was a slow progress. She hadn't been there in at least a year. Avoiding it was high on her priority list.

Still, she was safer with Graves than she had ever been alone. So, she followed him onto the 3 train that rattled noisily into view. For the time of day, it shouldn't have been busy, but it was New York, so…it was swamped. Graves wrapped one hand around a pole at the center of the car. She placed hers under his and braced herself as the train rolled south toward Times Square.

"What's in Times Square? Besides chaos."

Graves's mercurial eyes flicked around the crowded subway. A group of nymphs lounged on top of one another in the seat across from them. A haggard array of humans took up many of the other seats. She noticed a goblin against the far wall. No one here with advanced hearing, but it hardly mattered anyway.

She could sense the noise distortion as Graves flicked his hand, using his powers in public, and no one was the wiser for it. No one even looked up. The subway-goers were too concerned with themselves to think that *magic* was happening just around them.

"An entrance into Third Floor."

"There's one *in* Times Square?"

"Under," he corrected. "This is the most direct route underground. It takes us to a checkpoint that bottlenecks into the underworld."

Kierse shivered with excitement, that wrong smile returning to her face. Graves could only shake his head.

"Little thief," he murmured.

The train rolled to a screeching halt at the Times Square—42nd Street station. The nymphs burst from their seats in a riot of color. Kierse followed them out of the train and headed toward the exit. Graves directed her out of the flow and toward the S platform. She had no intention of complaining that they weren't headed through the frothing madness up above.

When they reached the S platform, Graves waited for the train to appear and all the other passengers to enter. Once the platform was entirely empty and all that lay before them was silence, Graves hopped onto the tracks.

He held his hands up as if he meant to catch her. "Come on."

"I'm no damsel, Graves."

She landed easily on her feet, crouched like a cat on the tracks. She rose to her full height, arching an eyebrow at him.

"Right," was all he said with a ghost of a smile. "This way."

Then he set off into the darkened gloom of the subway tunnel.

She jogged to catch up. "What if a train comes?"

"The shuttle shouldn't swing through here for another five minutes. We have time."

"Lovely."

Kierse kept looking down at the time on her cell phone. Five minutes wasn't that much time. Already four minutes had passed since the last shuttle. Things weren't always on schedule—in fact, they hadn't been on schedule *before* monsters—but she didn't want to bet on it.

She tapped her cell phone as the five minutes dwindled. "Graves."

He stopped abruptly. "Here we are."

Darkness swallowed him whole as he stepped off of the train tracks. She gaped in shock. One moment, he'd been at her side, and the next, he'd just vanished.

"This way," Graves said through the gloom.

Suddenly, the tunnel began to rattle. She jerked her head to the side and saw the lights of the train barreling down the shaft. Fear ripped through her. There was no other option; she took a deep breath and joined him. The darkness seemed to be more of a boundary than anything. Once she was on the other side, she could see that spotty electric wiring lined the roof of the tunnel, illuminating the space.

This was an entrance to Third Floor.

She exhaled slowly. "That must not have been warded."

"No. There are hundreds of entrances that allow access below, but there are far fewer checkpoints." Graves stepped over a rotting rat carcass. "The tunnels branch out beneath the city like a web. Even more expansive than the subway system. The checkpoints control entrances to King Louis's domain. Walter controls the checkpoints with his warding. So he controls access to the market and thus access to King Louis."

"Kind of brilliant. Are you sure you should have kicked him out of warlock training?"

Graves shot her a look. "It was the right idea at the time."

"And just think—if you hadn't done that, we never would have met."

He frowned as if he didn't like that assessment one bit. "I highly doubt that."

So did she. Something tied them together. One way or another, he would have crossed her path.

"Third Floor is its own sprawling city. The checkpoints let them charge for people to get into the market, to live in the market, to work in the market. It will not be easy to find a way in or out other than the checkpoints."

She nodded. "Got it. Where is the actual market located?"

Graves was silent a moment before saying, "Underneath Grand Central."

"Ah," she said in understanding. That made sense. Few ventured to Grand Central anymore. It was as anathema as Times Square, even if it had retained its former glory.

"They still operate the Grand Central Market with a mix of monster and human wares," Graves explained.

"Only tourists are stupid enough to go there."

"Precisely," he said. "This is a mockery of that market. Third Floor is located in the subbasement below the public-facing market. The few humans that venture below either spend enough to *maybe* ensure their safety or have a death wish."

"Sounds right," she said without emotion.

Humans could be just as monstrous as monsters when they wanted to be. But the majority hadn't asked for any of this to happen. She wanted to see them safe for the safety she had lacked in her youth.

"And King Louis's residence is at the center of Third Floor?"

"No, actually. How much do you know about the rail system?"

"It gets me where I need to go."

Graves shot her an amused look. "Ah, well, it's a fascinating read, if you ever want to try something other than fairy tales."

"I'm at your disposal. You're setting the reading materials," she reminded him.

"I'll give you a brief rundown. When the rail system was designed in Manhattan, a secret platform called Track 61 was built in 1910 to transport presidents in times of crisis. You can access it via a locked gold door on 49th Street, which leads underneath the Waldorf-Astoria building."

"Never been in it."

"It's under new management."

"Which monster?" Because she couldn't imagine there was another explanation in these times.

"Who do you think?"

"Louis," she guessed.

He nodded. "He purchased the building, gained access to the secret platform, and instead of taking up residence in the penthouse, he holed up in the bunker."

"Naturally. I'm guessing the door on 49th is warded?"

"It is. You could get in and out of it, but it's under constant surveillance. We need a more reliable exit."

That, at least, she could agree on. Exits were part of her repertoire.

Jason had taught her that the hard way.

Chapter Thirty-Nine

"The checkpoint is ahead," Graves told her, finally slowing several blocks later. She could hear voices coming from the end of the tunnel. "Through there, you'll get into Third Floor to the monster market and gain access to Louis's residence through Track 61."

Kierse and Graves stopped together when the checkpoint came into view, staying just out of sight. She'd seen a picture of it, and it was still disappointing. She'd wanted a filigreed archway with a glittering blue light inside or some kind of substance that would give way beneath her hand. But it was just a tunnel with monsters milling about, guards patrolling, and some kind of machine. If the goblin guards hadn't been there, she never would have known it was a checkpoint into the monsters' lair.

"How does it work?"

"Walter carved wards into the walls," he said. Kierse craned her neck and saw markings on the wall that she'd have easily missed under normal circumstances.

"So, they're pretty powerful."

He nodded. "Carved is always a more permanent marking. With what he's using to hold up all these wards all over the city, I'd imagine he *has* to carve them or else he couldn't sustain them all."

"Or he's more powerful than you give him credit for."

Graves shot her a look. "Doubtful."

"Always so sure of yourself."

He smirked. "For good reason." He pointed to the machine she'd seen before. "The computer is what controls the wards."

She furrowed her brows. She understood technology enough to break it when she needed to. But she didn't understand how to *build* it, let alone what kind of power Walter would need to channel his magic into an electrical device. She couldn't even ward her wooden box. "How does it control the wards?"

"I have no idea," he begrudgingly admitted, his jaw set. "Walter designed the computer system as well. He had to have a way for people to enter the underworld while his wards were up and still keep people like me out."

"He hates you so much that he warded it so you couldn't get inside?"

"That's one way to look at it," Graves said dryly.

"What's the other way? You threw him out and abandoned him in the middle of his training," she told him. "It's not surprising he'd want to keep you out."

"Yes, well, I always assumed it was because I was powerful."

She laughed. "That probably doesn't help."

"Anyway, at first, Walter left open a few key points to funnel people in. They were frisked. People didn't like it. They complained."

"Customer service at its finest," she muttered.

"His solution was the machine. People are screened, pay a fine, and are given an access card. They just have to swipe it, and it works with the wards to let them pass. Like a MetroCard."

"No one complained about that?"

"They like the exclusivity."

"Of course they do. Do I need to steal a card?" she asked, watching the growing crowd.

He held up a card. "That was the final business I was working on the day of the museum. I had one made for you."

She snatched it out of his hand triumphantly. "This will get me through?"

"My contact told me that it would make the system recognize you, but he couldn't do anything about the wards. That only Walter could code them properly. Each person has their own card, but ultimately, it's the warding that let them pass."

"So we can trick the machine but not the magic," she mused.

"Correct. And the reason I need a wardbreaker is because the wards are carved and written specifically to keep me out."

"You really messed it up with Walter," she said.

Graves crossed his arms and said nothing. He couldn't even deny it.

She watched the checkpoint for a few minutes as monsters scanned cards and were let through. Did the wards deactivate every time the card was swiped and approved? Or did the particular monster just get to pass through them with the card as their means of protection? Either way would probably be a simple function if he ran it like code. She knew how to break code but not create it. A programmer who also had magical powers could probably do it with ease.

"Wren?" Graves asked.

She blinked and met his gaze. "I was analyzing the situation. I need to get closer to look at the machine and test the wards. Do you think the card brings the wards down momentarily or just lets the person pass through them?"

He relaxed slightly as her expertise took over. As if he trusted that she knew what she was doing.

"The latter," he assured her. "Bringing wards up and down that are carved like that is nearly impossible, especially with how much he's sustaining. The machine is the work-around to let people go through them."

"But he doesn't know about me."

"He does not."

Her smile was dangerous as she scanned the crowd. "Got it. Where is everyone coming from?"

There were two bulky goblins carrying M16s. A woman swaying on her feet in a slip of a dress with a vampire in a gown from the nineteenth century who held her by the back of her neck. A couple clinging to each other that everyone else gave a wide berth. She shuddered a little when she recognized them as a succubus and incubus. Even most monsters didn't like the sexual predators, who almost always worked in pairs. Finally, a group of douchebag-looking bros all laughing and cajoling. They were the type that had more money than sense.

She didn't know what perverted appetites they had that brought them down here when they could have their fun above ground. There were no other human women waiting in line. None but the vampire's female companion.

"The main entrance is through a private tunnel in Grand Central, but there are hundreds of tunnels that empty here. I think it's why Walter chose this for one of his checkpoints."

Kierse chewed on her lip and then dug through her pockets to find a hair tie. She needed to look a little less feminine. She tugged out the bobby pins and slipped them up her sleeves. She brushed her hair forward into her eyes, giving her a shaggy look, then tied the rest back into a ponytail. She used a few of the bobby pins she frequently broke into residences with and tucked the hair up underneath itself. Then she flipped up the hood on her jacket.

The biggest problem was her height. She was about average height for a woman, short for a man. But perhaps an adventurous boy.

"How do I look?"

"Like you're going to get in trouble."

She winked at him. "Give me some credit."

Then fell into step with a figure that passed her.

"Keep your phone on," Graves insisted.

She tapped her pocket to let him know she'd heard, but otherwise he was completely out of her mind. He'd given her the plan. She now knew how to execute it. Kierse integrated herself with the frat boys. She stepped forward, bumping into the nearest guy. "Oh, sorry."

"Hey, man, no problem," the guy said with a laugh.

She put her hand on his shoulder, careful to keep her gaze down as she slipped her hand into his back pocket. "Always running into people."

But the dude-bro had already stopped paying attention. He hadn't even felt her slip out his wallet. He'd been too focused on her running into him, the hand on his shoulder. Diversion. Slip of the hand. She stepped in front of him, making sure she was clear of the frat boys before rifling through his wallet and finding the access card. Didn't hurt to have a second card to look into later. Plus, it would cause a distraction at her back when he realized his was missing.

The vampire went in ahead of her, paying extra for the girl at her side. Kierse watched the machine with curious eyes as it let the pair pass. No indication from the machine or the wards other than a picture of the people then a green light to indicate it was okay to go through. And then it was Kierse's turn.

She held her breath as she came up to the machine. If it didn't take the card or she couldn't go through the wards, then she'd be found out. Walter and King Louis might even discover they were trying to access the underworld. But if she didn't test it, they'd never know if she could get through.

Finally, she tapped the card onto the touchscreen. With her heart in her throat, she watched a picture of herself appear, and then the green light flicked on.

"Pass," the goblin who manned the checkpoint grumbled.

Kierse grinned to herself, but the real test was next. Graves's contact had gotten the machine to work for her. Now her magic had to do the rest.

She took a step into the checkpoint. She could almost read the language carved into the wall now that she knew what she was looking for, but it always stayed out of reach. Walter's wards were unique, as Graves's was threaded with holly and Imani's were with sankofa. She could make out what appeared to be a sun symbol at its core. She wondered how that reflected in Walter.

With a deep breath, she waited to see if she could feel the magic absorbing into her skin, but it felt much the same as it always had. Walter's wards felt like nothing at all as she absorbed the magic and stepped through to the other side. First test passed.

She looked back only once to see Graves watching her. He looked hungry. This was a victory for them. A big one.

Now on to Third Floor.

Chapter Forty

The tunnel didn't immediately open up to the market beyond. Instead, Kierse wound and curved for a while before she finally came upon it. Swallowing her fear, she marveled at the market before her. It was an underground cavern so big that she couldn't even see the other side. Dark and ominous and yet full of life. And monsters. Monsters were *everywhere*.

Solid structures had been built around the perimeter while the inside had hastily erected tents and shanties. Kierse moved with the flow of traffic as she entered the bustle of the market. The main thoroughfare deposited her at the center of a market square, and in the middle of the row of vendors was a statue of Coraline LeMort.

Kierse blinked in confusion. She didn't want to draw attention to herself, but what the hell would a statue of Coraline be doing in the underworld? She was a symbol of revolution and peace. Her statue outside of the Met had been erected post–Coraline Convention, when the world was ending the Monster War, but the underworld was the antithesis of that. King Louis and the Men of Valor wanted to end the Monster Treaty.

Curiosity got the better of her, and she sidled up to the statue, reading the plaque at Coraline's feet.

Sacrifice reaps the greatest reward.

– Coraline LeMort

So King Louis saw Coraline's death as a symbol of the *new* revolution he wanted, a necessary evil, and he'd twisted her words to fit his agenda. Typical.

Kierse gritted her teeth and turned around to find a dark tunnel blocked by elaborate gilded doors traced with wards. She could see a sun image at the heart of the wards just like on the checkpoints. Walter's wards. On the front of the gate was the Men of Valor logo—angel wings with an arrow shot through.

Giant trolls manned either side of the entrance with a disapproving look at anyone who came too close. Well, this must be the way into King Louis's residence. He certainly didn't hide his place. And why should he, here at the height of his power?

Eager to avoid the trolls' gazes, she moved back into the flow of traffic through the market, getting the lay of the land as Graves had suggested. She blended in well enough. There were plenty of men or monsters in hoods, hiding their faces and keeping to themselves. She silently mapped out her surroundings for Graves.

It was hard to imagine that this had once been a basement level of Grand Central. The place had clearly been gutted and made into this enormous monster market. She could see relics of its past use in the ventilation system, piping air out of the cavern, and old human workspaces now used as stalls.

She passed a meat vendor and tried not to let the shock show on her face. The shifter running the place was serving raw meat, and monsters sat on barstools, feasting on the flesh. She swore she saw something on a plate that looked vaguely human. Which hadn't been legal since the Monster Treaty, but no one was policing this place.

The next stall held potions and elixirs. There was a full black witch's cauldron brimming with fog. She wondered if that was to provide the right feel of the shop or if she was actually brewing something. She wondered how Dr. Mafi would feel about the stereotype.

Kierse moved on. She saw severed heads and blood bags and trinkets of all shapes and sizes that promised the wearer any number of magical properties. The next stall caught her eye, and she scanned the weapons with delight. Knives and swords and daggers. Handguns and machine guns and even a grenade launcher.

"You like what you see?" the man working the stall asked.

Kierse startled when she looked up. The man was no man at all. He was a phoenix. A rare breed of monster that could shift into a giant bird and burn to ash. The stories from before the war left out how a phoenix could use that fire to burn others to ash, too.

"Uh, no thank you," Kierse said quickly. Though her fingers itched to filch something off the table, she didn't particularly want to be burned to cinders today.

She took in the market, drawing blueprints in her mind. It was bigger than she'd anticipated, and she could have spent days walking around, but she had two main objectives: scope out the place and find a way to sneak Graves inside.

But she couldn't help having a third reason for being down here. Nate had known when Torra was kidnapped that she'd been brought to Third Floor, but they had never found a way inside. Nate was too much of a human sympathizer. He helped with the Monster Treaty. No one was letting him or his people down here, even if they *had* known where to start looking. Now it made perfect sense that they never would have been able to get in.

And she knew the bastard who had taken Torra was a monster named Orik Thompson. She'd found that name and a phone number in a scrap of paperwork in Torra's abandoned apartment. She'd looked into the name and discovered he was a vampire known for trafficking humans into Third Floor.

Maybe the last thing she should do is search out someone like Orik Thompson, but this might be her only opportunity to get answers…or to kill the monster who had done this to Torra.

With her hood low over her eyes, she ignored the passing monsters and headed toward the nearest bar—a constant source of information above, and she doubted it would be any different below. A lumbering troll nearly ran into her. A shirtless, muscled mer passed so close that she could smell the ocean on him. A werewolf strode by with a stalking gait. Vampires and werewolves had been on opposing sides of their own war for eons. The treaty must upset a great deal of monsters for a werewolf to be in a vampire's market.

Finally, she stepped into an aptly named bar: Blood. The place looked exactly as any grimy dive bar did above, save for the monsters and pitchers of what appeared to be human blood on *tap*. Kierse took up a seat in a corner of the bar and ordered a beer that she refused to touch. She sat there long enough for the bartender to ignore her and for her to hear way too much from a goblin crowing about how King Louis had forty-eight acres down here and still he couldn't find space for his new human-murdering business. He didn't say it like that, exactly, but it was both disgusting and terrifying to think of the breadth of King Louis's reach if he had Walter handling nearly fifty acres of property plus his private quarters.

Finally, she found her opportunity as the bartender came over to investigate if she'd want another drink. She slipped him a fifty-dollar bill and leaned forward. "Actually, just curious if you know where I can find someone."

The monster palmed the fifty and waited expectantly. "Depends on who it is."

"Orik Thompson."

He held his hand out for more money, and she handed over another fifty.

Good thing she'd added cash to her pockets just as she'd added her heavily concealed weaponry.

"Sure. Orik works at a place around the corner." He eyed her crudely up and down. "Why? You want a job?"

"No, thank you," she said, sliding another bill toward him. "Directions?"

"Place is called Red Velvet." He smirked as he told her how to get there.

"Okay. And how will I recognize him?" Another bill.

"Can't miss him. Short and bald with a long, blond beard." He grinned, showing off his pointed vampire canines. "He's going to like you, if you know what I mean."

She was afraid that she did know what he meant. But at least she had a lead. The first one she'd had in a year. It was time to get some answers.

She dropped more money in his tip jar as she left.

"Forget I asked," she added.

The bartender waved her off like it was normal business.

The directions were good, and Kierse successfully navigated the market to find Orik's workplace. Kierse's blood ran cold at the sight. She'd known exactly who the monster was and the crimes he'd committed, but seeing it in person made it all so much more real.

Red Velvet was a vampire brothel. Humans hung in the windows, their bodies on display, their necks exposed. The lavish red exterior was a stark contrast to the blacks and dark grays of the rest of the market.

Was this where Torra had been taken? Had she been sold to these people?

She was furious at the thought, but there was nothing to do but use her anger and disgust.

First, it was time to have a little chat with Orik Thompson. A bullet might not kill a vamp, but it sure would slow him down long enough for her to cut his head off.

Chapter Forty-One

Orik Thompson was a lackey.

The fact that she had been thinking he was a player in these games for a whole year made her sick to her stomach. He didn't even own the brothel. He just kidnapped people from above and kept a steady supply of humans available to the vampires below. He was one in a string of cronies working for the actual owner of Red Velvet.

It took more time than she'd planned to dedicate to the task to finally get Orik alone. She'd clocked him coming out the back of the brothel with some other vamps, shouting about the "good time" they'd had. She'd wanted to kill them all right then and there.

Unfortunately, she couldn't make a scene. This was revenge, but she wasn't stupid. She couldn't jeopardize the mission with Graves. She still needed access to Third Floor and to find that exit to get Graves inside. Time was running short, but now that they knew she could get inside, she could recon night and day.

The other vampires patted him on the back, and he continued off alone through the market. She trailed him at considerable distance. He was a vampire brute, exactly as described by the bartender, with a stout build and wrinkled brow, as if he'd been turned many years into his human life. It didn't make him any less deadly.

When he entered an empty alleyway and pulled out a cigarette, she took her chance. Kierse checked the auto-silencer on her pistol before putting a bullet in his leg.

Orik cried out, falling to the ground and clutching his knee. It wouldn't keep him down long. She needed to make her move *now*.

She stepped out of the shadows at his side and felt all her pent-up energy from the last year unleash from her. She didn't give him a second to speak before burying her fist in his face. It didn't do enough damage. There was a reason she didn't normally go up against a monster. Not like this. She was usually stealth, not muscle. But this time, it didn't matter.

"What the fuck?" Orik cried out.

Two knives whisked out of her jacket, strong and sturdy. She poised them crossed at his neck.

"You brought a woman here a year ago," she snarled.

He laughed. With a bullet in his leg and knives at his neck, he still laughed. "Bring a lot of girls here."

Maybe she should have just killed him. One less asshole on her streets. But fuck, she wanted answers.

"A *woman*," she corrected. "Roughly five feet tall with a pink pixie cut and blue eyes."

The vamp laughed again. "Could have been me. Who's to say?"

Kierse felt fury in her veins. She kicked out at the wound in his knee, and he screamed in pain. "You might want to reconsider whether you remember."

"There's lots of girls. Lots of boys, too," he cried out. "I don't remember them all."

She narrowed her eyes at him, wondering if she'd made a mistake. Was he lying? Was he stalling for time to recover before he got the jump on her? Was he just heartless? Could they all be true?

"Torra. Her name was Torra Hastings," Kierse spat. "Ring a bell?"

His eyes flared wide. Now *that* name meant something.

"Oh, Torra?" he asked with another stupid laugh. "'Course I know Torra."

She blinked. *Know.* He *knows* Torra. That didn't make sense. Her brain couldn't pick up the present tense fast enough.

"What did you do with her, you bastard?"

"I delivered her to King Louis, of course," he said with a vicious smile. "That's who all the Red Velvet workers owe their debts to."

King Louis.

Her blood ran cold. She should have known it would all lead back to him. The true villain and mastermind of Third Floor and all its depravity.

"What happened to her?"

"Last I saw, she was on break," Orik said.

"On break?"

"At Red Velvet."

The pieces all fit together at once. He knows Torra. Not knew. Knows. She belonged to King Louis. She was on break. At Red Velvet. Torra was there now. She was still *alive.*

Kierse looked away from Orik, her gaze going back to the red monstrosity in the distance. Torra was alive.

And that was the moment Orik struck. He snarled and lunged for her.

His vampire teeth sharpened and elongated as he used his considerable strength to try to overpower her.

She was distracted by the revelation, but instinct took over. She slipped into slow motion just before he could reach her. She turned back to him, sidestepping his approach. Her arm continued on its trajectory, and because he hadn't been anticipating that she'd have any kind of super speed, he moved right into her. With the force of her slow motion meeting his vampire speed, the knife went straight through his jugular.

His mouth formed an *O* of shock right before she lopped his head off.

"Fuck," she hissed.

She jerked out of the spray of his blood, which missed her by inches. He was dead. She'd killed a monster in *monster* territory. This place seemed lawless, but she needed to get the fuck away from the scene just in case they came looking for who'd offed one of King Louis's lackeys.

She didn't regret killing him. *Couldn't* regret killing him. Not just for Torra but for all the people he'd taken over the years. All the humans he'd treated like chattel. For them. Good riddance.

Anyway, she had a new mission.

She needed to find Torra and get her the hell out of here.

Chapter Forty-Two

Her boots stomped hard against the ground as she backtracked to the brothel. She didn't know how long she would have before Orik's body would be found. Or if anyone would even care here. It was a gamble. Time to improvise her plan.

She reached the back door of the brothel without anyone stopping her. She'd spent years inside Colette's and knew that the back door was the best way to get in and out without raising suspicion. The workers were always going to be more helpful than the goons. She loved the Roulettes, but they were hired muscle. And hired muscle didn't want anyone inside who could mess with business.

A group of workers sat together in a room on the first floor. She ducked her head in and kept her voice slow and steady.

"Hey," she said. The group glanced up at her, saw she wasn't an employee or likely a customer based on her attire, and dismissed her. Then she used the one card she had to ask, "Orik said that Torra was on break. Do you know where she is?"

"Probably her room," a man said, lounging back on a divan.

"Second floor, third door to the left," a woman said.

"Thanks," Kierse said.

Kierse climbed the flight of stairs that led from the back of the brothel. It was primarily used by the workers themselves, so it was blessedly empty. She pushed open the stairwell door to the second floor and scanned the hallway. She waited for a female vampire to pass before she hustled down the hall and knocked on Torra's door.

Up until this moment, she had been moving on pure adrenaline. The news that Torra wasn't just alive but had been *living here* in Red Velvet this whole time hit her like a freight train as she waited for the door to open. She'd been trafficked. She'd been stolen from her home and forced into this blood brothel. And she'd survived it for *a year*. A whole fucking year.

While Kierse had been up above, living her life and trying to move on, thinking she was dead. The thought broke her. And a tear came to her eye that she hastily brushed away. She couldn't fall apart. Not yet. Not until Torra was out of here.

The door was yanked open, and Kierse stopped breathing.

Torra stood before her. Her once-pink hair was now a dark brown with blond ends. Her blue eyes were vivid against her creamy white skin, which was so pale that Kierse could see the veins running underneath. As if this place had leeched the color from her skin. But the sway of those hips, the careful tilt to her head, the swell of her breasts in the red corset. Those were all things Kierse distinctly remembered.

"Torra?" she gasped.

Her eyes rounded. "Kierse?"

"You're alive," she said, her hand going to her mouth.

"What are you doing here?" Torra grasped Kierse by the arm and yanked her into the room. She slammed the door closed behind her and leaned back against it as if she, too, could barely stay standing at the sight of her.

Kierse's eyes traveled over Torra like she was a ghost come back to life. She was the same and wholly different. More fragile, more frail, and with the unmistakable white outlines of bites across her neck and delicate wrists. But she was still completely Torra.

"Torra, you're alive," Kierse repeated.

She couldn't stop herself. She moved toward Torra and pulled her into her arms. For the last year, she had believed that she was dead. She was the last person Kierse had ever had a relationship with, and she'd just given up after that. She and Torra hadn't been perfect. They'd fought, and little things had always blown up to bigger things between them. But she hadn't wanted her dead. And she certainly didn't want *this*.

"I'm alive. I'm alive," Torra said, brushing at the tear that had rolled down Kierse's cheek.

"I can't believe you're here," she said. "We need to get you out of here. I just killed a vampire and…"

"You did what?" Torra gasped.

"I killed the fucking vampire who did this to you, Tor." She straightened, forcing a sense of calm back over herself. "I cornered Orik Thompson in an alley, and I cut his head off when he lunged for me."

"Oh my god." Torra's lips quavered. "I'm glad he's dead. I'm glad for it, Kierse, but the entire place is going to go on lock down as soon as they find him. You need to get out of here."

"I'm not leaving without you!" Kierse insisted. "I'm getting you the fuck out of here."

"And go where? Do you have a plan?"

"Fuck," she spat.

She did have a plan. She had one from Graves. And it was find a fucking exit.

It was important, had always been important to the success of the mission. But now it was something else. Now it meant a way to get Torra out. She hadn't thought she was alive, so she hadn't even considered that she would need the exit first. She had *her* exit but not one for anyone else. And she had never hated herself for that fact more.

"I can get you out. I just need more time," Kierse said. "We can hide you until I figure it out."

"You can't hide me. I'm okay. I'm safe. I'm alive."

"Tor," she said, swiping at her eyes again. "You're not safe. Please."

"No, you listen to me. You are going to get the fuck out of here, and then you're going to find a way to get me out. I don't care that I'm indentured to King Louis and that he might find and kill me if I leave."

"He won't find you. I'm going to kill him."

Torra looked frightened then. "I believe you mean that, but first we need to get you out of here. Come back. Find a way out. I'll go with you. But I *cannot* live if they put you in this place, too. It'd be so much worse if you were here."

An alarm wailed in the brothel. Kierse jumped at the abrupt sound.

"They know. They know he's dead," Torra said, her voice frantic and horrified. She pushed Kierse toward the door. "Please just go."

"I will find a way to get you out of here," she promised. "I swear it. I'm coming back for you."

Torra threw her arms around her once more. "Don't die. Please."

Then Torra grabbed her and dragged her out the door.

Kierse flew out of the bedroom in Torra's wake. The brothel was in chaos, much the same as the night of the gang raid at Colette's.

"This way," Torra told her.

Kierse followed Torra to the stairwell that Kierse had taken to find her. They hurtled down the stairs past other panicked workers. No one looked at Kierse twice when she was with Torra. But she knew that it was only a matter of time before a vampire started rounding the workers up, and Kierse would look out of place.

"Here," Torra said.

They took a separate landing from the rest of the rush and came to a side exit. *Bless Torra for having another exit.*

"Now go."

"I'll come back," Kierse promised.

"Thank you," Torra said with tears in her eyes.

She took one last look at her ex-girlfriend. The tear that tracked down her cheek, the red in her eyes, the terror on her face and trembling of her too-thin body. She memorized what Torra looked like in this moment. Because this was the true cost of King Louis's power.

This was his real villainy. She had wanted to get the spear for many reasons. For money, for the safety of her chosen family, for Graves's collection, to keep it out of the hands of monsters who would start a new war with its power.

But this…this was the real consequence of him ruling.

She had wanted the spear to finish the job.

Now, she wanted it to slit King Louis's fucking throat.

Chapter Forty-Three

K ierse evaded the vampire guards that put Red Velvet on lockdown. But the rest of Third Floor seemed to continue as if nothing had happened. What was one dead vampire in a place that served fresh meat and blood on every corner? She was shaken up, but she needed to make sure she had covered her tracks at least.

She didn't have any blood on her. The alleyway had been dark, and her hood had been up. If there were cameras, she might be caught, but she hadn't noticed any in the gloom. In fact, she hadn't noticed them anywhere except on the gates of Louis's residence. As if the only thing he really cared about in his lawless world was his own well-being. Fucker.

Once everything seemed to calm down, she texted Graves to let him know she was on her way and backtracked down the long corridor that led to the checkpoint. She rescanned her card, passed through the wards, and was on the other side.

Graves waited for her at the mouth of the tunnel. "Well, how did it go?"

"Not to plan," she said. She couldn't seem to get her hands to stop shaking.

He took one look at her face and her trembling body and asked almost gently, "What happened?"

"Not here," she said.

But she could barely get the words out.

Graves just nodded. He understood the need for secrecy more than anyone else she'd ever met. More than herself, even. So, when he guided her away from the tunnel, she followed mutely.

She needed to get it together. She could not have a breakdown. She could not lose control. She had to get back to the library, back to the safety of Graves's home. Back to the safety of…Graves.

When had she started to think of him as a safe place? Hadn't he been just another monster? But now he…wasn't. That much, she knew.

She trusted him. Not just with her body the other night, but with her safety, and now her…secrets. She could trust him with her secrets about Torra.

"This is far enough," Graves said, pulling her to a stop. "You're shaking.

Tell me what happened."

Kierse leaned back against the tunnel. She *was* still shaking, and she couldn't get herself to stop. "A year ago, I was dating someone. Her name was Torra."

"Okay," Graves said uncertainly.

"We met through the Dreadlords, and things got serious fast. She wanted me to move in. She wanted a relationship. A real life together," she told him, remembering it like it was yesterday. "I was still...not ready for that. She thought I would never be ready. We had a huge fight and broke it off." She met his gaze. "And then she disappeared."

"Disappeared?" he asked.

"Into Third Floor."

Graves stilled. "And you found her?"

"I thought she was dead, Graves," she said around the knot in her throat. "I thought she was gone forever. Vampires raided her apartment and stole her. I only found the information after the fact, but Nate couldn't get into the underworld. He couldn't get in because he was a human sympathizer. We didn't know about the wards. He lost a wolf trying to get below, and he had to stop. We both had to stop."

"Fuck," he whispered.

"So, I planned to find the people who did this and get answers."

"You never mentioned this."

"I know," she said, letting him see the desperation in her expression. The vulnerability that she so rarely showed anyone. "I don't talk about her. Not with Nate. Not even with Gen and Ethan."

"And yet you're telling me," he said slowly as he realized the implications of this.

"I want you to understand."

"Tell me." But it wasn't fierce; it was reassuring, as if she could talk to him, as if it could always be like this.

"I found the vampire who stole her. I killed him."

Graves's smile was dangerous. "Good."

"You don't judge me for it?"

"Why would I? He deserved it."

"Yeah," she said, breathing out. It wasn't her first kill. No, Jason had claimed that honor, but she had always fought to stay out of those situations. She had never gone looking for trouble like that. "Yeah, he deserved it. I'd do it again."

"I'd do it for you."

She nodded, mutual understanding settling between them. "He told me Torra was alive. I saw her at the brothel. She's working for King Louis." Fire sparked in her eyes as she let him see her fury. He met it with his own need of vengeance. "I promised to get her out. I promised to find an exit for her. And I promised to fucking kill him in the end."

Graves was silent for a moment before nodding. "He's earned it."

"Yes, he fucking has."

"And you?" he asked, taking that last step forward toward her.

"What about me?"

"Are you going to be all right?"

Her fire extinguished at that look in his eyes. Not pity. Not that horrid word that she could never accept. But understanding, acceptance, vulnerability. An instant where they both let their guard down in the wake of unequal tragedy.

"I don't know," she admitted.

"Come here." He held his arms out toward her.

And for a moment, she couldn't process the offer. Couldn't put together this Graves who was offering her comfort with the hardened monster she had first met. Couldn't believe that he could change this much for her, as she had changed this much for him.

She wanted it.

She wanted it every bit as much as the sex.

So she stepped forward into his embrace. She flinched at the first touch, but once his warmth enveloped her, she released the last wave of tension holding her upright and settled into his arms.

Then she began to cry.

Chapter Forty-Four

Three trips into the dark market, and Kierse had found nothing. No way out that wasn't controlled by one of Walter's checkpoints. No concealed exit. Not even gossip about how to get in. She'd followed people through three other checkpoints, but that hadn't been any more help than the one Graves knew about. The extra card she'd filched that first time had proven useless as well.

And they were running out of time. The winter solstice was in four days.

At least while she was within the walls of Third Floor, she could confirm that Torra was still alive. Even if it was torture that she couldn't get her out. And if she couldn't find an exit in time, then all the plans were fucked. Graves couldn't come with her, and Torra couldn't get out of that hellhole.

Which was why she was back in Graves's library, trying to find a way to make this work. The door creaked open behind her, and she smelled the cinnamon before she looked up.

"What is that?" she gasped.

"Sustenance," he said with a small smile that she recognized as something specifically for her. She didn't know when she'd started to judge them for herself, but she knew them.

"It smells like heaven."

He set the parcel on the table, next to the map she had been scouring. It had every entrance and route that Graves had discovered into and out of the underground. She glanced inside and saw the cinnamon babka. Her stomach rumbled at the same time her heart flipped.

"Babka?" she asked.

"Your favorite."

It was. But she hadn't suspected that he was going to get her any. Even if he'd been mad about Lorcan sending her some. Even if she'd had a complete breakdown on him and felt the warmth of him as a balm. She could hardly believe it.

"Thank you," she whispered as she broke off a piece and popped it into her mouth. She groaned at the taste of it. She'd thrown away the loaf from

Lorcan before she could try it. And it was better than she even remembered. "So good."

Graves ate a small bite of his own and nodded with approval. "I see why you like it."

"Best in town." She ate a few more bites as she looked over the map. "That poor man."

"What do you mean?"

She glanced back up at him. "Hopefully you didn't scare the shit out of him like Lorcan."

Graves looked offended. "I do not frighten little old men."

"You're pretty frightening."

"I appreciate that," he said lazily as he snatched up another bite.

"We need him to keep making this bread. So I hope you turned it down a notch."

"I paid him handsomely." His eyes met hers. "For you."

She swallowed and nodded, quickly returning to the map again. She could feel Graves's eyes on her, but she said nothing. Just waited for him.

"I've been thinking," Graves said. He came to stand next to her.

"Dangerous," she told him.

Ever since their moment in the tunnels, it was like she could feel his awareness all the time. Like there was a string that guided them back together. And when they were this close in proximity, her heart began to beat frantically. She couldn't seem to cut her gaze away from his face or the lines of his body in his suit.

"We need to find that exit."

"What do you think I've been doing?" she asked.

"I am not denigrating your reconnaissance work," he assured her.

"Fine. If you have a new suggestion on how to get you in and Torra out of there, I'm all ears."

"Well, when I believed that you had immunity, I wasn't sure if you could use your passive gift at all. If you could, then we could have tried to see if you were capable of projecting your immunity on to me."

"Thanks for running that one by me."

"Projection like that is advanced magical work." His eyes cast over her face. "There wasn't enough time for you to learn that level of magic."

"I still can't even ward a stupid box," she grumbled.

Despite working on her magic training in the hours she wasn't in the underworld, she had come no further than before. She was starting to think that her absorption must be just as passive as the rest of her magic. Or that because she wasn't a warlock maybe she couldn't even do it.

"Maybe we've been focusing on the wrong thing," he admitted.

"Did you just say that you're wrong?"

His smile was quick as he leaned toward her. "Surely not. What I mean is, maybe we need to get you to focus on actively absorbing. I want to test to see if your absorption can not just bypass the magic but also *break* wards."

"How would that work?"

"Right now, your absorption is passive. You walk through my wards. They brush against you. You absorb whatever touches you and continue on. But what if you could absorb more than what touched you? What if you could absorb the entire ward?"

She furrowed her brows. "You think I could do that?"

"If you've spent days on making your own wards and aren't getting any further, then it's worth trying something else."

"All right. I'm willing to try anything at this point." She turned to face him and caught his gaze sweeping to her mouth, but then quickly back up as if he hadn't done it at all. "And if I *can* do it, you don't think it'll be like the wish powder all over again? That I'll absorb more than I can process?"

"Limits," he said. "We find out how much you can absorb. When you start to fatigue, we back off."

"That sounds like a super fun time, but if I brought in too much magic with the wards, wouldn't the wards then start to deflect me? As in I could be trapped inside Third Floor without a way to get out."

"It's possible," he admitted slowly. "Too much magic does override your system, but I don't believe Walter's wards are strong enough to hit your limits."

"Why? They're strong enough to keep you out."

He shot her a smile that was all teeth. "But he's afraid of me. He doesn't know about you. Plus, you have the advantage in this situation because you know how to release your magic."

"I do?" she asked, furrowing her brow.

"You can go slow motion, as you say, to dispel some of the magic you absorb. I suspect that's why you were passing out from it."

She straightened at that. She hadn't exactly considered that option. "You think that would work?"

"We have a lot of tests ahead of us. So, let's get started."

Graves beckoned her over to the center of the library, where he'd placed the illusive warded box she'd opened at their first meeting. She wished she could figure out how to ward her *own* box, which was currently upstairs.

"Oh, do we get to play open the box again?" she asked with a short laugh.

"Not quite."

"Intent, right?" she guessed. "I need to focus my intent on the box to absorb it."

"No. That's basic warding. This goes beyond that." He rested his hand on top of the box. "Kingston told you some of this to start, though I'm not sure if you were paying attention. Magic has a feel to it. A sense, of a sort. It opens something inside you."

"I was paying attention. What does magic feel like?"

"All magic has a different sense to it, depending on what the person is capable of. But magic itself, raw magic, has always been pure energy. Like when the sun shines on your skin, warming you, or the crackling of a fire. You can feel the energy from the fire, from the sun."

She nodded. "I can feel the energy off of you all the time."

He quirked an eyebrow. "Can you?"

"Your heat, fire. You're constantly burning up."

His look heated her up right then. She had never told him that she could feel how warm he was around her. He seemed impressed.

"Then you have the first sense of it. I am constantly using low levels of magic to maintain my wards. I always run warm, but it's the magic you feel. There's more than the physical heat. There's the magical energy. There's a life to it. Sometimes a smell to it. I've been told that my magic smells like leather and parchment."

She frowned and wondered if she'd ever smelled that on him. But she didn't think so.

"That's where we're going to start today. I want you to find my magic. Sense it. After that, we'll work on having you actively absorb my magic into your body."

Doubt crept through her. She had never been magical except by coincidence. Her slow motion was a natural extension of herself. She'd never known it *was* magic. She hadn't even known she was absorbing magic, and she couldn't seem to get any of the warding to work. She didn't know if she could do this.

"Breathe, Wren," he reminded her, settling his hands on her shoulders to get her to focus on him. Her eyes met his, and even though the contact should have made her uneasy, it relaxed her.

She released a breath and nodded as he added, "It's just practice."

"Okay, I'm ready."

Once she had finally calmed, Graves withdrew and then slowly removed his gloves. Knowing how much work it took him to be comfortable around her without them, she loved when he took them off. Loved every glimpse she got of that hidden tattoo.

"I'm going to touch you, releasing my energy into you as my magic tries to read you. You'll naturally absorb it, but I want you to focus on it. Feel the energy."

"I'll try." She hesitated. "Will you be able to read me?"

"No. Not unless you're overwhelmed by magic."

"Okay," she said softly.

"May I?"

She nodded. This time, he was asking permission. How different that must be for a man who always took what information he wanted. Even knowing he couldn't take from her, he was still being careful. She appreciated it.

His fingers curled invitingly around her wrist, the pressure of his palm gentle against her bare skin. She was distracted as she got lost in his swirling gray eyes. He so rarely touched her that it was hard to focus. She had to bring her concentration back on the magical training.

Kierse tried to sense something other than his touch and the heat of him sliding up her wrist. She narrowed her eyes. There must be something. She wanted so badly to smell that tang of the leather and the fresh parchment from him. To know what he *really* smelled like. Not just the man he appeared on the outside, but the real person underneath it all. No matter how hard she tried, all she felt was him touching her.

"Any luck?" She shook her head, and he released her. "I have some other ideas as well. It won't come automatically. Especially since you have never had to be intentional about your own abilities. It's new. We'll keep working on it."

"All right," she said, disappointed.

It wasn't like she had learned to steal in one sitting. She couldn't expect herself to get it immediately, but she still wanted to.

"Do you think all of this isn't working because I'm not a warlock?"

He shook his head. "No. I think it's just new. And there's only one way to get better."

"Practice," she said, and they went back to work.

After hours of training, Kierse was no better off than when she had begun. She couldn't feel the magic that she was absorbing. There was no buzz or rumble or sense to it. There was just Graves, touching her.

Or her hand on the ward against one of his boxes that felt like cold wood. Or an ounce of red wish powder that he produced in a vial. Just looking at it had made her want to throw up. But he'd assured her it was nothing like what she'd inhaled at Imani's house and then unhelpfully told her that she might be more susceptible to it after what happened. Be able to feel its power.

She couldn't.

Instead, she broke out into cold sweats and had to try another day.

That was how she found herself back inside Third Floor.

Chapter Forty-Five

Torra hugged herself tightly in the back shadows of Red Velvet when Kierse approached, as promised. "I don't have a lot of time. Did you find a way out?"

Kierse shook her head, hating that she was bringing bad news. "Not yet. Did you hear anything?"

"I don't want to raise suspicions, but we had a meeting about an upcoming party and I tried to ask around." Torra frowned. "They're all still pretty upset about Orik. I didn't want them to think I was plotting an escape. People don't escape this place."

"You will," she assured her.

She hadn't thought that Torra would be able to find a way out. If she had, then she'd already have left this place a year ago. No, Kierse knew she had to find it.

"What about this upcoming party?" Kierse asked.

"It's King Louis's winter solstice party. He throws it every year. Last year was…a bloodbath," Torra said with a shudder.

Kierse shivered. Torra was going to be at the same party where Kierse and Graves were planning to steal the spear. She needed to get her out before the party.

"What?" Torra asked.

"Nothing."

"I know you better than that. Why do I have a feeling you'll be at that party?"

"I'm running a job there," she admitted.

"Don't," Torra said. "How would you even get in? You're human. They'll kill you."

"I have an invitation."

Torra grasped her arm, fear crossing her face. "They will kill you."

"I'm going, Torra, and I'm going to find a way so that you don't have to go."

"We should use the party as cover," Torra said instead. "You find your exit. I can get you safely into that party and give them a reason not to immediately kill you. We can get out together from there."

She shook her head. "I'm not putting you in danger."

"I'm already in danger," she hissed. "I'm trying to think of how we both get out alive."

"I need the exit first."

"Then get to work," Torra admonished fondly. "But think on the party. I don't know how you got an invitation, but I promise you, I know King Louis. And you do *not* want to use it to get inside."

Torra stumbled back toward Red Velvet, leaving Kierse wondering exactly how Graves had gotten the invitation. Torra had been down here long enough to know how these things work. Maybe she was right. Maybe she and Graves needed to go back over the plan.

But first...a fucking exit.

She circumvented the brothel and headed back to Blood. Since crisscrossing through the Third Floor entrances didn't seem to bear any fruit, she'd decided to do the more boring side of recon work: wait, watch, and listen.

Thankfully, it was a different bartender today, and the goblin seemed to care even less that she wasn't drinking, though she kept a glass in front of her the whole time. She was here to listen for pertinent information. Except that no one mentioned anything relevant in the hour she sat and listened in on conversations. Nothing on ways in or out. Nothing on King Louis. Nothing at all.

Today was a bust. Kierse put some cash on the bar and stood from her chair. Sure, there were plenty of monsters. An incubus leaning against his succubus pair as they stared lasciviously at a goblin enjoying a beer across the bar. A mermaid on two legs with hair the color of seaweed speaking to a sketchy shifter. They all made sense. All allies of the vampires during the Monster War. But the pack of nymphs surprised her. They were closest to humans, along with wolves. More monsters had gone underground than Kierse had even realized.

She'd just pushed through the double doors, ready to do some more traditional reconnaissance, since her wait and watch hadn't helped anything, when something caught her eye.

A flash of thick, black-rimmed glasses, a distressed superhero T-shirt, and a pair of dirty black Converse. He looked out of place amidst the mayhem of the market, which made him stand out. She knew him instantly from the photograph in Graves's library.

Walter Rodriguez.

She hastened around the corner of the pub. Her eyes scanned the crowd, and she nearly walked directly into a wraith.

She skittered backward, edging away from the soul-sucker. "Sorry," she said, pitching her voice low.

Then she saw him. Just a wisp of his curly, dark-brown hair.

There and gone. He'd disappeared down a side alley.

Kierse raced after him. She rounded the corner and found him standing at the back entrance of a restaurant. Sliding into the shadows, she concealed herself in the darkness of the cavern to listen in on the conversation.

"Ah, you're here again already?" a mer asked Walter with anger scrunching his face.

"Yeah. It's that time, Ulster," Walter said.

Ulster huffed. "We have a few in the back. He likes them young, yes?"

He cleared his throat. "Yeah. Yep. Young."

"Fine. I'll send the lot over."

"Good. By tonight," Walter added.

"You know," Ulster growled.

He reached out his hand as if he were going to yank Walter up by the collar of his superhero shirt. But once he got within inches of Walter's body, he bounced harmlessly off. As if he'd hit an invisible wall.

A force field.

Kierse blinked. Well, that was pretty clear. She had just seen how Walter's force field worked. It was an invisible barrier around his own person, several inches in front of his body.

Walter tsked, suddenly losing his uncomfortable, dopey demeanor and straightening his long limbs out. "King Louis won't like that one bit. You might want to send the girls over right away, or else I might have to tell him."

Ulster cowered backward a step. Even here, magic terrified people. What a trussed-up little shit. He was King Louis's lackey. He put up wards, maintained the checkpoints, and even collected humans for his feeding.

She shuddered at that thought. He liked them *young*. Gross.

Walter took off, and Kierse decided to tail him to see exactly what he was up to. He stopped once to pick up his *own* dinner, which were mouthwatering empanadas that made her stomach grumble. A second stop to check a faulty ward at the door to some sort of weapons facility. She must have passed right through one at Red Velvet and not even noticed. No wonder no one seemed concerned by her appearance.

Another machine was hooked up in front of the door, and the tall, black-clad shifter owner gesticulated wildly about him taking too long to fix the broken ward. Walter ignored the monster and got to work, fixing it in a matter of minutes.

Then, finally, he ended up at another brothel. This one seemed more like what she expected from above as well. Not vamp specific but likely still trafficked humans. Fucking atrocious.

Reconnaissance could be so boring sometimes. So much more waiting that felt pointless. She yawned and covered the gesture with her hand, slinking back into the shadows as a vamp passed too close to where she was standing. She doubted Walter would last that long inside with the prostitutes, but maybe they'd try to draw it out. Get their money's worth and all that. She knew all the tricks of the trade even if she'd never been a part of it.

However, Walter appeared only a few minutes later. He frowned at the establishment. As if he too found the whole thing distasteful. That was a surprise.

Kierse trailed him past the brothel and along the outskirts of the market. The farther from the center, the seedier the locations got, but he seemed unperturbed. Of course someone with a natural barrier against danger would feel that way. She'd love to come upon him with a knife at his throat just to see his shock. His force field wouldn't work against her. Which made her feel like a lioness stalking her prey.

Then, in the blink of an eye, he disappeared.

She frowned. Where the hell had he gone? He'd been right in front of her, and she doubted he had some sort of magic invisibility, too. Graves insisted that two strong powers were rare.

After a minute of indecision, she walked over to the wall he had been standing in front of, running her hand across the surface to look for an explanation. It looked the same as the rest of the wall, except it wasn't. It was like the darkened entrance she and Graves had walked through in the subway tunnel. Not invisible at all.

With a deep breath, she stepped through it into another narrow tunnel. She ran her hand along the wall and felt his warding in place. Bingo.

She was quiet as a mouse as she stalked forward. A secret entrance into the market. She almost beamed with excitement. Because if there was a secret entrance…that meant there was a secret *exit*.

And she *liked* exits.

Not just that—she desperately needed this one.

Walter's footsteps were heavy ahead. With the din of the market gone, she realized he tromped like an arrogant fool. He had no need to step quietly, to learn stealth. Not with his ability. Graves had said magic had consequences. And Walter had learned to not fear pain or retribution, because who could touch him with his force fields up? He'd gotten careless. She could exploit that.

She walked behind him until they came to a fork. To her shock, this fork was *labeled*. She listened for Walter going on ahead to the left. But the right read RESIDENCE.

Walter's home? Or King Louis's? Was this the back entrance into Track 61?

The tunnel she was on said MARKET. But the one Walter walked down wasn't labeled, which meant she needed to find out where exactly he was going.

She followed Walter's clomping feet. She made a point to memorize the twists and turns through the darkness, but she was losing the trail. If not for the sound of Walter before her, she might have gotten hopelessly lost.

They continued for roughly a half hour. She guessed they'd gone about a mile at this pace before she saw light flare in the tunnel ahead. Walter's figure was briefly illuminated before he climbed up a ladder into the light.

Walking into the light was not ideal, but she needed to see what lay ahead. Kierse waited five full minutes and then eased forward, coming to the top of the ladder and finding herself at another subway tunnel. A light lit the trapdoor, but unless she was looking directly at it, it was essentially invisible. She recognized the wards etched into the opening. Which meant even if someone else found it, no one could get inside. Except her, of course.

And if she could learn to absorb the wards in time, Graves and Torra, too.

She hauled herself up through the door and trekked to the nearest subway platform. Luckily, no one was around when she towed herself up onto the southbound platform of 23rd Street station. Signs showed service to R and W trains. She racked her brain. 23rd and 5th Avenue. That was the Flatiron District. She'd come out right in front of the famous Flatiron Building.

Kierse pulled out her phone, and Graves answered on the first ring.

"Are you okay?"

"I found my exit," she told him.

"You did?" he asked, surprise layered in his voice.

"I followed Walter through a secret tunnel out of the market. Do you have a way to track me so that we can get a route through the tunnel?"

He paused a moment. "Yes."

"Do it. I'm going to backtrack to the market."

"Done," he said. "Be careful."

"As always," she joked. "I'm going to go back in the tunnels now."

"Hey," he said into the phone before she could step back off the platform.

"Yeah?"

"Good job."

She grinned and then hung up.

Just that one little compliment made her giddy. She probably should have hated how she preened under his praise, but it was all the sweeter when she'd earned it.

Chapter Forty-Six

I t took her forever to figure out how to backtrack through the tunnel. Now that she wasn't following the sound of Walter's stomping and scuffing feet, she made a few wrong turns but eventually made it. She wanted to check the residence but decided to leave it for tomorrow. They had three full days to figure out how to get around down here and how to break the wards to use it as the entrance and exit for the heist. It wasn't enough time, but it would have to do.

Kierse returned to the original checkpoint and out the Times Square subway entrance.

As she hauled herself back up onto what she thought was an empty platform, a hand reached out and grasped her wrist, yanking her up. She snarled, reaching for her one of her pistols. She had it out and leveled at the man's head before she recognized him.

She didn't lower the gun.

"Lorcan," she said.

"What a welcome," he said with his same charming smile.

"Why are you following me?"

"I did say that we'd meet again."

"Yes, but I didn't think that you'd come to me." It didn't seem his style. Even if he'd said that he would the last time they met. The babka had felt like more of a warning than anything.

"I didn't, either," he admitted. "But…I feel compelled to you."

She narrowed her eyes behind her gun. "Try again."

"Can you please stop pointing that thing at me? I am here on good faith."

"Like that time you tried to have me killed or the time you kidnapped me?"

"I did apologize for the first, and the kidnapping included dinner. That has to count for something?" His smile only widened.

"Does it?"

"I just want to talk. I promise," he told her, stepping forward. He put his hand up and gingerly pushed the barrel of the gun down toward their feet.

"Now, there, isn't that better?"

"Not particularly."

He laughed that real, easy laugh, like he didn't have a care in the world. "Let's go up top and walk."

"It's freezing outside."

"I can give you my coat," he offered with a quirked eyebrow.

"I'll pass."

"On the coat or the walk?"

"Yes," she responded. "Stalking isn't cute. It's how people get killed."

"Says the woman still holding the gun."

She and Graves had already agreed that they could use Lorcan's interest in her to their advantage. The same way that she had considered it for Nate. But when it had been with Nate, it had felt like planting a bomb in the monster's path. Here, it felt like Graves was offering her a way to get information out of his enemy. And while she wanted to find out how much he knew about their mission, she honestly wanted him to stop stalking her more.

"Okay. I will go for a walk with you under one condition." He waited as if anticipating a blow. "You agree to stop stalking me."

"I will agree to your condition on one condition. You give me your number."

"What?" she asked, startled. "Why?"

"So that I don't have to continue to stalk you."

"Insufferable," she muttered under her breath. "You know it's Times Square up there."

He smirked. "You'll be safe with me."

And for some reason, she believed him.

"Fine," she said, holstering her weapon and then walking toward the exit with Lorcan on her heels.

She headed up the stairs, past the troll, and up into the cold of the city. She'd been underground so long that it felt good to breathe in clean air rather than the circulated air below. But it was Times Square, and she couldn't let her guard down.

While she had been in the subway below many times now, she hadn't been on the street in Times Square in at least a year. She was surprised to see that half of the enormous screens were back up and running. Even familiar name brands and Broadway shows were advertising on the streets again. A handful of powerful shows had started new runs this year. Monsters *and* humans were welcome.

And the tourists had returned in full force. Kierse expected them on Fifth Avenue. Those who could afford the high-end boutiques would always find a way. But she hadn't expected this many people to brave Times Square… as if things were normal.

"It's been a while since you've been here?" Lorcan asked.

"I pretty much avoided it at all costs before it was decimated."

She had only been twelve when the war started, but she'd already been working with Jason for years. She hadn't been a normal kid by any stretch of the imagination. Tourists were only good as easy marks. Otherwise, they made her break into hives. NYC being free of tourists had been one of the only good things about the war.

"It's good to see it get back to normal."

She nodded, a smile almost tugging at her lips.

"Come on. I like a little café nearby. We can get out of the cold." He brushed a hand back through his dark hair, his big, blue eyes guileless, and smiled at her. All perfectly straight teeth and the hint of a dimple in his right cheek.

"Why are you doing this?" she asked. "We're on opposite sides."

He looked personally offended by that sentiment. "Are we?"

"You hate my boss."

"Not everything is black and white." Then his smile widened. "Plus, I'm only asking for coffee."

She might as well see what she could get out of him. "Fine. I could use some coffee."

Lorcan liked to hear himself talk. So he kept up the chatter as they headed down 42nd Street toward Bryant Park and an innocuous twenty-four hour coffee shop. Kierse ordered a black coffee, and he got a cappuccino, looking pleased with himself. Once they got their coffee from a harried barista, they settled into a booth.

"If you don't wipe that smirk off of your face, I'm going to regret coming here with you."

He brought his coffee cup to his lips, trying and failing to not smile. "I thought we could pick up where we left off."

"Which was…?"

"You wanted to know about my history with Graves," he said smoothly.

She stared down into her mug. Did she let him know that she knew something of his history? Would it be a better play to see what he said?

And what was Lorcan's play in all of this? He clearly wanted to poach her or at least figure out what Graves's next move was. Not something she was going to give to him. But she wouldn't mind determining exactly what *his* next move was.

"And why should I trust anything you're going to tell me?"

"That's fair," he said, taking a sip of his coffee. "I know it's hard to see, but I'm not the bad guy in this. Graves is your villain."

Kierse smiled, leaning forward on her elbow. "You think sending me babka is enough to make you a good guy?"

Lorcan shrugged it off with a laugh. "I thought you'd enjoy it. That's all. I couldn't help myself."

"Nothing to do with Graves at all."

"You got me," he said good-naturedly. "But when you're working for someone like that, you should see him for who he really is."

"A monster," she guessed.

"Exactly." Lorcan leaned forward to match her posture, as if they were sharing secrets. "A girl like you shouldn't get involved with someone like him. I don't know what he has you doing, but it can't be good. Is this why you've been going into Third Floor?"

She arched an eyebrow. He was really fishing for information. "Did you follow me there?"

"Into that disgusting place? Heavens no." He wrinkled his nose. "But I can guess based on the entrance. Though not why."

So…he didn't know about the spear. Or at least not that they were trying to steal it. Despite him seemingly interrogating her, he was sure giving her easy information.

Kierse threw down a hand to see if he'd bite. "I have a friend in there," she said, letting her voice tremble a little and staring into her coffee. It wasn't hard to conjure. "She's in debt. I've been going to see her to try to find a way to get her out."

"No one leaves that place while in debt," he said as if he knew for a fact.

"Yeah. That's what she says."

"And this friend…she's the job?"

"She's not a job," she snapped at him, looking up at him with watery eyes. "She's a person."

"I'm sorry," he said softly. "I didn't mean to sound insensitive."

"It's fine," she whispered. She took a drink of the piping-hot coffee.

When he cleared his throat again, he asked, "Does all of this have something to do with Walter Rodriguez?"

Kierse kept a carefully neutral expression on her face. "Who's that?"

Lorcan laughed, easy and bright. "He was a failed pet project of Graves. A rogue warlock working in the market sounds just like something Graves would want to stop. You're armed to the teeth. I suspect you're...what? Bait?"

She gave him an innocent look. "Never heard of him. But he sounds like someone I should avoid."

"For your safety, you probably shouldn't associate with warlocks at all."

"Little late for that, isn't it?"

"Never too late. I'll be frank with you: Graves and I used to be close. We were like family." Kierse stilled as she heard the shape of the same story tumble from Lorcan's mouth. And he seemed rightfully sad about it. She wondered how much of it was an act. "The only reason we're not anymore is because of his betrayal. He's going to hurt you the way he hurt me, the way he hurts everyone." He traced the rim of his cup. "You don't have to work for him. Others have tried to work with him as you are now, but there's a reason no one else stays at his side. I don't want to see you like that. I don't know what he has over you, but you could leave. You'd be safe with my Druids."

"I'll take that into consideration."

Lorcan jerked his eyes back up to her. "You look like you want to cut me again. Am I really that distasteful to be around?"

The answer was no. He wasn't. He was a little too confident, but something about him felt so easy and comfortable.

That didn't mean she didn't see through him. He was trying to make her second-guess Graves, and she'd just began to feel like he made sense.

"Are you insecure enough that you have to ask?" she asked him instead.

"Around you...maybe." His expression was earnest. "You put me off-balance."

Fuck, he was really going for it. Really put it all out there. This *must* be a front. He had to be acting in the same way she had when she told him the story about Torra—fishing for information. No one could be this clueless.

"Because I don't grovel at your feet?"

"I am a man used to getting what he wants," he said casually, rubbing his hand across his beard. "But I just like to spend time with you. You're different."

"I'm different," she said sarcastically. "Try a different line. That one is a little cliché."

He chuckled and put his hands up. "You're right, of course, but it doesn't change how I feel."

Kierse tugged her hair out of its ponytail at the nape of her neck. It was starting to give her a headache. Or maybe it was this conversation. Or the time. God, she was tired. She downed the rest of her coffee. The caffeine would help for a whole minute.

"I should go. Thanks for the coffee."

"Wait," he said.

She was half out of her seat when the word fell from his lips. She glared at him. "What?"

"Your number," he reminded her.

"I didn't agree to that."

He slid his phone across the table without another word. "Come on, trade with me. I know that you didn't add my number to your phone." She hadn't. She still had the business card, but she had never intended to use it. "Look, I won't follow you anymore. We can just try...talking. Friends."

"Do all your friends threaten to kill each other?"

He considered. "Yes. I'd say that's accurate."

She couldn't help the smile that tugged at her lips. The bastard found a way to make it come out when she wanted to keep it hidden. Despite herself, she passed him her phone while she input her digits into his.

"Have a good night," she told him, retrieving her phone.

His hand slipped out and took her wrist. As if he couldn't stop himself from touching her one last time. "Good night, Kierse."

She gently pulled her hand free and stalked out of the coffee shop. She considered Lorcan's angle. Was he trying to recruit her to his cause, or did he just hate Graves that much?

She was glad that Graves had suggested this. It was easier this time to get caught and sift through Lorcan's supposed sincerity. Too much was on the line for Lorcan to be this close to their mission. The last thing she wanted was for him to try to interfere.

Plus, she liked that Graves laid down the same cards she did. It was always better to know where your enemy stood.

Chapter Forty-Seven

The brownstone was silent when she made it back. But the silence was no longer overwhelming or deadly. Instead, it was something good to come back to. Almost like…a home.

She headed up the stairs and was surprised to see Graves's light on in the room across from his second-floor study. She'd never seen what was in the room. A part of her little thieving brain said to find out, but as interested as she was, as much as she wanted to know all his secrets, she found that she wanted him to confide those secrets in her. That learning them from him was much more satisfying.

So, she turned toward the stairs, leaving him to his night, but just as she climbed the first step, she heard the doorknob turn. And when she glanced back, Graves came out the door in nothing but a pair of black running pants.

Her breath caught. She'd never seen him undressed. Even when they'd had sex, he had been fully clothed. He'd even had his gloves on. She was regretting that decision now.

His chest rose and fell rapidly as if he'd been out for an evening jog. Sweat gleamed on his muscled torso, the droplets collecting in every curve and crevice of his rippled abdominals. And that tattoo was finally, *finally* visible. Holly vines started around his wrists and snaked up his tense, veined forearms, up the ridge of his biceps and over his shoulder to the edges of his chest. The vines constricted around the muscles, and thorns bit into his skin as if they were physically piercing the flesh. It was intricate and mesmerizing and easily the most lifelike tattoo she had ever seen.

Her heart pounded in her chest. Just the sight of him standing there made her belly dip and core pulse. She wanted him again just as she'd had him when he'd pinned her against the library shelves. Rough and ready with the monster off the leash.

But much more terrifying was the fact that she wanted *him*. Graves the man. Not the monster. An all-new feeling.

Graves looked up then and saw her watching. Let her watch.

She swallowed, stepping back down the stairs and facing him. "Late-night run?"

"It clears my head," he confessed. "You're back late."

"I had a run-in with Lorcan," she said, her eyes drifting lower and lower to the Adonis *V* at the top of his pants.

He smirked when she glanced back up at him, not self-conscious in the least. Just walking toward her and filling the space. "How did that go?"

"You were right. He doesn't know about the spear. He bought the half truths that I fed him. I told him I was there to see a friend. He guessed we were going after Walter because he'd gone rogue."

"Good," Graves said, pleased. "I knew that we could use him stalking you to our advantage."

Her eyes floated over his corded arms. The biceps that bulged and those broad shoulders. "Uh-huh."

"You look exhausted," he said, closing the distance.

"I am," she admitted with a yawn. She covered her mouth and wished she could have suppressed it. She was tired, but she wouldn't mind if he kept her up all night.

He bridged the distance, tucking a loose strand of her hair behind her ear. She normally would have pulled away from that touch. Yet she didn't pull away. More importantly, she didn't want to pull away.

Not from Graves.

Something had shifted between them. And it wasn't purely physical. In fact, it was terrifying mostly because they hadn't hooked up again since that night in the library. Still, things had changed. She had grown more open. She was beginning to be able to interpret the man who was impossible to interpret. And he was looking at her...

God, he was looking at her as if she was something...precious.

Something worthy of protecting.

How long had it been since she let anyone protect her the way that Graves had? She had her friends. They would go to the ends of the earth for her, but it was always her protecting them. And Nate was family, but she watched her own back and he knew it. Even Colette, who cared for her, was looking out for herself first and foremost. It was why they had always gotten along. These were her people.

And yet...Graves held her life in his hands, and she believed he would bring her to the other side. Her stomach fluttered at the thought.

"You're shaking again," he said, tipping her chin up to look at him.

"I've never seen you like this."

"Out of a suit?" he asked.

"Exposed," she whispered.

He tipped his head. "I'm not exposed when I'm with you."

Then he dropped his lips down onto hers, and she lost all thought. He tasted like bliss, and she wanted to drown in him. Wrap herself up in this feeling forever and never break free. She wrapped her arms around his neck and drew his bare skin against her. Felt his heat and the hard planes of his stomach and the firm grip of his hands on her back as he clutched her to him.

For so long, every gentle touch had come with a volatile price, where she had no idea whether or not this was the time she would end up dead. And even with her closest friends, when they could never hurt her, she still flinched at the thought of that level of intimacy. Now here, with Graves, that washed away.

He wasn't going to hurt her. Her entire body melted into him at the realization.

And that was when her phone started buzzing.

Graves jerked back, his eyes narrowing. "What is that?"

"Uh, nothing," she said, realizing in a panic exactly which phone was currently going off.

Her burner.

And only two people had that number—Colette and Nate.

"If it's nothing, then let me see." He held his hand out. His eyes had gone flinty, as if he'd realized that this wasn't something she was supposed to have at the same time she realized he shouldn't know about it.

She'd kept the phone on her at all times, but it was on silent except for emergencies. She hadn't anticipated it ringing in front of Graves. Or at least she figured she would have been able to silence the phone and call them back at another time.

But that was not what was happening.

She dug the phone out, revealing the burner, which had switched off and then quickly began to buzz again.

Graves plucked the thing out of her hand, and before she could stop him, he answered it.

"Kierse!" Nate gasped on the other line before Graves could even say anything. "You need to get out on the street right this minute. Make any excuse you have to. I'm the closest one to your location, since I was on duty, and I'm picking you up."

The whole time Nate had been speaking, Graves's eyes were locked on her. And whatever kindness and understanding had been in them evaporated at the words coming out of Nate's mouth. He knew that she'd been speaking with them, that Nate had been patrolling the house, that she'd given him a way to contact her.

He was knowledge; he could easily infer what all of that meant.

She'd broken their bargain.

"Graves," she whispered.

But Nate was still rambling. "Kierse? Do you hear me? Ethan and a bunch of my wolves were drugged. We don't know if they're going to make it."

In that moment, she didn't care what Graves thought. Ethan was in trouble, and her brain short-circuited. She snatched the phone out of Graves's hand and pressed it to her ear.

"Nate? What happened with Ethan? He was *drugged*?"

"They think someone slipped him something in his drink and they're ODing."

"His drink?" she asked in incomprehension. Ethan wasn't supposed to be anywhere where someone could spike his drink.

"I'll tell you when I get there," he said, swearing foully. "Two minutes or I'm barging in that fucking house, Kierse."

And then he hung up.

Graves's hands were clenched into fists, and his eyes were like ice. He turned on his heel and disappeared. Shit.

She followed after him. "Graves," she called.

But she didn't dare cross the threshold into his room. Whether the door was open or not, it wasn't an invitation. She didn't fucking have time for this, but she had to say *something*.

Just then, Graves returned with a shirt on.

"You've been in contact with your friends and the Dreadlords," he said, his voice frozen over.

"I haven't been in contact with my friends."

"And Nathaniel O'Connor?"

"This isn't about Nate. It's about Ethan."

"Go save your friend," he said, gesturing to the door. "Your wolf should be here any moment."

"Don't do that," she said. "Don't close yourself off right now. This is life or death."

"I would never keep you from your friend's side in a time of need," Graves said. "But this isn't about Ethan. This is about our broken bargain. I made it *very* clear that any contact with your friends and associates would put them at risk and jeopardize this mission."

Kierse shook her head. "That's not what happened at all."

Graves had opened his mouth, ready to breathe fire like the dragon he was, when a banging sounded on the front door. Edgar and Isolde were long gone for the day. And there was only one person who had been sent to pick her up.

Kierse shot Graves a panicked look before hurrying down the stairs and yanking the door open. Nate stood on the stoop in all his glory, real fear on his face.

Graves had followed, looking furious. Nate couldn't set one foot inside the house because of the wards, but he wasn't stupid enough to try anyway.

"Hello, O'Connor," Graves said smoothly.

Nate nodded at him. "Don't mind my intrusion."

"Oh, I don't mind at all," Graves said in a manner that made it certain he did quite mind Nate being at his door. "Our bargain has already been broken." He was still staring at Nate as if just the wrath in his expression could make the wolf disappear. "So go."

"You don't mean that."

"You know that I do."

She snarled back at him, "I know you fucking don't!"

Kierse glanced between the two men. She could hardly process that it was all crumbling down around her right now. Right when Ethan was dying. When no one knew what was going on with him. She had to be there.

Mission or no. Betrayal or no.

She couldn't stay when part of her heart was dying across the city.

"We'll talk about this when I get back," she told him fiercely as she crossed the threshold to where Nate was standing.

Graves took a step away. "We both know you're not coming back."

Then he closed the door in her face.

"Fuck!" she cried.

It couldn't all be over. There was too much at stake for both of them for it to be over.

"Kierse," Nate said urgently behind her. He sounded ready to haul her down the stairs and into the idling car.

In the end, he didn't have to. She would choose Gen and Ethan every time. She would have to fix this thing with Graves after.

She turned on her heel and left his house, broken bargain and all.

Chapter Forty-Eight

K ierse vaulted into Nate's car as he skidded around the corner and dropped into the driver's seat. He put his foot to the pedal and revved the engine.

"Didn't mean to blow your cover," Nate said.

"I don't want to talk about it. All I care about is Ethan right now," she said as she watched the city zip by in the night. "I can deal with Graves later."

"All right," he said.

"Tell me what the fuck happened. Ethan was in the club? What the fuck was Ethan doing in the club?"

"Look, he started learning to bartend with Cara," Nate said, running a hand over his curls.

"Excuse me?" she asked lethally low.

"He wanted to," Nate said. "I told him it would be fine to learn from her but not to be officially on the floor. It's hard being locked in your room, Kierse."

"His life was in danger! He's been drugged!"

"I know. Fuck, I know. The place should have been safe. There are plenty of drugs that run through there, but basically none of it works on my wolves like it does on humans. And three of them are just as bad off, including Cara," he said. "So I take it fucking seriously, and I'm fucking sorry."

"Sorry?" she snapped. "You were supposed to keep them safe."

"They were safe," he insisted. "But fuck, they still have to live. Gen has been working with Maura, training to be a nurse. She fits right in."

"Has she been going *out* with Maura?"

"No, no, just after her shifts and stuff. She's safe. I swear."

"If Ethan dies, Nate, so help me God."

He blanched and nodded. "I know."

Kierse couldn't relax on the entire drive to Five Points. She closed her eyes to calm her racing heart. Freaking out would only make things worse. She needed to be levelheaded. There had to be a solution.

Nate jerked the car into a garage a block from Five Points, and together they hustled through Dreadlord territory. After staying up for nearly twenty-four hours, Kierse was bone weary, but she had to keep going. Nate directed her to a back door where Finn stood guarding the entrance.

"Boss," the man said with a nod and a sad smile when he saw her. "Kierse."

"Hey, Finn."

Finn reached for the door, yanking it open for them.

"Update?" Nate barked. Ronan fell into step beside them as they headed up the stairs.

"Cara, Elijah, and Haylee are all fighting whatever is in their system, but they're reacting worse than what drugs normally do to us wolves." Ronan chanced a dark-eyed glance Kierse's way. "Ethan hasn't progressed further, but he hasn't gotten any better, either. We moved them all to the conference room when Mateo shifted."

Nate's eyebrows rose. "He shifted?"

"Involuntarily."

Nate ground his teeth together. "Fuck. And the substance?"

"We interrogated the bartenders, the doormen, and the regulars who were there when it happened, but no one noticed anything out of the ordinary."

Nate nodded. "Good. Return to your position."

Ronan tipped his head at Nate, then Kierse, before disappearing back into the shadows.

Nate pulled Kierse up another flight of stairs and then thrust open the door to the conference room. She burst inside with Nate on her heels. The room would have been crowded without two full-grown wolves lying on the table. Cara was the last wolf to remain in human form. Her pallid skin was bleached white, and she was shaking as if fighting the shift.

Ethan lay sprawled on a table with Corey clutching his hand. His complexion was sallow, and his scar puckered against his now-sickly face. If it wasn't for the labored rising and falling of his chest, Kierse would have thought he was already dead.

"Oh, Ethan," Kierse said and rushed to his side, taking his other hand.

Gen threw her arms around her. "You made it."

"Of course I did." She pulled back to look into Gen's red-rimmed eyes. She looked thinner, as if this had drained the life out of her, too. "How's he doing?"

"I don't know," Gen said. "Maura is the nurse. I'm only her apprentice."

"And we need a doctor," Maura said tightly. Nate went to her side, pressing a kiss to her cheek. Maura looked at Kierse with a neutral expression, but Kierse saw what wasn't there. It was bad. "Ethan's alive. They're all alive, for now. I already administered activated charcoal to try to keep the drugs from absorbing. But it's not working."

Maura's gaze went to Gen's as if seeking reassurance from her own assistant. Gen had that effect on everyone.

"I can give Ethan another dose," Gen insisted.

"But we can't give it to the wolves. Not without injury to ourselves," she said clearly. "I don't have the equipment to intubate anyone here to pump their stomachs. I'd have to take them to a hospital."

"We could take Ethan," Gen said. "Cara maybe. But what about the wolves? In their shifted form?"

Kierse knew the perfect hospital. "There's a monster hospital. In Queens. They could treat your wolves."

"Queens?" Maura asked. "They'd never make it. I don't even know if we could move any of them."

Cara cried out in that moment, and they all froze as claws suddenly carved divots into the conference table. Her back arched. Her eyes opened wide, going from large and blue to pinpricks in a second. Then, between one breath and the next, she shifted. Her body extended, fur appearing, and when she collapsed back on the table, she was an enormous honey-brown wolf with fangs that could cut a person in two.

"Fuck," Nate cried. "They shouldn't be shifting involuntarily. That's not natural. Maura?"

She shook her head, her calm demeanor nearly shattering.

Gen went to her. "What do we need to do?"

Maura closed her eyes for a split second before saying, "We have to try to get them out of here. I can't do anything more."

"You have to," Corey cried. "If we move him, he's not going to make it."

"If we do nothing, he definitely won't," Nate told him, putting a hand on Corey's shoulder.

Maura sighed. "We don't have time to figure out which one it is. We just need to get him to the hospital."

"I was there when it happened," Corey said mournfully. "One minute, he was completely fine, and the next, he went wild—like completely uninhibited. I'd never seen him like that. I thought it was cute at first, and then…"

Kierse looked into his distressed face. He wasn't crying, but his eyes were distant, lost. As if someone was carving out a piece of him while Ethan lay there on that table. To see this strong Roulette breaking down almost put Kierse over the edge.

"Do we even know what drug could do this?" Kierse asked. "Make wolves shift like that?"

Kierse shoved her hands into her pockets, feeling helpless as fuck. She wished Graves were here. She wished that she had asked him to come with her. Not because he could have done anything to help. He didn't have healing powers. If he did, then surely he would have done something to speed up her own healing when Imani's magic had almost killed her.

What kind of drug could make someone do this? Go completely uninhibited. Make a wolf shift involuntarily.

Could it be that it wasn't a drug at all?

Could it be magic?

And *that* was why the human methods weren't working?

"I've never heard of anything that can force the shift in my wolves," Nate said.

"There's that new drug on the market," Corey suggested. "We don't even know what it looks like to overdose on the red powder."

Kierse froze. "Wait…*red* powder?" Maybe it wasn't just magic. Maybe it was *Imani's magic*. "Is the new drug called wish powder?"

Nate nodded. "Yeah…how did you know that?"

Kierse shook her head. Graves had said that Imani's powder wasn't dangerous. That the product she was producing for her parties just intensified sexual desire. She didn't know if this was an attack from Imani, but someone had clearly wanted to hurt Ethan to get to her.

Either Ethan needed a hospital or Kierse would have to try her magic. Except she didn't know how to use her magic. She'd worked with Graves unsuccessfully for hours. Not once had she been able to even sense him; not once had she been able to use her intent to draw a ward.

But if they took Ethan to a hospital and it was the wish powder, then even if they got in, which was a slim chance at best, there was nothing the doctors could do for him. It would all be for nothing. They could pump his stomach, and the magic wouldn't dissipate. His wish could still kill him.

Graves would know if there was magic involved, but they didn't have time to go get him.

They only had her.

Chapter Forty-Nine

"Let me in," Kierse said, pushing Maura aside to get to Ethan.

"What are you doing?" Maura demanded.

"Kierse?" Gen asked as if sensing the shift in her.

Without warning, she pressed her hands to Ethan's chest and closed her eyes. The magic was there. She just needed to find it, sense it, and feel the weight of it. She'd never done it before, but this wasn't practice. This was life or death.

So, she delved deeper and deeper. She pushed at the spaces of her awareness that she had never tapped into. All those moments she had been quicker, faster, stronger than others her age and older. When she should have been a small runt of a girl who died on the streets, but she had survived. It was those instincts that had kept her alive. It was her own magic and strength that had done that. She would need both for this to work.

Like a sudden awakening of her senses…it was there.

Soft at first. A gentle brush against her awareness. A yearning breeze that said winter was over and spring was coming. Kierse latched on to that feeling, the strange newness within her mind. She clung to it, calling it forth until it came fully into focus. A bright light in the darkness.

She'd been *right*.

Magic suffused Ethan's body. Head to toe, he was tainted with it. The vessel for Imani's powers, the heat and brush of her magic made manifest.

And still there was something more—flowers. She could smell flowers. Specifically lily flowers. She'd never been able to smell another warlock's magic before, but now she was certain that Imani's magic had the cloying, overpowering smell of lilies. Kierse nearly gagged on the taste and oppressive smell of it.

But she refused to lose focus, because next up was the tricky part. She had to absorb the wish magic from Ethan's body and draw it into hers. Kierse had never consciously absorbed magic before. Fear clogged her senses. Not the fear that she couldn't do it, but the fear that she *could*. That she would draw it into herself and drown in that magic again.

Would she survive this? Could she come out whole and strong again after what Imani's magic had reduced her to last time? Without even the antidote from Graves to stabilize her. She opened her mouth, wanting to tell them to call Graves. Please let someone else bear this burden.

But as she did it, the threads slipped. She almost lost Ethan, and he began to seize.

"Kierse!" Corey cried.

Maura tried to shoulder her way in, but Kierse held firm. She closed her eyes, reached for that cloying fragrance, and dug in again.

Graves couldn't help her right now. She was the one who had to figure this out and deal with whatever came after once she was through.

Her hands trembled against Ethan's chest, and for a second, it felt as if something clutched her around the middle. As if she were completely immobilized by that crushing ache. It felt like a ten-ton brick weighing down on her, overwhelming her from all sides and trying to sever the connection.

Then there was a hand on her arm. Just the faintest brush of Gen's fingers. And under that touch, she took in a breath and another. Kierse felt it then…Gen's own magic, of a sort. Not warlock magic. Just a light at the end of a long tunnel. The part of Gen that had always let her read tarot cards and made her medicines so potent. The part of Gen that collected broken strays and nursed them back to health. The part of Gen that was just…Gen.

Gen's touch said she was here. She believed in Kierse. That Kierse could do this. Gen didn't need to know what was happening to trust that Kierse could do it. It was what she needed. Gen always knew what she needed.

And as Kierse wrapped her magic around that kernel of Gen's powers and brought the combined weight down toward Ethan, she felt *another* flicker respond.

Ethan.

A different light than within Kierse or Gen. The part of Ethan that made his plants grow. The part of Ethan that kept him buoyant even in the dark times. The part of Ethan that was purely Ethan.

It pulsed to life at their touch and made a bridge to finish off their triangle. Threefold. A trinity. The beginning, middle, and end. Just enough to bind them together.

With a deep exhale, she held on to Gen and Ethan, knowing now that she could do this. On the next inhale, she breathed in as much air as she could, and with it came the magic.

The energy that had settled onto Ethan's body snaked its way up, up, up, out of him…and into her.

The magic didn't look like anything to anyone else in the room. Up until that moment, even Kierse hadn't been able to see it. But suddenly the smell and fire of the magic turned into a soft golden glow across his entire body. Her eyes widened at the new awareness. The sense of it all coming together, just as Graves had said.

As she reached out for that golden glow, she could *feel* the magic like a rising tide. The magic soaked into her skin and made its way through her body as lilies consumed her and the fire reached for her. *Hello, old, familiar friend.* It ached. Bit into her like it was trying to snap her bones and leave her in a million little pieces. The pain gripped her, tightened, and twisted. With it came agony and a deep look into the abyss. But she held on. Refused to let go.

There was more magic. So much more.

Kierse wanted to throw up, to empty her stomach and rid herself of this vile coating, but she couldn't move her hands. Not even if she'd wanted to. They were glued to Ethan's chest, soaking up every ounce of that golden glow and bringing it into her body. Her eyes burned. They had caught flame. Her hands shook, then her arms, and into her body. A buzzing settled into her ears, and everyone disappeared save for her, Gen, and Ethan.

Time held no meaning. Not in this realm where she was working. Somewhere in the distance, she could hear her friends. Colette had finally arrived. Others, too. Finn and Ronan. They were shouting and trying to hold down the other wolves.

But Kierse couldn't stop. Not until it was all out of Ethan's system. Not until he opened his eyes and looked up at her with his beautiful smile.

Not until he lived. Even if she died.

"Almost there," Gen said softly.

As if she knew how close Kierse was. Intuitive, beautiful Gen.

Then that last tendril of magic curled into Kierse's fingers. She cradled the bit like a small flame in her hand. Then it flew into her body, and she felt it burrow down deep.

But she wasn't done. She was suffused with power. It was overwhelming her system, and still there was so much more.

She reached her hand out and grasped Cara's paw. Kierse dragged the magic out of Cara. She was determined to drain it all into her. Then she could go slo-mo and drop Imani's magic. But she could only do it once she was completely and totally done. Because she wasn't sure she'd be able to hit this connection again so soon.

As she tugged on the energy around the wolf's body, something shifted in Cara. As if she were resisting. Cara thrashed around. Nate was shouting again, trying to get her to stop. Claws dug into her skin, and Kierse screamed.

The pain overwhelmed her. She tried to fight through it and drag more magic toward her. But the feeling wasn't just the pain from her now-bleeding arm. It was the magic. Her absorption was running out. She couldn't take anymore. She wasn't strong enough.

"No," she whispered, fighting the pain and the magic. "No."

"Kierse, please." Gen grasped her around the middle and hauled her backward.

When she lost her touch on Cara, the connection severed and Kierse crumpled against her friend.

Ethan no longer glowed, but Kierse burned as bright as the sun.

"She saved him," Gen breathed.

The world was spinning. Everyone was in shock, but she couldn't get any words out. She couldn't shift into slow motion. She could barely think Graves's name before the floor reached out for her, welcoming.

And then it all went blissfully dark.

Chapter Fifty

Kierse was in a bed.

It was not as soft as the one she normally woke up in.

Where was she? Everything felt so fuzzy and distant.

She peeled her eyes open and blinked rapidly at the harsh lighting. Her eyes didn't adjust fast enough, and she sluggishly raised her arm to shield them.

"Ugh," she groaned.

"Kierse!" a voice gasped.

Kierse recognized that voice. And when she lowered her arm, she saw Gen leaning over her. *Gen?*

"What…what are you doing here?" Kierse asked her.

Gen frowned. "What do you remember?"

She thought back to it, tried to remember, but it was blank. She'd been working with Graves. She'd gone to Third Floor. Talked to Torra. Seen Lorcan. What happened after that? How had she gotten to Gen?

Another face appeared over her. Ethan.

Kierse blinked rapidly. Was she dreaming? "What are *you* doing here?"

"You're at Five Points," Ethan said, sinking into the chair next to Kierse's bed. "You saved my life."

Kierse's eyes lifted to Ethan's. He didn't look like she'd saved his life. "I did?"

"Ethan was drugged," Gen said softly. "You showed up and drew the drugs out of him with your…with your bare hands."

Her bare hands? What were they even talking about? And then she felt it—the magic. "Oh god."

She turned her head and vomited into a wastebasket next to the bed. She threw up the entire contents of her stomach. And then she threw up some more.

She hadn't been this sick since the wish powder. Right. The memory of what she had done flooded back to her all at once. This *was* wish powder.

After she emptied her stomach, she flopped back in the bed and waited for the room to stop spinning. She was a wreck, but at the same time, everything about her awareness felt different. As if the world had settled a second layer over her consciousness. Now she didn't understand how she had missed it. Would it always feel this overwhelming in its intensity? Or would it eventually feel normal? As if the world had never once been so dull?

"I remember," she told her friends. "I remember everything."

Gen and Ethan exchanged a look.

"You used...magic, right?" Gen said. "Did Graves teach you that?"

"Yes," she said. Then also: "No. I mean, he tried to train me, but I only figured it out to save Ethan and the others."

Gen blanched, and Ethan dropped his gaze to his hands. There was something they weren't saying.

"The others," Kierse whispered. "What happened to Cara and the other two wolves?"

Gen swallowed. "They...they didn't make it."

Kierse realized then that her other arm was bandaged. She remembered Cara slicing her claws into her as she tried to dredge the magic from the wolf. But Kierse hadn't been strong enough. She hadn't trained long enough, and she had broken the connection.

"I let them die," she whispered in horror.

"This isn't your fault," Ethan said at once.

Kierse felt tears gather on her lashes. But it was, wasn't it? The wish powder in the city was because of her thievery. The wish powder to Ethan was targeted at her. It all came back to Graves, but none of this would have happened if she hadn't accepted that first job. If she had decided to back out because she didn't have enough information. She was so focused on the score that she didn't prepare enough. And now people were dead on her watch.

"It is," she said hoarsely. "It is my fault."

"You saved Ethan's life," Gen reminded her.

"I wasn't strong enough to save the others."

"It wasn't your responsibility," Ethan said, taking her hand gently. "You did what you could do, and I'm forever grateful."

Kierse nodded, closing her eyes and holding the tears at bay. This was because of Imani. This was revenge. She would remember it, and she would get stronger.

No one would ever die on her watch again.

"Kierse," Gen said. "When you drew the magic out of Ethan...I felt something, too."

She pushed down all the guilt and pain and opened her eyes to look at her beautiful friend. "You felt your magic."

"*My* magic," she said in awe.

"And Ethan's."

Ethan balked. "I don't have magic."

"You do," she told him. "I don't know how, but you do."

"I felt it, too," Gen told him.

"I don't know what either of you can do or what you are. I still don't have any answers for myself, but we will find them out together," she promised. "All I can say is that there's a reason you can read tarot." She shifted her gaze from Gen to Ethan. "There's a reason you can grow plants in the winter."

Ethan's eyes flicked to the dozens of new plants he had growing all over the room. "That's not magic."

"It's something," she told him.

"And we're all together in it," Gen said.

"Yes," Kierse said. "Like a thread that's knotted between us."

Gen looked hopeful. Ethan was skeptical. But she'd felt it, just as Gen said. Her friends weren't as perfectly human any more than she was.

And there was only one way to get answers.

Her eyes widened in alarm. "Wait, how long was I out?"

"Three days," Ethan told her.

Kierse reeled. "Three days?" She counted the days in her head. "Oh fuck, is it the solstice?"

"Day before," Gen told her. "The night of the twentieth. The full moon is tomorrow. So the wolves are all on lockdown under the club. We were going to meet Maura as soon as you woke up."

"Fuck, fuck, fuck," she said, flinging the blankets off of her.

Three. Fucking. Days.

"I have to get to Graves."

"You're going back?" Ethan asked in disbelief.

"I have to," she said, coming to her feet and wobbling. She felt woozy, but she needed to get to him as soon as possible.

"You can't even stand. You can't go anywhere," Gen said, putting her hand out to stop her. "You have to go on lockdown with us. It's safe."

"I love you both. I made the right call coming back to see you, even if Graves disagrees." The thought of him slamming the door in her face still infuriated her. She covered her irritation by reaching for her clothes on the nightstand. She was in nothing but a hospital gown, and she needed to get going. "He said I broke the bargain by coming here, but there is too much at stake to walk away now."

"What is at stake?" Ethan asked. "The money? We're fine here, Kierse. I was skeptical at first, but I like being with the Dreadlords."

She shook her head. "It's not safe. This is *proof* that it isn't safe. And it won't be safe until I finish."

"And that's why you're going back?" Gen asked. "For our safety."

"Torra is alive," she gasped out.

Gen and Ethan looked at her in shock.

Gen whispered. "How?"

"She can't be," Ethan said.

"I found her," Kierse said. She steadied herself against the wall. Fuck, she needed to do something about this. "I found her, and I promised that I would get her out. Plus, this heist is so much more than what I first signed up for. Just trust me when I say that we cannot leave this object in the hands of King Louis unless we want another Monster War."

Ethan's jaw dropped.

"You're serious," Gen whispered in shock.

"Deadly."

Kierse tugged on her T-shirt and then slid her arms back into her fitted jacket. She hissed as she drew it over her hurt arm.

"But surely you can rest one more day."

"No, it's happening tomorrow night," she said. "I need to go back now. Graves has to see reason about all of this. Broken bargain or no." Kierse bit her lip and wavered. "He has to."

Gen's expression softened at those words. "You want to go back to him."

Leave it to Gen to see to the heart of it.

"I do," she said like an admission. "He was…different. Kind, in his own way."

Ethan cringed. "I thought he was a monster?"

"So did I," she whispered.

Her thoughts went distant as she remembered him giving her his coat, the way he'd held her in the tunnel, the tuck of her hair behind her ear as he stared down at her with those inimitable gray eyes. The taste of the babka and the crush of his lips. That little smile that she had just begun to interpret. All the many little ways in which Graves the monster had become Graves the man in her mind.

Gen touched her hand. "You sound like you actually like him."

"He's a monster, but he's *my* monster."

Gen and Ethan were silent at that proclamation. And it was the truth about Graves. The whole truth. One she wasn't even sure she had taken the time to look at.

"My entire life, I've been running from my past. I don't want to run anymore. Not from him." She cleared her throat and looked up at her friends. "So, I love you, but you're going to have to enter lockdown without me, because I have to leave."

"You do," Ethan said as if he finally understood, too.

"One thing before you go," Gen said, retrieving a card from her belongings and offering it to Kierse. "I pulled a card for you."

Kierse turned it over and revealed the Magician. *Graves.*

"Thank you," she said.

Then she pulled her friends into a long hug, gathered her strength, and walked out the door.

A weight settled on her as she stepped out of Five Points. The door sealed shut from the inside. She tugged on it twice just to make sure that no one was getting in after her.

She looked at the edifice with resignation. This was the right thing to do, but she didn't feel right leaving them undefended. If wish powder could get inside once to hurt her friends, it could happen again. Maybe it was Imani; maybe it was someone else trying to get to her or Graves. But she didn't care. They wouldn't hurt her friends.

She had something to protect now. Something to ward. And when she focused her intent on the building, her magic came to her with ease. She drew the ward for the entire building. She didn't stop to wonder if she was doing it correctly. She just used her magic how it came to her intuitively. When she was done, Five Points was a wish-powder-free establishment. No one would be able to bring it inside. Her friends were safe.

The hum of magic was just a small buzzing in the back of her mind as she saw the little wren in the shape of her ward.

Now, she could walk away.

Interlude

Isolde came into work early.

Something felt wrong.

She'd woken up in the middle of the night feeling like bugs crawled all over her skin. She hadn't been able to fall asleep after that. Nor think of anything else.

Instead, she'd gotten dressed and come to Graves's house before sunrise. She decided she was going to bake a few loaves of bread. He loved having fresh bread in the morning. Loved the smell of it wafting up through the house to greet him.

But when she'd arrived, he had been seated in the kitchen. As if he knew that she would be there. A crystal glass sat before him, empty. Just a few melting ice cubes in the bottom. He stared down in it like it would refill itself. Or he'd drown in it.

It wasn't that different than the first time she had met him. She had been working as a pastry chef far away from here. He came in every day, asking for one of her latest creations. She'd admired his handsome build, but there was something dark inside of him. Something that twisted him up. She had only been twenty-five at the time. Still bold and reckless.

When he stayed after hours with his head buried in a drink, she had struck up a conversation. They had never been romantic. She had seen too quickly that he could never *love* someone. Not the way she wanted. He was a man of a thousand broken pieces.

When he offered her the job, she hadn't thought twice before agreeing. He needed handling. She could see that. And strangely, she wanted to be the person who did it.

Over the years, she had watched people flit in and out of his life. Women and men entered her kitchen and swiftly departed. Few stayed for long as he trained them.

If there was one thing that was constant about Graves, it was leaving.

The people in his life were temporary.

He never got close enough to another living soul to feel anything more than passing interest. It infuriated most. Some left with sad resignation. Maybe they saw what she saw. That a broken man could not love, for no one could put those pieces back together once they were sufficiently shattered.

Worse, who could ever love him? She loved him in her own way. A dutiful way. She was devoted to him. But he only showed her the best of him. To be loved, you had to show all your worst, too.

Isolde knew the man she worked for.

He was the villain of his own story.

She didn't mind. He paid her, cared for her, looked after her all the same. But for more than that, you had to meet someone right where they were. See who they were, all the damaged parts, and want to be with them anyway.

When she saw him sitting there in her kitchen, she knew in her heart what had happened.

Kierse had gone.

And he had let her.

Isolde stepped quietly into the kitchen. She got out her ingredients and carefully mixed the flour, salt, and yeast. She added the water last, bringing the dough together as she'd been taught so long ago. Her old arms didn't like kneading, but she found it better than using one of the new mixers. Faster didn't mean better. It didn't imbue it with love.

It wasn't until she had poured the dough out onto the counter and begun to knead it that she finally spoke. "Kierse has gone?"

Graves nodded. He didn't even seem surprised. "She's returned to her family."

"For good?"

He nodded again. "Yes." He paused there. Some fire came into his features before quickly dissipating. As if he couldn't even find the anger anymore. A small sigh. "Her time here was always tenuous."

"What will you do?"

"What I always do." When he glanced up at her, he looked pained. "Start over. Again."

Isolde saw the truth under those words. He was hurting. He had been so different these last weeks. Kierse had been good for him. She didn't put up with his morose behavior. She made jokes with him. They had similar interests. It had been a true blessing to watch them both begin to open up. She'd never thought she'd see the day. For the first time in her tenure with Graves, she had wondered if she was wrong about him. If he *was* capable of love after all.

"But what about Kierse?"

"She made her decision. They always do. One after the other after the other. They choose…" He waved his hand and then reached for the bottle and poured himself another drink. "Whatever they find important."

Over him. Over learning magic. Over this life.

She understood in her own way why someone would want a simple life. The magic he wielded was not in any way simple. It was dark, deadly, and dangerous. Most people couldn't handle it. She had thought that Kierse was different.

She couldn't help but say it out loud. "I thought that she was different."

As she looked down at her master, she realized…he had thought so, too.

"Aye," he agreed.

And it hurt all the worse to know that he had been wrong.

Part VI

THE WINTER SOLSTICE

Chapter Fifty-One

T he last thing she wanted was to trek fifty blocks north in the cold. But without the Dreadlords to drive her or cash on hand to take a cab, she had no other choice. She braved the 14th Street subway entrance, paying off a particularly irritable troll, to take the 1 uptown. She pickpocketed her way through the platform to rejuvenate her magic, and by the time she exited onto the Upper West Side, she was starting to feel better. The magic burn was dissipating.

Her previous disdain for the neighborhood was completely gone. Even a few weeks ago, she would have sneered at the clean, well-lit streets, and now, this felt...right.

She breathed a sigh of relief as Graves's brownstone came into view. There was so much more inside those four walls than she had ever dreamed. Though it felt like coming home, her steps were tentative as she approached the front door and its ostentatious dragon knocker, knowing the firedrake that lived within. She smiled at the thought. But the look vanished when she lifted it and knocked.

She could easily just walk across the threshold. His magic couldn't keep her out. But she felt more a guest now than the last time she had knocked on this door. She didn't know if she was welcome.

The moment lingered. She lifted the knocker again and banged on the door. A moment passed, and then the door heaved slowly inward.

Graves appeared before her. He was dressed in a rumpled dress shirt and slacks. The first three buttons of his shirt were undone at the top, and the sleeves were rolled up nearly to his elbows, revealing his holly tattoos. A half-empty bottle hung from his hand. His hair fell over his forehead, the streetlight catching on the midnight-blue strands. His eyes, those dark storm clouds, took her in in one long, lingering look. He looked like he'd had a worse few days than she had, and that was saying something.

"Kierse?" he asked in what could only be described as shock.

She had never heard the tone from him before. Never heard him even use her name on his tongue. She had always been Miss McKenna or Wren.

It was unnerving.

He looked at her for a moment like she was a complex math equation. "What are you doing here?"

"Can I come in?"

"I don't believe you have ever asked permission." He recovered his bravado long enough to sweep his arm out and allow her inside. He dropped the bottle of bourbon on a console table as he toed the door closed behind her.

She rubbed her hands together and then blew on them. "Why is it so cold in here?"

"I'm alone."

They stood together on the cold threshold. No words crossed between them, just silence. Graves was rattled by her appearance. As if the string that ran between them was tenuous and at any point could snap.

She needed to get the words out, but somehow seeing him like this made it all the worse. They both had their backs to the wall. Neither of them had fully put their faith in the other. Not even as everything began to change over the weeks together. And now she had to find a place within herself to let go. Something she never did with *anyone*.

Before she could begin, he asked stiffly, "Are you here for a reason?"

"I came back to…apologize," she forced out.

He arched an eyebrow. "Apologize for what, exactly?"

"For what happened with Nate." She stared down at her hands. "Can we sit to discuss this, please? I have a lot to tell you."

His Adam's apple bobbed once before he nodded. They stepped into the sitting room, and Kierse couldn't bite back the smile. The little green book sat on the side table. Her blankets were folded neatly next to her favorite seat. No sign of Anne, but she came when she pleased.

Graves went immediately to the dead fire. It made the room feel so much colder and less welcoming. He got it going again in silence as she settled on the couch. Soon the warmth from the fire radiated throughout the room, and the feeling slowly returned to her hands.

She waited until Graves settled into the chair across from her before continuing.

"I don't know how else to explain it," she said, dropping her gaze and trying to find the courage to open up to him. "My love for exits isn't manufactured. My father abandoned me young, and I lived on the streets. It was a terrible situation," she said with a shudder. "I don't even like to think about those years."

Graves nodded in understanding. He, too, had been abandoned. He knew the weight of that.

"So, then I was picked up by my mentor, Jason." She took a deep breath. Oh, how she hated saying his name out loud. "I was raised in his thieving guild—a prodigy," she added with disdain. "There is nothing positive that I can say about him except that he kept me alive. Barely."

She wanted to tell him more, wanted to say all the ways in which Jason had cobbled her. But the pain that she endured at his hands still burned like fire in her veins.

"The best lesson he ever taught me was how to escape. Even if it was to escape him." She gulped, forcing herself to continue. "So, when I moved in here with you, I saw a cage."

Graves frowned. "That wasn't my intention."

"Wasn't it?" she asked. "I was free to come and go but not free to live my life."

He clenched his jaw but said nothing.

"So, you can't blame me for reeling at the cage and immediately putting into place ways to save myself when this inevitably went south." She glanced down at her shaking hands, hating the sound of the words. "I was prepared to die on this mission, but my brain couldn't stop me from putting contingencies in place. But then…things changed."

Graves straightened at those words. "How did they change?"

"You don't know?"

She saw that he really didn't. He had no clue how she felt. They'd both been so closed off, so unable to be exactly who they were. They'd been hurt in their previous lives, and now even admitting to feelings of caring felt interminable.

"At first the job was just a job. But you went from being a monster to a stranger to a friend and then…more. Someone I could almost…trust," she volunteered. She pushed forward. "I'm not just doing this job for the money or to help my friends. I'm doing this to help Torra get out of that place. I'm doing it to keep the spear out of King Louis's hands. I'm doing it for *you*."

"I thought you were gone."

Kierse sighed. "I didn't mean for it to all go down the way it did, but you had to know things were different. You had to know I was coming back."

"You were gone for three days," Graves said. "I admit that I blew up on you, but I thought you made your choice."

"I know," she said tenderly. "But I came back." Her heart was in her throat. She was baring herself to him, and she didn't know if it was going to be enough. If she had shattered the modicum of trust they'd gained over the last couple of weeks, maybe she'd never get it back.

Finally, Graves asked solemnly, "This wasn't your exit?"

"No," she said fiercely. "No, this wasn't my exit at all." He seemed startled at her vehemence. "I only left because of Ethan."

"And is he okay?" Graves asked carefully.

"Yes. It wasn't the kind of overdose that my friends originally thought. Someone slipped him and three of Nate's wolves wish powder. I absorbed the magic out of Ethan, but the wolves... They died."

Graves came swiftly to his feet. "And no one came to get me? I have the antidote. I could have helped to heal them."

"We didn't know that's what it was when Nate came to get me. We just thought it was drugs." Tears came to her eyes again. "I don't know, Graves. It all happened so fast. By the time I realized it was magic, I did what I could."

His eyes rounded in shock. "Their deaths are not your fault."

"They're because of me. I wasn't strong enough. I don't know enough about my powers."

"They're *my* fault," he insisted.

"Blame doesn't matter. It doesn't bring them back." She swiped angrily at her eyes. "I need to be stronger. I need to learn to use my magic so I don't end up in another situation like this." She looked up at him sadly. "But that's why I was gone these last three days. That's why I didn't come back. I woke up and came straight here...after pickpocketing a few unsuspecting strangers."

"I'm glad you're back," he said, releasing a harsh breath. "I'm glad you saved Ethan. I'm glad you figured out your magic and how to rejuvenate it."

She nodded. "Almost good as new. It was like my powers were waiting for the moment when I really needed them. I was able to see and smell the magic. I understand what you mean by intent now. I understand everything. I even warded Five Points to keep wish powder out of the establishment."

"As I knew you would with practice. Unfortunately, sometimes magic only awakens during a trial," he said.

"At least it did awaken," she said. "So, you see, now we have all the pieces to finish the job tomorrow. I want to do this. No, I *need* to do this." She swallowed hard, letting him see her vulnerability and earnestness. "I'll go in either way, but we're better off together. You know that we are."

Life flickered back into Graves's eyes at those words. She could see a new plan lighting there.

"We are better together." And the words he uttered were like music to her ears. Soft and seductive. He came to his feet. "A new bargain?"

"We don't need a bargain to seal this anymore. We do this together. Get in, get the spear, kill King Louis, and get us all out of there."

He nodded. "Done."

Chapter Fifty-Two

With their mission restored, Kierse felt lighter than she ever had with Graves. Maybe with anyone.

"I truly thought you had left for good," he told her.

"You shut down as soon as you found out about Nate. I told you I would come back. I swore we would talk about this."

He ran a hand through his hair, and when he looked at her next, she saw that he was thrown off. That she had surprised him when he was not usually surprised. He truly had thought that she was never coming back. Even when she had been yelling at him and telling him she would be back, he'd immediately thought that she was like everyone else in his life. That she would abandon *him*. Right after she had finally let her guard down around him.

But of course, he had no idea how important that was. She'd never told him her past. She had been as closed off as he was. So closed off he'd thought that she'd leave and never look back. That was written all over his beautiful face. All because she couldn't share her own pain. As he couldn't share his.

"I will try to explain. I never talk about my history," he began. "You see, I was born a monster." He clenched his hands into fists. "On the day I was born, I killed my mother. Not a natural death from childbirth; a death from my being born."

"What's the difference?" she asked.

He met her gaze, wholly empty. "Giving birth to a warlock kills the mother. They can't survive the magic or the loss of it."

"Oh," she whispered. Then the realization lit in her mind. "That's why you assumed I was a warlock. Because my mother died as well."

"Yes. See, my mother was Irish and fled her people to be with my father, who they would never have approved of. She was the light of his life. He would have done anything for her. But when she died, my father blamed me for her death."

He glanced away at that admission. She wanted to tell him he was worth so much more than what had been done to him. She hoped he already knew.

"On the same day, King Henry VII of England died," he added. "He blamed me for that, too."

"That's absurd."

He nodded as if he knew it to be so and it didn't change the years of hurt. "It was. He died of tuberculosis. Something that I found out much later. It was just a lucky coincidence. Something for my father to beat into me for the six years that I lived with him." His jaw clenched. "Years later, I went back to my little hovel in a town that no longer exists to repay him for those years of kindness, but he was already dead." Graves's brows furrowed. "It was for the better. I didn't need his blood on my hands, but I'd never forgive him. You see, he sold me."

"Sold you," she said gently.

"Yes. Like a cow."

She'd seen and heard of terrible things in her days. Her heart ached for a child purposely sold by a parent. Kierse had just been left to fend for herself. She couldn't imagine the pain of knowing his father had done it on purpose.

"A merchant came through our village right after my sixth birthday. He gave my father a pittance and took me away. I lived and traveled with the man for several years before I managed to escape." His eyes went distant. "They weren't easy times. It took another couple of years to find a way to get on a boat that would take me to Ireland and my mother's people. Because I thought surely they would accept me, even if I was only half Irish."

"And did they?" she whispered.

"They did. For a time." He met her gaze, distant and hurting. "But that's a different story." He let her see the man that was underneath all the bravado. As she had done for him. "So you see, it was from my father that I first learned nothing is permanent. The longest I stayed anywhere was in Kingston's company. But even then, two master warlocks don't suffer each other long. We moved in and out of each other's lives. No one who gets close to me lasts. They all end up leaving." He reached out slowly and took her hand into his. "I assumed that you were the latest in a long line of disappointment."

She swallowed. "You assumed wrong."

He was silent for a beat before saying, "I did."

And then Graves leaned forward, fitting his mouth to hers.

Kierse released into him. He tasted as delicious and inviting as ever. But as her magic wrapped itself around him, for the first time, she felt more than just his fire. She felt *him*.

The magic that made him so powerful radiated off of him—a pure golden light. Endless, boundless, eternal. It felt like infinity. And then underneath the sensation, she could smell it. The musky scent of leather and new books. Just as he had described and yet so much more. Those were base scents. His magic was more nuanced than that. She could breathe in the smell of the first snow of winter, rosemary, and a hint of tea. All were distinct, and all were distinctly *Graves*.

"You were right," she said against his mouth. "Your magic does smell like leather—and you said parchment, but I smell books. Like your library."

He grinned. "Yours smells faintly, too."

"Of what?"

"Spring."

She wrinkled her nose. "Spring? That's not distinct."

"There's this lake in Ireland. It's tucked away far from prying eyes, and in the springtime, thousands of wildflowers bloom. They're the brightest yellows and sharpest purples and darkest blues. The grass is so green it looks like a sea. Everything smells fresh and new. As if anything could be possible. That's what you smell like."

Graves kissed her again. Deeper. She felt herself drift away. Felt like she could let this moment happen. Let him consume her in a way no one else ever had.

But at its heart, she hadn't given him all that he had given her. She pulled back slowly, hating that she had to drag herself free of him.

"What is it?" His hands were still tangled in her shirt.

She looked down and swallowed. "I understand your story. About being given away, that is. I was abandoned on the streets when I was very young." Graves released her shirt and watched her intently, waiting for her to continue. "I told you that Jason picked me up when I was young. That he trained me to be his protégé. But that isn't all of it."

Graves tipped her chin up to make her look at him. "Tell me."

His command spurred her forward. "He wanted to teach me how to be a better thief and bring me into his circle. I learned everything I could from him. He was a great thief. Though, to his chagrin, I was better."

She froze up at the thought of what was next going to come out of her mouth. But his calm, steadying presence kept her together.

"Jason was…volatile." A harsh laugh escaped her. "God, why is it still so hard to talk about him? He was an asshole and terrible and unforgivable."

"It's always difficult to speak of those who hurt us most," Graves said softly as if he, too, understood her pain.

"Maybe that's it." She glanced down, wanting nothing more than to hide from Jason's memory forever. For him to never again hold this sway over her. "Because I was special, we were together more frequently. He treated me like…family. And you have to understand that when it was a good day, it was like the sun was shining on a summer afternoon. He made the world turn."

"But what about on a bad day?"

She shivered. "On a bad day, I was never sure if I was going to live or die by his hand."

Graves went deathly still. "He hurt you?"

"Hurt me?" She looked up into his eyes with a disquiet in her mind. "For years, I never knew which step was going to end up with a kind touch and which was going to have me thrown off a building."

"He threw you off a building?"

"To get over my fear of heights," she said. "He broke my arm once in three places. It was reset wrong. So he broke it again just to be sure I wouldn't have a disadvantage in his schemes. And all of his other guild members hated me for being his favorite." She laughed hollowly. "What I would have given to be anything else. The level of abuse that I suffered at his hands…"

She couldn't even say.

"Then Gen…Gen found me. She saved me," she explained. His hand covered hers, so strong, so comforting. "I'd wanted to find my exit from Jason and his thieving ring. He caught wind of my plans to leave. He was… let's just say less than pleased. I tried to run, but he'd been in this game far longer than I had, and he found me. He stopped me." Her voice shook, and her hands trembled. The harsh words were the truest ones, and yet she'd never said them before.

"You don't have to keep going," Graves told her, low and menacing. "I already want him dead."

"I have to," she forced out. "He told me that he was just taking back what was his. That he owned me and that I could never leave. That he would kill me before allowing it. And he must have thought I was dead after he beat me to within an inch of my life and left my broken body in an abandoned alleyway." She hiccupped over the next word. "Even in death, there was no escape, no exit from him."

Twin flames danced in his eyes.

"And they call us monsters."

Kierse nodded. Men could be just as much monsters as the ones with claws and teeth.

"That was what I saw," he said faintly as if afraid of spooking her.

"What do you mean?"

"The one time I could read you, when you were overwhelmed with Imani's magic, I saw you bloodied up and lying in an alley. I saw what Jason had done to you." Graves clenched his hands into fists.

She gulped. "Yes."

"I didn't realize that at first. I wasn't sure why your brain was stuck on that image."

"Now you know," she whispered.

"How did you escape him?"

"I was mere blocks from Colette's brothel. Gen brought me in," she explained. "I was terrified at first that I would be forced to work in the brothel or run jobs for people. That every person I came in contact with was only being nice to me as a ruse before they would hurt me." A long breath escaped her lips. "But that wasn't the case. That wasn't Gen. It took me a long time to figure it out, but she was always just my friend. She helped me heal."

"And where is Jason now?" Graves asked with deathly quiet.

She shook her head. "Dead, I think. I stuck a knife in him." She looked down at her hands, picking at her nails. "He should have suffered more, but when I went for my revenge, I took what I could get."

"Good," Graves said, slowly removing his gloves. "I wouldn't have been able to suffer him being alive. I would have killed him myself."

"His death belonged to me," she told him, brushing back her hair with trembling hands. "It's why I have trouble with accepting comfort, accepting any sort of actual intimacy." She took a deep breath before adding, "It's why I couldn't love Torra."

Graves went still at the name. She hadn't spoken about Torra since he'd held her as she cried in the subway tunnel. But here was the truth. The one even she hadn't been able to face.

"There wasn't enough left of me that wanted more than just casual sex." She looked up to meet his eyes, every ounce of openness on her face. "It's why when I came to you in the tunnels, that was… It was different with you."

"Ah," he said, swiping a tear from her cheek. His face softened. "That is why you couldn't fathom that I would think you would leave."

"How could I leave the one person I'd allowed myself to be vulnerable with? The first person I ever considered more with."

He cupped her cheek. "I see it now."

"What a pair we are," Kierse said with a choked laugh.

"What a pair, indeed."

Then his lips were upon hers again. She opened her mouth to him, letting his tongue slide across hers. His hands, his blessedly bare hands, came up to cup her cheeks, and she leaned into him. She wanted this. It wasn't a matter of just sex. This was so much more. She had confessed her darkest secret and revealed exactly who she was. And he still wanted her.

She wanted more than the sum of its parts. She wanted it all.

"Graves," she whispered. "I want this. I want to be with you."

"You're sure?"

"Yes."

He pressed a kiss to her lips. "Come with me."

Chapter Fifty-Three

Her heart rate picked up as he pulled her away from the comfort of the sitting room, up the first flight of stairs, and then toward his rooms. These weeks, she had never gone inside them and always respected his privacy. She would be lying if she said she wasn't curious. But she was naturally curious, and there were few things left secret to a thief with a good set of picks.

When he pushed the far door open, she found his bedchamber. It was stunning in both the simplicity of the furniture and the richness of the pieces he had chosen. Unlike the opulence of the rest of the house, this felt more like a sanctuary. It felt like Graves.

"I've never done this, either," he admitted.

"Done what?"

He pulled her into his inner sanctuary. "Brought someone to my room."

She swallowed. "An all-new experience."

"It doesn't happen often when you've lived as long as I have."

She wandered his inner sanctum, taking in the small details that must have mattered to him. The carved wood bird figurines on top of a dresser; a copy of Edgar Allan Poe's *The Raven* on his dark mahogany nightstand; a handful of European coins, as if he'd just returned from a trip, though they looked far out of date; a portrait of the *real* Anne Boleyn in her signature B pearl necklace; and another painted in muted colors with two figures in a field of wildflowers, looking down at a little green book. One of them could have been Graves for all she knew.

She understood then why his privacy was so important to him. A place where no one else could see him, where he could just be himself. And he was allowing her to invade that space.

"I'm glad you showed me this," she said, fingering a clear vase full of winter flowers.

Then she returned to him, taking his hand and drawing him to the bed.

"We don't have to…"

She put a finger to his mouth. "Shh…I want this." She slowly peeled off her top, tossing it to the floor next to him. "I want this with you."

He didn't object further, just skimmed the top of her pants as he pushed her back on the bed. He popped the button as his lips came to hers. Her own hand came up to the buttons of his shirt, slowly sliding them open.

"I've never been with someone I haven't been able to read before."

"We did just fine in the library."

He laughed against her mouth. "That was rushed. Now, I want to take my time."

"I just want you." She gasped as his bare hands ran across the sensitive skin of her stomach.

"I'm going to have to learn what makes you make those incredible noises," he said with a cocky, devilish smile on his lips.

His fingers dipped under her waistband, stroking lazily along her hip bones. She groaned and tried not to squirm under his touch. His eyes were curious and hyper-focused on her.

"And how I do love to learn new things," he purred.

He removed her bra in one fluid motion. Her breasts spilled out of their enclosure, and his eyes moved straight to them. Next came his hands, commanding and firm as he reacquainted himself with them. She tipped her head back as he kneaded a nipple.

"You didn't even touch me last time," she said as she reached for him.

"I assure you, I touched you."

She chuckled. "I mean, you had your gloves on."

"For most people…it's protection," he said, his head going to her nipple and taking it into his mouth.

"I like to feel your heat." She pushed her own hands against his warm chest. "And those hands on me."

Graves stripped out of his shirt to reveal the muscled chest she had marveled at. The full tattoo on display. Now she dragged her nails across the inky lines of holly vines, down across the thorns piercing his skin, and around the leaves that trailed lower into his pants.

"Your tattoo is so vivid," she mused. "Can I lick every inch of it?"

He groaned, pressing himself against her. "You can do whatever you want with me," he promised.

Then he claimed her mouth again. He wasn't the only one learning, and oh, how she liked his reaction to that. The way he forced himself hard against her, the feel of his erection bulging against his pants.

Carefully, she drew her hand down the front of his pants, cupping him in her grasp. He jerked against her hand. *More.* She released his mouth and began to kiss her way down his perfect chest, over every intricate detail of his tattoo, noticing the spattering of scars along the way.

She came to her knees before him and then looked up at him from under her lashes. "And if I want this?"

"And I thought I was supposed to learn your body," he said through gritted teeth.

"Plenty of time for that later."

His breathing was ragged as she undid his pants and drew them over his narrow hips. His boxer briefs followed, revealing the full length of him before her. She had barely gotten to touch him the last time. Just a firm grip on him before he'd thrust into her.

Now, she wanted *all* of him. She grasped his cock in her hand, slowly stroking him up and down. Then she fit her mouth around the head of him.

He moaned deep in the back of his throat. She pushed forward, taking in the length of him. When she drew back again, his hips flexed as if he wanted to thrust into her again. She rolled her tongue over the tip teasingly before taking him in again, lingering longer at the base.

His hands slid into her hair. He wasn't exactly gentle, but he wasn't hurting her, either. With the grace of a predator, he began to direct her against him.

Anyone else who would have dared try, she would have walked away so fast. She'd always enjoyed women over men for this. It felt so much less expected. So much less…dominating. Or at least that had always been her personal preference.

But with Graves, it just felt right. It was how it should be. She was not nor had she ever been a submissive woman. This didn't feel that way. It was like he was giving her pleasure as much as taking his own.

She was full of him, full to bursting. Him hot in her mouth, and *she* was the one prime to climax.

Somehow, he still got bigger. Big enough she almost gagged on him. Then, in one slow pull, he removed himself from her mouth. She instantly felt bereft. She looked up at him through tearstained lashes, on her knees before him.

"Graves?" she whispered.

"Seeing you like this, Wren… I have to have you."

She shivered. "Yes."

He lifted her to her feet, and she slid out of her jeans and useless panties.

Then she crawled backward on the bed, spreading herself before him. She watched his naked body from between her legs. All he did was stand there like a Greek god—no, a Celtic god—and she was panting for him.

She bit her lip and beckoned him forward. "I need you."

He settled between her legs, his cock jutting toward her waiting pussy. All she wanted to do was shift and have him inside her once more. Then their eyes snapped together as if drawn by a magnet. And in that gaze, she saw that she was precious to him. Something new in a world that had always been the same.

"You'll stay, Wren?" he asked.

She nodded, the nickname sliding pleasantly over her. "Yes. I'm staying."

He pressed his lips to hers, almost gentle, before thrusting inside of her. She arched her back. Her eyes shut, her gasp audible. This was what she wanted. The way they seemed to fit just right, as if one had been waiting for the other and it was finally how it always should have been.

"Eyes on me," Graves commanded. "Show me what's hidden."

She slowly opened her eyes and blinked up at him. He couldn't read her. He couldn't use his magic on her, and for once, he had no idea what she wanted from him. So she kept her eyes on him as he began to move in and out of her, a steady, easy rhythm. She wanted more. Harder. Faster. And yet, she'd never really had this before. This feeling between them that made sex so erotic.

"What's hidden?"

"Everything," he said. His thumb ran across her bottom lip. She opened for him, flicking her tongue against the pad of his finger. "And now, I can see you."

She gasped as he pushed into her harder, their gazes never breaking as she met his thrusts with her own. Their fires mingled, the heat blooming in the room like a furnace. It centered in her core, and as they crashed together one last time, she felt it erupt. They climaxed together with such intensity that it felt as if a wave of energy had just been released from their bodies.

Graves fell forward over her, pressing his forehead against her own. "My wren."

"Mmm," she hummed breathlessly.

His lips found hers again. Just a light brush. "I'll be right back."

Then he was gone, sliding out of her and striding toward the bathroom.

She lay there, staring up at the ceiling in wonder. So, this was what she had been missing. Sex *wasn't* just sex. With Graves, it was so much more.

Water gurgled in the other room, and Graves reappeared, hauling her off of the bed. She nearly crumpled as her legs tried to give out under her. He laughed under his breath and then threw her easily over his shoulder. She protested, but he was already moving as if she was as light as a feather.

The bathroom was nearly as large as the bedroom, with a sunken tub that could have doubled as a small pool and a heated jacuzzi next to it. Graves dropped her lightly to her feet on the edge before stepping into the jacuzzi, beckoning her forward.

"I could have walked," she teased.

"And miss the chance to carry you?" He tsked. "Never."

She grinned as she stepped inside the bubbling water, then nearly groaned at the warmth.

Before she had a chance to take a seat, Graves drew her against his naked body. She settled onto his lap, curling into him. His warm arms wrapped around her, and she closed her eyes, sighing happily.

"I'm glad you came back," he said softly into her hair as he ran his wet fingers through the strands.

"Me too." She trailed her hand up and down his bicep. "I have a question."

"Yes?"

"What year did King Henry VII die?"

Graves rumbled a laugh. "1509."

Kierse startled. "Oh."

"Are you doing the math on my age?" he asked. "Warlocks are especially long-lived."

She looked into his eyes. "Over five hundred years."

"And still learning to trust," he said, sweeping a hand down her face and tilting her head up so their lips nearly met. "But I trust you."

"Good. Then kiss me again."

And he did, running his tongue along her plump bottom lip as all thought fled her mind.

Chapter Fifty-Four

"Kierse, stop fidgeting," Torra hissed at her. "You already look out of place. Try to glaze your eyes over and look a little more drugged."

Torra had suggested that Kierse sneak into King Louis's Winter Solstice party with the rest of the people from Red Velvet. Though she would have much preferred Kierse not go at all, it was their best chance of getting Torra out on the other side. Plus, Torra had been dealing with King Louis for a year. If she said the invitation that Graves had wasn't going to get her in, then she believed her.

Graves had agreed, too, and he planned to get in through the underground tunnel she had mapped out that day with Walter. They would meet up once they were inside, with Torra escaping to the tunnel before the carnage occurred and meeting Kierse and Graves at the exit after they retrieved the spear.

All of the heist planning came down to this moment, when Kierse had to convincingly look like a Red Velvet girl.

Except that Kierse didn't look like one at all. She'd seen the sun and didn't appear to be wasting away. But with a ton of makeup, the scanty outfit, and heeled boots, she thought she did an okay job of fitting in. It helped that all the workers were wrapped in white Red Velvet cloaks with high collars as they were escorted toward a back entrance. The cloak did the job for now, but Torra had insisted she tell everyone she was new if they noticed she had no bite marks.

Kierse held her breath and tried to look more like a zombie as she reached the front of the line. The vampire guard scrutinized her. "You're from Red Velvet?"

She dipped her chin and looked back at Torra with what she hoped was timidity and concern. "I'm new," she whispered, barely audible.

"What was that?"

"She's new," Torra spat, forcing his attention back to her. "Just a new debtor hoping to pay her shit off with this tonight. Can we move along? I want to get paid."

The monster glared at Torra, and Kierse hastily slipped through the door. She'd worn many costumes and disguises in her line of work, but this was next-level. There was a slim margin of error for this to go right and a huge window for it to go terribly wrong.

Torra touched Kierse's back, and they scurried into the entertainment holding area. It was a diverse group being housed in what appeared to be a seldom-used warehouse. Boxes were stacked high against the walls, and the rest of the room was full of humans who would be the main course and entertainment for King Louis's party.

"At least try to be careful," Torra hissed into her ear.

"You know me."

"That's why I'm telling you."

"Just stick to the plan," Kierse told her. "And if all goes well, we'll both be on the outside before the end of the evening."

They were closer to the party entrance now. Workers from Red Velvet shucked off their robes, revealing various tiny white lingerie—a white satin baby doll on one, white leather briefs and nipple tassels on another, a sheer lace bodysuit on the next—and passed them to a handler before stepping across the threshold.

Torra turned to Kierse then. Their eyes met across the short distance. She looked pained, as if she wanted to say more, to tell her to stop, go back. But she said none of it.

She just nodded her head with wide doe eyes. And then it was her turn. Torra shrugged out of her robe, showing off the white teddy that buttoned up to a choker around her neck, and entered in front of Kierse, who had no option but to do the same.

As soon as Kierse discarded her robe, she felt exposed. With Kierse's muscle mass, a lot of the lingerie was too tight on her. They'd had to go with a white corset that lifted her breasts practically to her throat. Graves had gotten the outfit tailored with slots for throwing knives, since they were sneaking in the back way now. The corset was coupled with a frilly panty-and-garter set attached to white thigh highs. Her white boots came up just over her knees, where she'd hidden two handled knives that were better for fighting. Torra's eyes had gone distant when she saw the outfit, swearing they were never going to believe she was one of them.

Now she was here. And she could be nothing but one of them. So, she swayed forward down the hallway and into King Louis's Winter Solstice party.

Kierse hadn't known something so beautiful existed in the underworld. Everything was usually so dark and mysterious. An air of staleness and vulgarity. But this ballroom held none of that. The marble flooring had been polished until it gleamed. Tall, towering columns lined the room made of the same white marble. The ceiling was something out of one of Graves's storybooks. An intricately detailed painting stretched across the length of the domed ceiling that was half glorious, winged angels fighting a godly war — blood rippling down bodies and pain written across faces — and half angels lying naked in comfort and luxury. The message was clear. Only through war, death, and suffering could the comforts of life endure.

Kierse tried not to get swept up in the rest of the gilded hall. Gold chandeliers hung from the ceiling. Waiters carried golden goblets on golden trays. Monsters lined the room, predominately male but some female. Gold pins were on the lapel of every monster in the room. As she peered closer, she saw it was a set of wings with an arrow struck through them. The mark of the Men of Valor.

She had assumed that it would be only vampires at the party, and while they were the majority, they were far from alone. Shifters rippled at the periphery. A mer spun a Red Velvet girl in a circle. A troll trudged through the hall. A goblin downed a bottle of wine with her compatriots. Nymphs danced to a tune only they could hear. And wraiths were everywhere. They were only missing werewolves in their midst. It appeared even monsters didn't want to deal with a wolf on the full moon.

Her breath caught as she realized that she *recognized* one of the wraiths — Gregory Amberdash.

Her face flushed. He was in the Men of Valor? He wanted to end the Monster Treaty? Her vision blurred at the edges at that thought. He'd sold her out to Lorcan, but she hadn't thought he was stupid enough to want *this*.

She backtracked away from Amberdash. The last thing she wanted was for him to compromise her mission. But as she turned to escape, she nearly ran into a vampire. Her gaze snagged on her Men of Valor pin.

She grinned at Kierse. "Are you admiring our signet pins?"

She cleared her throat. "Quite."

"They mark us as the Men of Valor."

Kierse forced herself to keep smiling. "What is the meaning of it?"

The woman ran a bloodred nail down Kierse's jaw. "It's a reminder that wings can always be broken. That those who attempt to fly free can be cut down. More importantly, it's a symbol to remind us of where we belong —

monsters ruling once more."

"As you are doing here?"

"Rightly so," she said, passing her a goblet. She thought it would be blood but saw that it was just wine. "Have a drink, my angel."

"I have no wings."

"Not anymore," she purred.

Kierse pretended to take a tentative sip of the wine and then handed it back to the vampire. "Thank you. I must go find my benefactor."

"Oh? I thought all of you were up for grabs." She clutched Kierse's ass to make his point.

She had to brace herself not to draw the dagger from beneath her snow-white corset and ram it into her throat. "Almost all of us," she said with a conspiratorial wink and then hastened away from the vampire.

Thankfully, she didn't pursue her. But when she flicked her eyes back to her, she had already entertained herself with a young boy. Kierse cringed. It made her think of Ethan, and she didn't like that one bit. Not any of it.

She just needed to remind herself of the plan. Just…where the hell was Graves?

He should have been here before she had to parade around this party in nothing but lingerie. It was a disguise, but it wouldn't hold long if he didn't make it inside. And she had no intention of being bitten tonight…or ever.

Kierse made a slow circuit of the room. Her training as a thief had taught her how to work a room and remain unnoticed. It was harder to stay in the shadows in a white corset, but it wasn't impossible. Most of the workers *wanted* to be noticed. It was their job. So, she took in the sight before her. The horde of monsters and their meals for the evening. How quickly the Red Velvet workers were snatched up. No sign of Torra, though. Hopefully that meant she'd gotten out already.

There was still no sight of King Louis. Perhaps he planned to make a grand entrance. It seemed his style. He liked the mystery that surrounded him all while he ran things behind the scenes.

Kierse ground her teeth together and slunk deeper into the depths of the colossal ballroom. She was halfway to the other side of the room, nearest the dais, when a hand snaked around her wrist.

"Hello there, pretty thing," a man said from the shadows. He was tall and fair skinned, with eyes like those of an eagle about to catch a mouse. "What is your name?"

She stilled and tried to appear coy and drugged like the others. It was hard as she stared into the eyes of a vampire. "Hello," she purred. "I'm Kendra. And you are?"

"Wilson Bellack," he said evenly as if it should mean something to her. "Where are you off to in such a hurry?"

"Off to?"

"You were sneaking about the ballroom. Looking for someone?"

He was closer than she liked to admit. But he didn't know it.

"I'm promised to someone," she said breathily. "He is of high rank among the Men of Valor."

"Is he now? Then perhaps I would know who he is."

"Perhaps," she said. She twisted her wrist gently, and her hand slid out of his.

"Then who is he?"

"When I find him, I'll introduce you."

"I think not," he said instead. His hand slid around her waist, holding her tight against him. She fought to keep from shivering as he radiated cold. "All of you lot are available. It's his fault that he left such a wild rose free to bloom alone."

Kierse batted her eyelashes. "I think that perhaps…"

"We didn't pay for you to think," he snarled.

Then he slapped her across the face.

Shock stung her more than the hit itself. It wasn't to cause pain. It was to keep her in her place. He had clearly done it many times. He'd probably even known exactly how hard to hit her so that it wouldn't leave any kind of mark. She knew, because Jason had hit her like that more times than she could count. She pushed down the familiar memory of that hit. Pushed it far, far away.

Her hand went to her face, but she kept her eyes carefully away from his. Because she knew that in them smoldered a dark intensity that said she would kill him where he stood for touching her.

"Now, you will be with me. I already have a room," Wilson said, grasping her upper arm with more force and shuffling her toward an exit.

Kierse almost sighed with relief. Yes, a room would be lovely. That would mean she could incapacitate him somewhere private instead of in front of everyone in the ballroom. She'd have to be sure not to get too much blood on her corset. Though with this crowd, who would even notice?

She was nearly to the door when a hand clamped down on the man's shoulder, dragging him to a halt. "Wilson Bellack."

Kierse had to fight to keep her face neutral when she saw Graves standing before the sniveling vampire.

"Yes? Are we acquainted?" Bellack asked.

"I don't believe that we are," Graves said, dominance on full display. The force of his magic made him nearly blinding to look at. She hadn't realized that the fear he inspired was, in part, a product of his magic. It was easy to see why others shrank from him. "But you do seem to have my property."

"And who the hell are you?"

Graves just smiled at him. Something cold and lethal. "That's not any of your business."

"Are you of the Men of Valor?"

Graves nudged the winged pin at his lapel in answer. "Now, would you *release* my property?"

Wilson flung her arm aside as if she were a doll. He looked like he wanted to say something more, but he just strode away furiously.

"I don't think he likes you," Kierse reasoned.

"No, I suspect not," Graves said.

"What took you so long?"

He flashed the pin at her. He must have taken it off of someone.

"Miss me?" He drew her closer. His eyes skated down the skimpy outfit.

"Hardly," she teased right back.

"I approve of the outfit. Wear it for me later?"

She wasn't sure if he was joking. And part of her shivered at the thought, but she couldn't consider it here.

"We're wasting time," she told him.

He nodded just as a hush fell over the room and the exits were barred. Kierse swallowed and glanced at Graves. He shook his head minutely.

"His Royal Majesty, King Louis," an attendant declared.

And onto the head dais strode the King of the Underworld.

Chapter Fifty-Five

"Greetings, my fellow monsters," King Louis crowed.

Kierse met Graves's eyes, and together, they took a step farther from the ring of monsters. They were supposed to be gone before Louis's big announcement, but Graves had been delayed. And now she was finally getting her first look at the monster.

King Louis was larger than life in every way imaginable. From his over-the-top seventeenth-century Sun King outfit, complete with a long golden waistcoat, puffy sleeves, knee-high tights, and heeled boots, to his long, curly-haired powdered wig, his look reveled in the moniker he had taken for himself. He held a staff in front of him and strut forward to his awaiting audience, who cheered wildly.

Graves sighed at her side. "He couldn't even get a historically accurate wig."

Kierse forced her face neutral to keep from laughing. "What?"

"They weren't powdered for another hundred years."

She shook her head at him. "Only you would know that."

King Louis continued, raising his arm and gesturing into the air. "Welcome to my Winter Solstice celebration!"

Despite the ridiculous powdered wig, he cut a formidable figure. He had a manic look in his eyes, and power radiated off of him—it was easy to see how he had come to rule despite his eccentricities. His very presence exuded authority and danger, as if he might start murdering everyone in attendance just for looking at him wrong.

"The longest night of the year belongs to *us*," he said, tapping forward with glee. "It belongs to the creatures of the night. Those who have fought to claim their rightful place."

Another cheer went up in the crowd hungry for his approval.

"Only to be cut down by the insidious human hand. To be cut down from power by the insufferable Monster Treaty. As if being stronger, faster, and living longer than the humans were some sort of illness rather than what we all know it to be." He paused for dramatic effect. "Salvation."

The response was deafening. All manner of monsters cheered for his glory and his promised salvation. This was what they were all drunk on. Not promised blood or entertainment. It was about reclaiming what they believed had been taken from them. And it made them ravenous.

Then, her eyes found Walter at the base of King Louis's dais, staring up at him in concentration.

She nudged Graves. "What's he doing?"

"He's protecting King Louis," he breathed against the shell of her ear. "His force field encircles them both."

Kierse's eyes narrowed as she focused on Walter's magic. She could see a shimmer of gold shadowing him and weaving around King Louis, too. They'd have to take out Walter before getting to him. "Did you know he could do that?"

The flicker in Graves's jaw was enough to say that he hadn't known. Another new ability. Walter was shaping up to be more than Graves had ever anticipated.

King Louis continued. "You already know what I believe, what I stand for. This isn't an election, where I recite my triumphs for you to know that I am strength. I am the height of vampire strength, the height of all monster strength! I will not back down. I will not fall. Not like my brothers before me. I will fight for our rights, for our ability to live our lives how we see fit. Not how the baser, *lesser* humans deem to be fair." King Louis held up his hand as the crowd foamed at the mouth for his offer. "They want us to grovel at their feet when *we* are the apex predators in this world."

Kierse turned her focus to the humans in the room. The *meals* these monsters had purchased for the night. Most seemed just as enthralled, but Kierse found a few humans who looked as disgusted as she felt. They didn't deserve this. None of them did.

"We are the Men of Valor! We will not grovel. We will not compromise," King Louis shouted to his supporters. "We are the rightful rulers of this world. It is time to take it back!" The crowd cheered, and King Louis called over them, "Feast tonight, brothers and sisters. Enjoy the spoils of our war. Tomorrow, the real work begins."

Everyone cheered for King Louis, chanting his name.

"The doorways are clear," Graves said.

Kierse turned to leave, but Graves went suddenly still. "What?"

And then she saw Dr. Mafi at his back, a gun pointed at his spine.

"Not so fast," Dr. Mafi said darkly.

"What are you doing, Emmaline?" Graves asked.

"You are here to kill me."

"I'm not."

"Liar," she hissed.

"Let him go," Kierse growled, retrieving a knife from her boot and positioning it under Dr. Mafi's ribs. An easy shot upward would drive it into her heart.

Mafi froze. "Kierse?"

"We're not here to kill you. Now, let. Him. Go."

"I can't," she whispered.

Kierse dug the knife in deeper. "I don't want to kill you. Let's go somewhere and talk about this."

"To give him a chance to kill me?" she snarled.

"Emmaline, I am not here for you."

"You sent your dog after me," she said in fury. "I came to Louis, knowing you wanted me dead."

"I sent Edgar to offer you protection."

She laughed. "I don't believe you."

But Kierse saw the truth in his words. Mafi might be holding him at gunpoint, but Graves had magic. She didn't doubt for a second that he could have gotten away from her if he wanted. Which meant he wanted to talk. So, even though Kierse hadn't known that he'd sent Edgar after Dr. Mafi, she wasn't surprised by it, either. There was no reason to lie here.

"He's telling the truth. We're not here for you," Kierse said.

"We're here for something else," Graves said.

"Something...not someone?" Dr. Mafi asked.

"Yes," Kierse said. "Now, drop the gun."

Kierse saw the pain war through her features.

"How can I trust you?"

"Don't trust him," Kierse said. "You know he could stop you at any point. If he hasn't, it's because he doesn't want to hurt you. Neither do I. Please, trust me."

Mafi glanced at her, and whatever she saw there made her lower the gun a fraction. "I have a room nearby. I will take you there." Graves turned to face her, and she said, "Don't think about reading me."

That was the moment Kierse realized...Graves wasn't wearing gloves.

"After you, Emmaline," he said darkly.

Dr. Mafi looked like she wanted to raise the gun again and shoot him, but instead, she pocketed it inside the folds of her black-and-gold-trimmed abaya. "Follow me."

They moved to the exit like specters in the night, stealing away in the hallways and maneuvering through the sprawl of King Louis's house. The enormity of it hit Kierse in the chest. Not because she wasn't aware of how big the location was, but because the longer they followed Dr. Mafi, the farther they tracked from the vault.

Finally, Dr. Mafi stopped in front of a door. Her fingers rested upon the handle, and she spoke a few words. A stream of silvery light encased her hand, the lock clicked, and she pushed the door open. Kierse had known Mafi was a witch, but it was the first time she'd ever seen her use magic.

"Wow," she breathed.

"Parlor tricks," Graves scoffed before striding inside.

Mafi had already entered the bedroom, and she closed the door behind Kierse. The room was sparse: just a small bed in one corner, a side table, and a desk across the room with two chairs.

"If you're not here for me, what are you really doing here?"

"First, can we discuss you selling your soul to King Louis?" Graves said.

Mafi looked like she wanted to rake his eyes out with her nails. "I did no such thing."

"No? Just your medical integrity?"

"What are you talking about?" Kierse asked in confusion.

"Emmaline sold your blood to King Louis," Graves said.

Kierse felt sick. "You *sold* my blood?"

Mafi sank onto the bed across from them. "It wasn't like that. I was doing some under-the-table work for some politicians. Louis got wind of it and blackmailed me. I would have gone to jail. He had me under his thumb, and there was nothing else I could do."

So she was just like everyone else in King Louis's world, beholden to him and unable to escape. It didn't excuse her giving King Louis Kierse's blood, but it made her just another victim in a long line of victims.

"What did he want with her blood?" Graves asked.

"He was looking for blood with magical components. He believed it would make him stronger, enough to win this war. So, I told him that I would find candidates with different blood from people who came through the hospital."

"And does it make him stronger?"

Mafi rolled her eyes. "Of course not. Her blood is like any other blood, but he wouldn't listen to me."

Graves paced away from her. "Why didn't you come to me?"

Mafi laughed. "I owed you a favor. I couldn't owe you a second."

Graves looked like he wanted to say more, but Kierse stepped between them. "The world is a hard place. It makes monsters of us all."

Mafi's face fell at those words. "It does, doesn't it?"

"We should tell her," Kierse told him.

Graves shook his head. "We've spent enough time here as it is." He turned to Mafi. "You should get out of here while you can. Get to my brownstone, speak to Edgar. He'll give you everything you need."

"Why are you helping me?" she asked skeptically. "You only ever do things for your own aims."

His gaze cut to Kierse's, and she nodded, understanding sinking into her stomach. "Because I should have done more the first time."

Mafi reared back in shock. Her eyes flickered between the pair of them. "Maybe you *have* changed," she said thoughtfully. "Fine. I'll get out of here. But you two should as well."

"That's the plan," Kierse said. "We just need one more thing before we do."

"I can't change your mind about whatever you're about to do?" Dr. Mafi asked.

Kierse shook her head. "We're set on it."

Dr. Mafi sighed. Her gaze cast to Graves. "How much of the blueprints have you seen?"

"I know my way around," he assured her.

"Of course you do." Then she stood and held her hand out to him. "Just in case, check against my map."

He stared down at her hand as if he couldn't believe she was offering it to him. "You *want me* to read you?"

Dr. Mafi tipped up her chin and met his eyes. "I want you to get her out of here so she's not more collateral damage."

Graves stiffened. "She isn't."

"Then let me help."

He straightened to his considerable height and then slowly wrapped his hand around her wrist. This was the first time Kierse had ever seen Graves read from someone, since it never worked on her. She knew that he did this as part of his business, but now she could see it.

The gold light of his magic flared to life at the contact: a shimmering, mesmerizing aura that smelled strongly of leather with just a hint of fresh paper. Kierse could hardly fathom that he was currently *reading her mind*. Even if he claimed it wasn't that. That he could only skim what people were thinking, and Mafi was clearly showing him a way through the hallways. Laying a map she was familiar with over the one they had been studying to get inside.

But what else could he skim from her in this brief contact? What else was she thinking even subconsciously that Graves could learn? No wonder he was so powerful, if he could gain access to people's minds.

Graves released her a moment later. The light and fire and smell dissipated all at once. "Ah, it looks like some of our information was out of date. But our pathway is still clear."

"Thank you," Kierse said to Mafi.

She just nodded gravely. "Be quick. He intends for tonight to be a slaughter."

Chapter Fifty-Six

They left Mafi at the entrance to her rooms and wound through the labyrinth of hallways with practiced ease, bypassing patrons and security. Kierse stayed close to Graves's side, recognizing the layout of the passageways as they got closer to the vault.

"I'm surprised Mafi let you read her," Kierse said. "She seemed particularly upset about it in the past."

"She had every reason to be. I didn't hold her trust well in the past," he said. They turned down another hallway.

"What else did you get in that touch?"

He frowned. "Enough."

Which was why Dr. Mafi hadn't wanted Graves to read her in the first place.

"I have never been more thankful that you cannot read my mind."

"Again, I don't read minds," he said in exasperation. "She practically shouted the blueprint over to me. It threatened to give me a headache. The other stuff was what I already knew. Sometimes when people try so hard not to think of something, all they do is think about it."

Kierse shivered. "No wonder everyone is terrified of you."

"Hence the gloves," he said, showing her his bare hands. "Around this corner."

She peered around the next corner and saw two vampire guards standing in front of a door. "We have arrived at our destination," she told him. "It's the only guarded door. It practically has a sign on it that says, *Steal from me*."

"You have a twisted mind."

"Says the man who reads minds."

He shrugged. "I come by my powers honestly."

"As do I," she said as she retrieved a knife concealed in her corset. "How should we do this?"

"You take one. I'll take the other."

She took a deep breath. She knew she could take down a vampire. She'd killed Orik one on one in a darkened alleyway by hitting into slow motion.

She didn't want to burn out her reserves before she even got to the vault, though. Thankfully, she didn't need to kill these vampires. Just knock them out. Maybe head-on wasn't the right call.

"I have another idea."

"Which is?"

She twined her hand around his waist and glued herself to his side. "Remember what you said to me at Imani's? I'd have to play the part of your pet?" She gestured to her outfit. The white lingerie that screamed Red Velvet girl.

"I adore your mind," he rumbled with affection.

Graves waited for her cue, and then they turned the corner with Kierse slumped against his side. His hand brazenly cupped her ass as he staggered forward, apparently drunk. He swayed with the force of his act while she giggled nonsensically beside him.

"Hey, you there," the first vampire said. He was a beefy sort. Tan skin, dark eyes, and more muscles than brains. "No guests down this hallway. Go back to where you came from."

Graves kept walking and flicked his pin at them, his British accent growing thicker and more imperious. "I am a Man of Valor. I can…do what I want."

The guards rolled their eyes, relaxing at his inebriation. "Sir, we're going to have to ask that you find a room." Their eyes lingered on Kierse now, assessing her scantily clad form, the pulse of her blood through her veins. "Take your…companion with you, and all will be well."

As the first guard stepped forward to intercept them, they moved as one. Graves went for the beefy guard as she intercepted the second. He was slighter than the first. But he had keen, hungry eyes, and they were squared on her.

She darted forward, throwing a knife from her corset toward his jugular. The guard backpedaled, narrowly missing her deadly aim. He was fast. Vampire fast. She had to be as fast or faster to survive this. And in heels at that.

He came at her then, raising a baton and striking toward her head. She grasped another knife from her boot as she ducked and dodged his swings. He had a longer reach, and she needed to get in close to use her knife. She was really missing her gun right about now. Too bad they wouldn't have fit in her outfit.

The guard brought the baton forward, nearly smashing into her face, and she said, "Fuck it."

Time slowed to a crawl. Her magic buzzed all around her as she actively engaged it. A swirl of golden light that only she could see swam around her.

The baton flew toward her face as the guard tried to crack her jaw. She dodged the blow and then stepped into his space, not giving him a chance to bring his baton up again. She kicked him in the kneecap, whirled around, and brought her knife across his chest. He gasped in shock more than pain, then blocked her next hit, sending the knife tumbling out of her reach.

"Motherfucker," she swore as she skidded away from the monster and back into regular motion.

"Going to enjoy feasting on your blood, you little bitch," he snarled.

She dropped to her knees, sliding his feet out from under him. She rolled to her back and kipped up to standing. The vampire had crashed unceremoniously to the floor, but he was already lunging for her as she returned to her feet. She moved out of the way, jerking into slow motion. She retrieved her second knife from her boot and rammed the side of it into his skull with blunt force.

The vampire stumbled. His eyes went wide with surprise, but he was still heading toward her. She would have to be quick and decisive. Maybe her knife wouldn't cut through bone, but it could do some damage.

Then, just as she darted toward him, Graves appeared. He moved at shocking speeds—such that even her slow motion could barely track him. A blur of heat and gold light as he intercepted the blow of the vampire, deflected it with his forearm, then twisted the vamp so he had his back to Graves's chest. Time slowed even further as the vampire realized he had been bested. Then Graves snapped the vampire's neck, and he crashed to the floor, dead.

Kierse came back into motion with a wince. Everything had been so quiet. But as soon as she returned, it was like the world magnified the sound.

"Thanks," she said, breathing heavy. "Think anyone heard us?"

Graves shot her a look that said all she needed to know. "Open the door across the hall."

Kierse jumped into action. She jiggled the locked door handle and then tested it for magic, but there were no wards. She smiled and put her other skills to work. She withdrew a trusty hairpin and flipped the lock in a matter of seconds. So much for Mafi's parlor tricks when her bobby pin could do the same thing.

A closet. A totally normal janitor's closet. Excellent.

Kierse and Graves hauled the guards inside. She frisked the vamps, removing a handgun from one guard, stuffing it into her boot. The second guard had a key card like what they used for the checkpoints, but it had the Men of Valor logo on it. She slid the card into her opposite boot, then closed and locked the door again.

Graves drew a ward on the doorknob, applying his magic to it in a sizzle. The smallest hint of golden light and the smell of leather and new books wafted in the air. Sometimes she still couldn't believe that she'd never smelled it on him before.

"Now for the fun part," she said.

They turned back to the vault. It was relatively innocuous, just a large, gray metal door with a handle, save for the key card reader on the wall next to it.

"You're up," Graves said.

Kierse straightened her shoulders and felt the excitement rush through her body. She loved this part. It made her blood sing. All of that magic she had used was about to be restored. Her hands pulsed with excitement, and she quickly shook it off and got into position.

She tested the handle. Locked, of course.

Then she drew her magic to her and felt around for the wards. She blew out a breath. Walter hadn't skimped on this. The warding system was like trying to break into a bank vault. It had a pattern and what appeared to be a warded combination lock. She'd never seen anything like it before.

"What is it?" Graves asked.

"It's a combination lock like on a vault. I have to break the wards in a certain order for you to go inside with me."

"Or what?"

She frowned. "Do you want to find out?"

"No."

"Do you have to go inside with me?"

He just leveled her with a flat look. He wasn't coming this far and not going inside that room.

"Fine," she said with a laugh. "Go be a lookout."

Kierse got to work as Graves hung back at the other end of the hallway. She steadied herself and pretended like this was any other lock she had opened before. She ran her hands across the various wards, recognizing the sun symbol threaded through Walter's warding. The wards didn't touch her—she just absorbed them—but if she didn't want to be caught doing it, then she needed to figure out this code and figure it out fast. Quick hands, skill, and intuition made a thief valuable.

She looked at the problem from Walter's point of view. From the basics that she knew of computers from her time deactivating security systems and taking down cameras, a computer worked with a series of zeros and ones. Coded correctly, it functioned as a brain, figuring out complex problems and generally running daily life. But if the code was wrong, the back brain stopped working. She needed to find the system code.

Unfortunately, there were an infinite number of possibilities. Without the ability to hear the clicks of the vault, she didn't know how she was supposed to solve it. She couldn't just try at random. That would trip an alarm.

Her eyes roamed the carved marks. There had to be something different about them. Some of the wards were darker than others, as if they had been carved in harder. She didn't know why that was. Why would he even set it up this way? Then she saw that there appeared to be something else in the whorls and swirls than what she had seen before. This was a different kind of ward. Possibly one he had invented himself.

Her finger stilled over the top ward. XII. Roman numerals. Her eyes drifted around in a circle. She shifted to the next one. I. And the next. II. And the next. III. The next was IIII, not the IV she had expected, but she still saw it for what it was.

It was a clock.

But why would only certain numbers be darker? Maybe they were used more often. She could see the numbers I, III, IIII, V, IX. Which only marginally narrowed it down.

Kierse slid the key card out of her boot. She ran it across the slot like at the checkpoints, but instead of it opening, a password punch code appeared below the card.

"Graves," she called. "There's a password on the wards. I can't break them separately. I'm ninety-seven percent sure that will trigger an alarm. I have to know the password."

"Great," he growled in frustration. "What can I do?"

"You knew Walter. Think of what he would use as a password. A numerical password that includes one, three, four, five, and nine. I'm thinking tech related. Think code or math or something."

"What if it's Louis's code?" Graves asked.

"Would *you* let Louis pick the code?"

"Of course not."

"I doubt Walter would, either. It's his system. It's his code," she said with more certainty than she felt.

She just thought of the person she had trailed through the market that day. Walter had so much pride in his work. It was obvious in every inch of his systems and the way he repaired them that day. She didn't think he would give away any more control than he had to.

Graves looked at the keypad for a span of a few seconds, and then, without even running it by her, he punched in a series of numbers.

"What are you doing?" she gasped, waiting for an alarm to blare and for someone to come and stop them.

Then the system disarmed like magic. The door began to slowly slide open.

"How?" Kierse gasped in relief.

"Pi was Walter's favorite number. He liked that it was a constant. 3.14159."

"Thank god that you love knowledge," she muttered. "I never in a million years would have guessed that. That could have been a disaster."

Graves shrugged. "It felt like a solid gamble."

He was fucking lucky he was right.

The door finally opened all the way, releasing with a soft hiss. Kierse's breath caught at the sight before her. The gallery was even more beautiful than the ballroom, with black marble floors ingrained with gold. The walls were a silky-smooth red, and built-in white display shelves lined one wall, full of all manner of objects, including jewelry, gemstones, a large gold crown, and some very old-looking books. The other wall displayed what she assumed was priceless artwork. Kingston would kill to be in this room.

But her eyes came back to the item at the center.

A closed black box that contained the most valuable item—the spear.

Finally within her grasp.

Kierse still needed to break the wards just to be sure the system didn't come back online while they were stuck inside. Now she could do that without setting off an alarm. Walter was smarter than Graves had given him credit for. This system was genius.

She carefully deactivated each of the wards, absorbing the golden glow into her, getting a brush of Walter's magic—incense and rainstorms. She didn't want someone to bring the system back up and lock Graves inside. This was her exit strategy for a room with only one exit.

"All right," she said with a nod.

Then, with a held breath, she stepped into the trophy room. No alarm tripped. No sound went off. There was perfect silence.

"Graves, look at this place," she said, turning to face him.

But he was still on the other side of the door.

"Get out of there," he yelled just as an alarm blared.

The door slammed shut between them before she could cross the threshold. The lights went out, and she was cast into pitch blackness.

Kierse lurched for the door only for arms to roughly grasp her. "No!" she screamed, reaching for her knives or the gun in her boot.

But a heavy object came down on her temple, and she collapsed, unconscious, to the floor.

Chapter Fifty-Seven

The floor was cold under her cheek.

Her head swam, but as she came to, she could hear voices. Many voices. A chill ran up her spine that told her not to move, not a single muscle. She'd felt that terror before as she faced down a monster. This time, it was all-encompassing.

From her position, she could tell that whoever had kidnapped her had been thorough. The knives in her corset and boots as well as the pilfered gun were gone. She had no weapons. And she was about to face down a party of monsters without an exit strategy. Her worst nightmare.

At least Graves was out there somewhere. She hoped.

No, Graves *would* show up. He would save her.

"Ah, she's awake," a voice said from beside her.

No use pretending now.

Kierse opened her eyes as she was roughly hauled to her feet by a pair of vampires. Her greatest fears were immediately confirmed. They had brought her to the full ballroom of monsters, where King Louis was seated like a conquering hero on a throne, drenched in the blood of his victims: three young women—one already dead, the other so drugged out on his venom that she would likely follow, and the last one—Torra.

Her breath caught at the sight of her lying at the feet of the throne. Her head slumped against the leg. She was supposed to have already made her way to the exit to meet Graves and Kierse. She shouldn't have been lying at King Louis's feet with only a subtle rise and fall of her chest.

She tore her eyes from Torra to confirm that Walter was still standing at the front of the room. A shimmering force field stretched around the vampire that only magic users could see.

Then she saw what sat before the vicious monster—a clear box, humming with ward energy. The Spear of Lugh.

Kierse lunged for the box. If she could just get to the spear— But before the thought could even process, she was wrenched backward and secured in place.

A chorus of laughter rang from the ballroom, and King Louis's demonic eyes shifted fully to her.

"Our guest of honor!" he boomed.

He rose to his full height, standing half a head taller than Kierse, and dumped the girls unceremoniously to the floor. Kierse held his gaze, steady. She did not flinch. She did not break his stare. She was afraid, but she refused to show it.

"Ah, come now. I can sense your heartbeat," he said quietly. "You can drop the act."

She refused. She wouldn't give him the benefit of seeing her fear.

"Fuck you," she spat eloquently.

He chuckled. "No need for vulgarity. It's a party. We're here to celebrate." He gestured to their ravenous audience. The monsters hungering for her. The meals slumped over from blood loss. As if this wasn't vulgar. "After all, I've gone to a lot of trouble to get you here."

She blinked at those words. Keeping her mouth clamped shut was an effort, but he must have seen the questions in her eyes.

"See, I've been looking for tasty little morsels like yourself. Power, true power, can't be bought or made or purchased. It can only be inherent in a person. Like me." He straightened, holding out his cane and preening. "But it can be *enhanced*. And your blood is an enhancer."

"Bullshit," she spat.

Mafi had said that her blood didn't do anything for vampires. It was just blood. Her being able to absorb magic didn't do anything to him.

He smirked. "No? Should we test it, then?"

Then his act dropped, and she saw the moment when the killer instinct took over, the moment when he changed from the pantomime performance to the true deadly beast within. He moved so fast that he was merely shadow before he was at her side. Walter's force field swarmed around her as well, as Louis grasped her wrist in his meaty fingers.

Her gaze found Torra against the throne. Her eyes were pleading and sad.

She mouthed, *Breathe.*

Kierse's eyes widened in panic. No, he couldn't drink from her. She looked around wildly for another way out.

Graves. Where the hell was Graves? He hadn't been captured. He hadn't even made it into the room. He had to stop this.

But no one came.

No one stopped it as he lifted her wrist to his mouth. She was stealth and intrigue and secrecy. She had her slow motion, but she was still woozy from being incapacitated. Her mind was swimming, and she couldn't shift fast enough, couldn't escape his goons.

Then he sank his fangs into her wrist. She hated herself for the gasp that escaped her mouth. Blood flowed from her veins, and then he went *deeper*. This time, her gasp became a scream as he gulped down the blood.

With a satisfied sigh, he wrenched back. Her blood just barely tinted the edges of his mouth.

The venom hit her system like a shot of espresso. Where pain had been only seconds earlier, now there was nothing. She'd never been bitten before, but she had heard from enough people to know the sensation was like a mix of alcohol and ecstasy. A little drunk, a lot aroused. She'd thought nothing could be as bad as wish powder. But she would take that every day over the blanket that was thrown over her senses now.

"Delicious," King Louis said. The raucous cheer from the crowd brought her back to reality. "And *full* of power." He took a deep breath and spread his arms. "Brimming with power. With you and my spear, I'll be unstoppable. We'll end the Monster Treaty. We'll take back what was ours."

Kierse swayed on her feet.

He laughed at her, tipping his head at his minions. They released her, and she stumbled forward.

"The venom works swiftly," King Louis informed her. "Mine in particular is incredibly potent, as you can tell." He gestured to the girls at his feet.

Her eyes were unsteady as she looked for an exit. She still hadn't seen Graves. What was he waiting for?

"I assure you. No one is coming for you," he said with a sinister edge as if he knew her thoughts. "You're *mine*."

He put a steadying hand on her back. She tried to wrench away, but his grip was firm.

"Come along. Let me show you my other prize. You can't touch it anyway," King Louis explained. "No one can get through my young apprentice's wards."

So, King Louis didn't know about her powers. He only knew what Mafi had told him about her blood absorbing magic. Good.

She needed to stay coherent. If only she could shift into slow motion and burn the venom off—but it wouldn't come. Her magic was as sluggish as her senses, and all she could do was follow King Louis toward the box.

Her breath caught even in her addled state as she looked inside the clear glass and got her first real look at the spear.

It was somehow more ordinary than she had expected *and* more glorious. The blade was about a foot long, razor-sharp with little adornment. It was attached to a dark wooden handle that showed no signs of wear despite its age.

Her heart thudded. So much energy put into acquiring this one item, and finally it was right before her.

"Wow," she breathed despite herself.

"Isn't it glorious?"

King Louis raised his hands and began a diatribe about the spear and his rightful place at the head of their maniacal monster organization. Kierse was barely able to stand, but she knew her cue when she saw it.

With a quick lunge, she pushed her hand through the wards of the box and wrapped her fingers around the spear.

A tidal wave hit her. The vampire venom in her system evaporated upon contact. Suddenly, her addled senses sharpened. Her slow motion sat so close to the surface that it practically shimmered in front of her in a haze of gold energy. Filaments of light dotted every bare scrap of skin, revealing all the magic she'd absorbed. For a second, she felt as if she could suck all the magic out of this very room like a vacuum just by concentrating hard enough.

Oh yes, *this* was the spear they had been looking for.

It hummed with untapped energy. Magic so depthless as to be overpowering. As if lightning were trapped in the blade, desperate to be released. As if it *recognized* her. The spear had a will of its own, and right now it wanted to release its power. She had to force down the desire to do just that.

Use me. Wield me. Unleash me.

And oh, it was tantalizing.

Oh, how I have longed for you. Destroy our enemies.

How many times had she wanted something to give her the power to destroy her enemies? She'd wanted her parents to come back and save her from poverty. She'd wanted someone to come and stop Jason in her darkest moments. She'd wanted someone to take care of her after she was broken so that she didn't have to steal any longer. She'd wanted a safe city and safe streets and no monsters.

But wishes were for the weak.

She pushed back against that hum—that draw to its energy. The spear bucked against her, angry that she was imposing her will against its own. She had to remain like steel, building an impenetrable shield against its nature. Then she locked the door and buried the spear's energy behind it. Finally, it settled.

No one had been there to save her.

She drew the spear level with King Louis and spat, "I'll save my fucking self."

Chapter Fifty-Eight

The shock on King Louis's face morphed almost instantly into disdain. Walter's force field had snapped back into place around the vampire. He believed he was protected. He'd watched her get through his wards, and he *still* believed in Walter's force fields.

"What are you going to do with that thing? Surely one little girl can't wield the Spear of Lugh."

She *could* in fact wield this spear. Though she was bucking under the strain of its power.

"Surely your master told you what you hold?"

Oh, she knew. Graves had her reading all of those assignments to prepare her for this moment. And she had walked right into the answer about the spear. Not that it had actually prepared her to hold the thing.

But that didn't matter. All that mattered was that it felt right in her hand, and nothing Louis said was going to change her mind.

"The Spear of Lugh," he said for his audience. "Slaughterer. One who has never been defeated in battle." He taunted her. "A little girl can't hope to harness the power of the gods. You're not powerful enough."

It was a god's weapon, but that didn't change its purpose.

At the end of the day, it cut all the same.

And the person she wanted to destroy stood before her with Torra beside his throne and two victims at his feet. Two in a line of hundreds or even thousands.

Humans who hadn't had an option to escape. People he would just throw away for a meal. Kierse could have been any of them. Jason was his own monster and had abused her beyond comprehension, but even he didn't have a long line of dead people in his wake. If she let King Louis live, how many more people would end up like Torra? Like Mafi? How many more would suffer at his hands and the hands of his pathetic Men of Valor?

No, she had promised Torra that she would kill King Louis.

And she kept her promises.

The spear latched on to her thoughts, saw into her heart, and knew what she wanted. This time, she didn't dispel it. She didn't ignore its sinister voice, because it matched her own.

"You are no king," Kierse said, taking a step forward. "You are a puppeteer, pulling strings. Your reign ends today."

Kierse lifted the spear, muscle memory from hours of training kicking in. It had never felt as comfortable as a knife or a gun in her hand, but that was because she had been waiting all of her life for *this* spear. The perfect weight in her hands, the dark voice in her ear. She knew what to do.

She stepped through the force field, watched the shock register on Louis's face, then raised the spear and thrust forward. Louis dodged just barely as an alarm blared to life around them. His guards hurtled for her, but she slashed the spear blindly toward them. She felt the sickening crunch as she sliced through bone. Heard the squelch as it sank through flesh. Barely altering her focus, she was on Louis again.

He brought his arms up to dodge her strike. She sliced deep grooves of dark blood into his arms. He cried out as the world fell into pandemonium behind them. His hyper speed kicked in as he tried to backpedal, but Kierse went instantly into slow motion, pulling it over her like a blanket. And suddenly, Louis was swinging his arms as he backpedaled.

He was within reach a second later as she came out of slow motion. His jaw opened, revealing the gleaming white fangs. His eyes were wide with shock and a satisfying amount of fear. He couldn't win this, and for the first time, he'd realized it. She had outmaneuvered him. A little human woman with nothing and no one to help her.

"How?" he gasped.

"Magic."

With all the force of her training, she drove the spear deep into the vampire king's heart.

King Louis fell to his knees as she yanked it from his chest. "Who are you?" he muttered as blood poured out of his mouth.

"I'm the monster in *your* nightmares."

Then she slashed the spear sideways, decapitating him.

Louis's head fell off of his body to a chorus of screams. The rest of him toppled forward, blood sputtering onto the white marble and soaking the white of her lingerie.

Her eyes rose to the monsters before her. Walter had already vanished in the crowd, among the rest of Louis's followers, his pathetic Men of Valor. The scum that he empowered with his propaganda. These monsters had spent their entire lives oppressing humans. They deserved a similar fate.

Then a figure appeared on the dais.

Graves.

He assessed the state of the world as it had just shifted off its axis to accommodate her. He took in her bloodstained clothing, the wicked grin on her lips, and the spear held firmly in her grasp. He nodded once, a slow smile coming to his devastating features. The power pulsed relentlessly through her, between them.

She lifted her chin to meet that gaze. She'd accepted her place as a monster. A monster at his side. And he accepted that in a glance.

No, not accepted. Reveled in it. Devoured it. As if it were destined from the start.

He took a few long strides across the dais, ignoring the remaining carnage. Stepped through the blood of the dead vampire king, slid his hand to the back of her neck, and kissed her with the hunger of a predator. She met him where he was, refusing to give even an inch. A fight, a challenge, a sundering.

Because she had never been kissed the way Graves was kissing her, standing in the blood of their enemy.

Their mouths fitted together. Tongues volleying for dominance. Power coursing through them like a conduit igniting and blazing for everyone to see. Their magic met. A gold glow that twined around each other, not quite melding but mirroring.

When the kiss ended, the world felt as if it had tilted back and this was how it was always meant to be.

"My Wren," he said.

"I got the spear," she said, hoisting the thing up.

His eyes flickered to it and back as if he'd been so blinded by her that he hadn't noticed. "Good. We have to go."

"We have to get Torra."

Graves reached for the spear, but she couldn't let go. The spear didn't want her to let go. So, she left Graves facing down the impending monster horde and fell to her knees before the vampire's throne. "Torra. Torra, we have to go. We need to get moving."

"Kierse," she said, her voice unsteady. "I don't think I can move."

"You can. I'll help you."

She put her weight underneath Torra and lifted her slight form off of the ground.

"You killed him."

"I told you I would," Kierse said.

"Thank you," she whispered.

"We *need* to go," Graves said, swearing under his breath.

"Then fucking help me."

He swore under his breath and then swept Torra into his arms as if she weighed nothing.

It had been a matter of seconds between killing their king, Graves's kiss, and freeing Torra, and already the monsters were forming up to come after them. That wasn't good. The spear was powerful, but she didn't know if it could take on a vampire army.

Do not underestimate me.

She shuddered at the voice in her head, uncertain if it was her own thoughts or…the spear's.

"This way," Graves said.

They ran.

She tucked the spear to her side. The weight of it felt right. No, perfect. Impossibly balanced and like an extension of herself. She understood why she'd dealt with all of the training to get to this very moment.

Graves had been busy while he was gone. Every guard between her and the exit had been efficiently incapacitated. Seeing the carnage was not just impressive but terrifying. They came across only a handful of frightened guards as they made their escape toward the secret tunnel out of Louis's residence. Some fled from the sight of her. The others, Kierse made quick work of. Torra fell unconscious at some point as they got away.

They'd just turned toward the secret tunnel when they came face-to-face with none other than Walter Rodriguez wearing a loaded-down backpack and looking panicked.

His jaw dropped open. "Graves?"

"Hello, Walter," Graves said.

"You," he said to Kierse. "You…you walked through my force field."

"And reached through your wards," she said with a dangerous smile.

His gaze shifted frantically between Graves, Kierse, and the spear as if he couldn't decide which was the bigger threat. She could smell a faint scent of incense and rainstorms when his shields strengthened at their perceived anger. He'd just admitted that she could get through them, and still he reacted by instinct. "Wh-what are you doing here?"

"Using your exit," Graves said smoothly. "What a clever little mouse."

"How do you know about that?" He glanced behind them, inching backward.

"I know everything you've been doing for King Louis. But you chose the wrong side, Walter. Your master is dead."

His eyes widened. "I didn't *choose* a side. You discarded me like old garbage," he said, his voice quavering even as he stood up to Graves. "I went for the next highest bidder, and now I'm getting *out* of here."

"We don't have time for this," Kierse said. "We need to leave."

"He's a threat," Graves said.

"No, please," Walter said, backing away. "I just want to get out of here. I don't want to hurt anyone."

"You heard him. He got roped into this," Kierse said, blocking Graves. "And you did discard him after not seeing his potential."

Graves met her gaze with what looked like admiration. He'd come to the other side with Mafi. And for the first time, it seemed like he had realized his mistake with Walter as well.

"I did," Graves said. "You're done working for the Men of Valor?"

"I'm done," Walter said frantically.

"We don't have time," she said. She pushed past Walter. "Graves, let's move."

For a second, she thought that he wasn't going to listen to her. But after staring at Walter another beat, he followed Kierse down the exit. Then they took off at a run.

The tunnel was long and winding, but she remembered the way through. The entire time, she held tightly to the spear, its constant hum a reminder of how very alive and deadly this thing was.

"What the fuck am I holding, Graves? I know you said it was the Spear of Lugh, but I didn't know that it was going to feel like this." She shook her head. "The gods," she muttered under her breath. "This is a god's spear."

"Yes. I already told you that it was. This was why we had to get it from Louis."

There was a difference between knowing and *knowing*. If all of it was true. If the spear was literally a magic spear from the gods. If all of the stories she'd read from her assignments weren't just a kernel of truth but fact—then what was she? What was Graves?

He used the holly as his symbol. Of course he would see the wren as part of him. He hadn't said anything, and yet she knew it. Maybe she'd always known it. Because they'd been twined by that first night. As soon as he'd seen her wren necklace. The moment she'd glimpsed his library. They'd been tied together like their magic in that kiss—an inextricable link.

But she still had to say it.

"You're the Holly King."

His throat bobbed before he nodded. "And you're my wren."

Chapter Fifty-Nine

The Holly King.

In the flesh.

And she was his wren.

She shuddered at the shape of the words. They sounded the same as when Gen made a prophecy. They sounded *true*.

It seemed impossible that myth and legend could be manifested in this way, and yet it was impossible to ignore. Her winter god was before her, and today was his day—the winter solstice. No wonder she had felt their linking. It had been as destined as it felt.

"What does that mean?" she gasped. "How am I your wren? I don't understand."

"The Holly King is the power of winter," he said through gritted teeth. "It's a manifestation of the energy of the season itself. I come into the height of my power on the summer solstice, and it wanes after the winter solstice."

"I know that. Because of the battle with the Oak King."

"Yes. The Oak King has his robin, his bird a symbol of the coming fall. And I have a wren, my symbol of the oncoming of spring."

"But I'm a *bad* omen," she said. "I'm...the bird that dies after Christmas."

"You are, but until then, you enhance my power," he admitted. "I'm at my height right up until the end of the longest night of the year."

"Tonight," she whispered.

"That's right." His gaze slid to hers as they took another turn deeper through the tunnel system.

"But Kingston said...he said that it didn't work out for you," she said, slotting together all the pieces from the last couple of weeks. The words others had said about her being a wren that she hadn't understood until now.

Graves averted his gaze again. "Yes, well, I gain more power, but ultimately, after the solstice, you are my downfall."

She blinked in shock. "Then why...why would you work with me?"

"Our mission ended tonight. It was a gamble worth taking," he admitted just as the light of the end of the tunnel came into view. Then he shifted his grip on Torra. "I never…" He actually stumbled on his words. "I never planned to fall for you. That wasn't part of the plan."

She swallowed. "I don't…understand."

"It's poetic," he said softly. "To fall for the source of your own destruction."

She still had so many questions. More questions than answers as always with Graves, but then they reached the end of the tunnel.

Graves hoisted Torra over his shoulder and then climbed up the ladder. She followed with the spear in hand. When she reached the top, Graves hauled her up into the subway tunnel.

They continued in silence, jogging to the exit and scrambling up into the longest night of the year. The winter solstice. The last night of Graves's heightened power. They had made it. They had survived with the spear in hand.

Torra roused as they exited into the evening air.

She shifted groggily. "You can put me down."

Graves put her carefully onto her feet, shucking off his jacket and sliding it around Torra's bare shoulders.

Torra wobbled slightly. "Thank you."

"Can you give us a minute?" Kierse asked Graves.

He gestured to the car idling on the street. Their escape plan. Kierse nodded at him and watched him head toward it.

Torra tipped her head back and took a good, long breath of fresh air. "I never thought I'd see the sky again."

Kierse frowned. "I'm so sorry, Tor."

"But you saved me. You got me out," she said with a harsh inhale. "I'll never be able to repay that."

"No repayment needed. This was righting a horrible wrong."

"And he's really gone."

Kierse nodded. "He's really gone."

Torra swallowed back tears. "Hard to believe."

"What are you going to do?"

Torra smiled, and it was the first happy expression Kierse had seen on her face since they reunited.

"Whatever I want. I'm free."

Torra pulled her into a hug. Kierse held her tight, relieved that she had saved at least one person in all that madness. She hoped Louis's downfall would put a stop to the Men of Valor's machinations, but she didn't know that it would for a fact. At least he wouldn't be able to prey on innocents anymore.

"You could come with us," Kierse said. "Graves could help you."

Torra's eyes went to the monster waiting at the black car. "I don't think that's my path."

"Then go to Colette," Kierse said when she pulled back. "Nate is on lockdown for another night of the full moon. He can help you after that."

She swallowed. "You think they'll still want to help me?"

"We've all missed you," Kierse insisted. "They'll help whatever you decide."

"Thank you, Kierse." She started to take off Graves's jacket.

"Keep it. I'm sure he has a million of them." Torra nodded. "Are you sure we can't drive you somewhere?"

"I think tonight, I just want to walk," she said, and then, before Kierse could utter another word, Torra turned and headed the other direction.

Kierse hated letting her go, but she knew a freedom walk when she saw one. She'd done what she had set out to do. Torra was free.

Graves pulled the door open for her without a word as she headed his direction. They climbed inside, and Graves said, "Drive."

The car lurched forward. And the silence was filled by the sounds of their heavy breathing. Kierse set the spear carefully in her lap. She was glad to not be holding it, but a part of her wanted to pick it up again. It was a sickness.

"Let me see it," he said.

She shook her head. "I don't think it wants me to let it go."

"It speaks to you?"

"If that's what you call it." She shivered. "It seems to want to impose its will on me."

"That is the essence of the spear. It derives from the story of Lugh himself, who was so skilled that he outsmarted the doorkeeper to be allowed into the court of the Tuatha Dé Danann," Graves explained. "Only when the gods were outmatched in a great battle did they appoint Lugh their commander. There, he used the spear to slay their enemies."

"Well, it would certainly like to do that right now," she said, her fingers grazing the long handle.

"Then it is alive as well."

She raised her eyebrows as a sinking feeling settled in the pit of her stomach. "What do you mean, '*as well*'?"

His eyes were still on the spear as he spoke. "You already know that of which you ask."

Kierse racked her brain. "You have another one."

But he didn't answer that question, to which she surely already knew the answer. Instead, he said, "There are four magical objects—the spear, the sword, the cauldron, and the stone. After the gods left, the artifacts were thrown across the world, their locations unknown for centuries. Only whispers popped up about each of them. The spear was always the loudest, as it is nigh unstoppable. I have been searching for them for many years."

"For all four of them?"

"Yes," he said simply. "They belong to me as much as any other. My mother was descended of the magical line who worshipped the Tuatha Dé Danann. Anyone who is of the line could lay claim to them. Why not me?"

She remembered him saying that he had gone to Ireland, to the people of his mother's line. She hadn't realized that he meant *this* line. Magical worshippers of ancient Celtic gods.

Frankly, she couldn't process that at the moment. What was important was that he had another object than the spear. He was halfway to his goal.

"Which one do you already have?" she asked.

"The sword," Graves said. "You hold the spear. There are two more out there yet to be discovered."

"What are you going to do with them?"

He considered for a second. "A spell."

"And what does this spell do?"

Graves's expression went perfectly flat at the question. "Very powerful magic."

And that was all she was going to get.

Despite everything that had happened between them over the last couple of weeks, he still didn't trust her with the full truth. She had known from the beginning that this was how it would be. She had wheedled answers out of him the entire way, but he had been keeping his actual intentions close to the vest the entire time. She shouldn't even have been surprised, but somehow, she was.

Kierse kept her hand on the spear as they drove through the wintry New York streets and into the underground garage.

As they pulled to a stop, she asked, "Will you show me the sword?"

"If you like."

She picked up the spear, ignoring its tempting words, and headed out of the car. Kierse followed him to a wall of the garage, where he ran his hand down to reveal a slit in the stone. Graves used his magic to unseal it first. Next was a retinal scanner and a fingerprint before it made a puff of air and opened to reveal a hidden room. Inside the room was a vault—very new, very shiny, very impenetrable. And on top of the high-tech system, wards were etched into the giant thing. Graves was not fucking around.

After he disengaged a system of locks and released the wards, what lay within was finally revealed.

Only one object—a shining blade.

"The Sword of Truth," Graves said, taking it in his hand.

Kierse's eyes widened. She could feel the blinding light, its own perfect blend of magic. The opposite somehow to the spear that she held in her hand.

Destiny and power enough to make the world tremble.

"What does it do?" she whispered in awe. The spear radiated in her hand, this close to another artifact.

Graves lifted the blade parallel to his face. "It shows the truth in all things."

Another truth was whispering in her ear.

Something is wrong.

Then she felt it. The house was…silent.

Not just sound but *magic*.

"The wards are down."

Graves's gaze cocked toward the house. "Someone is here."

They rushed out of the vault, spear and sword in hand, taking a set of emergency stairs that led to the first-floor landing. Then up the next flight to the Holly Library, where the doors lay ajar and a sliver of light shone through.

Graves raised the sword, blazing his path as they entered the room as one. She nearly lost her grip on the spear when she saw what awaited them inside the library. Gen and Ethan were held by Druids with knives at their necks.

At the center, seated like royalty, was Lorcan Flynn.

Chapter Sixty

"Gen!" Kierse gasped. "Ethan!"

She stepped toward her friends, but Graves held her back. She wanted, needed to go to them. But she couldn't. Not with Lorcan and those knives between them. Even with the spear, they would be dead before she got to them.

"Kierse!" Ethan cried. "Oh god, Kierse."

"Are you hurt?"

"We're okay," Gen said. A tear ran down her cheek. Her chest heaved slightly. "It'll be okay."

Kierse whirled on the Druid. "Lorcan, what are you doing? They're innocent. Let them go."

He straightened at her assessment. He was dressed in a navy three-piece suit, his tie knotted at his neck, his brown leather shoes polished to perfection. His beard had been trimmed, and his dark hair fell over his forehead. She could see a holster for a pair of guns against his sides, and his hand lay casually on a black blade.

"Hello, Kierse." His eyes were welcoming. Not at all the predator he posed in Graves's home. "You didn't answer any of my texts."

"You'd think you'd get the message."

"He broke through the wolf lockdown," Gen said through tears.

"The Dreadlords were all chained up for the moon. There was nothing we could do," Ethan added.

"This isn't your fault," she insisted. "I'm so sorry."

"This goes against our arrangement, Lorcan," Graves said with lethal calm.

"Oh, does it? I wasn't aware," he asked with amusement. "Did you think I would miss tonight?"

A muscle feathered in Graves's jaw. "What do you hope to get out of this?"

"I thought that was rather obvious. The magical artifacts that belong to my people." Lorcan's gaze drifted from the spear in Kierse's hand to the sword in Graves's. "You had to know that it would come to this, Brannon."

Graves flinched at the name.

"Oh, does no one call you that anymore?" Lorcan laughed, but it was a cold, vicious laugh. Like he'd known how it would hit. "You cannot go around collecting Druidic artifacts and expect no one to notice."

"I knew you would notice," Graves growled. "It is another matter for you to enter my home unprovoked. There are consequences."

"Tonight is the only night that isn't true."

"Why?" Kierse demanded.

"Have you not told her?" Lorcan asked. "No, of course not. Secrets all around."

"She knows," Graves said. He adjusted his grip on the sword. "It's not quite midnight. Why don't we take this outside?"

Lorcan chuckled. "No, I think this is the *perfect* place for this. The Holly Library, you're calling it now, Graves. A little on the nose, don't you think?"

Then she looked between them. Graves surrounded by holly, a wren beside him. Lorcan across from him on the winter solstice. She remembered the oak trees lining his property. The acorn on his business card. The clean, crisp scent whenever she was around him. All he was missing was a robin, and he'd be the consummate Oak King.

"Oh," she gasped as the pieces all notched into place.

Lorcan sketched a bow in her direction. "The Oak King at your service."

"How?" she whispered.

"I wish we knew. No matter what we do, we can't escape each other. Unfortunately, you're part of this now, Kierse. I would have spared you and your friends. But there are consequences to the theft of my property." Lorcan smiled like a fox as his attention returned to Graves. "You can give it back, and then no hard feelings."

"I don't care about stories or your artifacts or your stupid petty war," Kierse snapped at Lorcan, taking a menacing step forward. "Release my friends now."

"If you don't care, then hand it over." Lorcan held his hand out.

The spear. She could hand Lorcan the spear and get her friends.

But Kierse couldn't give the spear to Lorcan. Despite whatever persona he showed to her, however friendly or connected he wanted her to believe they were, this was proof of what lay beneath that facade. He was a killer. She should have never unlearned that lesson. He would do whatever it took to get what he wanted. And if he had the spear, then he'd win.

The weapon hummed at her touch, pushed into her dark emotions. But she was more clearheaded than she had been while running for her life. She ignored the thoughts. She wouldn't risk her friends.

"I didn't think so," Lorcan said.

"How did you find out?" Graves asked.

"Well, I suspected for a long time. I knew that you had the sword. Thank you for getting it for me," Lorcan said with a smile. "We already turned the place over looking for it, and now, it's right here. But the spear—we didn't know where it had been lost. Just that you wanted it." Lorcan shifted his gaze to Kierse. "Then Kierse started disappearing into Third Floor like a little mouse, which I found…curious. And what did I find when I got someone inside? The spear was with King Louis *and* he was having a winter solstice party."

"Fuck," Kierse hissed.

"I know how you work, Graves," Lorcan said with a head tilt. "That was your play. I just had to wait for you to bring it back to me."

Graves's eyes darkened. She could read in the clench of his jaw that he *hated* that Lorcan knew him well enough to be right. "How did you get the wards down?"

"How do we do anything, brother?" Lorcan threw the word at him like an insult.

Graves ground his teeth. Kierse looked between them in confusion. *Brothers?*

"You performed a ritual to take them down, using the liminal time to heighten your abilities."

Lorcan performed a slow golfer's clap. "Indeed. We picked the day for the same reason you did. Magic is stronger on a solstice. It's all about balance."

"Fuck your balance," Kierse spat.

"Are we done with the Q&A?" Lorcan asked pleasantly, as if they were meeting over tea and he didn't have her friends behind him crying. He rose to his feet, casually dusting invisible dirt off of his suit. "I would like to get on with the show."

"What show?" Kierse asked.

Lorcan withdrew a pistol from his jacket and slung it up, aiming at Ethan's chest. "Give me the spear or I kill your friend."

Graves was motionless. "Lorcan," he hissed.

"No!" Kierse was frantic.

This couldn't be happening. It was an impossible choice. And yet so easy. She would give Lorcan the spear. But…she couldn't possibly give him the spear. He'd just kill them anyway.

"Why are you doing this?" Kierse asked. "We could have worked together."

"No, we couldn't," Graves said simply.

"Graves and I have been fighting for five hundred years," Lorcan said. "Why stop now? That's no fun."

"You're a monster," she snarled.

Lorcan narrowed his eyes slightly. He looked offended. "I am not the monster. Whatever story he has spun for you is a falsehood. I can assure you of that, because I was *there* five hundred years ago when he ruined our friendship. When he went from being my brother to being the sick, twisted thing he is today. He is scum, and he is *using* you, Kierse. As he uses everyone in his life. He destroys them all bit by bit, day by day. A virus, a parasite, a leech. No better than the other monsters he has such scorn for. He drains you of your life energy and then tosses you aside when you prove no longer useful."

"*He* is not resorting to death threats!" she shouted.

"You see how he doesn't even defend himself," Lorcan added, gesturing to Graves. "He can't. What I say is the truth. It's hard to see from your position, little songbird, but I am the hero of this tale. The Druids are beacons of good in this world. Graves and his ilk are the demons in the night, the villains."

"If you are so good, then *let them go*."

"I'm afraid that I can't do that," Lorcan said almost regretfully. "You have something I want, and I know Graves too well to think that talking will change his mind. Only action. Isn't that right, *brother*?"

"I will not change my mind," Graves agreed, "but you are not innocent in this."

"Not innocent?" Lorcan looked furious, as if he might fling the gun in Graves's direction and shoot. His eyes switched to Kierse. "You want to know why we hate each other so? Graves *murdered* my sister in cold blood with his bare hands."

Kierse's stomach twisted. Her eyes flicked to Graves in question. But he wouldn't even look at her. He was wholly focused on Lorcan.

"Emilie was sixteen years old, and he took her life just like that." Lorcan snapped his fingers. "And we'll never get her back."

Kierse swallowed. "I am sorry for that. But two wrongs don't make a right. If you kill my friends today, then you are no better than he is."

"It brings me no joy to have to do this. You simply don't understand what you carry," Lorcan said.

"Don't condescend to me. I can feel its power. I know what it is."

"You can feel it, but you can't possibly know. You have never been to Ireland. You have never strode across the Moors. You have never stood where the gods once stood on our lands. This is just a spear to you," he growled. "To us…it is heritage. It is home."

"That doesn't give you the right to kill anyone."

"Sacrifices are part of our rituals, and rituals produce power. So, it won't all be for nothing. You have a choice. You can either hand me the spear or watch your friends die. It's your choice."

"Lorcan, no," she snapped.

The gun went off with a loud *crack*. Kierse screamed, wrenching forward as if she could stop the bullet from hitting her friends. Gen's and Ethan's screams mingled with hers, but then they all saw that a shot had hit the floor in front of them.

"Next time, I won't miss," Lorcan threatened. "The spear, Kierse?"

Fear raced through her. He was only going to fire a warning shot once. The next one would land in a body, not the floor.

"Okay," Kierse said. "Okay. Just stop. Please!"

"Good," Lorcan said with a triumphant smile. "Much better. Now, hand it over."

Kierse nodded. "All right."

Graves put his hand out to stop her. "You can't."

"I know," she told him as tears tracked down her cheeks. "Don't you understand? I can't lose them. I can't lose my family."

The fire in his eyes guttered out, but still he stepped forward. "You cannot give this to him."

"I can't suffer the consequences."

"That's right," Lorcan said. "Give me what is rightfully mine. Don't let him deter you."

Graves grasped her arm, a firm, steady grip. "Listen to me. Lorcan will kill everyone in this room if you give him that spear. It is the only reason you are still on your feet. You can't be foolish enough to do this."

Her eyes were wide and cloudy as she looked up at him. "He has my weakness. That is how he can do it. I am sorry that you have no weakness."

"Hmm," Lorcan said softly. He glanced between them. "Oh, but he does." He swiveled in place, aiming the gun at Kierse's chest. "Does the villain believe this is love?"

"Stop," Graves said, cold and lethal.

"Do you think you deserve to feel this way after what you did to Emilie?"

"This is not about our past."

"Isn't it?" Lorcan demanded furiously. "You think that you can move on. That you need to no longer suffer for what you stole from me, from our people, from the world. You do not deserve someone like her. You do not deserve *anything*."

"If you shoot her, it will be the biggest mistake of your life," Graves snarled.

He tried to inch his way in front of Kierse, but Lorcan fired his gun at their feet. Kierse shrieked and jumped backward, away from the bullet.

"Ah ah, don't move." Kierse froze in place, and Graves mirrored her. "I don't think this would be a mistake. You give me the sword, and I don't shoot her. That seems fair."

Kierse couldn't even process his words. Graves wouldn't give up the sword for her. It was impossible.

"You will regret this," Graves warned him.

"Why? Because you'll come after me?"

"I will," he said easily, "but no. Because of this."

Then Graves moved at his blinding speed. He shifted in front of her, blade raised. For a moment, she thought that he was going to lunge at her. That he was going to finish it so that Lorcan couldn't use her against him. But instead, he held the blade up to her face.

"Show the truth," Graves told the blade.

He dragged the sword down her body from her shoulder diagonally across her navel and to her other hip. She shuddered under the weight of it. Her instinct was to pull up the spear to use against the sword. But those weren't her thoughts; it was the spear. It was the power the sword wielded. The truth it released.

She trembled, a cold sweat spreading across her skin. Her heart rate picked up, and she thought she might pass out. She gasped and clenched her hands into fists. Her knuckles were white where she grasped the spear tightly in her hand. This wasn't painful but disorienting and uncomfortable. As if she had always been walking underwater and was now on land.

She flexed her fingers and felt light as a feather. Fiery blue light threaded with gold suffused her entire body, a swirling glow that slithered and pulsed as if it had a life of its own. Then, as the last of the power of the sword unleashed upon her, the magic burst like fireworks, breaking apart into a million little pieces before settling back into her skin.

Then he finished. And she felt lighter. As if she had been in chains and now was set free.

"What...did you do to me?" she whispered.

"I revealed who you truly are...*what* you truly are."

Lorcan's eyes went as wide as saucers as he jumped to his feet. "It can't be. They're all dead."

"Not all of them, apparently," Graves told him.

"What...what am I?"

Fear crept into her voice. Finally, the answer to all of her questions. And yet, she almost didn't want to know. Couldn't bear it. Yet, at the same time, she *had* to know.

Lorcan dropped his arm, lowering the gun to his side. His voice was reverent as he told her the information she had she had always wanted.

"A wisp."

Chapter Sixty-One

"A what?"

"A will-o-the-wisp," Lorcan told her. He looked like he was going to bow his head and swear his allegiance. "The last of your kind."

Kierse's eyes flicked back to Graves. "A wisp? Like a little ball of light? Like in the stories?"

"Not a ball of light. That is just all the stories remember—that wisps lure people into the dark. But real wisps are of the Fae."

"Fae? Like a fairy?"

Her fingers went to her ears, and she gasped. They were no longer completely round. The tips were pointed at the ends. But not just that... everything felt different. Like all of her limbs were stretched and smoothed over. The glow had remained on her skin as if she could now *see* exactly where her absorption-magic levels were at rather than just feel them.

Graves nodded. "They were very powerful magic users who came over from their world millennia ago. They were aligned with the Druids for centuries until their kind disappeared."

"They were slaughtered," Lorcan growled. "Hunted down and massacred. One by one until there was nothing and no one left." Lorcan took a step forward as if he needed to touch her to make sure that she was real. "But now, you are here. You are a miracle."

Kierse stepped back at his sudden change of heart. One minute, ready to kill her; the next, admiration mingled with devotion. She couldn't handle that. She couldn't handle any of it.

She was a wisp. And wisps were Fae. And...she was the last wisp.

Then something else filled her heart. A revelation she hadn't considered. Graves had *known*, and he hadn't told her. This wasn't a secret about his history or his past. This was a secret from *her*.

She whirled on him. "How long have you known?" She could see the machinations working in his mind. See him trying to find a way to get out of this conversation. "How long, Graves?"

"I have suspected since we saw Mafi that night you absorbed magic."

Kierse took it like a blow. "You knew that night. You said that you had heard of someone like this. Did you mean a wisp then?" He clenched his jaw. All the answer she needed. "Wisps absorb magic. And yet, you never shared your suspicions with me. Why?"

"I suspected, but the wisps never had your limitations."

"But you could have used the sword," she pointed out.

"I didn't know you were bound. Or that your magic and your self were tied up by whoever did this to you."

"You mean you didn't trust me to know about the sword."

"That's exactly what he means," Lorcan said.

"I broke what was there and revealed the truth under the lie," Graves said. "I always planned to do it tonight."

Bound. He had broken her binding. Now she was truly a wisp in more than just name. Still…she couldn't dissolve the anger. The real Kierse, the one who had been left on the streets and abused by Jason—that one was still furious. She didn't know whether he had actually planned to tell her the truth or not tonight. Only that he had purposefully withheld this.

"But you suspected that I was a wisp," she said, lethally calm.

"He didn't tell you for a reason," Lorcan said. "He knew you would go looking for what you were capable of."

"Why?" Kierse demanded, whirling on Lorcan for the answers Graves refused to give. "What would I find?"

"Wisps can kill warlocks," Lorcan told her.

Kierse's eyes widened in horror. "You thought…I was a threat."

"No," Graves said automatically, pain in his voice at that accusation. "Never."

Kierse took another step back. A step away from them both.

How had she gotten here? To this moment when the man she had finally taken her guard down for, who she cared for, who she had confided her secrets in, would truly believe this about her. Would hide the one thing she wished to know from her out of fear.

"I don't care about your petty history or the reasons you two have been trying to kill each other. I don't even care if you're actually the Oak and Holly Kings," she said, holding the spear aloft between them.

It spoke into her veins, humming into her magic, telling her how powerful she was and all the things that they could do together.

You are of my line, too.

If what the spear said was true, that the Fae were of the magical line just as Lorcan and Graves were, then she had every right to this spear.

"You both lied to me," she accused. "If I am a wisp and of the Fae, then this spear is *mine*. I claim it by *my* birthright as a Fae, and neither of you will take it from me."

"As it should be," Lorcan agreed without pause.

Fire shot through Graves's eyes. For a split second, she thought that Graves would regret what he'd done when he realized he had lost the sword, but he was too absorbed in his feud with Lorcan to see that he'd shattered her trust along with the binding on her true identity.

"This is over," Kierse declared.

"It's *not* over," Graves barked, his gaze still settled on Lorcan. "He broke our arrangement. He had your friends kidnapped. He doesn't get the right to walk out of this room."

"You think that you can stop me?" Lorcan asked.

Graves narrowed his eyes. "It's time to finally settle this."

"I should have killed you for what you did to Emilie," Lorcan said. "My sister deserved better."

"This has nothing to do with Emilie."

"It has *everything* to do with Emilie, and we both know it!" Lorcan yelled. He raised the gun and gestured to Kierse. "I was wrong. You'll use her and discard her like all the others. You're the same as you've always been."

Something snapped in Graves's carefully calm veneer. He lunged for Lorcan. The gun was still aimed lazily in Kierse's direction, and Graves knocked it out of Lorcan's hand with a swing of the sword. It went off with a crack. Gen and Ethan screamed. Kierse ducked, but the shot had gone wide, barely missing Kierse and embedding in a bookshelf beyond. A cat's shriek came up from nearby, and Anne darted across the library in a hurry.

With the gun out of play, Lorcan jerked out of Graves's path and grasped the handle of the black sword he had at his side. With a swing that said he had been training for centuries, he lifted the sword and met Graves with a clash.

An ancient battle had begun.

Spring and fall.

Summer and winter.

Light and dark.

This was just the new catalyst to this age-old tale. The Oak and the Holly Kings raged against each other to either bring back the light and spring or keep the world in perpetual darkness. And on this night, the tides felt as if they could go either way.

As they were entrenched in the battle, Kierse took her chance. She shifted into slow motion and came at the Druids holding her friends. She could feel the ease with which she shifted in and out of her powers. The way it moved through her like liquid. Never before had it felt this seamless. In fact, it was so easy that she overshot her exit and came out *past* her friends.

The Druid holding Ethan barked out a shout at her swift movement. Kierse leveraged the spear the way she had been training and directed the instrument toward the woman. She balked at the sheer ferocity of Kierse's actions, dropping the knife that held Ethan. Kierse kicked out, sending the woman sailing back a few feet, and she landed in a heap by the coffee table and chairs.

"Aisling!" the second Druid cried.

"Get her, Niall," Aisling groaned.

As soon as he was free, Ethan turned and jumped at Niall, who was holding Gen. Kierse was there a second later, popping out of slow motion to bash Niall in the head. She didn't know what new fighting styles she could achieve, how much faster she could go, or what other consequences came with this. Only that she had to get her friends out of here alive.

Niall landed hard on the ground. Blood welled on his temple from the force of the strike, and for a moment, she feared that she had killed the guy. That hadn't been her intention. When he groaned and tried to roll over, she released a sigh of relief. She didn't know her own strength.

"Look out!" Gen cried.

Aisling had gotten back up and held a gun level with them.

"Get down!" Kierse shouted.

But Niall threw himself between Kierse and Aisling just as she pulled the trigger. Niall gasped, choking on his pain. Kierse's eyes flared wide. He'd just *saved* her.

"Not the…wisp," Niall said to Aisling.

Aisling gasped in horror, dropping her weapon and holding her hands up. "I didn't think…" Then she fell to her knees. "Niall."

But Niall was already gone.

The sounds of swords clashing brought them back to reality. She couldn't do anything about the Druid who had died for her. Not while her friends were still in danger.

"We need to get out of here," Kierse said.

"The window," Ethan suggested, glancing backward.

"It's too far of a drop for you two. You'd break something," she said, knowing full well that she had been prepared for the same thing only weeks earlier. But Ethan and Gen weren't even as strong as her. "We need to get past them to the stairs."

The historic fight raged before her, and all that mattered in her world was escaping.

Kierse squeezed Gen's fingers, and Ethan took Gen's other hand. A trio. A unit. As they always had been.

"Together," Ethan said.

"Together," Gen repeated.

Kierse knew the library like the back of her hand. She had spent countless hours between training sessions reading in the privacy of its shelves. And the fastest exit was straight through the battle. The worst exit was the window with its impossible drop. They needed another out.

"This way," she said and then dragged them from the sword fight. The two beings were no longer cognizant of the world around them.

She maneuvered through the stacks. In the process, she found Anne cowering in a corner.

"You too, kitty," Gen said, then scooped the cat up in her arms.

Kierse gaped at her. Of course Anne Boleyn loved Gen.

They hustled around the next bend of shelves and came out on the other side of the fight. But the battle raged nearby with no end in sight. It wouldn't be easy to get past them, not for her friends, but there wasn't another option. Not a real one.

She had to get the doors open and then get the fuck out of there with her two friends and a tempestuous black cat. Fuck.

"Once I get the doors open, you run faster than you ever have in your entire life," she told them. "Let me deal with Graves and Lorcan if they come near. Understand?"

Her friends nodded, terror on their faces.

Then she pushed herself to max speed. Her limbs barely processed what was happening as she raced for the door. Everything slowed, and for a moment she could almost see the finer points of the battle. Graves and Lorcan were so much *more* tonight. With the solstice and the full moon and the approaching witching hour, the stars were aligning for this fight.

It was strange to see them haloed in the golden glow of their magic. The Oak King and the Holly King. A summer god facing off with a winter god. Dark facing Light.

Though she had no idea which was which. There was no good guy in all of this. Graves had said that from the start. There were only the consequences of their actions. It didn't matter their intentions when the outcome was the same.

Both liars and monsters and murderers.

Both capable of love and laughter and life.

No heroes.

No villains.

Just people blessed and cursed with magic.

As she was.

But there had to be a winner.

And the second before she pulled out of slow motion, she saw the tide shift. She wrenched the library door open the same moment that Lorcan moved. He pushed aside the tip of the Sword of Truth and pierced the black sword into Graves's shoulder.

Kierse gasped as the weapon clattered out of Graves's fighting hand. It hit the library floor with an otherworldly loudness as Graves was forced onto his back. Lorcan bent down and picked up his prize. He held aloft in his hand the sword that made him the self-proclaimed winner. The Oak King. The bringer of light. He claimed his victory as he always had at the end of the fight on the winter solstice.

Graves wasn't focused on his opponent any longer. Lorcan had disappeared for him when he met Kierse's gaze. She was furious with him. He had lied and schemed and hidden the truth from her. And yet, in that look, she knew that he hadn't faked his affection. That at the end of this battle, his eyes were only for her. A depthless longing and affection lay in those storm-cloud irises.

"Kierse," Ethan cried, reaching for her. "Come on."

"We have to go," Gen said as she clutched a terrified cat to her chest.

But as Lorcan raised the second sword toward Graves, Kierse knew she couldn't let it end like this. She simply couldn't imagine a world, *her* world, without Graves in it. No matter what he'd done or what he'd withheld from her. No matter what she felt right now.

Kierse moved faster than she had ever moved in her life. One moment, she was by the doors, and the next, she raised the spear over her head, placing herself between two primordial beings.

She met the bone-jarring clang of the sword as Lorcan brought it down to end the fight. It clashed against her spear, but the full force of the ending wasn't in the magical artifacts. It was the power of the Oak King in his victory.

Magic pulsed out of him in an explosion of white light that pierced Kierse straight through the heart. She gasped as the magic enveloped her senses before blasting out of her and reverberating through the brownstone and out into the world beyond.

What was left of Kierse exploded with it.

Chapter Sixty-Two

God magic.

That was what was coating her body. An unbelievable, all-consuming fire of god magic.

Her Fae heritage was desperately trying to keep up. An impossible task, and still her absorption powers were working overtime. But there was no way she could absorb the amount of energy that had just been unleashed on her. She'd hardly been able to contain wish powder. Even with her new abilities, whatever they might be, it wasn't possible to absorb the full might of the Oak King in his ascendance into power.

Like the click of a vault opening, she felt the moment her powers were overwhelmed. Felt the second that she was pushed over the edge and cast into a fire of molten magic. She was being burned alive at the stake. Every nerve ending, every sense, every fragment of her being erupted with pain, and then there were only her guttural screams as it tore through.

"No," Graves and Lorcan cried at the same time.

She could hear the shrieks from her friends, but they were drowned out by her own screaming.

"That wasn't meant for you," Lorcan gasped.

"You did this," Graves accused Lorcan.

Then, he wrenched the sword free of his body with a grunt and cast the black blade aside. He heaved his torn body off of the hardwood floors, blood leaking out of his injury as he came for Kierse.

"You can fight this, Wren," he told her as he gripped her by the shoulders. "You can fight it. You can win. Just…just give it to me. It was meant for me."

But she could do or say nothing. There was only the pain. Only the searing, endless pain.

She had trained her magic well enough to make a ward, to absorb magic, and to go into slow motion. None of that could help her here. She'd absorbed too much. She couldn't even find slo-mo if she wanted to. Not while her body was fried from the inside out.

If she was capable of releasing her powers into someone else, she had no idea how.

"Please, Wren," Graves said, his voice breaking. "Please. You have to try. You have to try to give me the power that was meant for me. It was *my* undoing, not yours."

Tears leaked from her cheeks, but she couldn't even tell him no. She couldn't even try.

"You don't die until the day after Christmas, remember?" His voice was hoarse. His hands moved up her arms to cup her face. She stared into her favorite pair of gray eyes. "You can't. You can't go early. You have to herald spring."

Kierse dug deep. She fought back against an overpowering tide of magic and pain to the center of herself. The spark that held all of her magic. It was just a flicker, barely an ember. And then she stoked it. Tried to force herself to do something she had never done before. To shift the full might of the Oak King into its intended target.

A tendril of magic shifted. It flicked off of her and curled into a loop before their eyes.

"Yes," Graves said. "Yes, give that to me. You can do this. Try again."

Tears poured down her face, and she shook violently.

She would try. Another bit of light escaped her body. She pushed it forward, tried to propel it out of her. It touched the front of Graves's suit and singed into him. He grunted as if the barest flick of pain was his undoing.

"Good," he said.

She couldn't keep going. She just…couldn't.

"Again," he commanded.

And this time, he brought his lips down on hers. A kiss that for the barest trace of a moment made the pain cease. Made the entire world disappear. Her magic was so overwhelmed that Graves could easily read her, though she didn't know what he would find other than the fire coursing through her.

But then something happened. A memory moved *into* her mind.

Not her memory. Graves's.

She was looking through his eyes as he traipsed through a field of wildflowers. Bright yellows, dark blues, and vivid purples were on display all around him. And tucked away against the moor was a lake so large and green as to look an endless sea. He carried a book under his arm as he made his way to the shore. The sun shone on his face and hands. His wrists were bare. No tattoo. No scars. No markings at all. This was the man before he became the monster.

"Everything smells fresh and new. As if anything could be possible. That's what you smell like."

This…this was what she reminded him of.

Hope.

And home.

Then the image burst like a soap bubble and she was back in the library fighting for her life. She used that moment of distraction to dig deeper and push another spark out of her. It found its way into Graves, and then another.

"What's happening?" Ethan asked.

"Tell us what's going on," Gen demanded.

"She's doing it," Lorcan said in awe. "She's transferring the magic."

And she was…barely. A single tendril at a time. She needed to do more, to fight more. But it hurt *so* much. It hurt more than she could ever comprehend.

Worse, she was fighting against an all-encompassing blackout. At any moment, she could feel it pressing against her. She was strong, but was she strong enough to defeat *this*?

"I can't," she managed to get out.

Her legs gave out from the pain, and she fell to her knees. Graves went with her, groaning as he caught himself on his injured arm.

"You can," Graves said, pulling her toward him. "It's mine. Give it to me, Wren. Let me end this."

She tried again, but the last ember winked out. She gasped and saw black at the edges of her vision. This was it. This was the end.

"Fucking help her," Graves yelled at Lorcan. "Do a ritual, use your spells, *heal* her."

"That was *all* of my magic," Lorcan shouted back, frantic and in pain. "The time for spells is past."

"She's fading," Graves said in horror. "Kierse, Kierse, you can do this."

The sound of her name on his tongue roused her. She met his gaze, a ghost of a smile appearing. But there was nothing left to fight. Not as the god magic consumed her.

"Neither of you can save her?" Gen screamed at them. "*Save* her!"

"Please!" Ethan yelled. "She's dying."

And then Gen was at her side. Her smooth hands touched Kierse's face as her vision tunneled. Ethan next, burying his face into her hair. She could hear soft sobs as he cried against her.

She wanted to tell them that it would be okay. That they would be safe now. But the words wouldn't come. No words would.

"Say your goodbyes," Lorcan said.

"No," Gen said, her voice like ice. "No. Maybe you two don't have the power to save her. Maybe none of us do. But I will not stop trying."

Gen held her hand out for Ethan.

"But I cannot do it alone."

"What can we do?" Ethan said.

"Together? Anything."

Ethan nodded and then placed his hand into Gen's. They placed them over Kierse's heart. At that moment, a flare of light rose up in Gen. The little bit of magic that Kierse had first felt that time they connected when Ethan had been drugged by the wish powder. Her magic reached out for Ethan, and at the same moment, to his shock, it snapped into place with Ethan's own shoot of magic, a little sapling just like the ones he'd cultivated all these years.

Once they connected, there was only a second before the triangle was complete, latching on to Kierse's torrent of energy. But she was too far gone. Her vision went black. Her breathing went shallow, barely rising and falling. And her heart…stuttered and paused and then stopped.

Then a new light flared as their trio, their knot forged anew.

Gen and Ethan gasped as it took on a life of its own. Gen's healing, Ethan's growth, and Kierse's energy all flowed freely between them. It rose and rose and rose until all three of them were pulled wholly off the ground. The force of their joining an all-new magic.

And out of that, the Oak King magic released upward in a torrent—a blinding white light that ripped through the roof of the Holly Library, tearing a hole to the full moon.

Everything hovered, suspended in midair as the last of the energy passed from their bodies and out into the world.

Then all three of them dropped back onto the library floor. Debris fell atop and around them. And as Gen and Ethan scrambled to Kierse's side, her heart kicked into gear once more.

She groaned, the aftermath of the magic still a live wire on her nerves.

But she was alive.

She was *alive*.

And when she opened her eyes, it was to tears streaming down her friends' faces. To Lorcan staring in shock. And Graves.

Graves, who was still bleeding on his floor. Graves, who looked like he had seen a ghost. Graves, who crawled toward her and brought his lips to hers.

The memory of his lake and wildflowers bloomed in her mind again. She didn't know what it meant. Didn't know he was even capable of inserting memories in other people's minds. Or maybe he'd only been able to do it for her as she was dying.

"I'm okay," she told him, pushing back gently. "I'm okay."

"Kierse," Gen said with relief.

"You're alive," Ethan said, brushing aside a tear.

"You saved me. I don't understand how. I was…" Kierse couldn't say it. *Dead.*

"You joined," Graves said. "Three became one like the three parts of the soul in Celtic heritage."

"Three is our holy number," Lorcan agreed. He looked to Graves. "It was a triskel. You saw it, too."

"What is a triskel?" Kierse asked.

"It's an ancient symbol of a triple spiral connected at the center. It was used historically to describe when a Druid, a High Priestess, and a wisp connect their magic."

Gen choked on that.

Ethan blanched. "But we're not…"

Kierse looked between her friends. At the magic that they'd had hidden beneath, just like her. How Gen had been able to find her and Ethan and save them. How together they had grown and healed and been stronger.

Always stronger together.

"Yes," Lorcan said, looking at Ethan. "You're a Druid."

"And I'm a High Priestess," Gen said in shock.

"You are *my* people," Lorcan continued. "You belong with me. Only I can help and train you." He held his hand out. "Let me guide you."

Kierse barked out a laugh, surprised that there was no more pain. She rolled to standing, reaching for her spear, before helping Gen and Ethan off the floor.

"Like we would ever trust you after all that you have done." She put herself between Lorcan and her friends. "You would have to go through me first."

"I am not your enemy," he told her.

"You will leave this place and never come back," Kierse commanded.

Lorcan's eyes roamed over her as if seeing something in her for the first time. His eyes widened, and his voice pitched low with emotion. "I have missed you so."

Kierse whirled the spear around. "Leave, Lorcan."

Lorcan eyed the spear and Graves still lying on the floor before looking back at Kierse. "We will meet again."

"And if we do, then pray I let you walk away a second time."

Lorcan grinned and nodded. "Until next time, a chuisle mo chroí."

Kierse furrowed her brow, not understanding the words coming out of his mouth. She wondered what they meant. But then he just nodded and helped Aisling carry Niall's body out of the library.

She waited until they were finally gone before turning to Graves, who had risen once more to his feet. "What did he say?"

"Pulse of my heart," he said softly.

"Why would he call me that?"

"Wisps and Druids were aligned."

She could tell that wasn't the whole of it. Lorcan had gone from reverence when he found out she was a wisp to something else in that moment. Something much deeper.

"Do you need Gen to look at that?" Kierse asked, gesturing to his shoulder.

"I don't know that I could do much more than get you a sling right now," Gen muttered.

He shook his head. "I'll…be fine. Fast healer."

Gen and Ethan disappeared behind her as she stared at Graves. She had saved his life. He had tried to save hers. Nothing would change that. But nothing could change the betrayal she felt, either.

"Could you see the vision?" he asked.

"The wildflower fields by the lake?"

He closed his eyes and breathed a sigh of relief. "You saw it."

"Yes."

When his eyes opened once more, he dipped his head. "Lorcan's offer isn't the only one. I can train you as well. You can learn from me here."

"I think we're going to make our own way now." Gen and Ethan came up to Kierse's sides, taking her hands.

Then, together, the three of them walked out, leaving the ruin of the library behind.

Chapter Sixty-Three

Five days later, no wrens died in New York City.

Kierse inhaled the crisp chill as snow collected in her dark hair. Wren Day. *Her* day. And she had survived it after all. If only barely.

Nate's black car came to a stop before her. He rolled the passenger window down. "You ready?"

She touched the wren necklace at her throat. The legacy her parents had given her, whatever may have happened to them. She still didn't have answers, but she was going to get them.

"All set," she said.

She yanked the door open and slid inside. Nate took off like a bullet down the crowded streets. Christmas traffic had returned in force. Christmas markets had sprung up overnight. A tree at Rockefeller Plaza. She hadn't seen any of it from the sanctuary of Five Points, but Colette had told her about it all happening. Like this season had redoubled its efforts to bring Christmas magic, cheer, and joy to the city.

After the events of the solstice, Kierse, Gen, and Ethan had gone to Colette, who had put them up in a different room. None of them could say it, but they weren't quite ready to go back to the attic. When the wolves had woken up a day later, they'd returned to the Dreadlords. Nate had apologized a thousandfold for what had happened while he'd been on lockdown. But she couldn't blame him. She wasn't sure that Nate would have been able to succeed against Lorcan that night anyway.

"You're sure about this?" Nate asked.

"Positive."

"I'm still sorry," Nate said, cutting his hazel eyes in her direction. "About everything."

"You don't have to apologize, Nate. The whole thing was fucked."

He nodded, and they drove the rest of the way in silence. He cut the engine a block from Colette's, taking the first parking spot available on the slushy streets.

"You know that you're welcome with me anytime, Kierse."

"I know," she told him. And she did.

But she couldn't remain at Nate's. Nor could she stay with Colette. She had too much to do, too much to learn. And she needed to start now.

"Don't make it another year, okay?" he said, pulling her into a hug. She didn't fight it, just let his wolf warmth radiate over her. Oh, how things had changed.

"I'll be back," she promised.

She pushed open the door and was hopping out when he called, "Wait." She stuck her head back into the car, and he passed her an envelope. "I wasn't going to give this to you. He doesn't deserve access to you, but... Fuck."

Kierse turned the blank envelope over and saw that there was a green wax seal with an acorn pressed into it. Lorcan. She stuffed it into her jacket pocket.

"Thanks, Nate."

Then she darted across the street and up the front steps of the brothel. Corey stood sentinel on the steps and had a wide smile for her.

"Kierse! Glad you made it."

"Hey, Corey," she said with a wave. She was surprised that he could still smile, considering what she, Gen, and Ethan were planning to do. But maybe Ethan hadn't told him yet. Leaving it to the last minute.

"They're waiting for you inside." He pulled the door open for her.

Inside, she found Colette, her lush, red hair in a gorgeous wave down her back. She was in a floor-length black dress with a mink around her shoulders. She arched an eyebrow at Kierse's appearance. "Welcome back."

"Are you going soft on me?" Kierse asked, fighting for the familiar.

"Never." Then her voice dipped. "I'm just glad that you brought my Genesis home to me. And Ethan," Colette added. "And you, of course. All three of my children."

Kierse's throat closed up at those words. And when Colette held her arm out, Kierse let her hug her as well. A day of hugging for a day of leaving.

She took the old, familiar stairs, running her hand along the banister, listening for the same creaks that were always there. She took her time, reminiscing. Then, just before she reached the landing for the attic, she withdrew Lorcan's letter.

She hadn't been sure she'd read it, but she was too naturally curious.

Kierse,

I know you don't trust me. I haven't given you reasons to do so. But you cannot trust him, either. I won't beat a dead horse and list the ways of his deception. I believe you have finally seen the truth of the matter.

I could wax poetic about the ways in which you are sacred to my people, how you have changed my entire world, but from our short acquaintance, I can tell that would not sway you.

So go.

Go see the wide world beyond. Learn your answers the way that I did. The way that he did. And when you return home, I will be waiting.

L.F.

P.S. I'd start at the Goblin Market on Grafton Street in Dublin.

Kierse folded the letter and stuffed it back into her pocket. Arrogant, insufferable man. As if he hadn't threatened to kill her and her family innumerable times after making his *own* promises that he would not. Like she couldn't see the web of his own deception. Now he was groveling because she was somehow *sacred* to his people. Not good enough.

She ground her teeth together and then released her anger before walking the last few steps up and pushing open the door to her attic.

Somehow, it felt…smaller.

Had all three of them really lived up here?

Their beds were the same against the far wall. The abandoned training facility in the center of the room. A space reserved for Gen's tarot cards and herbal work. A couch where they lounged. She ran her finger along a dresser and found dust collected in the crevices. Ethan had been so tidy that it was hard to believe. Most of the plants were dead or their pots were empty. Gen's discarded harp, a side project that had never taken root, was lying atop her messy table. Kierse's clothes still filled the closets or lay scattered on the floor. The place where they lived.

"Hey," Ethan said, sliding a full backpack on his shoulders.

"Kierse," Gen said. She turned toward the sound of Kierse's footsteps. "We were just packing up."

All of Kierse's clothes and belongings had been delivered in neatly packed boxes from Graves's residence on Christmas morning. No note or anything from him. Just the boxes and another five million dollars deposited into her account. A closing to her services.

She wasn't surprised. She was just another person he'd pushed away. Just another person who had left him.

So, she didn't actually *need* anything from the attic. All of Graves's clothes were higher quality and better fit. It was the closure that she needed.

"You have to tell her," Gen hissed.

"Tell me what?" Kierse asked, coming back to herself.

"I'm…I'm going to stay," Ethan said.

Kierse blinked. "What do you mean?"

"I mean," he said, breathing in deeply and then releasing it. He was actually afraid to say this. "I'm going to go train with Lorcan."

This time, Kierse froze completely. "Come again?"

"He said he could train us…me. I'm a…Druid," he said as he floated his hand over his coils nervously. "I don't know what that means. I don't even know how it's possible. But he has answers. He has them *now*, Kierse."

"He's going to play you," she said. It was hard to keep her tone light.

"He's not Graves."

"No, he's not," she said, and it wasn't a compliment.

"He's going to go whether you approve or not," Gen said. "So just be happy for him."

"Happy for him," she repeated. "He tried to kill you. Both of you. He almost *did* kill me."

"I know," Ethan interjected. "But I want this. I have magic; I want to know how to use it. So, I'm going to go train with him. You made your deal with the devil. Let me make mine."

She didn't want to. She wanted to beg him not to do it, but she couldn't make his choices for him.

"Of course," she said instead. "Of course, if that's what you want."

Ethan blew out another breath. "You…you could come, too."

"I couldn't," she said. "I need my own answers. Not ones that come with strings. I hope he gives you what you're looking for, and if he hurts you, remind him that I will kill him."

Ethan laughed before clearing his throat when he realized how deadly serious she was. "Yeah, I'm sure he'll love that." He turned to Gen. "And you?"

"I agree that you should do what is best for you even if we disagree," Gen said quietly. "But I'm with Kierse."

He nodded. "I figured."

"We'll be back, though," Gen insisted. "Can't keep us away forever."

Gen beckoned Kierse in, and she let her friends hug her. This triskel, as Lorcan had said, that had created between them. She knew they were stronger together. The thought of Ethan going off with Lorcan was…wrong. And yet, she couldn't stop him any more than he could stop her. But she felt bereft at the thought of his absence.

Gen patted Kierse's arm and then followed Ethan to the door.

"Kierse," he said over his shoulder. "Until next time."

She smiled back at him, fighting down tears. "Until next time."

When he was gone, she let the tear track down her cheek. She swiped it away angrily. Ethan had made his choice. That was all there was to it.

A creak on the stairs brought her right back to reality. She whirled around, hoping that he'd changed his mind, but against all odds, the figure that walked into the attic was Graves.

She inhaled sharply at the sight of him. He cut a sharp figure in a stark black suit. His wound must have fully recovered, since he wasn't even in a sling. No one else would ever know that he had been stabbed less than a week earlier. But Kierse knew. She could see it in the tilt of his head, the clench of his jaw, the weight of him. She knew him too well not to see the strain. It hit her so much harder, knowing that. That she *did* know him.

And her tangled feelings made it all so much worse.

"I never thought I'd see you in here," she admitted as he came fully into the attic.

"I wanted to see you before you left."

"You didn't send a car? Or wait for me to show up?"

"I came to you," he answered simply.

Kierse looked away from him. "It's not much, but it was home."

"I understand its importance in your life."

"Well, are you going to ask me to stay?" she asked, glancing up at him again.

His eyes were soft. "Would that work?"

She laughed slightly. "A question for a question. How very Graves."

"Stay," he said, a note like pleading in his voice.

"I can't," she told him.

She had wanted those words from Graves. She had wanted him to want her like that. To need her in that way. She had thought for a time that they were the same. And at their core, they were.

They fit together not just because he was the Holly King and she, his wren. But because they were two broken pieces of the same tapestry, and being with him was like being sewn back together. Only he'd sliced his sword down that mended seam. And she didn't quite know how to repair it.

Which was how she knew that she needed to go. Go and get her own answers. Here, she would only be a part of Graves's mission. She would only know enough to suit him and not enough to suit her. She wanted more than that. But if she was to return to the city, her home, to Graves…then she wanted it to be on her own terms.

"I understand." He spoke in a way that said he didn't approve.

"You could tell me where to start, though," she suggested.

He considered the request. "If I was starting, I'd go to Dublin," he said. "There's a place on Grafton Street called the Goblin Market. It's probably your best bet if you won't stay."

Kierse almost laughed. The Goblin Market. The same place that Lorcan had suggested. Well, if she had doubted either of them telling the truth before, having the same answer from both of them confirmed it.

"Thank you."

He nodded. "You'll be safe?"

"As safe as I ever am."

"That's what I am afraid of."

"Give me more credit," she said, reaching for playful.

"And the spear?" he asked hesitantly.

"Is mine," she told him. "Your spell will have to wait."

He grasped her hand. She realized in that moment that he wasn't wearing his gloves. Skin to skin. His heat melted into her.

"What we had was real," he confessed. "It was real for me."

"I know." She met his gray gaze, saw the fiery emotions so blatant there. She wanted to lean into it. She wanted so much more from him. "It was real for me, too."

The door to the attic creaked open then. "Kierse, Ethan just left…" Gen trailed off when she saw Graves standing in the room. "Oh, should I come back?"

She looked around the attic that had been her sanctuary. But it was just a room now. It was the people that mattered in her life. Gen, Ethan, Colette, Nate. They were what mattered. And maybe…maybe Graves, too.

"No," Kierse said. "I think I got everything that I need."

Then she walked past Graves, took Gen's arm, and closed the page on her life in the attic.

Graves's voice carried over the threshold. "Are you going to come back?"

"New York City is my home," she said. "I'm not done here yet."

Interlude

G raves stood in his renovated library. All the books were back where they belonged. The roof was repaired. Even Anne had returned to his side.

Spring was fully in swing, but he still felt the cold.

Felt Kierse's absence from the city.

He remembered the first time that he saw her. The little thief who had gotten in past his wards to steal a diamond. She had been limned in the dim light, her brown hair a chocolate wave extending out of the ponytail. Her figure was not quite starved—a look he'd seen on many in the city in those days after the war had ended. She had more muscle than most. Her cheekbones were defined as she pocketed the diamond and checked her surroundings.

But she didn't see him.

Didn't expect his fury. And when he caught her and had her within his clutches, there she had stood with a wren necklace around her throat, her skin refusing to give him the answers he so desired.

He had known then that she was powerful. But not how powerful.

Or that all that power would sunder him.

For he had lived many lives, but none had been worth living compared to these weeks with her.

He poured himself a drink and scooped up the black cat, who snarled in irritation at him. Anne nipped at his hand, and he dropped her. She landed on all fours and pounced atop the couch, giving him an angry side-eye before sinking onto a cushion.

She'd been like this ever since the night of the solstice. He could hardly blame her.

"I know. I miss her, too."

Graves drained his drink and then set it down on the table. He leaned over the materials he had collected on the spell that he had been working on for much of his life. He needed all four objects to complete the spell. He'd had two in his possession on the solstice, and now, he had none. He was back at square one.

In a momentary burst of anger, he swept his hand across the table and cast all of the documents and papers to the floor. The glass went with it, shattering into a million pieces. He wanted to rage. He had lost both objects…and Kierse. His wren. And what did he have to show for it?

He leaned his palms on the table and dropped his head forward, his midnight-blue hair hanging into his eyes.

He knew who had the sword.

He knew who had the spear.

That was at least something. It was better than nothing, which was what he felt like he had.

He was knowledge. His powers could read the answers to life's great mysteries, and yet he could not accomplish what he truly set out for. The knowledge he truly wanted. The woman he truly wanted.

And worse, Lorcan now had his hands in all of this. Sure, Druids and wisps had been allies for millennia until the wisps had all died out, but that wasn't the reason that Lorcan wanted to keep Kierse close.

His mind drifted back to that moment when Lorcan had called her "a chuisle mo chroí."

He couldn't even get the word out when Kierse had asked. He'd seen fiery fucking red at the thought. Because of course, *of course*, after all was said and done, he would have to contend with *this* as well.

The pulse of his heart indeed.

He remained there, his chest heaving, trying to rein in the anger that still coursed through him. He only moved when he felt the vibration of his phone in his pocket.

With a sigh, he pushed back from the table and answered, "Hello?"

"Graves," a gruff voice said on the other line.

He stilled. That was a voice he hadn't heard in a long, *long* time. "Laz?"

"I have a lead if you're still interested."

"That depends entirely on what you found."

Laz snorted. "You know what I went looking for."

A smile stretched across Graves's face as he straightened. "You found the cauldron."

"Bingo."

"Tell me everything."

The more Laz spoke, the more Graves realized one very important thing—he was going to need a very clever thief for this job.

Acknowledgments

When I sat down to write *Wren*, I never guessed the journey that this book would take me on. The six years it would take from the first kernel of an idea to having this beauty in your hands. So many times we see the completed project and forget everything it took to get to this moment. So here are the people who went on it with me.

First and foremost, I want to thank my husband, Joel, who was there from the very beginning when I wrote Graves. And I proposed that I wanted to write a monster Avengers and he didn't laugh at me but said to do it. Thank you for the years that we spent honing this book into what it is and for listening to me go through edits until my eyes bled. And of course, to my baby boy, who was grown, born, and raised in the intervening years as this book came to life.

To my agent, Kimberly Brower, who heard the idea for Graves and said, "Write the whole book. This is the one." You were so right. It was a road. A long, winding road, but you were at my side the entire time. My fighter who let me cry and vent and cheer and jump up and down. Thank you, thank you, thank you. I wouldn't be here without you.

To my friends who dedicated any amount of time to this book. Rebecca Yarros for every two-hour phone call, text message, and virtual hug as we went on this journey together. Nana Malone for always being on the other end of the line when I needed you. Plus the sensitivity read on Imani and Montrell that pushed me to write diversity that I could be proud of. Staci Hart for every writing session and ounce of editing help and your incomparable friendship. Diana Peterfreund for reminding me time and time again of my worth and refusing to let me settle for less. Also for the title, which I wouldn't have without you! Sierra Simone for having all the same IDs as me and encouraging me to go there whenever I thought of holding back. Rachel Van Dyken for all the long text messages that helped me get through this journey. Kandi Steiner for being my forever cheerleader. You make this industry a brighter place. Amanda Bouchet for your beautiful quote and for saying that the couple reminds you of Barrons. Highest of praise!, Also, Laurelin Paige, CD Reiss, Mari Mancusi, Carrie Ann Ryan, Lexi Ryan, Holly Renee, K.A. Tucker, Adriana Locke, Claire Contreras, Lisa Baker, and Virginia Carey.

To my alpha readers—Anjee, Becky, and Rebecca. You read so many drafts of this book, and I am forever grateful for your guidance and cheerleading. We're here, y'all!

To my incredible publicist—Danielle Sanchez. I couldn't thank you enough for your tried-and-true advice and all the moments you lifted me up. My incredible assistant and friend, Devin McCain, everything you do is so valuable, and this release was so much easier with your help.

To Liz Pelletier and the team at Red Tower who championed this book from day one. So thankful that you read it before the imprint was even announced and called it a six-star read. Bree Archer for the *stunning* cover. It was beyond my wildest dreams. Molly Majumder for the perfect edits that brought this book to life. Hannah Lindsey for the tireless copy edits. The many sensitivity readers as well as the Celtic folklorist that were brought on for this project.

Thank you to Gillian Green and the team at Tor UK for all your work behind the scenes and especially for the stunning UK cover. Also, big thank you to all of the foreign publishers who are translating *Wren*.

And finally, to all the readers who championed this book. To each of you who picked it up and read it and loved it. This is the book of my heart, the one I always wanted to read, and I hope it's the one for you, too!

CONNECT WITH US ONLINE

⟩ @redtowerbooks

𝐟 @RedTowerBooks

♪ @redtowerbooks

RED TOWER
BOOKS™